BEST NEW AMERICAN VOICES 2005

GUEST EDITORS OF
Best New American Voices

Tobias Wolff

Charles Baxter

Joyce Carol Oates

John Casey

Francine Prose

BEST NEW AMERICAN VOICES 2005

GUEST EDITOR

Francine Prose

SERIES EDITORS

John Kulka and Natalie Danford

A Harvest Original • Harcourt, Inc.

Orlando   Austin   New York   San Diego   Toronto   London

In memory of James R. Frakes,
an extraordinary teacher

CONTENTS

Preface   ix

Introduction *by Francine Prose*   xiii

THE GOLDEN HORDE OF MISSISSIPPI *by Charley Henley*   I

GARDEN CITY *by Frances Hwang*   28

ESSAY #3: LEDA AND THE SWAN *by Eric Puchner*   50

FULL-MONTH CELEBRATION *by E. V. Slate*   75

LIKE VACLAV *by Keith Gessen*   89

FARANGS *by Rattawut Lapcharoensap*   115

MORE ABANDON *by Joshua Ferris*   134

ROSIE *by Vivek Narayanan*   155

SILENT SKY *by Lachlan Smith*   167

PINE *by Hasanthika Sirisena*   177

BRIDES *by Aryn Kyle*   195

YOU ARE HERE *by Michael Lowenthal*   216

SANGEET *by Bhira Backhaus*   252

CREATURES OF A DAY *by Matthew Purdy*   280

DOG CHILDREN *by Tamara Guirado*   290

THE COSMONAUT *by Ian David Froeb*   320

SNOW FEVER *by Rebecca Barry*   354

Contributors   369

Participants   372

PREFACE

Best New American Voices, now in its fifth year, is an annual short-story anthology that introduces emerging writers. By emerging writers we do not mean writers who are still doing apprentice work but rather skilled writers who are embarking on their professional careers. The stories the reader will encounter here are highly accomplished. This anthology is intended for those who value the pleasures of discovery above the reassurances of the familiar. Few of the names in the table of contents will be known and, as in past years, some of our contributors make their debuts in these pages.

Here is how the Best New American Voices series works: rather than solicit story nominations from the publishers of magazines and literary quarterlies, we request nominations from writing workshop directors and teachers. These nominations come to us from arts organizations such as the Banff Centre for the Arts and the PEN Prison Writing Committee, from summer writing conferences including Bread Loaf and Sewanee, from university-affiliated writing programs like Iowa and Columbia, and from community workshops like those held at the 92nd Street Y in New York City. Hundreds of writing programs across the U.S. and Canada participate in this process. A directory at the back of this volume lists all of the participating institutions.

Many of these programs are highly selective and justly famous training grounds for our best new talents. Consider, for example, that the following writers all came out of the Iowa program: Flannery O'Connor, Wallace Stegner, John Gardner, Gail Godwin, Andre Dubus, and T. C. Boyle, to name just a few. And the Stanford program has produced its own credible national literature with such famous alumni as Robert Stone, Raymond Carver, Evan S. Connell, Tillie Olsen, Larry McMurtry, Ernest J. Gaines, Ron Hansen, Ken Kesey, Scott Turow, Thomas McGuane, Alice Hoffman, Allan Gurganus, Wendell Berry, Harriet Doerr, Al Young, Michael Cunningham, Blanche Boyd, N. Scott Momaday, Vikram Seth, Dennis McFarland, and Stephanie Vaughn.

If the names of our current contributors are not so well-known as these, that is certain to change with a little time. Many of the contributors to past volumes have since gone on to great success: David Benioff (*The 25th Hour*); William Gay (*Provinces of Night* and *I Hate to See That Evening Sun Go Down*); Ana Menendez (*In Cuba I Was a German Shepherd*); Timothy Westmoreland (*Good as Any*); Adam Johnson (*Emporium*); John Murray (*A Few Short Notes on Tropical Butterflies*); the late Amanda Davis (*Circling the Drain* and *Wonder When You'll Miss Me*); Maile Meloy (*Half in Love* and *Liars and Saints*); and Jennifer Vanderbes (*Easter Island*). This is far from a complete list.

For *Best New American Voices 2005* we received many hundreds of prescreened nominations. We read all of the nominations at least once, as we do every year, and winnowed them down to a much smaller group of finalists that we then passed on to our guest editor, Francine Prose. Francine has selected seventeen stories from our finalists for inclusion in *Best New American Voices 2005*. Her selections make for a diverse, multicultural anthology whose contributors probably have little in common—except this, that they are all talented. The stories speak for themselves.

We would like to extend thanks to Francine Prose for her careful reading of the manuscripts, for her professionalism, and for her enthusiasm for this project. We would like to thank our past guest editors for their ongoing efforts and support: Tobias Wolff, Charles Baxter, Joyce Carol Oates, and John Casey. To the many writers, directors, teachers, and panel judges who help to make this series a continuing success we extend heartfelt thanks and congratulations. To name just a few others: We thank our editor Andrea Schulz for her patience and guidance; Andrea's assistant, Jenna Johnson, for her unfailing attention to detail; André Bernard at Harcourt, Inc., for his enthusiasm; Lisa Lucas in the Harcourt contracts department for the obvious and maybe not-so obvious; Gayle Feallock, managing editor at Harcourt, for her unflagging efforts; and our families and friends for their love and support.

—*John Kulka and Natalie Danford*

INTRODUCTION

Francine Prose

What reckless bravery it takes to sit down before a notebook or a blank sheet of typing paper or a computer monitor and start writing! What resolve and patience and stamina is required to put down one word and the next and the next, and then shape and form and revise that phrase into a sentence that anyone might want to read. And what an admirable and peculiar recipe of arrogance and humility is needed in order to finish a single piece of fiction—let alone to show it to another human being!

That's what I found myself thinking frequently as I considered the thirty-five short stories that Natalie Danford and John Kulka had chosen as finalists for the Best New American Voices anthology. In fact, by the time I had read and reread and winnowed down the submissions—fictions from a notably wide range of men and women with apparently little in common but talent, the desire to write, and the fact that they had studied at a writers' conference or in a writing program—I had come to see the selections before me less as a stack (well, a shopping bag full) of manuscripts than as the ultimate result of thirty-five separate, impressive acts of individual courage.

As hard as it is to generalize about writers as a species, it's probably safe to say that it would be hard to afflict a writer with a fear or anxiety that he or she hasn't already suffered, without outside help. But at the risk of doing so, let me list a few of the myriad worries that must be overcome, or at least subdued, before that first word can be written. The fear of writing badly; the fear of being rejected, ignored, unread, misread, misunderstood; the fear of offending those loved ones (Mom! Dad!) whose lives might have at one point resembled those of our fictional characters; the fear of self-exposure, of suggesting that we may, for a fleeting instant, have experienced, or even imagined, a reprehensible or socially unacceptable act or emotion; the fear of devoting our lives to something that will never make us rich or popular or beloved, when we could just as well be doing something useful and/or lucrative: becoming a brain surgeon, or a movie star. The hideous necessity of confronting these terrors on a regular basis is why, I would imagine, Rilke advised us not to become writers if we could bear to do anything else.

Yet even as I was moved to conjure up this catalog of understandable reasons for dread, I was struck by the nerve that animates so many of these stories—by the limbs, so to speak, on which these writers have so courageously dared to go out. "More Abandon" transports us into the mind of a sympathetic office worker who also happens to be an after-hours voyeur and a vandal, while the graduate student at the center of "Like Vaclav" is notably and quite impossibly full of hot air. The hero of "Creatures of a Day" is a kind of Walt Whitman of the poultry world—a man whose deepest desire is to lie down with the chickens. The fictional "author" of "Essay #3: Leda and the Swan" is not only treacherous and self-serving, but has a conspicuously wobbly command of grammatical English. "Silent Sky" tracks two half brothers in the criminal act of poaching wild sheep, out of season.

It would spoil the ending of "Brides" to reveal the unwholesome and unwise way in which its narrator embarks on her first sexual experience. And the young woman whose dazzlingly acute perceptions brighten the dark world of "Dog Children" submits to the kind of exquisite psychological torture that, certain critics would suggest, we should never permit our "empowered," self-activated female protagonists to endure in return for the semblance of male affection. In all these works, obviously, the writers are more interested in saying something about the way we live now—or would like to live now—than in charming us or reassuring us with flattering platitudes, redemptive epiphanies, happy endings, or improving moral lessons.

In many cases, the bravery of these stories involves the quiet, firm, and absolutely essential insistence that a writer can and should be able to imagine characters whose connection with their creators is forged entirely by empathy and imagination, and has little or nothing to do with surface details of gender, class, age, and race. Though I can only guess about the age of the writers, I would assume that the authors of "Full-Month Celebration," "Garden City," and "The Cosmonaut" are a good deal younger than their protagonists. However much these stories have drawn on experience and observation, few seem more than tangentially autobiographical, and reading them, I was heartened to see so many authors writing so naturally and confidently across the narrow boundaries of identity.

The other thing I found myself thinking about was the basic question of what makes writing interesting—or, anyway, interesting to me. What was I looking for? What initially snagged my attention and ultimately won my heart?

For the most part, what I found myself responding to most strongly had less to do with character, theme, and plot (though there is no denying the pleasure of an expertly crafted and well-told story) than with language—specifically, with the way that language determines tone and voice, enlivens dialogue, and works in a kind of felicitous partnership with the dead-accurate observation and the perfect, revealing detail. In fact, what pleases me most is the way that language can be deployed to depict a character's inner life—a sensibility sparkling with sophistication, imagination, and intelligence, qualities that might be less immediately apparent if we encountered the character outside the story and in the dimmer and less revealing light of everyday reality.

A perfect example of what I mean occurs at the beginning of "Dog Children," in those words and phrases—*nickering, shrieking gamely, enclosure* vs. *penetration.*

"In an effort to save their relationship, Maggie and Avashai were watching pornos in Maggie's barn apartment. Both front and back doors were open, and they could hear the soft nickering of the neighbor's horses while on the television screen, a small blond woman in a red neckerchief straddled the supine body of Long Dong Silver. The woman slowly skewered herself, shrieking gamely, as Long Dong lay perfectly still, looking vaguely embarrassed. Maggie was reminded of a feminist philosophy course she had taken in which the professor had suggested that *enclosure* might be a better word than *penetration.*"

Or in the loopy biology lesson provided by "The Golden Horde of Mississippi," as a young woman attends the funeral of her biker hard-metal-musician cousin Bobby.

"Eye level with the urn, she could picture his nasty little eyes floating around in there with a few pieces of bone and patches of charred flesh in the otherwise uniform ash of a human being. She could tell you from the classes she took at the university, that when you boil him all down to gravy, there's perhaps a dollar's worth of chemicals in a human being. If you unfolded his organs down to their proteins and his proteins down to their amino acids and his amino acids down to their constituent elements, you're not left with much to bargain on. *The magic and wonder are all in the folds,* she thought."

Or in the piquant and hilarious cultural analysis compressed into the opening paragraph of "Farangs," a story about the son of a motel owner at a Thai resort:

"This is how we count the days. June: the Germans come to the Island—football cleats, big T-shirts, thick tongues—speaking like spitting. July: the Italians, the French, the British, the Americans. The Italians like pad thai, its affinity with spaghetti. They like light fabrics, sunglasses, leather sandals. The French like plump girls, rambutans, disco music. They also like to bare their breasts. The British are here to work on their pasty complexions, their penchant for hashish. Americans are the fattest, the stingiest of the bunch. They may pretend to like pad thai or grilled prawns or the occasional curry, but twice a week they need their culinary comforts, their hamburgers and their pizzas."

Or in the pitch-perfect tone of this conversation early on in "Snow Fever," between two men in a bar watching a woman play darts:

"'She has a good arm,' said Hank, sitting down next to Bill after the third game. 'I haven't seen that on a woman since that lesbo mail carrier, Fat Betty.'

"'I haven't seen that on a man since the last time your mother was in town,' said Bill, since Fat Betty was his friend and she was a meter maid, not a mail carrier."

Or in this passage from "You Are Here," which economically conveys nearly all the vital statistics of the young priest working a gig on a cruise ship:

"He can tell she expects a priest to be older than twenty-seven, with a puffy, underwhelming body and burst-capillary face, not his firmly gym-enhanced physique. The sunglasses probably don't help, either. He removes them and says, 'Step into my office.'

"Ordained just last month, he's yet to hear his first confession, which is what the *Destiny Daily* touts as his role here. But given the holiday atmosphere, and because it's his twenty-something style, there will be no 'Bless me Father, for I have sinned.' In this floating village where every imaginable service has been arranged, Father Tim is the hired shoulder to cry on."

I also found myself drawn to stories set in unfamiliar (at least to me) cultures, stories whose authors were not only able to create believable characters but to convey detailed and intriguing information about the communities in which they live. "Rosie" revolves around the racial and social tensions that inspire a Tamil Brahmin family—residents of an African city beset by a terrifying crime wave—to buy a guard dog that, at least in theory, will protect them. In "Sangeet," two Sikh sisters in California must negotiate a balance between family tradition and the promptings of their own hearts. In "Pine," a Christmas tree becomes a symbol of the stresses that have already fractured a Sinhalese family in North Carolina.

What interested me, too, was that the members of the subcultures these stories so deftly portray are as likely to be native-born as immigrant or foreign. Reading about the hapless Pacific Northwest punk slackers in "Dog Children" and the Deep South headbangers in "The Golden Horde of Mississippi," I was struck by how atomic our society is, by how many separate subgroups continue to prosper and thrive, to live by their own lights and their own rules: stubbornly and blessedly indissoluble lumps in our so-called melting pot.

Finally, what intrigued and cheered me most was the simple fact that these stories exist and are as accomplished as they are. Daily, it seems, we hear from someone who can't wait to tell us the bad news: Literature is in its death throes. The cool (or in any case, cooler) worlds of film, music, video, and electronics are attracting the talented kids who might once have wanted to become authors. Novelists have become a rare and antiquated breed, as quaint and outmoded as icon painters or manuscript illuminators.

And yet the quality of stories like these, and of an anthology such as this one, effectively argues against those particular harbingers of gloom. How can the written word be dead when it is being deployed with such spirit and vitality? Indeed, the very opposite seems to be true: Every day and everywhere, someone is sitting down at a table or desk, in an office or library or café, and somehow—improbably, miraculously—finding the heart to begin.

CHARLEY HENLEY

Florida State University

~~~

THE GOLDEN HORDE
OF MISSISSIPPI

~ 6,800 words

All that long morning of her cousin Bobby's funeral, Jessica Sue had meant to tell Grandma Lucy about the Golden Horde of Mississippi, but she and the old woman had been fighting as usual and the music video just hadn't come up. To be fair, Jessica Sue *was* wearing a ratty pair of Dickies jeans and a faded Megadeth T-shirt, which she knew perfectly well was not proper funeral attire. But she hadn't come home for Christmas vacation expecting her cousin Bobby to slide his Harley-Davidson up under an eighteen-wheeler. And anyway, *this* was how Bobby would've wanted her to dress, and wasn't it *his* funeral after all? Wasn't *he* the one cremated and packed into that lavender and gold cloisonné urn up there on the mantelpiece?

Eye level with the urn, she could picture his nasty little eyes floating around in there with a few pieces of bone and patches of charred flesh in the otherwise uniform ash of a human being. She could tell you from the classes she took at the university, that when you boil him all down to gravy, there's perhaps a dollar's worth of chemicals in a human being. If you unfolded his organs down to their proteins and his proteins down to their amino acids and his amino acids down to their constituent elements, you're not left with much to bargain on. *The magic and the wonder are all in the folds,* she thought. *And folded within the billions upon billions of cells that make up a human body there is over six feet of DNA. Six feet.* But here in this urn was Bobby, unfolded, brought by fire to his basic state. And yet, thinking of her cousin Bobby, Jessica Sue couldn't help but wonder, were there chunks of him in there that had simply refused to go peacefully?

"My Bobby was a good boy," said Grandma Lucy. "He'd want you in a black dress, with your hair all combed nice like a young lady."

Bobby had been a lot of things, but "good boy," had never been one of them. Not even Grandma Lucy, who could see the good in a tornado—Grandma Lucy lived for a tornado—not even Grandma Lucy had ever called him a good boy when he was alive.

"Bobby was a little freak," said Jessica Sue, maybe louder and more emphatic than she'd meant to.

"There's not a thing wrong with him," said Grandma Lucy. "I'll have you know, he never once talked back to me in the manner you just have. That's for sure. He had respect for his elders."

All the long drive up Star Road to the church, Grandma Lucy, with the lavender cloisonné urn clutched to her chest, fumed over the usual suspects of her misfortune. How could her own children have grown up to abandon such monsters as these, her grandchildren—by which she meant the one: Jessica Sue—into her care? Why had she sent Jessica Sue off to college, where all the girl had learned was disrespect for her elders, the denial of God, and to go around wearing not even a stitch of underwear in a ratty pair of Dickies about to fall right off her, and T-shirts with pictures of the devil on them? So, keeping silent, Jessica Sue hadn't gotten around to mentioning the video.

The night before the funeral, she and her cousin-in-law Shauna, Bobby's widow, had sat up until three in the morning at the Waffle House plotting it all out. They'd video the band playing in the sanctuary, and then the service. They'd splice it all together with home movies of Bobby as a child and whatever weird stop-action stuff they could find off the Internet: flowers growing in seconds, the spinning dome of the stars. They'd really gotten into it, and by the time they were done working it out, she really thought they'd managed to capture the spiritual essence of just who Bobby was, of just what Bobby stood for. And when they parted ways, she told Shauna not to worry, to just get the Horde out to the church early and set up. She said she'd have Grandma Lucy well in hand by the time they got there. "You just tell Reverend Duey it was Grandma Lucy's idea," she said. "He's scared shitless of my grandmomma."

But then there was the fighting, and she hadn't said a thing all morning. Nor had she said a thing all that long drive up to the church. Truth be told, she'd lost a good bit of the reckless abandon of the night before. So she was a little nervous as they pulled into the parking lot at First Methodist of Brandon and saw it all spilled out and reeling across the asphalt and the flower beds. There were a dozen Harley-Davidson motorcycles, little demons of steel and leather, one with a sidecar, another one a chopper with six-foot chrome forks. There was a jacked-up Malibu, and a ragged-out Econoline, painted black with house paint, and the words, GOLDEN HORDE OF MISSISSIPPI, in dripping red. Parked in the handicapped zone was Bobby's brother-in-law's trike. Made from the back half of a Volkswagen Beetle and painted purple, its doors were decorated with pictures of stacked skulls and crawling rats. The driver, Shauna's brother, a great round gut of a man, all sunglasses, cheeks, and grease-crusted denim, a completely bald head and a two-foot long fork of beard, sat in the parking lot revving the trike's motor, slow and methodical, just to hear the blast. Rising to either side of him, flames shot out the silver pipes of the exhaust manifolds. In the flower bed by the front steps of the church, these latter-day Tamerlanes had planted their standard. A six-foot-long weight bar sharpened to a point at the bottom, it had two long black horsetails falling around the hubcap off a '59 Edsel. Welded to a crossbar and painted gold were the letters GAM. Bobby claimed it was Latin. "Fucking Latin, man. Like fucking ancient Rome. *Grex Aurum Mississippae, motherfucker.*"

A necklace of cat skulls hung around the disk of the hubcap. It was something Bobby used to wear over his shirtless and pale— almost translucent—and emaciated chest when he sang. In the parking lot, little knots of people milled about greeting and shaking hands. They were big men, most of them older than Bobby, in T-shirts and faded denim, biker leather and thick-soled boots. The women with them looked hard, in stiletto heels and leopard print. Some wore Metallica and Ironmaiden T-shirts, with more pictures of devils on them, jean jackets and leather against the chill. All around the parking lot sloped masses of long greasy hair, dark bloodshot eyes, twisted and scarred faces, missing teeth, missing limbs, a mechanical arm, all of them gathering toward the church, all pressing in toward the doors. These were Bobby's people, his friends, and members of his band. Spaced out at the far extremes of the parking lot, a few groups of family clung to one another, making their way slowly or not at all, some just standing in bewilderment, and some getting back into their cars and leaving.

"That godforsaken little tramp," said Grandma Lucy. Jessica Sue traced her finger along the necklace of cat skulls. She thought of Bobby in the garage screaming into a microphone. "Where is that slut? These are her people," said Grandma Lucy.

"Come on," said Jessica Sue. Since Grandma Lucy had the urn cradled to her chest like a football, Jessica Sue couldn't get her arm, but she took the old woman's elbow and led her up the steps and into the sanctuary. At the altar, Shauna, Bobby's widow, her bleached blond hair done up like the top end of a pineapple, crawled along the baseboards, dragging an electrical cord behind her. Commotion was general in the church. Two groups of bikers attempted to erect klieg lights at either side of the altar. A couple of other men had video cameras. They argued about angles and shadow. One man, dressed more as a Klingon than a warrior of the Asiatic steppe, wandered the sanctuary with a light meter. A small circle sat by the pulpit, pounding out a rhythm on bongo drums. The Horde's lead guitarist—one of Bobby's coworkers at the Jiffy Lube in Brandon—stood in front of a Marshall stack playing with feedback. "What in god's name?" said Grandma Lucy. "Where's Reverend Pickett?"

"Reverend Duey," Jessica Sue reminded her.

The Mintons—led by their matriarch—had been members of First Methodist for fifty years. Ever since Granddaddy'd come home from the war, with that great splash of color across his chest, testament to Minton superiority, and told her he'd converted to Methodism in a foxhole on Guadalcanal. Leastwise that's the way Grandma Lucy told it. There were bombs going off all around his head, and Japs charging out of the darkness, and Granddaddy down in that mud pit with nothing but a busted shovelhead and a Bible. Granddaddy never talked much about it. Truthfully, he just never talked. But Grandma Lucy could talk the horns off a goat. She said, when the Light come on Granddaddy in the darkness of that foxhole, he just stood right where he was, and walked out, killing Japs left and right with that busted shovelhead, and sending them on down to hell. That's what Grandma Lucy used to say. Jessica Sue and Bobby had grown up with this image of Granddaddy in their heads. He was

miles tall, walking his way up the ring of fire. Just hopping from island to island like they were stepping-stones across a creek. He sowed
the land with atom bombs, laying them down like he carried them
around in his pockets. A kind of apocalyptic Johnny Appleseed.
"Atom bomb," Grandma Lucy'd say, smiling, her eyes twinkling
bright. They'd all grown up knowing, if there was one thing Grandma
Lucy loved besides her grandbabies, Jesus, and a tornado, it was an
atom bomb. And that's how come the Mintons were a churchgoing
family, to thank Jesus for seeing Granddaddy home alive and for
sending our great nation the bomb. The day Granddaddy got home
she took his medals off him, and she sewed them into a square of
black velvet, embroidered on either side with the images of Douglas
MacArthur and Robert E. Lee. She hung it on the wall over the
mantelpiece. On one side was a painting of Jesus and on the other a
piece of Elvis Presley commemorative flatware, the one with him in
that shiny gold suit. It was the perfect shrine for Granddaddy's little
pewter urn full of ashes, which now sat before that mantelpiece display on a lace doily, just like Grandma Lucy'd planned it all along.

So ever since the war the Mintons had been members at First
Methodist. And Mintons were everywhere. They sat on all the com-
mittees, taught Sunday school classes, and sang in the choir. It was
Grandma Lucy's sister played the organ. And in all those years it'd
been Reverend Pickett up at the pulpit. He was one of those godly
men who are born old. He had the soft and pliant skin of the sunless,
and his sermons were as regular and ordinary as a metronome.
Grandma Lucy insisted he was the wisest man she'd ever met. Jessica
Sue thought him a complete fool. They'd bickered about that for
years, but it was pointless now. Reverend Pickett had died that spring
of a coronary embolism. Reverend Duey had been with the church
for seven months now.

The changes hadn't been to Grandma Lucy's liking. Reverend Duey must've been about thirty years old. He was full of passion and vigor for the Lord. And his righteousness had a tendency to manifest itself in spontaneous song and guitar plunking. He was earnest to a fault, and he drove Grandma Lucy nuts saying things like, "People have to find their own paths to Jesus," and "The Lord works in mysterious ways."

"Reverend Duey," said Grandma Minton, letting the revulsion roll around in her mouth before she spit it out. "Where is that fool?"

"Hey," Shauna Minton shouted from the altar. "Y'all done brought Bobby. Hey, everybody, Bobby's here, we can get rolling."

Shauna flopped the electrical cord over the pulpit and bounced down the aisle to see them. "Ain't it just great?" she said. "I ain't slept a wink all night. Soon as we left the Waffle House, I got the Horde all woke up and told 'em. We're almost ready to go. But y'all know where's an electrical socket up there?"

"There's one up by the choir box," said Jessica Sue.

"Where is Duey?" said Grandma Lucy.

"What are you plugging in?" said Jessica Sue. "I guess I envisioned something a little simpler, a camcorder maybe. Where'd you get the lights?"

"Duey!" Grandma Lucy screamed. "Reverend, you best get out here quick."

"They's a junior high up the road there. My brother'll put 'em back when we're done," said Shauna. "But I got to plug in Bobby's microphone."

Jessica Sue looked at the urn clutched to Grandma Lucy's chest. "Duey! Reverend!"

Reverend Duey stuck his head out from the back door. He had a slightly crazed look about him, his hair all electric and his vestments loose around him. He came hurriedly down the aisle to meet them, with his palms pressing the air in front of him, in the motion of a man trying to keep it all under control. "Now, this is all just fine here. Everything is under control," he said.

"Under control?" said Grandma Lucy. "This place is run amok with hoodlums."

"Microphone?" said Jessica Sue. "What's Bobby need a microphone for?"

"It *is* under control, Mrs. Minton," said Duey. "They're different folks. That they are. But they're the children of the Lord, too. And they've been very professional."

"What's he need it for?" said Shauna, utterly dismayed. "To sing 'The Dirge of the Dark Sun,' liked we talked about at the Waffle House."

"I know. I remember," said Jessica Sue. "But can't it just *look* like he's got a microphone?"

Grandma Lucy sniffed the air. Jessica Sue had noticed the faint odor of marijuana when they first came in the church. She'd been hoping Grandma Lucy wouldn't smell it. "Reverend Duey," she said. "This here is a house of God, for Christ's sake."

"It's that Dark Star," said Shauna. "Bobby was obsessed with it. You know what he told me? Right before he got on that motorbike and headed off for Biloxi, he said, it was the Dark Star that was *ultimately real,* not nothing else. And he said to sing it you had to sing it real."

"As Jesus tells us," said Reverend Duey. "My father's house has many rooms, Mrs. Minton. Now, Bobby was a different boy, you know? But the Lord comes to folks like Bobby, too."

"I see," said Jessica Sue. "Since the Dark Star isn't a metaphor, you can't have just the metaphor of a live mike, you got to have the real live mike even for the video?"

Shauna wrinkled up her nose. She put her hands to her hips and a couple of creases formed across her forehead.

"Different?" said Grandma Lucy. "There weren't nothing different about my Bobby. He was a good boy."

"Well," said Shauna, her enthusiasm on the wane. "I don't reckon I know nothing about no metaphors or nothing. I just know Bobby said it was ultimately real is all."

"He was a good boy," said Reverend Duey. "But he was a dog with a different set of fleas. He's in a better place now, Mrs. Minton. He sings with the angels. But we're all still here to carry on. And these are Bobby's people. They want to remember him in this way."

"Yes," said Jessica Sue. She was jumping to her toes as she spoke. "Yes, you see, Shauna, the Dark Star *is* ultimately real. All this time I've been thinking of it as just a metaphor, like maybe a metaphor for Bobby's social estrangement. But it ain't just a metaphor. It's *real.* I mean theoretically, anyway. So what Bobby's saying is that it's an *ultimately real metaphor.* You see?"

Shauna looked around. "I just need to plug his mike in," she said. "So's he can sing the song."

Jessica Sue looked to the urn. "Right," she said. She knew better than to have this conversation. "Of course. He needs his microphone plugged in."

"His people?" said Grandma Lucy. "His people? This trash ain't his people. Look at them."

"Shauna here was his wife," said Reverend Duey. He was kind of backing up as he said it, like maybe he'd be able to back all the way up past this morning, beyond last night and over the previous week, to a world where Bobby hadn't slammed his Harley-Davidson under that semitrailer, to a world where there were no Mintons at all even, but just shiny proper Methodists all lined up and ready to do good things and to be good people. Shauna must've really laid into him this morning when she sprung it on him.

"*I* am his grandmother," said Grandma Lucy, placing one hand over her heart and tucking the urn in the crook of her elbow. "I raised him myself. Raised up a good half dozen children in my day. Some were mine, and some were the children of mine, when my own children couldn't raise them, like Bobby and Jessica Sue right here. When their own fathers left out on them. I raised every last child the Lord seen fit to send me. And every last one of them was a good little boy or girl. You can believe that. And let me tell you something else. There ain't going to be no music video at my Bobby's funeral. The sheriff won't have any truck with it. And don't you think I won't call him, neither. I got me a cellular phone."

With the urn tucked in the crook of one arm, she dug through her purse with her free hand until she brought out the phone.

They were all dead silent after that. All the talking and murmuring drew to a close. Even the footfalls ceased, and all the eyes in the room focused on the group of them standing in the aisle. The Golden Horde had all spent nights in jail. Some had done ninety days. Jessica Sue knew for a fact Shauna's brother had spent six months on fish row. They were the sort who lived their lives watching in the rearview mirror. When they looked through their peepholes to the unexpected knock at the door, it wasn't a vision of thugs come to rob them that flashed through their heads, it was sheriff's deputies. Jessica Sue felt a slight churning of violence in the sweat-filled air of the church sanctuary. But that violence died in the thoughts of flashing strobe lights and squad cars, the crackle and static of radios, and the hard thunk of authority on the planks of the church floor. It was as if, spewed from Grandma Lucy's mouth, the deputies themselves came boiling into the room, swinging their batons and cocking their shotguns. The whole crowd seemed to heave as one, and then to sink into the pews before the propriety of the ma-triarch, her rights and prerogatives, and the threat of civic authority. Grandma Minton looked upon them with disdain. Reverend Duey tried to wipe the startled look off his face. But he only managed to blur himself into a long *O* of panic and uncertainty, as he no doubt saw his ministry evaporating. Shauna dropped the microphone. The Golden Horde seemed to deflate as one, and there was just that dead silence in the church.

It might've ended that way. But as Grandma Lucy always main-tained, Jessica Sue was prone to argument. The thing was she just couldn't get past the difference that had come over Bobby in this, the last year of his life. It wasn't that Bobby had been a lazy child. On the contrary, he'd always hurled himself full force into whatever weird-ness had captivated his infernal brain for the moment. It's just that growing up his interests had tended toward the destructive, not the creative. He'd built everything from zip guns to CO_2 and sparkler bombs. Under his mattress—where a normal boy might keep a swiped copy of *Playboy* magazine—Bobby hid his intricately detailed designs for a homemade nuclear device. Yet he had not managed to pass high school science. Nor for that matter had he managed to pass high school. He could spill out endlessly on the great crimes and psy-chopaths of world history. The banks of the Oxus River were more real to him than the state of Mississippi, as if he, too, had come rag-ing off the steppe to lay waste to the fatted children of the valleys. "To carry off their daughters," he'd scream at her, explaining his mor-bid desires.

And of their daughters—much to her distaste—Jessica Sue knew all to well. He used to tell her his perverted fantasies as they waited for the school bus in the mornings. It would take place in the Year of Four Emperors, as Vespasian's troops are sacking Rome in the midst of the Saturnalia, and the people, who just don't care anymore, are fucking in the streets. "Think of it," he'd say. "Slaughter to the right. And to the left, harlots and wine." He'd bring himself to a fever pitch, screaming "Don't you see? Don't you get it? Humanity will not truly be free, until there is fucking in the streets!"

And yet, his grasp of ancient history aside, she doubted seriously that at the time of his death, Bobby could've said who the president of the United States was, or—she suspected—that the United States was even governed by such things as presidents. It was as if Bobby lived at right angles to the real world, wandering through it, but in a wholly different direction from all other directions.

The band, however, was a different story. They were loud, yes, and morbid to the very core. In the beginning, they sang songs of the desperado, songs of trailer court love, gunfire and whiskey, galloping horses in the scattered drum. Whistling arrows. The flash of standards in the dust. Amid it all, the Scourge of God hurled himself among his audience, heaping vile epithets upon them. Blood flowed. His blood and the blood of his fans in a kind of maniacal oblivion and pure burst of rock-and-roll release that could never have lasted beyond the nine gigs and thirteen months that it did.

Of late, however, the Horde's music had begun to evolve. And Jessica Sue could not help but take a bit of credit for the new direction. In a summer session astronomy class, she had fallen in love with the theoretical notion of the Nemesis Star, a possible explanation for the periodic regularity of mass extinctions that take place on the Earth. This great clockwork of cosmic death, supposedly a black dwarf, swings round the sun every twenty-six million years, bringing from out of the Oort cloud a rain of ice and stone. The impacting comets turn the atmosphere to plasma, and the dust blots out the sun for a thousand years. It is an age of death. One evening, down on Grandma Lucy's pier, as they watched the Leonids and shared a joint, she told the Horde all about it. Bobby was beside himself with dread and excitement. He kept pointing into space and saying, "It's out there. Right out there. Even now the Dark Sun rounds the far corner of its evil path and sets its sights on the inner realms of the living."

That night he wrote "The Dirge of the Dark Sun." It was nine minutes of epic spacescape, with crashing cascades of electron rock. The tale of a fleet of Roman triremes commanded by the eight-foot tall Thracian general, Maximin Thrax himself, cruel barbarian emperor of Rome, on a voyage of conquest against the dwarves of the Dark Sun, those brainless and mute gods of the underrealm. Across a moon they wander in columns of despair, dragging their beards through the pooled methane lakes and crystalline jungles of that dark void. Tears of sulfur pour from their empty sockets, and in their throats rattle the croaking of toads, the flopping of broken wings, and the scutter of rats' feet. But there, streaking out of the sunlit worlds of the inner solar system, flies a great navy of triremes, their sails long washes of kaleidoscopic hydrogen and argon, trailing plasma across a light year in all the hues of the radiant spectrum. With a foot propped on the bow of his great flagship stands Maximin Thrax. He laughs, shaking whole star systems and galaxies from the wild nebulae of his hair. And with them, falling in spirals of infinite regress, come the marching hoplites, the columns of snowbound elephant, a multitude of legionnaires all assembled in square and wedge. There are horsemen in silver armor, the symbols of their gods emblazoned on their white robes. Pike men in hedgehog, before a charge. A cannonade, the hiss of gas and panzer troops, the rolling squeal of tank tread, a squadron of Zeros diving out of the nebulae. Circling overhead, like a great mirror-ball, there is a lone B-29, almost placid above the waters. And shooting out of it all, spewed out of that heaving galactic sex, out of that coursing plasmatic dark circus of human history and death, rides Bobby. He is bare-chested but for the necklace of cat skulls. He rides a winged Harley-Davidson, his fist high in the air gripping the standard of the Golden Horde of Mississippi. He screams across the eons of space, "Fucking in the streets! Let there be fucking in the streets." Thus was "The Dirge of the Dark Sun." Thus was rock and roll. And as far as Jessica Sue was concerned, they just couldn't have picked a better setting for the video.

"Grandma Lucy," she said, snatching Bobby's urn from her grip. "You're not calling the sheriff. We got us a rock video to shoot, and you just don't seem to understand. This here was Bobby's dream. He really put his all into that song, and all he wanted to do was make this video and send it off to MTV and get it put on the air. And you know what he told me? He said all he ever wanted to do in life was to show his Grandma Lucy he wasn't the fool everybody always said he was and that he was capable of something special in life and he wasn't just a nobody."

"He said that?" said Grandma Lucy. She reached for the urn, but checked herself, watching Jessica Sue, who towered over her now, young and flush and full of seething.

"That's what he said," Jessica Sue lied. "That's what he told me. He just wanted to be a success for his grandmomma."

"Well, it don't matter," said Grandma Lucy. "It's not fitting. This ain't fitting. It's—"

"It fits just fine," said Jessica Sue. "You give me that phone."

"No," said Grandma Lucy. But Jessica Sue had the phone away from her before she could flip it open.

"Come on, now," said Jessica Sue. "Let's have a seat and get on with this thing. We just need a good take of the band playing and then we'll film the funeral and that'll be that. Think of it, you'll be able to watch it whenever you want. Maybe it'll even make it to the TV."

"No," said Grandma Lucy. But she was already being led to her pew. Already she'd fallen. With a look of the lost about her, she watched the floor. Her skeleton seemed to dissolve into the pew when she sat. Suddenly she was eighty years old and no longer the matriarch, but just the afterimage of the matriarch. Nothing. Fallen and usurped. *No,* thought Jessica Sue. *That's not what I meant. That's not what I wanted at all.* The way she'd imagined it, Grandma Lucy sat tall and proud through the spaced-out Hammond intro of the Dirge, only to close her eyes, her mouth falling open as the blast of a sampled glass-packed 440 signaled the driving bass to come up to speed. It was to be a kind of ecstatic release of maternal cosmic energy and thought. But even more than the Dirge and the Horde and the video and even Bobby, Jessica Sue hadn't meant for Grandma Lucy to dissolve into eighty years. She hadn't meant to cause that. Already the Horde had gone back to shooting. She and Grandma Lucy were far, far away.

Through it all, Jessica Sue sat with her knees pulled up to her chest and her eyes on the floor. Grandma Lucy watched it unfold. Her eyes, beady and caged in the powdered rounds of her cheeks, darted around the sanctuary, in search of something that wasn't there. Even the Horde played with a lackluster air, each of them slipping back into the roles of the second-rate bar musicians they were without Bobby. Only Shauna tried to sustain the magic, with wild swinging camera work, and the adamant and incessant stamping of her feet when they weren't showing enough energy. Finally, disgusted, she shut off the klieg lights and hollered for Reverend Duey to get on with it, shooting was a bust for that day.

As the lights died and the church returned to the rainbow of stained glass, Jessica Sue was struck with the fact that not a single Minton, beyond herself and Grandma Lucy, remained in the church to pray with Reverend Duey. Not a single one had even come in. And neither her father nor Bobby's own had even shown themselves in the parking lot. All through Reverend Duey's stumbling service—he knew he'd be fired by next Sunday—she wanted to just stop everything and take it all back. It could've just been the funeral Grandma Lucy'd wanted. There could've been vases full of flowers and clean-looking, honest, Christian relatives. She herself could've gone to her grandmother's closet and found an old shawl-collared black dress and a necklace of pearls maybe, instead of this Megadeth T-shirt. There could've been people standing up at the pulpit with good things to say about a good boy, whom God had seen fit to call home so young. She could've stood up there herself and talked about riding in Bobby's go-cart and catching frogs and crickets and fishing and raising pigs in 4-H. Some of it wouldn't even have been lies. She wouldn't have to mention that he'd strapped M-80s to the frogs and used them as suicide bombers in the neighbors' mailboxes.

She might've talked about Grandma Lucy, too; about what a brave and honorable woman she'd been for taking them all in like she had. She might've looked out at the audience as she said it, and maybe her own daddy and Bobby's, too, would've been there in the front row with Grandma Lucy instead of wherever they were. Probably drunk. And maybe they'd have the nice and shiny well-fed look of nice and shiny well-fed Methodists. And maybe Grandma Lucy'd be smiling here on this pew instead of crying and maybe she wouldn't be crying either, because maybe Bobby wouldn't even be dead, but just shiny and well-fed looking and nice, instead of scrawny and evil and dead-looking and burned up to dust in that gold and lavender cloisonné urn. That rock-and-roll urn. That sure as shit rock-and-roll urn. Where Bobby lay. Probably chunks of him not wanting to burn up and go, but just lying there in the dust, refusing to unfold themselves and go back to nothing. So by the end she thought the video was just stupid, and the service was even dumber, and none of it was what she'd meant. Not at all, it wasn't what she'd meant at all.

The entire drive home they sat in silence; Grandma Lucy stared at the urn in her lap, and Jessica Sue stared at the road.

She saw Uncle Frank the moment she got home. He was down at the pier with a fishing pole and a cooler full of beer. She stood in the drive and watched him, but he never looked up. Grandma Lucy made no comment on his absence from the funeral. Grandma Lucy, with single-minded determination, walked in the house, the urn clutched in front of her. It was to go on the mantelpiece next to Granddaddy. But Jessica Sue stood in the drive a while longer, watching her uncle turn red in the sun and drink beer and pretend to fish. After a while she wandered down toward him, past Grandma Lucy's holly bushes, down past the cove and the rowboats, picking her way carefully and meandering a little, not really wanting to talk to him at all.

Back when she and Bobby were little, Uncle Frank used to disappear for long stretches. Sometimes he'd come home rich, all watch chains and wingtips, handing out dollars to all the cousins and whiskey, too. She'd sat on his knee one Christmas, taking sips of whiskey from a silver flask. Sometimes he'd come home broke. There'd be no whiskey and no silver, just flecks of blood in the commode for the week or so he was there, silent and brooding along the hallway. Nobody spoke much then. They all just waited for him to go.

Once when she was a child, she'd seen him try to kill a man. One Sunday they were up at a shot shack on Star Road, Uncle Frank and Granddaddy. She and Bobby waited on them in the cab of Granddaddy's truck. They sat with their faces pressed against the glass, fogging up the cab. One moment there was the sound of laughter from the shack. Then Uncle Frank and another man came boiling out the door and rolling in the gravel. The whole place spilled out, men howling and breaking glass. They heard the sound of wrenched and splintered wood. Uncle Frank had his man by the shirt collar, and he dragged him to the front of Granddaddy's truck. With his knee he got the man's head down a few feet behind the tire, and he was yelling for Bobby to drop the truck out of gear. Bobby crept forward. He put his hand on the stick. Uncle Frank kept yelling for him to just knock it out of gear, to just run this SOB's head over. She could remember watching Bobby with his hand on the stick, wondering if he'd do it. They were crying. Bobby had the stick gripped in his little fist. And when she reached out and touched his face, he just seemed to explode, hurling himself away from the stick and slamming against the passenger side door. Somebody came and dragged Uncle Frank away, and the men went back inside the shack. They all fell to drinking again. She and Bobby held hands in the cab. They said nothing between them at all. Finally, after a couple of hours, Grandma Lucy found them. She must've walked fifteen miles down Star Road from the house.

The day of Bobby's funeral Uncle Frank sat out at the end of the pier with his cooler. He must've heard her come up. The pier was an old and rickety affair with boards falling through to the water. She hadn't wanted to sneak up on him; Uncle Frank wasn't the sort of man you snuck up on. So she called to the dogs and she kicked at the rocks all along the path from the house. But when she got there, she found she had nothing to say, so she just stood behind him for a while. She thought about pushing him in. Just getting a good running go at it and slamming into him. The boards would give. See him splash. See the terrified look on his face as the water rolled across the top of him.

"It was a good service," she said.

He turned quick as a cat and threw a full beer at her. It flew past her cheek and crashed against a pine, spraying her with foam and glass. His eyes were cold and dead, and he stared straight into the space where she stood. She turned and without speaking further, she walked back to the house.

"What is the matter with that son of a bitch?" she said, rounding into the kitchen, where Grandma Lucy stood over the sink scrubbing the dirt off potatoes. Grandma Lucy dropped the potato she was holding. She'd been crying. "I'm sorry," said Jessica Sue.

"It's all right," said Grandma Lucy. "He is a son of a bitch, isn't he? I'd pull the switch on him myself if the governor would just get a hold to him. I don't know what it was I done wrong with those children."

"No, I'm sorry about—I'm sorry about that, too," she said. "I forgot he's your boy."

"He was," said Grandma Lucy. "I guess he still is, so I don't run him off when he comes by. I thought I'd do better with Bobby."

"You did," said Jessica Sue. "Bobby was a good boy."

"No," said Grandma Lucy. "No. You're right. You really are. He was a lot of things, but a good boy was never one of them. Come in here. Come take a look at this."

Grandma Lucy dried her hands on a kitchen towel. She smoothed her apron and seemed to take a last look around the kitchen to see if it was in order. They walked into the living room and Grandma Lucy led her to the mantelpiece where the urn display sat. There were two little lace doilies now, one for granddaddy and his dull-colored pewter urn, and another for the gold and lavender cloisonné explosion of Bobby's. Grandma Lucy had a stepladder she kept by the mantel for cleaning. She pulled herself to the top of it. Jessica Sue got on her tiptoes, so they were at about the same height, breathing the same air. She could hear the labor in her grandmother's lungs. The Elvis Presley commemorative flatware was dusty, cobwebs trailed from it to the brick chimney. Jessica Sue made a mental note to dust it off before she returned to the university. Grandma Lucy took down the picture of Jesus Christ. With her sleeve she wiped it free of dust. Grandma Lucy didn't say anything for a long time. She seemed to be studying the picture, her eyes darting across it as if she read something there. Jessica Sue stood beside her with her hands thrust deep in her pockets, watching her grandmother wipe the dust from the image of the blue-eyed hippie Jesus. She put the picture back on the wall and ran her fingers across granddaddy's war metals. She traced along the edge of the embroidered figures of Robert E. Lee and Douglas MacArthur.

"Such great men," said Grandma Lucy. "Such fine and honorable men, engaged in such valiant and noble causes. You should've seen how fine Windom looked in his uniform."

Jessica Sue had only ever heard Grandma Lucy refer to him as Granddaddy, and it took her a moment to realize who she was talking about. "He made corporal by the end of the war. He'd have retired a sergeant if he'd stayed in, you know? And when I think of those heathen Japs coming after him, it just curdles my blood. I just know it was God on our side. It was God sent us men like your granddaddy and Douglas MacArthur. And it was God's hand at Hiroshima, too. I can tell you that. That right there was the power of God."

This was the point where Jessica Sue usually broke in, but somewhere along the way she'd crossed that threshold to where it was no longer of any use to argue with her elder relations. "I reckon so," she said. "I reckon that was the power of God."

And Grandma Lucy must've known she'd crossed it, too, because she didn't bother to go on anymore about it. She didn't bother to talk about how Granddaddy drove a Ford until the day he died, and couldn't either of them believe it when their own children came home driving Datsuns and Toyotas, and the war not thirty years old.

She didn't bother to go on; she just stood there running her fingers across the medals. She didn't say any of that this time. And so Jessica Sue wished she had broken in and argued with her like she normally did, just so Grandma Lucy could have the satisfaction of talking down imported automobiles and the ungrateful children who drove them.

"Bobby really wasn't such a bad boy," said Jessica Sue. "I was just thinking of that time you came to get us out Star Road, when Granddaddy and Uncle Frank were down there drinking and remember I said Uncle Frank tried to kill a man?"

"Yes," said Grandma Lucy. "I remember that."

"And I remember fishing with Bobby a lot," she said, wracking her brain for anything like a decent story to tell. "I remember this one time I caught a ten-pound bass right out there off of that pier. And you know Bobby he cleaned every bit of that fish for me. He was so excited when I was reeling it in."

"Pick up Granddaddy," said Grandma Lucy.

"What?"

"Pick him up. Don't he feel light?"

"Light?" said Jessica Sue. She picked up the pewter urn and hefted it a few times as if to judge. "I don't know," she said. "I can't remember."

"Open it up," said Grandma Lucy. "Just unscrew the cap there."

Jessica Sue unscrewed the urn and looked inside. There was just the dark interior of the vessel. No dust at all. She turned to get a better look in the light from the windows. She had to turn it sideways and tap it a bit. There at the bottom was a couple of fingers worth of dust. "What?" she said. "Where is he?"

Grandma Lucy nodded. She climbed down from the stepladder and walked to the sofa and began picking through her junk mail. Jessica Sue looked at the pewter urn. "Where's the rest of him?" she said.

"Bobby," said Grandma Lucy. "I seen him one night. Maybe a week ago. He and Shauna'd been fighting like they will, and he was staying out here like he tends to. I had the sciatica so bad I couldn't sleep. So, I was up, and trying to walk soft so as not to wake him, and I seen him in here at the mantel. He was making himself one of those marijuana cigarettes you two smoke."

"Grandma, I don't—"

"I know you do," she said. "It ain't ladylike, I can tell you. But I don't reckon it's all that big a deal, really. Windom used to do it before the war. A lot of the country boys who'd come to Mobile did. It's not the marijuana, but he was putting Windom in there, you see. He was smoking them ashes in his marijuana cigarettes. Been doing it years now, till Windom's all but gone."

"Bobby smoked him?" said Jessica Sue. "Why on earth would he do that? It's—well, I don't know just what it is."

"It's morbid," said Grandma Lucy. "It's filthy. I don't know what could've possessed him. All I wanted was just a normal funeral. Just one moment of him being normal would've been enough for me. But it didn't matter, did it? Even dead and gone he had to be strange."

Jessica Sue rotated the urn so the dust spiraled around the lip of it. She had an urge to blow into the urn and send the particles flying in a cloud all around her, all the around the room, and out into the world, dispersing them back into the system. Into stone and water, grass and trees, the whole swarm of beetles and snakes, mice and dogs. She looked at her own hand gripping the urn, and wondered about the countless generations bound up in the meat of her own palm. If you sit quiet enough you can hear the flux of your own nervous system, that great collision of billions upon billions of tiny stones. She screwed the top down on the urn and set it back on the doily, walked to the sofa and sat, curling her legs beneath her. "Granddaddy was a dope smoker?" she said.

"He smoked it," said Grandma Lucy. "In Mobile, during the depression. You see, he had him a job waiting tables. But in those days you had to pay the restaurant for the privilege. That's how it worked. So he'd have a few pints of whiskey in his jacket and that there marijuana. And he'd take it around to the tables with him."

"Did you?" said Jessica Sue.

"Oh, no," said Grandma Lucy. "No indeed. It's not ladylike at all."

"No," said Jessica Sue. She put her feet to the floor and sat staring between her knees. "I guess not."

"Well," said Grandma Lucy. "I did once. It's not right, and I don't think you should do it. But I did do it once."

"Tell me about it," said Jessica Sue. She curled her feet beneath her again. "Please," she said.

"Oh, it ain't nothing to tell," she said. "I snuck it from Windom once, when he wasn't looking. I used to worry about it, but it just give me a headache. I figured if Windom got that much enjoyment out of smacking his head against a wall, I ought to let him. Lord knows, he could do worse. But he stopped all that after the war. He took Jesus as his Lord and Savior on Guadalcanal. He was fighting them Japs—"

"I know," said Jessica Sue. "But, you just snuck it—"

"—and they were coming into that foxhole. They just kept on coming. One right after the other and they just wouldn't stop. I can see it," she said. "I can see how it went. He found Jesus in that foxhole, and it was Jesus put that shovelhead in his hand; it was Jesus leading him then. And it was Jesus lifted him up out that mud and gore."

She was off and running. Jessica Sue let her mind drift as the story she'd heard so many times before fell into recitation. It was a children's story Grandma Lucy had always told them. She'd always known it was a children's story, with blue skies and puffy clouds that twisted to become rabbits and butterflies, great sailing ships and adventure. There was Granddaddy rising up from the mud, covered in it and stinking. He rises up from the mud with that busted shovelhead in his hand. He rises up, and he's a thousand miles high, like Jesus Christ. And he walks, stepping from island to island, up the chain of fire, casting atom bombs like grass seed. Thank god for Granddaddy and thank god for the bomb. Jessica Sue sat quietly and listened. She interjected where she was expected to interject. It was a children's story Grandma Lucy had always told them. Tomorrow Jessica Sue would pack her things and head back to the university. Maybe she wouldn't return again. It was all just a children's story; Grandma Lucy'd made it all up.

In the evening, after Grandma Lucy had gone to bed, she still sat on the sofa. She'd drawn her knees under her chin, and she sat with her arms wrapped around her knees. She hadn't turned on the lights and so it was dark in the house. But she could see the mantelpiece from the light of the stars though the window. After a while, she stood and began to wander through the house, turning on the lights as she went. She wandered into the bathrooms and the kitchen, remembering the rooms, and also seeing them fresh for the very first time. How small they'd become. She opened the refrigerator. A month-old pot of green beans. The turkey from Thanksgiving. She wandered down the hall to her old room. It'd become storage in the three years she'd been gone. Stacks of Grandma Lucy's magazines were piled on the floor. The closets spilled out with old clothes, slowly dissolving due to the moths. Across the hall, she opened the door to Bobby's room. Guitar parts littered the floor and a Marshall stack dominated one wall. The torn-apart corpses of electronics were scattered everywhere, even across the bed. She imagined he must've slept with it, rolling in the transistors and solder, awakening with it stuck in his skin. There were posters of Danzig and Black Sabbath, but also Gong and Camel. On one wall was a map of the world he'd drawn. Studying it, she saw that the countries were all different. There was the great nation of Zepplonia, for example, stretched across the north of Europe, from Ultima Thule to Siberia. It was covered with myth as well. On the southern tip of Africa sat Black Sert with his flaming sword, awaiting the end of time. Centered where a normal map would've had Mississippi was a gold star and the words CAPITAL OF THE UNIVERSE, in precise gothic script. She opened his desk drawer. There was a bag of marijuana in there and a box of rolling papers. She took these and put them in her pocket. She turned to go, but she stopped at the sight of Bobby's four-track recorder. She sat, pushing the junk out of her way, and put the headphones on. There was a stack of tapes. One by one she pushed them into the machine and listened, going through them in the best chronological order she could figure. There at the bottom of the stack was "The Dirge of the Dark Sun." It was a different version, earlier. Something Bobby hadn't meant for anyone to hear, much more raw, acoustic and plaintive.

When the song ended, she popped it out of the four-track and stuck it in her pocket with the rolling papers and the marijuana. On a shelf she found a Walkman cassette player. She went back to the living room and the mantelpiece. She thought about the meat of her own palms. She thought about the version of the song Bobby hadn't meant for anyone to hear. She thought about the children's story Grandma Lucy had always told them. And she thought about Maximin Thrax. When she was finished thinking, she took Bobby's urn from the mantel and found her shoes. She opened the door gently, so as not to wake Grandma Lucy and she stole her way down to the pier. Uncle Frank had long since gone. He'd never even stopped by the house. He'd left the cooler out there and his pole, too. He must've fished at some point in the evening, because he'd left a string of brim tied to the railing. There was no moon that night and the stars were wild and full of pale fire. *Pale,* she thought, *because light falls off at a rate of one over r squared. This is because it has three degrees of freedom,* she thought. *If we lived in a four-dimensional space, light would fall off at a rate of one over r cubed. And you would not even be able to see the sun. This is the interconnection of all things, even space. That is, all things are not merely interconnected* in *space, but* with *space. Things and space are one and the same.*

She set the urn on the railing. Beside it she laid out the bag of marijuana and the rolling papers and a lighter. She unscrewed the top of the urn, and set it aside. She reached in and drew out a pinch of dust. There were no chunks as she had expected. Fire had unloosed even Bobby. Even Bobby had unfolded himself to his basic con-stituents. Even Bobby was just an intricate weave of tiny stones. She took a rolling paper and put the dust in a line down the middle of it. She took some of the marijuana and she laid this over the dust. And then she folded up the paper into a tight cylinder and licked the gum and sealed it. She put it in her mouth unlit and let it rest there. Then she took the urn and turned it upside down over the lake, so all of Bobby's ashes fell into the water, returning to the system. She re-minded herself to fill it with earth on the way back to the house. Then she lit the joint and she sat back on Uncle Frank's cooler and she leaned against the rail and she smoked, looking at the stars.

She sat a long time thinking about him and listening to the acoustic version of "The Dirge of the Dark Sun" on his Walkman. The version nobody was ever meant to hear. She could see him out there, riding his winged motorcycle against the silent velvet of space. Out there, among the ice and stone of the Oort cloud. Out there, looking for the nether realms. He is alone and naked. He crawls, feel-ing his way along a shelf of ice. He holds a saucer of pale fire in his hand and he crawls slowly, feeling his way in the darkness. He turns, and looks back; the sun is just a star among the stars; he is so far out. At first he cannot distinguish it from the others. He believes it is that one. He is so far out. The ice he crawls along could be knocked loose of the sun's hold at any moment. Any passing body. Any wandering black dwarf would be enough to knock him loose. He is out there on his knees, with a saucer of pale fire. The winged Harley-Davidson lies bleeding and rain soaked. And the blood and the rain mingle and filter down along the grooves of the asphalt. Its wings heave a last sigh. There is no sound out here in the black of the Oort cloud. All his triremes are gone, swept away in the rain, with all his panzers and hoplites, the B-29 and all his trebuchets. Maximin Thrax is dead by the hands of his own men, his head sent back to the senate, and his body violated and hurled to the dogs. He has faded into memory with all the sideshow of human history. As the Dark Sun swings past, he neither hears it, nor sees it. He can only see the stars. He cannot hear the semi's hydraulics, nor the clatter of the cat skulls on the pavement, nor the high-pitched whine of the sirens. He cannot hear the ice knock against itself. His saucer of pale fire cannot illuminate the ice that knocks loose, beginning the journey inward. And it cannot illuminate the shelf of ice upon which he kneels, knocked loose, knocked outward, knocked free of the sun. There is Bobby against the black velvet of space, with a saucer of pale fire in his hand. He kneels, and he reaches out with his free hand, reaching out for the Oort clouds of other stars.

FRANCES HWANG

Fine Arts Work Center in Provincetown

GARDEN CITY

~ 5,300 words

No one wanted to rent the Chens' apartment. It sat vacant for three months, collecting dust and heat. Footsteps now and then echoed along the wood floors. Voices came and went. Sometimes the drone of a fly butting itself against glass. Eventually, the fly—its legs as thin as eyelashes—dried on the kitchen window sill.

In August, when Mr. Chen opened the door, he felt the apartment's hot breath as he entered. The Christian lady followed behind. The windows had become as cruel as magnifying glass. Mr. Chen's head swam, as if it were severed from his body and floating in the ocean. He blinked, trying to see the woman more clearly.

"A good apartment, this one," he heard himself saying. "Everything paid for. Garbage. Electricity."

His eyes were watering. For a moment, he could not remember what he was going to say. He walked over to the windows and began pulling down the blinds. Light glinted off cars and trees from the parking lot.

"Garden also," Mr. Chen murmured.

His wife called the apartment their worst investment. "Other than you and I getting married, this apartment has been the biggest mistake of our lives," she said.

No one wanted to live there. The rent was too high, even though the Chens kept lowering their price, stopping at eight hundred to break even. People called, but lost interest when they heard it wasn't near the subway station. The ones who actually saw the apartment examined the scratched floors, smiled politely at the 1970s plastic cabinets, inquired whether there was a dishwasher. There wasn't. Washing machine? Dryer? Mr. Chen shook his head. The laundromat was next door. After that, there was only the bedroom left to see. This was the moment Mr. Chen dreaded the most. He always felt an urge to apologize for how small it was—the previous owner had called it "quaint" when he showed it to the Chens eight years ago. If the people were kind, they went through the motions of opening the closet door and peering inside. A short while later, they thanked Mr. Chen, saying they would think about it. The door closed, and Mr. Chen was left standing alone in the apartment. He was a stout man, but at such moments his body seemed to cave in, as if his bones were softening. The apartment was quiet and hollowed out. A part of him wanted to rest on the dull wood floor, the same color as earth. He didn't want to go home to his wife and tell her of another failure.

They had bought the apartment because Mr. Chen thought it would be safe to invest in real estate. It wasn't like the stock market where you bought what you couldn't touch, your money rising and falling due to intangible economic winds. Mr. Chen had a literal mind. He promised his wife they would be able to earn four or even five hundred dollars a month once they paid off the mortgage. He hadn't realized that the apartment management would raise their maintenance fee every year, that the value of the property would fall, and that no one would be interested in renting. It was a bad sign when most of the people living there were the apartment owners themselves.

When Mr. Chen thought about it carefully, he was convinced that he had been fooled into buying the apartment. He blamed the garden—a conservatory pungent with the smell of overripe flowers that adjoined the lobby. Eight years earlier, he and Mrs. Chen had been beguiled by the magenta-speckled lilies as they sat together on one of the wooden benches. Mr. Chen had gotten out of his seat once or twice, pacing the garden in an excited manner. "Who wouldn't want to live here?" he said in Chinese to his wife.

Mrs. Chen knew that her husband was naive, that he had a habit of promising things he couldn't deliver. When he began exaggerating, her lips would wrinkle in disgust. "Don't be ridiculous," she would say, waving her hand impatiently in front of her face. Sitting in the garden, however, Mrs. Chen was distracted by the huge lavender peonies that looked clear and delicate as watercolors. She couldn't help but be lulled by the fragrances wafting beneath her tingling nose as she listened to her husband's boastful talk, all his plans for them and their son. She could not deny that the garden was a beautiful thing. In the end, she agreed that they should invest their savings in the apartment.

Eight years had gone by, and their son was now dead. Whenever Mrs. Chen saw the garden, she felt a bitterness rise up to her mouth. The smell of lilies reminded her of funerals now—their rich, exhausting perfume made her want to claw at her throat. The transplanted flowers were crowded too close together, and their thin, transparent petals gave off a ghostly luster. This was not a living garden, Mrs. Chen decided. Not a place where things came back.

When he first met the Christian lady, Mr. Chen was startled by the coldness of her fingers. He wondered if she had poor circulation. She slipped her bony hand out from his, glancing quickly around the lobby. She wore a dark blue suit in spite of the heat and a thin white blouse with faux-pearl buttons. Though she was respectably dressed, the suit was too large for her and made her seem almost pitiful, as if she were wearing another person's clothes.

When Mr. Chen first called the woman to set up an appointment, he got her answering machine. A listless recorded voice spoke to him. *And God shall wipe away all tears from their eyes; and there shall be no more death, neither sorrow, nor crying, neither shall there be any more pain.* There was a pause and then a beep. Mr. Chen hung up the phone, for some reason too embarrassed to leave a message. He called back later that night after he and Mrs. Chen had closed the grocery store.

A soft voice answered the phone.

"Yes. Hello," he said abruptly. "I am calling you back. You say you interested in the apartment? Garden City Apartments, 26 Harrison."

Mrs. Chen listened on the other extension as her husband spoke. It was a constant regret of hers that she had not married a more cultured man. Mr. Chen's brusqueness always became more apparent when he spoke English. It was even worse when he was on the phone, for then he shouted his responses as if he were deaf. What must these Americans think, she wondered. The woman said she was interested. Her name was Marnie Wilson, and she agreed to meet Mr. Chen at noon tomorrow. Mrs. Chen heard a click at the other end as the American lady hung up, and then she, too, put down the receiver.

"Did you hear?" Mr. Chen said to his wife.

"Yes," Mrs. Chen said, "but will she rent it? Bargain with her if you have to, but don't show her you're desperate. That will only scare her away."

Mr. Chen remembered his wife's words now as he stood in front of the shaded windows of the apartment, nodding and smiling at the Christian lady. He noticed that she stepped gingerly around the empty rooms, as if she were afraid of setting off echoes with her heels. Mr. Chen judged that she was twenty-six, maybe twenty-seven years old. Her formality and meekness made her seem outdated. Maybe she came from another country, though to Mr. Chen's ear she spoke perfect English.

As they rode down in the elevator to see the garden, Mr. Chen learned that the Christian lady worked as a receptionist at World Wide Travel. Had Mr. Chen heard of it? The office was only three or four blocks away. Mr. Chen said he had not. He didn't know of any office buildings close by. The woman wrapped her hand tighter around her purse strap and stared at the glowing display of numbers as they descended eleven floors. Mr. Chen scratched his forehead with the tip of his pinkie. He was hoping she wouldn't care about the subway station.

The elevator doors slid open, and Mr. Chen gestured for the woman to go ahead. They walked through the lobby, past the double glass doors that led into the garden. As had happened before, Mr. Chen experienced the curious sensation of leaving behind some part of himself. Everything suddenly was light and color and air. So many flowers he didn't know the names of—the same color as autumn leaves—gold and burgundy and rust. Sunlight streamed through the glass vault of the ceiling, yet because the conservatory was air-conditioned, it was cooler here than inside the apartment.

"Beautiful garden," Marnie Wilson said, staring at the chrysanthemums.

"Yes, beautiful," Mr. Chen agreed.

They stood in silence for a minute longer, and then Mr. Chen awkwardly cleared his throat. The moment had come to ask whether she was interested in the apartment, but before he could speak, he saw her pale lips moving slowly. "'And their soul shall be as a watered garden,'" she murmered, "'and they shall not sorrow any more at all.'"

Mr. Chen flushed but did not say anything.

She turned toward him, gently patting her skirt, which clung to the flowers. "I would like to live here," she said.

Mr. Chen showed his wife the check for eight hundred dollars. They had signed the lease that very afternoon, and the Christian lady would advance the first month's rent by the end of the week. Mrs. Chen was happy, but she pretended to find fault with her husband. "You were too hasty," she said. "Why didn't you check her references?"

"She looked respectable," Mr. Chen said. "She works at a travel agency near the apartment."

"And how did she dress?"

"A suit. Like she was educated."

Mrs. Chen snorted. "Christians are crazy, smiling at you all the time. Your child dies, and they say you should be happy."

Mr. Chen sighed, looking out the front window. "She didn't seem like that." From the living room he could see one of the two cypresses that grew beside their front door. Twelve years ago, when they first moved into their house, the trees had barely reached Mr. Chen's hip, but over the years they had grown into dark thin spires. When their son was diagnosed with cancer, Mrs. Chen wanted her husband to cut them down. "They're bad luck," she said. "They overshadow our house."

Mr. Chen grew angry at his wife's suggestion. "Don't be silly. Chopping down two trees won't make his sickness go away."

The tumor steadily advanced until the doctors told the Chens that their son's only chance of recovery was surgery. The Chens relented because by this time they were hoping for a miracle. But how stupid they had been, Mrs. Chen wept to her husband. A person cannot live when his head is sliced open like a watermelon, Western medicine or not. Why had they let the doctors touch him? He had died on the operating table with no one to comfort him. A terrible death that no one deserves, and he was only fifteen years old.

Mrs. Chen's tongue grew more venomous after their son died. When she opened her mouth, it was as if she were spitting out words to rid herself of life's bitter taste.

In contrast, Mr. Chen became softer, less defined. He rarely talked now, and the wrinkles on his face deepened so that Mrs. Chen said his forehead resembled a tic-tac-toe board. Mrs. Chen made her words sharp to wake him up. She didn't like to see him wading through the motions of life.

Neither of them mentioned the cypresses, which continued to twist toward the sky. It was as if their mutual silence were a tacit agreement to let them grow. Each willing for the bad winds to continue to blow.

In October, Mr. Chen received a four-hundred-dollar check from Marnie Wilson, accompanied by a note of apology. "Not two months and already she can't pay," he muttered, showing the check to his wife. When he called her number, he heard the same toneless voice recorded on her answering machine. *And God shall wipe away all tears* . . . Mr. Chen did not wait for the message to end before he hung up the phone.

A week went by with no additional check in the mail. On Saturday afternoon, Mr. Chen decided to let his wife manage the store without him and drove to Garden City Apartments. It usually took him forty-five minutes to drive into the city, and he had come to regard all the driving back and forth as a waste of gas and time. The worst was when people made appointments to see the apartment but then didn't show up. He would wait in the lobby, looking up from his newspaper at each person who came through the revolving doors. When an hour passed, Mr. Chen was forced to fold up his paper and drive back home. It was on such days that he believed people had no respect for each other.

In the lobby, Mr. Chen asked the doorman whether he knew if Marnie Wilson was in. "If you'll just wait a second," the doorman said, "I'll call up and see if she's there."

"No, no, I go up," Mr. Chen said. "She go out every morning?"

The doorman shook his head. "Not that I know of."

Mr. Chen took the elevator to the twelfth floor and walked down the close, dimly lit hallway. The walls were painted the color of dark moss, and the carpet was confusing for him to look at with its intertwining flowers. He knocked on the apartment door. "Miss Wilson?" He wondered if she was going to pretend not to be in.

A door opened loudly across the hallway. A large woman in a robe and sneakers peered at him from her doorway. Mr. Chen could hear her breathing through her mouth. He smiled and nodded, and the woman closed her door without saying anything.

"Miss Wilson?" he said, more softly this time. He put his ear against the door and tried to turn the knob. He hesitated before taking the key out of his pocket. If she was there, he would apologize, saying that he remembered a previous tenant complaining about a leak.

"Hello," he called as he opened the door.

It was late afternoon, a dusty gold light filtering through the windows. Mr. Chen could tell from the hushed stillness that no one was inside. He was surprised by the apartment's emptiness. Two chairs, a card table with rusting legs, a small bookcase with slanting paperbacks. A clock on the wall had stopped at 6:35. For a moment, Mr. Chen panicked, thinking the Christian lady had left her most worthless possessions behind. But then he noticed a small blue silk rug that changed to a silvery green when he walked to the other side of the room. It was the only valuable-looking thing in the apartment and at odds with the rest of her furniture.

Through the window, Mr. Chen could see the parking lot, a few trees, and the eight-lane highway. From twelve stories above, behind sealed windows, the cars glided soundlessly past.

In the bedroom, Mr. Chen was startled by the mirrors she had hung along the wall, at least a dozen of them, some as small as the palm of his hand. Oval and rectangular mirrors, mirrors in the shapes of triangles and suns, mirrors with smooth silver faces and dark blemishes reflecting hardly anything at all. They flickered to life whenever he moved. There was a single mattress with a wool blanket on the floor. An upturned box that she had decorated with an embroidered handkerchief and used as a night table for her Bible, lamp, and radio. He pushed open her closet door, saw her few clothes drooping from their hangers. The shelf above the rack was empty except for an old maroon hat with a wilted black feather. When he took it off the shelf, the hat was stiff and light in his hands, the velvet marred by dark oil spots.

On his way out, Mr. Chen saw two sun-faded photographs on the refrigerator door. Two little girls in orange bikinis were standing in a plastic pool in the front yard of a house. One girl's mouth was open like she was screaming in delight, her hands clutching her hair, her child's belly exposed to the camera, as the older girl gazed quietly on. In the second photograph, the same two girls were dressed in bright-striped shirts and bell-bottoms, holding a squash together in their arms. The younger one squinted in the sun, her lips parted, showing two large front teeth. Mr. Chen thought the older one, the girl who seemed more distant and self-possessed, was Marnie Wilson.

He let himself out of the apartment, quietly shutting the door behind him.

He found the Christian lady downstairs in the garden. She sat on a bench beside the roses, her head bowed over a book, her lips moving silently over the words. She wore a plaid gray dress and short black-laced boots. There was a painstaking neatness in her appearance that for some reason made Mr. Chen feel sorry for her. Her smooth brown hair was pulled back too tightly, revealing a high pale forehead. She looked up and gazed at him, and Mr. Chen began to smile, but then she hastily glanced down at her book, her index finger moving rapidly across the page.

"Miss Wilson?"

Her shoulder blades stiffened. She stared at her book a moment longer, then raised her head. Mr. Chen pretended to look around the garden. "You like this place," he said.

She shut her book, her fingers still caught between the pages.

"I receive your letter. You say you have a job?"

She gave a slight cough, clearing her throat. "It was only temporary."

Mr. Chen nodded. "You find another job." She set her book down on the bench without saying anything. "Why don't you ask help from parents? Your parents can help, right?"

She looked down at her lap, studying her hands as if they didn't belong to her. Then, in a calm voice, she told Mr. Chen that her parents were dead. With one hand, she smoothed the creases in her dress.

Mr. Chen was silent. He felt a curious lightness take over his body, as if he were watching proceedings from far away. For the first time, he wondered if the Christian lady was a liar. "Oh, too bad," he finally said. He was too embarrassed to bring up the subject of money now.

She looked at him, smiling faintly. "I will give you the money as soon as I can."

"Okay," Mr. Chen mumbled, turning away. "Thank you."

On the way home, Mr. Chen found himself stuck in traffic, amid a procession of alien, glittering cars. The image of the Christian lady sitting in the garden with her eyes half-closed and her lips moving seemed unreal to him, a fragment of a dream. A car honked, and Mr. Chen realized that the cars had begun to move forward. He pushed the gas too hard, the engine roaring to life as his car leaped forward a few spaces.

When he came home, he found his wife in bed propped up against her pillows. She was wearing cotton pajamas, the pants marred by faint circles of blood. She had scrubbed them again and again until they were only terracotta outlines. "Do you know what day this is?" she asked him.

Mr. Chen looked at her blankly.

"Today is our anniversary," she said. She narrowed her eyes, looking at him carefully. "I'm not surprised that you should forget. There isn't anything happy to remember about this day. Do you remember we spent two hundred dollars for the reception? Ha! That was a lot of money to us then."

"It still is a lot of money," he said.

"You always were stingy in your heart," she said. "That woman can't pay a few hundred dollars, and you go sniffing for it like a dog."

"What do you want," Mr. Chen muttered. "You complain if I go, and you complain if I don't."

"That's because you make me sick," she said. "Do you hear that? Nothing you do will make me happy." She began to cry and wiped her tears away with the back of her hand. She got out of bed and went into the bathroom, slamming the door. Mr. Chen heard a sound of something smashing. He was silent for a moment.

"Mingli," he said. He knocked on the door. He could hear his wife sobbing. "Open the door."

"Go away," she cried.

Mr. Chen went back to their bedroom. He sat down on the edge of their bed in a stupor. In a few minutes, he heard her opening the door. "Do you know what I regret the most?" she said. Her face was a terrible sight. He could stand any viciousness from his wife, but he couldn't stand her tears. They made him deeply afraid.

"I don't want to hear," he said.

"Do you remember that time when he cried outside our door? He was four years old and he cried outside our door wanting to sleep with us. We didn't let him in because we didn't want to spoil him. He cried for an hour maybe, and we listened to him for all that time, and when he was quiet, we thought he had gone back to bed. But in the morning, we found him lying outside our door, his forehead burning with fever. Do you remember?"

"Yes," Mr. Chen said.

Mrs. Chen got into bed, turning her back away from him. "That memory makes me feel bad," she said. "I can't ever forget it. It's what I regret the most." She reached over and turned off her light.

Mr. Chen received a call from the apartment management. People in the building were beginning to wonder about the woman who sat all day in the conservatory. "They thought at first she didn't live here, that she came off the streets," the office manager told Mr. Chen. "A resident saw her distributing pamphlets under people's doors." The manager laughed uncomfortably.

Mr. Chen grunted his assent.

"Believe me, we don't have anything against your tenant. But I thought you should know about her behavior. Maybe you could talk to her?"

"Me? What can I do? She hasn't paid rent for two months." The week before, the Christian lady had sent Mr. Chen a check for three hundred dollars along with a handwritten note. *Once I win my case with the government, I will be able to pay you the money I owe.*

"Is that so?" The manager sounded pleasantly surprised, then immediately lowered his voice. "You are the landlord, after all."

Mr. Chen sighed as he hung up the phone. He dug around the closet for his typewriter, which he used for official business only, and poking at the keys with two fingers, he fashioned a reply to the Christian lady. *I hear no more excuses. I come on Monday to speak to you.*

On Monday evening, he drove to Garden City Apartments, wondering whether she would be in. The weather man had predicted a storm, and the air had turned breezy and cold. Mr. Chen gripped the steering wheel whenever he felt the wind nudging his car into the other lane. The sky was dark and clear, without a hint of rain.

In the apartment building, he was surprised to find her door half-opened, like she was expecting him. He glimpsed through the crack and saw her kneeling on the floor. At first, it looked like she was patting an animal, but then he saw she was straightening the fringe of her rug. He knocked on the door, and she told him to come in. She stood up, slowly wiping her hands against her skirt. She wore a blouse with tiny red flowers embroidered around the collar.

"Hello," Mr. Chen said, nodding. He continued to stand even though she motioned to one of the chairs. "I like to talk to you about this check."

"You must forgive me," she said. "It's all I can give you."

Mr. Chen flushed. "I can't afford to have tenant that cannot pay," he said. "Isn't there someone—sister maybe—who can help?" Marnie Wilson gazed back at him without any expression in her eyes. "Maybe you find another roommate? Someone to move in here, someone you can talk to, you pay only half the rent?"

"I like living here alone."

"What about work?" Mr. Chen said. "You work, right?" She was silent, and Mr. Chen closed his eyes, shaking his head. A sound of hissing escaped from his teeth. "I'm sorry. You find another place to live."

The Christian lady turned her head to look out the window. "I don't like to go outside."

Mr. Chen looked at her. "Bad weather," he murmured.

From the windowsill, she picked up a green and silver box that looked as if it were meant to hold cigars. She traced the pattern with a finger before passing it to him. Mr. Chen held the box awkwardly in his hands. It was decorated with intersecting green and black lines in the shape of diamonds and three-petaled flowers with a streak of red in the center. He fumbled with the lid, thinking there might be something inside, but the box was empty. He saw only his blurred face upside down in the warped metal.

The Christian lady said he could keep it, but Mr. Chen shook his head, looking for a place to set it down. She said he could give it back once she paid him the money she owed. Mr. Chen stood with the box in his hands, feeling suddenly depressed. "You never go out?"

She pointed to the window. She was always looking for signs. Mr. Chen could see the first drops of rain tapping the window. He looked down to the parking lot and could hardly make out his small green car in the dusk, everything coated in a pale silver sheen. The trees were stirring to life, dry leaves circling the asphalt. It was a quiet world, Mr. Chen thought, waiting to be seized.

"It makes me afraid," she said. "I think terrible things will happen."

He heard the wind rising, an ocean in his ears. He could see lights flickering in the distance. The woman stood gazing out the window with her back toward him. His own body felt vacant and cold. The apartment had become a still life, he and the woman faceless, incorporated into the silence of the room.

The woman turned, and Mr. Chen took a step back. Though her mouth was moving, he couldn't hear anything. Only the sound of his blood in his ears.

"Mr. Chen, are you well? Would you like some tea?"

He shook his head. His body had broken out into a cold sweat, and he realized he was shivering. "Sorry," he whispered hoarsely.

"Mr. Chen, why don't you sit down and rest?"

"No, I'm okay," he muttered, moving toward the door.

"I promise to pay you soon," she said.

Mr. Chen barely nodded as he shut the door behind him.

Driving home through the rain, he caught glimpses of branches and debris scattered on the road. Black leaves streamed in the wind, slapping his windshield, getting tangled in the wipers. Mr. Chen felt as if his mind had been infected. At home, he found his wife sitting at the kitchen table drinking tea. When she saw him, she raised her eyebrows. "Well?"

"Nothing," he muttered.

"You need to kick her out."

Mr. Chen took off his coat and hung it in the closet. He had not known what to do with the box and had hidden it underneath the seat of his car.

"She can't continue living there for free," Mrs. Chen said.

"She isn't well," he told her. "Something wrong with her head."

That night, he dreamed he went to the apartment again, but it had turned into an endless cavern of rooms. An orange cat followed his heels, and this made him worry that the management would charge him a fine. When he found the Christian lady, she was standing before a mirror, wearing purple eye shadow and drinking a glass of wine. "My mother," she said, gesturing to the wall. Mr. Chen realized that what he thought was a mirror was actually a photograph of a woman sitting morosely in a chair, her thin dark hair plastered to her skull, her eyes vacant and heavily lidded. A white bow in the shape of a rose was pinned to the front of her long black dress. Her lips seemed to be waxed shut, and she grasped a startled baby in her lap between both hands. The Christian lady laughed. "No need to feel sorry for her," she told him.

He wondered about his dream. He did not know anything about the Christian lady really. When he imagined her, he always saw her alone, gazing out a window, studying herself in one of her mirrors, or examining her meaningless collection of boxes.

When December arrived, he did not hear from her. No checks or apologies. He tried calling her number, but there was a recorded message saying the line had been disconnected.

"That woman is robbing us blind," Mrs. Chen said. "But you continue to act as if we are running a charity organization."

Mr. Chen felt a terrible pressure in his head. "What can I do?" he burst out. "Throw her onto the street?"

"Don't be naive," his wife said.

He drove to Garden City Apartments the next day. No one answered the door, and he let himself in. The card table, the chairs, the bookcase—all her things were in the places he remembered, untouched as in a museum display. The silent, airless room made him feel trapped. It was difficult to imagine how anyone could live here.

In the kitchen, the photograph of the two little girls standing in the plastic pool was slipping from underneath its magnet. Mr. Chen straightened the photograph and opened the refrigerator door. There was a box of cereal, a shrunken apple, and a jar of floating olives. They seemed like odd artifacts in the empty white space of the refrigerator.

In the bedroom, the Christian lady's mirrors glimmered faintly as Mr. Chen walked by. The mattress had been stripped of its sheets, and dust had gathered in balls in the corners of the room.

He heard a sound of shifting from the closet.

"Miss Wilson?" he said aloud.

He tried to slide the closet door back, but it got stuck along the groove. The sleeves of her dresses poked through. In the dark of the closet, he discerned something moving, a tangled mass of hair, though he wasn't sure if it was a face or the back of a head. He looked down and saw chapped heels protruding from a blanket. The Christian lady lay on her stomach, her nightgown tightly wound around her body, her hands hidden beneath her. Her body was stiff yet seemed to be struggling underwater. She turned her head to look at him, and her eyes had a shiny faraway luster as if she were drugged. Mr. Chen thought she looked like some kind of animal. He did not say anything but hastily slid the closet door shut and left the apartment.

At the grocery store, his wife sat on a stool in front of the cash register watching Chinese videos. "So are you going to kick her out?" she said.

"I will call the lawyer that the Zhangs used," he replied.

His wife continued to watch her video, but after a while, her lips twisted into a strange smile. "That poor woman," she said.

Mr. Chen could not sleep. Though it was winter, he didn't need a blanket because his wife's body burned like a furnace all year long. When they were newlyweds, he had joked with her about the temperature of her body, pretending to burn his fingers whenever they touched her skin. She was a young woman then; her passion had been a great deal of her charm. But her temper had increased with age, and Mr. Chen feared that his wife was like a piece of burning wood that appears firm and unyielding until it suddenly collapses.

He turned over in bed and looked at the red eyes of the clock. Three a.m. In four hours, both he and his wife would be up—she to open their store, he to drive to Garden City Apartments. He wondered if the Christian lady would be gone by that time, the apartment as clean and empty as it had been five months ago, not a sign that she had ever lived there.

She had never shown up for the hearing. Mr. Chen learned about her absence from his lawyer. The judge had set a month's deadline for her to pay what rent she owed, but she hadn't been able to do this. Instead, she sent Mr. Chen a Christmas card. On the front, a quiet, even desolate painting of a lake turned blue with ice, a few spruce trees buried in a drift of snow. In mournful, slanting letters, she wished him a merry Christmas with a promise to pay back the money she owed. He turned over in bed once more, flipping his pillow to get to its cool side.

His sleep was no longer good. Even before his son became ill, Mr. Chen often woke up in the middle of the night, his temples smarting as his thoughts turned inexorably against him. He would escape by going to the bathroom, flicking on the light, and then he would wander down the hallway to check on his son. He would stop by the doorway, listening to his son's breathing, heavy and asthmatic in the darkness. Usually, he had kicked his blanket to the ground. Mr. Chen would stoop to pick it up, awkwardly pulling at the corners of the blanket to cover him.

It was Mr. Chen's lasting regret that they had never been close. His son had preferred his mother's company. Somehow Mr. Chen had never been able to find the right words. His questions were always gruff, and he didn't know how to smooth out his tongue. Where were you? Did you eat? Why didn't you wear your jacket? Have you finished your homework? To these questions, his son had replied in monosyllables. What Mr. Chen meant to ask was whether he was hungry, whether he was cold, whether there was anything that he lacked which Mr. Chen could provide? He hadn't been able to show his love in any other way than by providing for him, and so he gave him food to eat, clothes to wear, and a bed to sleep in. These things hadn't been enough to keep him alive.

Mr. Chen's head felt swollen as he waited for the sky to lighten. At seven a.m., he rose from bed, his brain throbbing with a swarm of useless images. His wife's face was slack against the pillow, her dry lips parted slightly. She seemed to be lost in sleep as he stood watching her, but then her eyes suddenly opened. "I'm leaving soon," he said. Mrs. Chen stared vacantly at him, and he wondered if she had understood what he said. "I'll be back before noon," he told her. She lay there, stiff and unblinking, and Mr. Chen finally turned away to change.

When he returned to the bedroom, the bed was empty and his wife was no longer in sight.

He found her in the garage, sitting in the passenger seat of his car. She wore a brown sweater with large yellow flowers and brown wool pants, and she was getting her makeup out of her purse when he opened the door. "That woman is a rat," she said. "I'd like nothing more than to sweep her out with a broom."

"What about the store?" he asked.

She smeared powder along her forehead. "I put up a sign yesterday."

When they got onto the beltway, there were rows of gleaming cars stretched into the distance ahead of them. They sat and waited, the inside of the car filling up with exhaust. By the time they reached Garden City Apartments, they were half an hour late. Large wreaths decorated with white and gold ribbons hung in the entranceway, even though Christmas had passed almost a month ago. The lobby was crowded with people, and when Mr. Chen inhaled the scent of a woman's perfume, he felt the same lightheaded sickness as if he were in a department store. Cold air blew along the back of his neck as people passed in and out of the revolving doors. Boxes were already stacked along the wall, and the movers he had hired were busy unloading furniture from the freight elevator. A man in a gray suit came up to him. "George Chen?" he inquired.

Mr. Chen nodded.

The man shook his hand and said he was from the Justice Court.

"Sorry to be so late," Mr. Chen muttered.

"Nothing to worry about. Your apartment is almost all cleared out. Miss Wilson will be coming down shortly."

"I want to go up and see," his wife said to him in Chinese. Before Mr. Chen could say anything, she stepped onto the next elevator, the doors sliding quickly behind her.

"An odd woman," the man from the Justice Court remarked. Mr. Chen thought at first that the man was referring to his wife. But then the elevator doors opened, and Marnie Wilson appeared, a faint smile on her lips. Her dark hair was pulled back into a tiny bun, and she wore the same blue suit that she had worn on the day that Mr. Chen had first shown her the apartment. He wondered what she had placed inside the small black suitcase that she clutched at her side. She stepped off the elevator, followed by two policemen. The doorman immediately approached her. "Miss Wilson," he said, looking embarrassed. "I'm sorry, but you can't leave your furniture and boxes here."

The Christian lady's face tightened, red splotches appearing on her skin. "Please," she said.

"I'm sorry, Miss Wilson, I truly am, but our manager has informed me that you can't leave your things in the lobby."

The movers were already beginning to carry her boxes and furniture outside to the street. Mr. Chen watched as the Christian lady dragged her suitcase across the lobby through the revolving doors. She stood nervously on the sidewalk beside her possessions, and people stared at her and at her things as they walked by. The movers continued to dump boxes and furniture on the ground, her possessions growing and spreading into an island around her feet. Everything was in a pile, jumbled together. Her chairs, her table, her bookcase, her rug, her mattress. The movers departed, and she was left standing alone amid the heap. She picked up her suitcase, walked a few steps, then set it back down again.

Mr. Chen tapped her on the shoulder, and she flew around to look at him. "I'm sorry about all this," he said. She stared at him with dazed eyes, and Mr. Chen looked away, pretending to study her possessions. "What are you going to do? You have so many things." He regretted his words as soon as they were spoken. The Christian lady owned very little actually. It could not have taken the movers more than a half hour to clear out the apartment.

"I'm sorry," he repeated, shaking his head. "I hoped you already moved."

The Christian lady's mouth trembled as she smiled. "I was so happy to live here," she said. She fumbled in her pocket and pressed something cold and silver into his palm. Mr. Chen looked down and saw he was holding the key to the apartment.

In the lobby, there was no sign of his wife. The elevator was empty, as if waiting for him, and Mr. Chen rode up twelve floors in silence. In the dim hallway, he could barely make out the edges of his body, and he stopped for a moment, trying to remember which way to turn. On the door, the Christian lady had taped a note in neat handwriting. "Forgive, and ye shall be forgiven," it read.

He found his wife inside the empty apartment. She stood in front of a window, looking down at the city. Mr. Chen's shoes echoed along the floor as he approached her. Everything was perfectly bare, just as he had imagined, but he knew he wouldn't be able to forget the Christian lady had lived here.

"Do you remember when we first saw this apartment?" his wife said. "We thought everything was going to be better then."

"Mingli," he said, and his voice sounded strange to him. It did not sound like his own. He touched her sleeve, but she continued to stare out the window. He wanted to say something, to ask her pardon, but he could only repeat her name, his fingers closing around her wrist.

"I feel," she said, and she covered her eyes with one hand. "I feel it would be easy to live in an apartment like this. I could live here for the rest of my life."

Mr. Chen put his hand along the back of her head. He could feel her scalp's warmth through the dry threads of her hair. Outside, there was winter, the cold gray surfaces of buildings. From where he stood, he saw tiny cars inching along the highway through a world that had fallen into silence.

ERIC PUCHNER

Stanford University

❧

ESSAY #3: LEDA AND THE SWAN

~6,400 words

Although the swan is not a delicate creature like a butterfly, and is not cuddly and cute like a kitten, it is a living thing that can feel pain and hunger just like any other living creature. In "Leda and the Swan," by William Butler Yeats, a perverted sort of swan ends up performing sexual intercourse with a loose girl named Leda. The motive of the swan is shown when he performs only a few foreplays, like caressing her "thighs" and gripping her "helpless breast," before revealing his "feathered glory."[1] He's got only one thing on his mind: shuddering his loins. This swan is clearly a sex-starved animal that doesn't belong in Ireland, let alone a city park! In this essay, I will argue that Mr. Yeats is actually a mentally ill person who lives poetically through swans and furthermore knows nothing about swans and their gentile mating habits.

---

[1] William Butler Yeats, *Selected Poems and Three Plays* (New York: Macmillan, 1986), lines 2–6.

First of all, Mr. Yeats is a mentally ill person who lives poetically through swans. I know this for a fact because my older sister, Jeanie, is mentally ill and used to write poems about animals before she ran away from home to become a missing person. However, since she isn't a pervert, the poems were not about intercoursing swans. Instead, they were about animals we see on our tables every day. One of the poems (which I still have) goes like this:

> *Cow, what do you chew?*
> *Big peace, bothering no one*
> *Who later chews you.*[2]

This is not an American poem, because it has syllables. In fact, it is a haiku, which is a popular form of expression in Japan. Jeanie wrote this after I stole her boyfriend and she started to become mentally ill. Mentally ill people come in many different guises, and for Jeanie the guise was Veganism, a religion where you can't eat eggs or dairy products, such as cows. Like many poets, she has a soul that she wants to communicate with others and liked to put her poems on the refrigerator for everyone to read. Unfortunately, my stepfather, Franz, does not have the soul of a poet, especially if we're having stroganoff for dinner. Franz would often get angry and make many remarks about cows being more stupid than chickens. Franz grew up on a farm in Bavaria and knows a lot about the stupidity of animals. One poem, in particular, seemed to upset him very much:

> *Turkey, my cousin*
> *We fail to be beautiful*
> *Punishment: oven.*[3]

---

[2] Jeanie Mudbrook, "Cow Song," lines 1–3.
[3] Mudbrook, "Ugliness," lines 1–3.

Franz was upset because he felt like Thanksgiving dinner wasn't the best time for the reading of poetry, especially when he was eating a wing belonging to the protagonist of the poem. He said that Jeanie and the turkey must really be related, if she would ruin a family get-together by reading a poem about the stupidest animal on earth. Franz said that turkeys were so stupid you couldn't leave them out in the rain or else they'd drown. In fact, his family had lost a perfectly good turkey in Bavaria because his father had left it out in a thunderstorm by accident. Jeanie asked him if we should kill retarded people, too, because they're less intelligent than us, and Franz said no, we should leave them out in the rain first and see what happens. This made me laugh, but Jeanie didn't think it was very funny. She called him a Nazi. This was very bad, and mentally ill, because Franz is not a Nazi even though he thinks Germany's better than anything.

Actually, Jeanie was upset because I'd invited Collin, her ex-boyfriend, to dinner. I didn't feel too bad because they'd only dated for two months before Collin dumped her, and surely Jeanie should have seen the perfect destiny of our match. Later Collin told me the truth, which was that he'd only gotten to know Jeanie in the first place because he was in love with me on account of my facial beauty. I can tell you right now that my sister's not so facially victorious. She's got our dad's nose, which is a shame because my mom's been married three times since my dad, and all of our stepfathers have had noses that didn't say from across the street hello I'm a nose.

Anyway, Collin's dumping her for my less visible features may have had something to do with Jeanie's mental collapse. Poets are very unstable people who often go crazy or die, and I should say that Collin is very handsome and popular and we were all surprised when he decided to date Jeanie in the first place. He is in a band called Salacious Universe and has long hair and these perfect gold arms like when you put honey on toast (except there aren't usually hairs in your toast). He is a construction worker on the weekends and looking at his arms kind of makes me wiggle my toes in an unvolunteering way until my sandals fall off. The wiggling was inaugurated at my first Salacious Universe concert. As it turns out, Jeanie couldn't go to the concert because she was attending a Vegan rally in front of the Safeway near our house. Vegans like to have rallies and personalize other Vegans to their cause. In any case, the concert was in the school auditorium (maybe you remember, Mr. Patterson, the flyers with Collin's hands shooting thunderbolts?) and I went with my friends Tamara and Tamara. It's a little weird how they have the same name, but neither of them wants to be called Tammy or Tams or Mara or any nickname I can think of because that would mean the other one got to keep their real name and she didn't.

So we were waiting for Salacious Universe to come out, sitting in the front row actually, when Collin pranced onto stage like a two-legged deer and picked up this guitar he has with a bumper sticker on it that says, FEAR ME, BRETHREN. It was very hot in the auditorium and I could smell the aroma of many armpits rafting in my direction. After the cheering died down, Collin started singing and his face kind of went fierce and angry and these very sexy wrinkles formed between his eyebrows. I said Tamara and she said what and I said no, *Tamara* and *she* said what and I said isn't he the most incredible human being of the male persuasion on planet Earth and she said yeah I don't know what he sees in Jeanie the haikuist freak. Salacious Universe plays speed metal music, which if you don't know is very difficult and requires you to change fingers all the time. They started right away to perform masterpieces and I knew immediately that I was destined to live my life with Collin Sweep, lead singer of Salacious Universe. The only problem was Jeanie, but I tried not to be a victim of negative thinking and dwell on the fact that she was dating my destiny. Collin is an idiot savant, which means he could play music with better lyrics than William Butler Yeats even though he was failing Trigonometry, Chemistry, American History, Spanish, and (far as I know) this class as well. In any case, Collin had us all riveted to his lips as he sang the chorus to one of his tour de forces:

All you mortals, I can and will bend
Cuz I'm the father of gods and men![4]

Believe me, everyone was screaming and wanting to intercourse him if they were either female or homosexual.

Then something happened that wasn't in the program. Right when Collin was achieving the height of his genius, there was a blackout and everything went dark. You could hear the band playing in the dark, but the electricity was gone and it was just a ghost-sound and not the real thing, like when you're talking to your stepgrandparents in Germany and your voice comes back to you all small and distant on the phone. Then the lights went on again and Collin was shocked. I mean "shocked" in the electrical sense, because the microphone made a weird zapping sound and Collin's hair stood up into a punk-rock hairstyle and he flew across the stage like a migrant bird. Everyone was concerned about his general health, including me, and I ran up on stage to give him mouth-to-mouth. By the time I got there, though, he'd already half-recovered and was blinking into space with a very sedated expression that said I'm having a one-on-one interview with the light.

That's how we ended up backstage, me and Tamara and Tamara. We were delighted to be official Salacious Universe groupies, even though I was clearly the main one and they were really just groupies of me. It was cooler behind the stage and I furthered the recovery of Collin's head by resting it against a papier-mâché stump. He knew

---

[4]Collin Sweep, "Pagan Liver," 2001.

who I was, of course, but I had to introduce him to the Tamaras since they were persistent in their appearance. He found it supremely cool that they had the same name and Tamara and Tamara were both sort of non-plucked because they did not secretly believe it was cool at all. Tamara asked him why the song was called "Pagan Liver" since it had nothing to do with body parts, and he explained that it wasn't supposed to be a part of the body at all but a person who lives, like you're a Pagan and you live that way.

After packing up his stuff, Collin asked me if I wanted to walk with him to the pay phone on the other side of campus. The stars were shining like distant balls of gas and you could see the janitors sitting on the roof of the library, sharing a cigarette. It was all very peaceful and beautiful with the janitors talking in Spanish and the imported words floating on top of our heads. Everything was really quiet except for the inside of Collin's pocket, which jingled with coins on account of his pinball-playing habit. That was when he told me that he liked the way I looked. His hair was still sticking magically from his head, all bright and glowing, like each hair was partaking in photosynthesis from the moon. He said he was going to call Jeanie and tell her he couldn't take her to Hailu's House of Tofu because something had come up, something unexpected, without telling her of course it was a secret crush on my face.

But then something truly unexpected happened. When he tried to put a quarter in the pay phone, it refused to part from his finger. He shook his hand, but the quarter just remained there magnetically attracted to his skin. Collin looked kind of worried and then stuck his hand in his pocket again and pulled it out and there were quarters stuck to each of his fingers, like a mini family of George Washingtons with very long necks. Of course, it scared me a little that his fingers could behave so strangely. After a minute, Collin's face sort of changed and he got this weird grin and wiggled his fingers and they glittered in the moonlight. He touched one of the coin-fingers to my mouth, which caused a tiny spark to enter my lips and electrocute the butterflies in my stomach. I have to admit, it was spooky and frightening and very breathtaking but also the most exciting thing that has happened in my life up till now.[5]

So that was how I ended up stealing Jeanie's boyfriend. I know it isn't cool to steal other people's boyfriends, especially if those people are your flesh-and-bones sister, and as a general rule I try to avoid it—but this was destiny and you only get one chance to fill it or else it flaps away into the starry universe. When I got home from the concert, I found Jeanie waiting on the porch in her favorite skirt and cow-safe high heels. I realized that Collin had forgotten to call her on account of his fingers being so talented. Because I'm a very honest person, I told her in a considerate way that Collin had fallen in love with me, that he was very sorry for the misunderstanding about dating her to begin with. Jeanie just stared at me with this little smirk on her face, like she was experiencing some gas in her stomach. Jeanie's got these very smirkable bee-stung lips that kind of complement the humongous bee that must have stung her nose. She had an unburning cigarette in her hand and she started to tear off little pieces from the end of it, sprinkling the pieces on the porch like she was trying to grow a tobacco tree. (Even though she's a Vegan, she smokes about five hundred cigarettes in her bathroom every day, which seems a little contradicting to her cause.) This was about when I started to appreciate her mental illness. I mean, if you're mentally with health,

---

[5]Mr. Patterson, I know this is supposed to be a paper about literature, and the particular literature named "Leda and the Swan," but you also said that we could use examples from our own life if we found something of "universal interest." That's why I've departed on a tangent and am writing this essay about love. I guarantee, universally, if you asked people which they'd prefer—a topic about LOVE or one about PERVERTED SWANS—they'd choose mine in a second.

and you've just found out that your boyfriend's dumped you for your sister, possibly because you're nasally obese, then wouldn't you be a little upset? An hour later, when I went downstairs to get some water before bed, I looked through the window and saw Jeanie sitting out there in the exact same place as before, hunched there in her skirt, even though Franz said it was cold enough to freeze the testicles off a brass monkey.

Jeanie didn't speak to me at all until Thanksgiving, when I invited Collin to the house and she read her Vegan haiku out loud before taping it to the refrigerator. To be honest, I was very hesitant to invite Collin at all, not only on account of Jeanie but because my mom is not a very gifted cook and likes to serve Bavarian Carp Salad as a tribute to Franz's ancestors. After Jeanie called him a Nazi, we were all sitting there very much alarmed because she stomped around the room and said "Hi Hitler!" until our plates shook and the salt shaker tipped over on the table. I knew she was really directing her Nazi-bashing at me and Collin, even though she'd ignored both of us since the beginning of dinner. She was wearing a Salacious Universe T-shirt with no bra underneath and her hair was very oily and Jamaican-looking. Franz grabbed her by the arm and forced her to sit down, saying he'd have her delivered to a mental institution if she didn't stop mistaking his identity. Hitler was a very evil man, but my step-father is just a bald person who owns a tire shop and likes to watch women's volleyball on Channel 39. My mom was incredibly plea-sureless because she'd made Jeanie a special turkey-free dinner with Not Dogs and thought it would be nice to put some gravy on them, not thinking that gravy is made from the destruction of living crea-tures and their boiled necks. She finished her glass of white wine and started to get very sympathetic with the turkey's plight, apologizing to the neckless bird when Franz broke off a wing or drumstick. (My mother drinks a lot in the evenings on account of her nerve-wrecking marriage.) We all kind of lost our appetites, even Franz, who just sat there silently chewing without looking at anyone.

Jeanie looked at me for the first time and then picked up a knife from the table and pointed it in my direction. Her face was very decomposed, and for a second I thought she might try to stab me. But then she turned to Collin and said that he was a slut who only cared about getting intercoursed and didn't he remember how she'd written all of his songs anyway and what was he going to do now, since he couldn't even spell *gargoyle*? What about moving to Hollywood and being speed metalists together, like they'd planned? She was kind of smirking and crying at the same time. It's true that they were friends before they'd started to date, but I didn't believe that she'd written any of his Salacious Universe masterpieces, even though he did look a little sad when she insulted his spelling. Obviously, Jeanie was just tortured with jealousy. I can't help it if I'm genetically attractive and have perfect skin and hazel eyes.[6] Sometimes she reminds me of Othello in the book we read by William Shakespeare, even though he was a mentally ill African American with no real reason to act that way.

The next day Collin took me to get a tattoo, my first ever, which I designed myself because I wanted something totally original if I was going to beautify my ankle on a permanent basis. Of course I didn't tell Jeanie, who avoided me the whole week, even when she came downstairs one night to watch a sleep-inducing documentary about the Animal Liberation Front. I couldn't help noticing that she was boycotting brassieres as well as meat. When the scab came off my ankle, though, I was so excited that I forgot about Jeanie's green-eyed

[6]I'm sorry to keep stressing this, Mr. Patterson, but I also want to make sure you know who I am since you always confuse me in class with Maria Zellmer, who sits in the back corner and digs the ear wax from her ears.

jealousy and actually stopped her in the hall to show it to her. She lost her smirk for a second and seemed genuinely very surprised. After a brief silence, we had a conversation that I've tried to record here for prosperity:

> JEANIE: You received a tattoo of a TV set?
> ME: It is not a TV set. It's a cobra.
> JEANIE: I know I'm a mentally ill person who suffers from hallucinations, but it looks just like a TV.
> ME: In reality, the cobra is coiled up in a basket. Like a snake charmer's. That's its head.
> JEANIE: Why the [intercourse] does it have antenna?
> ME: Those are bolts of electricity. From its eyes.
> JEANIE: Ha ha ha ha! (MENTALLY ILL LAUGHTER)

Obviously, this was all it took for me to reach a sad conclusion about Jeanie's mental future. To make things worse, she started to entertain nighttime visitors in her bedroom without anyone's permission. This was very sluttish and maybe could have been prevented by medication, which makes it even sadder. Since my mom and Franz are very leftist and allow us to have visitors whenever we like, and there's a staircase that basically leads right up to Jeanie's room from the back door, our slut prevention is not as implemented as it could be. Over the next few weeks, when I got up in the middle of the night to visit the rest room, I'd stop sometimes in the hall and hear sounds of nature coming through the door of Jeanie's room. These sounds of nature consisted of Jeanie and some boy intercoursing between the sheets. Or else, if they weren't intercoursing, I'd hear them talking in a private way that I couldn't hear. I knew she wasn't dating anyone at school, which means she was performing a major exhibition of her vagina. I must have heard her with six or seven partners. It's very sad,

Mr. Patterson, but I didn't like imagining my sister and some stranger making a beast with two backs.[7]

A few weeks after Thanksgiving, I asked Collin if Jeanie had ever been a slut with him, because frankly it was bothering my peace-of-mind quite a bit. We were sitting behind The Church, which is Collin's name for the big electric plant where we sometimes went to pet heavily in his Wagoneer. It did kind of look like a church, with its big voltage things sticking up like spires, but I felt like Collin meant it another way as well. Like there was something churchy about its relationship to his head. He looked at me all serious with his face shining in the lights from the electric plant and said he wasn't interested in intercoursing Jeanie, that he'd been waiting for her beautiful younger sister to turn sixteen, which made me feel better to the third degree. Then he said he wanted to show me something special. I was in reality a little nervous because of his incredible manliness, and because his eyes were gleaming in a weird way from the sulfur lights, like those reflector things on the pedals of a bike, but then he looked down and started to undo the buttons of his shirt with one hand in a very sexy method.

I was very stunned by what I saw. Starting near Collin's Adam's apple, and getting longer with each button he undid, was a big scar dissecting his otherwise perfect breasts and going all the way down to his bellybutton. It looked like a little pink snake crawling down his chest. He told me that when he was eight years old he had become very sick and unable to breathe, and that the doctors had had to give him open-heart surgery and repair his heart. What they did is take one of his valves out and put in a new one, except the new one was

---

[7] I know now this means intercourse, and not a camel like I wrote on my last paper, but I think that literature—and especially literature by William Shakespeare—should be less fascist in what it means.

bionic and made of metal. I put my head to his chest, because he told me to, and I heard the buzzing of the electric plant all around us but also a little sound under Collin's ribs, a secret ticking in his heart, like a watch when you put it up to your ear. It made me very sad and amazed. I asked him if he was still in any danger, but he told me that his new valve worked perfectly as long as he didn't go bungee jumping or scuba diving in some really great barrier reef. I closed my eyes and didn't see Collin the famous singer of Salacious Universe but Collin the sick boy who couldn't breathe, a little shivering boy thinking he might not live past age whichever, sitting by himself in the cafeteria or library or boys' locker room, and it made my insides melt into cream of Natalie soup. That's when I said I thought I was in love with him. Collin looked at me very carefully, like he was deep in thought and maybe remembering the suffering of his childhood. Then he said that he didn't ordinarily do this, not after knowing me such a short time, but that he felt an "electroaffinity" between us and thought that we should finalize our love in the back of the car, especially since the Wagoneer had collapsible seats.

The truth is, I was a virgin and therefore the anti-Jeanie, but I didn't really want to admit it out loud. I didn't want to intercourse anyone who didn't love me in the biggest, most eternal way possible—at least, not until I was positive of our mutual lives together. I told Collin I wasn't ready to go all the way and he kind of smile-frowned and said that he loved me, he just wanted to prove it to me—that's all it was, a way of proving his love—but I said it was extremely important to me and I needed time to think about it before yielding to his loins. I got home late that night because Mom wants to empower us with our own curfews and then stopped in front of Jeanie's door, listening for sounds of sexual abandonment. I knew Jeanie was a mentally ill slut, but I felt kind of bad because we used to be best friends when we were kids and now she was just a human sex appliance with no moral fibers. I remembered how we used to play orphanage every day and pretend to scrub the floors to please the evil house-mother, two orphans with very miserable histories, but then we'd escape from the orphanage and find a tree to sleep under in the backyard and sneak back into the house like it was a rich person's mansion, filling pillowcases with whatever things we could steal, candlesticks and spaghetti tongs and big hunks of cheese. We'd sit under the tree and take each stolen thing out one at a time, saying *Oh how beautiful!* until we were close to tears.

I saw that Jeanie's light was on and knocked on the door and she opened it in an extra small T-shirt, one of those slut-shirts that have numbers on them like football jerseys. She stood there smirking in that mental way, holding Hippo under one arm like she was performing a touchdown. (It's very interesting to me that she lived up to her slut stardom with great success but still slept with a stuffed hippopotamus on a nightly basis.) She asked me what I wanted and I told her I just wanted to see how she was, which was actually kind of true, though I also wanted to know if she could tell me anything about Collin's sexual résumé. She didn't invite me into her room so we stood there in the hall. I wanted to ask her if she remembered being kids, how we used to cry like stupid babies over spaghetti tongs, just to turn her mouth into something less smirky and more Jeanie-like—but I didn't, of course. Instead I peered into her eyes and asked her if she loved the boys she intercoursed, except I used a less ethical word.

She seemed very unshocked and even laughed. Love's a joke, she said. Do you think Mom loves Franz? Do you think the President loves the First Lady? Do you think anybody loves anybody? I told her that love *had* to exist. Why else would people keep getting married all the time? Jeanie seemed to find this very smirk-inducing. Mom's been married four times—do you think she ended up loving any of them? How many of your friends' parents are still married? I didn't know what to say to that. It's true that almost all of them are divorced: Tamara's parents are divorced, and so are Tamara's, and actually I couldn't think of any original parents who seemed very much in love. And certainly Mom hasn't excelled in the romance category, seeing how we've had a new stepfather every four years—and now she and Franz's heads weren't exactly over their heels either, if you take into consideration that they yelled at each other every night about who should have put gas in the car or did she recycle the newspaper article about American children having lower IQ scores than Europe.

Still, I felt like I had to defend the most important part of my life, even if I had my own doubts about the future. I looked Jeanie in the eyeballs and told her that anyway *I* was in love, and that nothing else mattered. This actually did end Jeanie's smirk, because she looked at me kind of like she was the rich mother of the mansion pitying a starving girl orphan. She dropped her head a little bit and said that she needed to tell me something about Collin, that he'd never actually broken up with her completely. In fact, ever since Thanksgiving, he'd been visiting her room in the middle of the night while I was asleep! It wasn't just to relieve his loins either: they'd talk until morning sometimes, about the universe and its general lack of meaning and how they were the only people at school who knew that we were all just animals. He could never dump her for good, because their minds were conjoined. Jeanie was staring at Hippo and wouldn't meet my eye, and really I had to guess that she was speaking to me at all.

You don't even know what's real! I said.

I felt very depressed after our conversation, even though I knew Jeanie was extremely diluted and making up stories. I went downstairs to see if I could locate my mother. Instead I found Franz sitting in the TV room watching beach volleyball on Channel 39 and eating a carton of Häagen-Dazs vanilla fudge ice cream. He did what he always did when I discovered him watching women's volleyball, which was to get a blushing face and then tell me how he enjoyed the game of volleyball because of its "strategic nuance." I didn't see much strategic nuance, whatever that means, except that the players kept having to brush sand from their buttocks after they dove, which meant that there were four buttocks on each side to de-sand. I sat down with Franz to try to appreciate the game of volleyball, but when I asked him what the score was he said he wasn't sure.

So I went upstairs and knocked on my mother's door. As usual, she was drinking white wine without reservation and lying in bed with the covers pulled up to her waist. I asked her if she was all right, and she said that yes, of course she was all right, if you call being married to a Nazi tire salesman with one ball all right, then I should send my congratulations to Eva Braun. I had no idea what she was talking about, at least with the congratulations part, and I was worried that she might be getting mentally ill like my sister because I'd heard about these things running in the family. She asked me if I knew who else had one testicle, and I said no, and she said, Hitler! I was very upset that Franz had the same testicles as Adolf Hitler, because I wasn't even aware that he was disabled. I wanted to make her feel better, so I crouched beside her and took her glass of wine away and then kind of tucked her into bed like she used to do when I was a girl. It's a weird thing, tucking in your own mother, and I don't really recommend it unless you're a professional nurse and have a diploma in drunk-mother-tucking. Before I turned off the lights, I asked her why she'd married Franz to begin with, was she in love with him, and she looked at me sadly and said she didn't remember now if she ever was, wasn't that the bee's knees?

I went into my own room after that and took out this picture I have of my father, my real and un-German one, who died in a car accident when I was six. I sat down at my desk and took it out of the CD case I keep it in and held it at the corners so I wouldn't vandalize it with fingerprints. In the picture, my dad and I are in a boat together, one of those ferries you can take to Alcatraz to avoid the sharks. He looks young and very smart in his glasses and you can see this funny detail above the enormity of his nose, how his eyebrows kind of join forces in a Unibrow. I sat there at my desk and stared at the picture for a long time. Our hair is levitating from the wind, which seems very fierce and bone-chilling, and by the way I'm tucked into my father's lap it looks like he's protecting me from the cold.

The next evening, Collin and I went to Pizza Man so he could play pinball on his favorite machine, which had a scoreboard featuring women in costumes from the future and very true-to-breast cleavages. I sat in one of the booths, watching him dominate the machine with his perfect skills. Then we drove to The Church like always and parked in front of the big transformer with the sulfur lights brightening the sky and putting the stars out of business. He tried to pet me for a while, but I guess I wasn't in the mood because I didn't return his advances in a right-away fashion. He stopped advancing and frowned for a second and then looked at me seriously, his eyes shining in that weird way they had. That was when he told me about his secret powers. He made me promise not to tell anyone and then explained that he could see into the future before it happened, which was why he could play pinball forever without losing a coin. He knew the itinerary of the pinball before it occurred. I was very startled and didn't speak for a long time. I asked him if he could see into my future like the pinball's. He said, yes, he could see my whole life and even beyond that, but that the knowledge was in his body and the only way to convey it was to pass it directly. The Gift, he called it. I didn't really believe him, but probably I was so in love with his

Collinness that it didn't matter what was true or not. I thought for a long time, about how he used to be a sick boy with no power even to give his heart enough kilowatts to beat, and about how I thought of him twenty-four hours a day until I couldn't sleep, and how if I knew my future for real, I might stop being so scared about everything in this great and mysterious world invented by God—about my own helpless feeling and my mom being a converted alcoholic and Jeanie being mentally ill when she used to be my friend—and then I told him that next Saturday, not the coming one but a week from then, December 22, 2002, I'd be ready in my room at nine P.M. sharp.

That week, I was totally aside myself. I must have been wearing Collin Goggles that I couldn't remove because everywhere I looked he seemed to be coming toward me, kind of scary and beautiful-looking at the same time. I couldn't get him out of my thoughts. On Wednesday I went to Open School night with Mom and Jeanie, which was very challenging because Jeanie and I weren't on one of our speaking terms and we had to meet all the teachers while pretending to be a happy family unpopulated by sluts and alcoholics. Perhaps, Mr. Patterson, you remember talking to us?[8] I kept looking around at the other families on the basketball court and seeing Collin's face attached to some distant boy's neck, even though I knew he wasn't coming on account of his own parents being in Hawaii. When the boy turned out to be a stranger, I'd Collinize someone

---

[8]YOU: Hi, Maria. This must be your mother.

MOM (*drunk since dinner*): He doesn't look like your dad one bit. Where do you see it? He looks like a . . . teacher!

YOU: Ha ha ha. Maybe I should get a tattoo or something to disguise myself better.

JEANIE (*smirking*): **Natalie**'s got a tattoo. My sister, **Natalie.** Go ahead and show it, **Natalie.**

YOU: Wow. Look at that. (*lifting your glasses*) A microwave?

ME: It's a cobra.

YOU: Gosh.

else's face instead. There were about a million families all squeezed into the arena, and I watched all the married couples following behind their offspring or stepoffspring and it suddenly seemed like Jeanie was right, like it was just some meaningless random thing who intercoursed who, like the moms and dads had just picked whoever was around because they were too lonely or desperate or sexually excited to wait. It's really weird, but I had this Jeanie-ish idea like maybe we were in a giant barnyard.

When Saturday finally arrived, I couldn't wait all day in my room without becoming mentally ill myself, so I drove to the construction site in El Cerrito where Collin was working. It was a very warm day for December, and I parked behind a trailer where no one could see me. Collin was up there on top of the house he was building, kneeling like a Japanese person and hammering nails into a two-by-four made of wood. A radio on the ground was blasting hard rock from the eighties, all metal all the time, so I don't think anyone heard me pull up. It was kind of weird that Collin was working, because I saw the other guys on the crew taking their lunch break on the gates of their pickups in a very chummy manner. Collin had his shirt off, and when I first saw him from the back, the way his muscles kind of remained invisible until he bent down to hammer a nail and they came up like a secret promise to Natalie Mudbrook, a volt of longing went through me and all my doubts about intercourse were exploded. I just sat there watching him with very weak knees. It didn't matter to me that I was only 99 percent sure of his devotion. I fantasized that Collin and I were already married and that he was building us a house, a big beautiful mansion where we could live out our days in endless eternity.

And then something very strange occurred. This woman walked by in one of those running tops that reveal your abdomen, walking a big dog in front of her, and the crew started yelling at her in this very discriminating manner. They were wiggling their tongues and making their hammers into phallic symbols and even performing air intercourse. I glanced up at Collin and wondered if he'd come to her rescue, because I knew he was very respecting of women. Instead, he put his hand on his sewn-up heart and called her a *mamacita* in Spanish and asked for her phone number in this loud voice that everyone could hear. Of course, I knew that he was just trying to impress his coworkers, that he didn't really want the little mama's number at all, but it gave me this weird feeling like my own heart was struggling to beat.

I left the construction site and drove around for a long time, sort of without knowing where I was going, like a ghost or something, until finally I stopped in at a random Burger King for a Pepsi. I sat in one of the booths by myself and stared through the open window at the neon sign, which said HOME OF THE WHOPPER in big buzzing letters. I remember thinking how everything was supposed to have a home, even the Whopper, but what if you weren't the Whopper but just a girl whose mom and stepfather couldn't get along and everyone you saw or loved—even a beautiful boy you were about to intercourse in a couple hours—seemed to belong to a secret home somewhere you couldn't find? I mean it was out there, but no one had bothered to tell you where it was? So you had to go and sit in the Whopper's home instead, like a burglar.

When it was dark, I drove around some more to tranquilize myself and then went up the back way of the house like always, passing by Jeanie's room on the way to my own. I was experiencing a desperate need to talk to her and started to knock on her door, but then I heard her plowing her slutdom and froze in midknock. I pressed my ear against the door. Jeanie was talking to someone in a strange voice, kind of loud and whispery at the same time, like she was trying to melt an ice cube in her teeth. Now and then a deep voice would interrupt her in a very personal fashion. It wasn't a slut-a-thon, I realized, but just a conversation. Then the deep voice said something and she laughed. It was a woman's laugh, ungirl-like and beautiful. The weird thing is, I felt kind of jealous. Not because I wanted to be a full-time premiere slut, or because a boy had never made me laugh like that—but because *I* wanted to be the one making her laugh. Then whoever it was she was talking to got up and walked around and I lost my breath for a minute, because his shuffles were united with a faint sort of jingling, like coins.

I went to my room and lay in bed, trying not to think about nine o'clock almost arriving. It was storming pretty hard outside and for some reason I thought about all those turkeys stuck out in the rain, all soaked and miserable, drowning maybe because they didn't know enough to get out of it. It made me very sad. There was this little worm of rain moving on the window, kind of wriggling for no reason, and I watched it for a long time.

Then I heard a knock and the room's energy changed completely. The energy collected around my body and seeped into my own skin, too, like I was a giant battery getting charged. Everything seemed connected: the rain squirming, my heart pounding, the Earth turning on its axle. Collin opened the door without me answering it. He looked more beautiful than I'd ever seen him, face glowing with confidence and his hair kind of floating around him like a commercial for Vidal Sassoon. His clothes were only a little damp, despite the undry weather. I was very scared. He walked over to the bed and knelt beside my face. He didn't say a word, just reached down and touched my lips, which made my eyelids sparkle at a very high frequency. I knew I wouldn't stop him from transmitting me The Gift. He stood up all of a sudden and walked over to the window—I guess to close the curtains so no one would witness my conduction. His jeans were kind of slipping down like usual, and I could see this strip of skin below his tan line that was all bumpy and wrinkled from the elastic force of his boxers. I imagined it was one of those Braille messages for blind people to touch that said BELOW THIS LINE IS THE REST OF YOUR LIFE.

But just as Collin was turning around to come back to bed, we heard a sound on the stairs that sounded like my mother's coughing lungs. This was very unusual, because she almost never came to visit me and when she did it was generally during the daytime when I wasn't being deflowered. But sure enough, her steps began coming up the stairs. For a second, I just lay there like an embalmed person. Then I grabbed Collin's arm and put him in the closet where nobody would find him, telling him to wait there until the coast was cleared.

I was glad to see my mom wasn't completely drunk yet, because she didn't have the sniffling nose and bare feet she got when she was inebriated. There was just a frizz of gray hair like a piece of tinsel hanging into her eyes and impacting her vision. She walked over to the bed and looked at me with a sad expression. She said she was sorry, and I said, What for? and she didn't say anything but just kind of looked around the room, like she sensed Collin's energy but couldn't put her finger on its origins. Then she bent down and hugged me. I held her back and didn't let go right away. Her hair was soft, and I could smell the maximum dandruff control of the Head & Shoulders she uses. She said, My god, Sweetie, you're trembling like a leaf. I wanted to ask her some questions about what it was like to be a full-grown woman with gray hairs in your face. Like, had a man ever solved her problems even for a week? Was being a woman, at least, something to look forward to? But I didn't. I just hugged her until I could feel her heart beating through my sweater. I was squeezing pretty hard because she eventually had to peel my arms from her neck on account of her historic back trouble.

And then she left, except I didn't tell Collin that she was gone right away. Instead I just lay there by myself and thought about this song Jeanie and I used to sing, the one with the double intentions in it. "Miss Lucy," it was called. I lip-synched it in my head, picturing us under our favorite tree and clapping each other's hands in a fast-motion rhythm like we used to:

> *Ask me no more questions, I'll tell you no more lies,*
> *The boys are in the bedroom, pulling down their . . .*
> *Flies are in the meadow, bees are in the park,*
> *The boys and girls are kissing in the . . .*
> *D-A-R-K*
> *D-A-R-K*
> *D-A-R-K*
> *Dark*
> *Dark*
> *Dark*

When I was a kid, I always loved the ending, how you spelled out *dark* with all its letters, like you didn't want the song to end and spelling the last word was a way of putting it off for long as you could. Sometimes, when my mom used to tuck me into bed, I tried to do the same thing in actual life and spell out the words of whatever I saw in my room, saying the letters in my brain, like it could maybe stop her from leaving and turning off the lights. C-L-O-S-E-T. There was a noise against the door, like the rustle-around of an animal. C-L-O-S-E-T. Soon I would know everything. C-L-O-S-E-T. I stared at the thing I didn't want to say, listening for Collin's breath behind the door, trying in my wildest brain to imagine what he'd look like when it opened.

Love exists. It has to.

I'm sorry, Mr. Patterson. I know I'm going to fail this essay, and probably the whole course, but it seems like William Butler Yeats has a lot of very talented groupies to explain his poem—but who's ever going to explain my story except me? Who'd ever waste their precious time to sign up for Natalie Mudbrook 101?

It's been two months now since Jeanie and Collin disappeared. Franz thinks they were in a conspiracy and ran off together, but perhaps it's just an accident that they vanished at the same time. My mom and Franz filed a Missing Jeanie report with the police, even though her duffel bag is gone and she clearly packed up her own things because she remembered to take Hippo with her. Some guys at school say that Collin kidnapped her and took advantage of her mental unfitness, or else that they're both crazy and made a suicide pact like those Davidist people in Texas. But I try not to listen to anyone else. Sometimes I think about Collin's face that night after we'd become single backs again, when it wasn't so wild and unhuman but more like a little boy's in the hospital, looking sad and far-off and not known by anyone—which was the way I was feeling, too. On the weekends, I drive out to the construction site where he used to work and watch the crew nailing our house together. I just sit there in the car, watching it get taller every week. Sometimes I close my eyes for sixty seconds like a game, imagining that when I open them again I'll see Collin walking toward me with his long hair and tool belt and glowing tan arms, the house finished and waiting to be peopled with newlyweds, like a movie version of my destiny.

But the weird thing is, with my eyes closed, I don't see Collin at all. I see Jeanie's brown eyes and size-challenged nose, which aren't the movie features I was thinking about. We're sitting in the half built house, all hunched together because of the wind, pulling candlesticks and egg-slicers and curtain-tier-uppers out of a pillowcase. Our eyes are crying at the beautiful objects. That's how I know Jeanie's really just run off like an orphan, except this time for real—that she's waiting under a tree somewhere, living out of her duffel like a duffel bag-lady, except I don't know where.

Other times, I drive up to the city and hang out in the park, watching the ducks and swans swim around in the little lake next to the paddle-boat dock. The swans are very peaceful and not at all like William Butler Yeats describes in his poetry. Perhaps they have "strange hearts," but how would you know without performing surgery?[9] I've never actually seen the swans intercourse, but I can tell that their mating habits are not perverted or interracial when it comes to humans. I look at how beautiful they are with their swan-shaped bodies and necks like question marks and imagine that there's a daughter growing inside of me already. I know I'll have a girl because of The Gift, which gets stronger and more giftlike every day. For example, I know she's going to be very beautiful, like that Helen Troy who launched a thousand ships with her face. I know for certain that no one will ever want to disappear without telling her. And I know just as certainly that she'll be famous and worshipped in the chests of strangers, that men will fight over her and even meet tragic endings.

Meanwhile, Franz hides in the TV room after dinner, and my mom complains to me every night while I tuck her in, and the elm in the backyard where Jeanie and I used to play is invested with bugs.

I wonder, Mr. Patterson, if you can change something that's not assembled yet. If you know the future, can you keep it from happening? The Gift is very strong, but actually it hasn't come all at once like you'd think. Instead, I'll be sitting in European History class with my eyes half-closed from boredom, or just staring out the window of

---

[9]Unless by "strange" he means like everyone else's and therefore alone under their swanny feathers, in which case I'm not going to argue with that.

my room while Tamara bitches about Tamara on the phone, and suddenly I'll see a whole scene flash through my head, a perfect smellable dream-picture except I'm awake, like I could walk into my own brain and snap a Polaroid. Sometimes they're people I don't recognize, but usually it's someone I know pretty well or at least have seen before in my regular life. I'm trying to make sense of the dream-pictures as they come. Like my mom with a black eye and slippers on her feet, hiding on the roof of our house while it's raining out. Or Rogelio, the school janitor, staring out the window of an airplane with his hands trembling a little bit under the tray table in its unlocked and downright position. Or one that I've seen more than once, which is Jeanie lying totally alone in an apartment somewhere without furniture, her ear pressed to the rug and listening to music through the floor. She's wearing one of her extra small T-shirts with stains under the arms, like maybe she hasn't changed it for a while, but she's smiling with this little-girl look like the music is the Secret of Everything and making her extremely happy, reminding her of something else, like maybe the secret really has to do with the *past* and not the future, but I can't get close enough in my head to hear it.

Or sometimes even you, Mr. Patterson. Take right now, for example. I can see you sitting in your office at school, reading this essay before I'm even finished with it. You're holding a coffee mug that says: READ BANNED BOOKS. Your office is very cold and sweet-smelling, because you just finished smoking a pipe filled with illicit marijuana buds that you hide in your glasses case (you blew the smoke out the window to prevent your being narced on by another teacher's nose). I've never noticed from the back row of class, but your eyebrows kind of connect into one. I see that you're wondering, as you read, how much you smoked. That the hair on the back of your neck is tingling. That you're finishing my essay. Right this second. And that you might even know now who I am.

E. V. SLATE

Boston University

⤳

FULL-MONTH CELEBRATION

Everyone was happy that Ah Fong was going back to China. For years she had said that even if she wanted to go, Ray, her "young master," wouldn't let her. She clenched her eyebrows when she said this, but anyone could see that she was pleased. Still they wondered, did she want to go back? She had been working for the Lim family for forty-five years, the elder Mr. and Mrs. Lim were long gone, and now there was only Ray, his wife, and their little boy, Harry, in that big colonial villa on Shelford Road. They thought of her as a grandmother of sorts, and even let Harry call her Mah-Mah, but in the end they weren't her family, she still wore her black and white amah uniform, so wasn't it time to retire?

There was no question of her going to the old folks' home run by the Taoist temple, with its attached columbarium filled with urns, or of moving into the room that she and her amah sisters rented in Chinatown for their two Sundays off each month. Only one sister lived there now, the others having died or gone back to the Old Country, and that sister, Ah Chin, was so very grumpy. Ah Fong was cheerful and usually quite pleased with herself. Since she had taken the vow of chastity before coming to Singapore, she had always felt that Ray was like her own child. Both of his parents had died by the time he was six years old, so whenever he fell down or was feeling the heat in his belly he always ran straight to her, and never to his grandmother, who had always been harsh with him. And these days Ah Fong hardly put herself out. She still cooked and dusted and looked after Harry when he came home from school—her favorite thing was to bring him snacks and pat his shoulders while he studied—but now the laundry was done in the washing machine and the Indian groundskeeper, who lived in a little room beside the garage, came in the afternoons to mop the floors. With all the money she had saved and sent back to her family in Canton over the years, they had been able to build three small houses, one for each of her brother's three sons, and to send one of the sons to university.

So what did she have to complain about?

Every old person born in China longed to go back there to die; that was as normal as bursitis and crooked toes. The amahs in the old folks' home talked about it all the time. But then they scared themselves with stories of other amahs being swindled by their nieces and nephews, of even being thrown out of the ancestral house once they had given away their savings. Ah Fong heard the stories each time she went to visit her friends, but she knew that it was only to comfort themselves that they said such things. They were really too old and too poor to go back. Compared to them, she was still quite young. She had some money that she had saved to build her own house, and each Chinese New Year her brother, Siang, wrote to her asking, *When are you coming back? Your place is here with your own family.* She went to Chinatown to have the letters read to her and came home feeling sick with longing. Then Siang died, and her nephews wrote to tell her that with his last words he had told them to write again and ask her finally to come home. After this, Ah Fong thought of little else and even told herself that she had always wanted to go.

Ray always said he wouldn't let her go back. He said it because he knew Ah Fong liked to hear it, and he had lived with her for so long that having her around was as natural to him as seeing the altar in the dining room with his grandparents' photographs each time he passed by. Anyway, to him, China was backward—full of ragged children and wandering dogs, no place for these little amahs who had grown used to the modern, sanitary conditions in Singapore. Also, everyone knew how greedy they were over there, thinking Singaporeans were rich, including the Chinese amahs, who had denied themselves all of the things that make women happy in order to send money back to relatives they hadn't seen in fifty years.

One day Ray was out in the garden picking mangoes with a long wooden plucker, twisting the fruit off the stem with a quick turn of his wrists, and then lowering it down for Ah Fong or Harry to take. The two of them vied with each other—Ah Fong was slightly taller, but Harry was faster and received playful smacks on his arm when he got to the fruit first.

"Hey Dad-dee, that one is not ripe, lah. Put it back in the tree," his wife joked from the veranda. She spoke English with a strong Singaporean accent and said *teef* instead of *teeth,* but she didn't know any dialects either, except for a few kitchen words that were the substance of her only interactions with Ah Fong.

"Ray, these are not ripe, try to reach the high ones," Ah Fong said in Cantonese.

"Mummy just said that, Mah-Mah," Harry answered her. He also studied Mandarin in school, which was very nice, but Ray was not pleased with the Singlish he spoke with his mother or with his grades in English at school, and had even tried to cane his son one night until Ah Fong knocked on the door, begging him to stop.

So it went in their household, where Ray relaxed and felt like an important man, though he had never invited over any of his colleagues from the bank, even during Chinese New Year. They were mostly foreigners or nouveau-riche Singaporeans with Filipina maids whom they mistrusted and sometimes even struck with switches.

While they were carrying the baskets of fruit inside, Ah Fong turned to him and said, "My nephew's wife just had a baby. Maybe I'll go back for the full-month celebration."

Ray sensed that this was not like all the other times, at birthday parties and New Year visits from her friends, when Ah Fong would announce, "I want to go back but he won't let me," and then slap his shoulder, a cue for him to look boyish and say, "It's true!" Now he looked at her and said, "If you really want to go, I'll bring you. When is it?"

"Oh, you are too busy. Next month, on the seventeenth."

"I'll check my calendar later, but does it have to be on the seventeenth?"

"Of course it's the *full*-month celebration. But don't worry, I can manage on my own!" she said and then laughed and clenched her eyebrows, so that Ray understood that he was now committed to arranging their trip.

Over time, Ah Fong let Ray know that this wasn't going to be a short visit. She began buying gifts for her nephews and grand-nephew, then came home from the pharmacy with five bags of her prescriptions and told Ray that since she was so busy packing for their trip, he had better hire another maid. So Ray and his wife drove down to a small office in Coronation Plaza and chose two photographs of girls from hundreds in a black binder. Both were Indonesians, pretty Muslim girls with shy, not sly, smiles; one was described as "not spoilt," the other as "likes children and hard work." It was not possible to engage them for the short term, as a payment was required for their plane tickets, and this was when Ray realized that Ah Fong would not be returning.

They threw her a farewell party the week before she was set to leave, and Ray even sent the driver over to the old folks' home to shuttle over the few amahs who were still able to walk on their own. They made a quaint sight, like relics of old China, in their white *samfoo* tops, black pants, and slippers. Together they seemed very small and shrunken, modest, and yet as self-assured as men. Although illiterate and afraid of everything from wet hair to ghosts, they had remedies for every ailment, though these usually tasted bitter or slimy or too sweet, like the bird's nest soup Ah Fong used to make after picking the down from the nest with tweezers and boiling it with sugar in a clay pot. All of them still wore their gray hair pulled back into the plaited buns that meant they had taken the vow of chastity before a Taoist priest, and it was easy to see in their soft, pale faces the girls they had once been. Ray felt very tender toward them, though he frowned when he stepped out onto the balcony and caught two of them smoking hand-rolled cigarettes as thick as cigars.

"Mr. Lim is kind to his servants and to the friends of his servants," one of them said, blowing out smoke.

"Yah, taking Ah Fong all the way to China himself," his brother-in-law called from inside. "I never thought it would happen, lah. Can't even get him to meet in Chinatown for a meal. No, must go to a *proper* restaurant!"

Everyone laughed, imagining Ray in his Brooks Brothers shirt and shiny Dunhill loafers strolling the muddy lanes of some Pearl River Delta village.

"It might be short trip," Ray said. "If I don't like the looks of it, Ah Fong and I have open tickets to come back straight-away, if necessary."

Ah Fong beamed at him from across the room, but Ray only looked away and said maybe it was time he went to China anyway, since Singapore was losing so much business over there.

The flight to Hong Kong was bumpy, as it always was during typhoon season. Ray flipped through the duty-free catalog and pretended not to notice Ah Fong vomiting into a paper bag. Once they reached cruising altitude, she unbuckled her seat belt and went to the toilet, remaining there for the rest of the flight, even after the warning light came back on and the stewardesses returned to their seats. Ray didn't know if he should go and find her or not. It had been awkward between them ever since the driver had dropped them at the airport, with Ah Fong fretting and asking Ray over and over if he had the passports and tickets. Finally, when they started to descend, a stewardess led her back with extra bags and tissues, calling her "auntie," then patted her on the back. Ah Fong shrugged away the caress and reached into her bag for a small brown bottle of medicinal oil that she rubbed with trembling fingers under her nose.

In Hong Kong, rain pounded on the taxi roof and blurred the view from the windows. Ray was relieved that Ah Fong couldn't see the steel and glass high-rises, the elegant clothes in the shop windows, the glamour of this very Chinese city. They boarded a hydrofoil at the Aberdeen Ferry Terminal, and Ray ordered tea and toast from the waiter. Ah Fong said she was feeling better, though she was glad that that was her first and last plane ride.

There were so few passengers on board that soon the waiter, a boyish-looking man with greased hair, came and asked them if they were mother and son, and where they were going. He had never heard of the amahs. He wanted to know if Ray liked to play cards. After a while the second mate joined them, bringing a bag of sunflower seeds that the men shelled in their mouths, spitting the soggy fibers onto a shared plate. Ah Fong fell asleep with her mouth open and then the two men told Ray a couple of dirty stories to "console" him for losing forty yuan. But forty yuan was not even ten Singapore dollars, and Ray had enjoyed their company, had even felt a surge of affection as they stood to attend to their duties before docking. "In Singapore you two would go far!" he told them. They blinked. This was China; they already had good jobs.

That night in the Red Flower Hotel in Zhuhai, Ray sat in his room flipping through the television channels. No cable, no BBC, and the state channels were mostly in Mandarin, which Ray did not enjoy listening to, so he turned off the set. Ah Fong was very quiet in her room next door. The rain had stopped, so Ray opened his window and breathed in his first smell of China: a mixture of exhaust, wet leaves, and something metallic, like hot ore. He wouldn't have said the odor was pleasant, yet he kept breathing it in, and was finally lured outside.

A rickshaw pulled up as soon as he stepped through the revolving door. "Keep on going!" The bellhop called, waving for a taxi. But the old man only pedaled forward and beckoned to Ray. "Fix the price first then!" the bellhop said when Ray climbed in.

"Don't worry, Boss, I'll charge you the local price." The old man stood up and put all of his weight on the pedal with a grunt, but once he got the bicycle going, it seemed to propel itself easily enough. From behind he looked like a muscular boy.

"Just show me around town," Ray said, leaning back in the seat and crossing his legs. He had never ridden in a rickshaw; the ones in Singapore, lined up in front of the Raffles Hotel, were only for tourists. Something about it felt right, though, being jostled down the street in this way. He had time to look at faces, at side streets, at the crowds in the neon-lit restaurants, and when they passed a fruit vendor he called for the old man to stop and bought a handful of rambutans for each of them. The old man drove with one hand, holding the rubbery, spidery skins to his mouth and then tearing out the clear orbs of fruit with his teeth. The red skins he spat to the ground. Ray laughed and tried it this way himself, not thinking of germs or pesticides, though he couldn't bring himself to litter in a country that wasn't his, so he piled the skins and seeds in a little mound on the seat beside him. Sweet, tangy, and cooling, it was the most delicious fruit he had ever eaten.

They came to a street market, and the old man asked him if he wanted to stop. Ray got out and walked the bright, crowded alleys. They really had everything here. He bought a woven handbag for his wife, a plastic machine gun for Harry, and a belt for himself. He sat on a small red chair beside a food stall, slurping a bowl of noodles, and listened to the chitchat around him. He couldn't remember the last time he had been out walking at night, and he was sweating pro-fusely in the muggy air. He decided to buy some T-shirts so that he would not have to use the hotel's laundry service. Also, he felt as though his lemon-yellow Lacoste shirt said something about himself that he didn't necessarily want to be true.

It was midnight by the time he got back to the hotel, yet people were still out walking and enjoying the night air, which was begin-ning to cool. So unlike dark Shelford Road, hemmed in by angsana trees and tall metal gates, everyone in their bedrooms by ten o'clock with the doors shut for the air-conditioning: Harry all alone, Ray and his wife lying back to back, reading magazines in bed. Sometimes when she fell asleep first, he didn't bother to switch off her light, and it burned all night over her head.

"Twenty-five yuan," the old man said. Twenty-five yuan. His expression had gone hard, and he got off his seat as though expecting a fight. But Ray handed him a fifty and turned away before the old man could react. The bellhop watched him with a sneer.

The next morning Ah Fong was feeling more like herself. She woke at dawn and made her bed and then went down to the lobby to wait for Ray. The girls behind the desk stared at her. She had made a new shirt for the trip, choosing a pale blue cotton, but she wasn't very creative at sewing and in the end had only made herself another *samfoo*. Everyone in Singapore knew about the amahs and felt kindly toward them; there was no shame in going out in her uniform. Here, she seemed to remind people of bad times, of famine and unwanted children, times those girls behind the desk might have heard about from their grandmothers. It would be different once she got to her village, she thought; then she would feel that finally she was home.

Ray came down at seven in a baggy T-shirt and a belt with a bright gold buckle. She hoped he would change before the driver arrived; she wanted him to look good, to look like himself. He was all she had to show for her forty years of hard work. She took his arm as they went into the hotel restaurant and ate porridge with pickles and fried dough.

"So, Ah Fong, are you nervous?" he asked. He was eating so noisily this morning, and with such a big appetite!

"Why should I be nervous?" Ah Fong answered, though she was. She had to run to the bathroom in the lobby while Ray signed for their breakfast, and down it went, all that money wasted. She had been sick last night, too. The chicken had been a little pink, the floor of the restaurant so dirty that she had lifted her feet under the table and held them aloft all through the meal.

The yellow taxi sped out of the city, past construction cranes and grimy, tiled buildings with blue windows, then newer high-rises that all looked the same. But as soon as they left the boundaries of the city they were back in old China and had to share the road with mule carts. Farmers in coolie hats trudged with their water buffaloes beside the flat, shining rice paddies. Ah Fong tried to imagine herself living in the meager stone houses they passed along the road. This would be her final journey, and in her entire life she had had only two. When she was fifteen, she had tried to be brave as she rode on the back of her father's wagon, carrying only a small bundle, her hair newly twisted into a tight bun. Now, she was glad that Ray was sitting up front and chatting so loudly with the driver, because they couldn't see her chin, which was trembling, or her eyes, which she had to dab now and then with the red silk handkerchief that her mistress had given her. Harry had told her it was red, for China, and silk because Ah Fong, like many amahs, had started out working in the silk factories of the Delta. She had never owned anything silk. It was not very absorbent and only spread the tears across her face.

Everyone in the village was excited about the full-month celebration. There would be long-life noodles, hard-boiled eggs, sweets for the children, and mao-tai for the men. The three houses of the Tong family had been decorated with red banners and paper lanterns, not just for the baby's one month birthday, but because Auntie Fong was returning home from overseas to live. All three sisters-in-law had been cleaning house and arguing over where this aunt would live. Finally it was decided that they would keep their father-in-law Siang's old room for the baby and put the aunt in an old storage room of the third sister's house.

People gathered in the courtyard while the sisters-in-law were still busy in the kitchen and the brothers were setting up tables and chairs in the courtyard. They all cooed over the baby, who was dressed in a red satin jumper that made him so hot that his cheeks seemed scorched. He squalled as he was handed around and held up and wished a happy birthday.

Just as the sisters-in-law were setting out the dishes and wondering how much longer they could wait, a yellow taxi pulled up by the stone gate. Out stepped a runty old woman with a smooth face, dressed in a historical costume. The driver and another man pulled two suitcases from the trunk, and the brothers rushed to take the bags. A crowd gathered around Auntie Fong and soon she was crying and patting her nephews on their arms and introducing one man, tall and fair-skinned, with very big teeth and a nice haircut, as her "young master," which made everyone titter, and the other man as the driver. Both were invited to stay and soon blended in with the crowd as they all sat down to eat.

Ah Fong sat beside her first nephew, who had a paunch and double chin, his wife, who was pretty but kept giving everyone sharp glances, and their red-clad baby. Ah Fong wasn't sure if she would be able to hold down her food, but she took a few bites so as to not insult her niece-in-law. Then she began picking the choicest pieces and dropping them into Ray's bowl. In this one tiny place in the world, she felt like an important person. She had helped pay for this party and for the new tile roof that her first nephew had just put on his house. He worked as an engineer in a factory near Zhuhai, but even after all these years, Ah Fong knew that her remittances came in handy.

After the noisy meal, the children ran between the tables, the men dragged their chairs together and brought out the mao-tai. The two guests of honor, Ah Fong and the baby, seemed to be forgotten. As

she was helping her nieces-in-law clear away the dishes, Ah Fong saw
Ray raise a glass of the liquor to his mouth. She had never seen him
drink, even on New Year's Eve. Now her first nephew clapped him on
the back and Ah Fong gasped; it must be that T-shirt. How could her
nephew know what an important man Ray was in Singapore?

"Auntie Fong, you mustn't help us!" her nieces-in-law cried. This
isn't your kitchen, they seemed to be saying. She didn't know where
to put the bowls. She didn't even know how to prepare the dishes
they had served, and yet all her life Ah Fong had loved to cook. Now
the third niece-in-law, a girl whose round face was speckled with tiny
moles, showed her to a narrow room with a plank bed and bare cement floors. With all the money she had sent, Ah Fong was surprised
by how small and basic the three houses were. Every wall needed a
new coat of paint.

"As soon as I settle in I want to build my own house," Ah Fong said.

"What for? You see we have three houses here. Why would you
want one all to yourself?" the third niece-in-law asked. She watched
while Ah Fong unzipped her bag and pulled out gifts for the baby, including a twenty-four-carat anklet with a little gold bell that would
tinkle when the baby started to walk. "You know, Auntie Fong," she
said, "my husband never got to go to college. It wasn't fair. Now he's
thinking of going into business as an entrepreneur. Maybe a shoe
store or a breakfast stall. Only, he needs a loan to get started, and
First Brother is so stingy."

"Of course I'll help if I can," Ah Fong said, sitting down on the
bed and fingering the woolen blanket.

"It's settled then! Now, why don't you take a rest? Your days of
hard work are over. We really don't need you to do anything around
here!" And she was gone.

After a while Ah Fong got up and wandered the houses until she
found Siang's altar. She lit incense, bowed and prayed, and then

stared into his stern, narrowed eyes. Nothing of the face in that photograph reminded her of the brother she had known. Now he was gone. His presence in the world lingered only around this little table, with the sounds of the full-month celebration drifting in through the open window. She imagined her own photograph on the wall and tried squinting to match his gaze. For the first time all day, her heart slowed down. The voices in the courtyard seemed far away. So this is what it will be like, she sighed. There was only one thing left to do. In a panic, she ran to find Ray.

He swayed and had to lean on the driver's shoulder to right himself. Lifting up his empty glass, he held out his other hand to let everyone in the courtyard know that he wanted to make a toast. "Now it's getting late, and I should be heading back to Zhuhai. At first, I was worried about this trip, about how all of you would treat Ah Fong." He leaned down toward the driver and whispered loudly, "I had never been to my homeland!" Standing straight, he went on, "But I shouldn't have worried. I didn't know! In Singapore, ah, we're all finished there. We swallowed the ways of the West, and now no one wants to go there. Why would they? You've got something we've lost," he said, waving his hand at the men sitting around him, and nearly toppled over.

"Something—" he faltered and at this everyone burst out laughing in embarrassment and said, *Poor fellow can't hold his drink!* Still, they were touched by his speech, and pulled on his arm, and the driver helped him walk toward the car. He had almost forgotten about Ah Fong, but when he saw her running across the courtyard he felt good about himself. Bringing a maid all the way back to China! It would be his one adventure.

"Ah Fong, you'll be all right here," he said, opening the passenger door.

"I've been thinking, though, Ray," she said, panting and tugging on his T-shirt, "why don't you stay in Zhuhai for a few days, and then come back for me? I'm sure Harry is missing me, and those other maids don't know how to prepare all your favorite dishes, and—"

"Always thinking of others! Don't cry now. She's been crying since we reached China! Have your nephews write and let us know how you're doing. And to think I never let you come before now—"

But the driver had already shut the door. The nephews and nieces-in-law came out to the gate, and Ray waved as the car sped off. He thought he would always remember them that way, with Ah Fong squeezing through and then waving as if to call him back, back to his roots, though the next evening, when he was sitting on the plane back to Singapore, he looked at the empty seat beside him. What would the house on Shelford Road be like without her? For the first time he saw that he was an orphan, that he had been one since he was six years old.

KEITH GESSEN

Syracuse University

‹❧›

LIKE VACLAV

I

Like Vaclav Havel under Communism, Mark Baumberg had decided, at the late age of twenty-seven, to live in truth. In Czechoslovakia this had brought down a tyrannical regime. In Syracuse, New York, it brought down a marriage and created a celebrity. Mark was that celebrity. The marriage, too, was his.

The exact order of events—who could reconstruct it? There were arguments, sentiments, tears, but in Mark's view the result was admirably ideological. For all he might have felt about the lovely Elaine, about her neck, about her stomach, his hands on her stomach while he walked behind her—he *knew* he should be out of it, *knew* that fundamentally his situation was false. So in the end Elaine returned to New York, to the literary agency with the magnificent 1920s elevator and the agents she could not abide, and Mark remained at Stickley U., free now at last to devote his undivided being to a dissertation on the Mensheviks, the grave gray truth-tellers of 1917.

Instead he played hockey, and in the afternoons wandered around the campus, bound on one end by the inadequate library and on the other by the great white bubble-domed stadium. The stadium seemed out of place, as if an alien spaceship had landed on the edge of a quiet college quadrangle and announced, in international space code, "Come. Come play football inside me."

To which the college had replied, "And basketball?"

"I love basketball," said the spaceship, which could seat fifty thousand.

The college pressed its luck. "What about hockey?"

"Sure," said the aliens, shrugging. "Whatever."

Beyond the stadium lay the ghetto, and on the other side, beyond the library, the fraternities and sub shops and defrosted pita wrap places. Mark always sensed the danger of absentmindedly walking to the campus edge and finding himself in the wrong part of town. It was all the wrong part of town. In the first few weeks of his freedom, before he became a guru of living in truth, he stumbled around from the stadium to the library, from the library to the stadium, blubbering. As though the cognitive function in his brain responsible for correspondences—that is, for connecting the sight of a tree to the mind's idea of "tree"—had begun to misfire, everything Mark saw connected in his mind to the idea of "Elaine." This in turn triggered the crying mechanism. He thought his brain might be running a self-diagnostic, for emotional functionality, and he succumbed. Ow-ow-ow, he whimpered. Oh-oh-oh.

But, too, he suddenly felt a profound connection to all this. Not the campus, which was cold and exposed to windstorms and populated by drunken idiots (his students), but the whole big universe. He was part of it again. Hello there! In the era of Elaine he had been an emissary from the Baumberg family, charged with returning home as soon as he'd gathered the necessary information, or groceries. To tarry longer—over coffee, a beer, over a left-leaning quarterly—was already the beginning of sin, and it was this sinning that had driven him mad. He couldn't do it to her. Now that nothing remained of them, he could. On the radio he experimented, tentatively, with non-public stations. The prattle of the DJs was intolerable, but the popular songs spoke to Mark. Baby, he thought, we only have tonight to feel alive. Girl, he nearly said aloud (did he say it aloud?), let's take a ride in the Benzie. There was a song that season by a woman, a diva, who claimed that she was "always on time." Ta-ta-TA-ta. Yes, thought Mark. He would try to be more punctual.

And yet he was always late to the history section he was teaching. The kids didn't mind, though, if they noticed; their blankness had been shored against all ruin. Stickley was a lazy and demoralized university, a place where no one was kidding anyone, but children traveled there from Long Island, from Westchester, dressed up for parties and for the bars, convinced somehow of its prestige—did it not, after all, boast a cavernous stadium? Mark tried his best to entertain them—this was, considering the tuition, the least he could do.

Nonetheless he could not help but collar one of his students after section one day, a history major in a blue hooded sweatshirt and a scraggly black beard. He demanded to know what they'd been up to. "Tell me," Mark said. "You haven't been reading. You haven't been writing. What have you guys been *doing?*"

The student didn't break stride; he merely offered Mark a look of great simplicity, of clear skin behind the faux-ragged beard. "We've been fucking," he said, smiled briefly as if at the memory of it, and left Mark standing, stricken, at the top of the stairs.

And how many women had Mark slept with? Ten? Fifteen? (As if he didn't know the number.) (But there were ambiguous instances!

There were some he wasn't sure of!) (Those don't count.) (He was *pretty* sure.) No matter, no matter—was it possible that beard-face, so pathetically misinformed on the midterm in his analysis of social conditions in the rural areas in 1917, had it right? Was what Mark needed in the wake of his divorce a series of meaningless encounters, a sort of primitive sexual accumulation, which, like its capitalist counterpart, would initially be ruthless, barbarous, and wasteful, but would eventually assume a benign, social-democratic form, with universal health care?

No, no. That would be living in truth as interpreted by the pool-cue-wielding brothers of Sigma Alpha Chi. After all, it wasn't really sex with other women that Mark had lacked during his years with Elaine, though he had certainly lacked it, and it wasn't the ritual coyness before the emphatic plunge. Rather it was the fleeting expressions, the tiny backhands of the spirit, the way in which American women managed, for all their seeming similarity of dress and manner, to distinguish themselves from one another, to defend themselves against vulgarity and still invite the sexual response. And then there were the moments, Mark vaguely remembered them still, pregnant with meaning, and anticipation, and the sending of signals, like prayerful cross-ice passes, across smoky rooms.

While in prison, Vaclav Havel was allowed to write letters to his wife, Olga. His jailers established narrow parameters—four pages, with three-centimeter margins, no stray marks or quotations or foreign expressions. When Havel, trained in Heideggerian metaphysics, started blathering on about Being, they banned that, too.

From the prison of his solitude, Mark wrote e-mails. He wrote a few daily encouraging lines to Elaine, an occasional teaser to Samara, the handsome management consultant he'd met at a party in Boston, and a steady stream of pedantic corrections to the editors of the political weeklies. And then he wrote long, Proustian e-mails to his friends. They were wonderful e-mails! Full of wit and wisdom, and brooding and charm, they were the distillation of a lifetime's considerations, a long relationship's repressions, that morning's reading in Soviet history. Above all they stressed his doctrine of truth, and secretly he lamented their disappearance into the Internet void, into the bustle of his friends' workplace inboxes. He was not so vain as to keep copies of his own e-mails, but he did have a faint vague hope that, post-9/11 maybe, the intelligence services might keep track of them, someday making the e-mails available to the reading public under the Freedom of Information Act of 1974.

"Friends," he wrote in the rousing peroration to a five thousand-word reflection,

> What are we doing? Why are we doing it? I remember the men we once were, and the promises we once made. Yeats: "I have grown happier with every year of life, as though gradually conquering something in myself." Are we? I saw Toby the other day—how diminished our Toby is! He wore Camper shoes and terrifying glasses. He said he hadn't read a book in weeks.
>
> I don't know why this has happened to us.
>
> Except of course I do know.
>
> Throw down your fishnets, dear friends! If there be women in the nets, cast them off! Come to Syracuse! There is plenty of parking.

He sent them out, he forgot what he'd written, he walked around between the stadium and the library, composing further e-mails in his head. But they were not lost. Like Havel's letters, which his dear Olga distributed to fellow dissidents, Mark's missives began to be discussed among his friends. They wanted to know more about truth, and living in it. Mark obliged with follow-up missives, further thoughts. "It won't be easy," he warned them. "Truth will not pay your rent, and it won't wash your dishes. If you send truth an e-mail, it won't e-mail you back."

Mark's friends were undeterred, his friend Dan least of all. Encyclopedic, neurotic, he abandoned his studies at Yale and drove the three hundred miles in one six-hour CD-changing dash. Dan had broken up with his girlfriend of eighteen months. For a day or two, he said, it felt great. "But living in truth in New Haven," he lamented, "it's too depressing."

"Yes," admitted Mark. "I should have pointed that out in my encyclicals: 'Don't try this outside the great metropolitan centers.'"

"Imagine," said Dan. "If Prague had been New Haven, or Buffalo—the regime would have lasted a thousand years."

Mark laughed and looked around. They were still half embracing in greeting as they stood outside his building. The name above the entrance, presumably "The Roosevelt," had lost half its lettering to vandals or neglect. A homeless man cajoled a three-wheeled shopping cart up East Genessee. Just before Dan's arrival, Mark had heard what might have been mistaken for a loud burst of firecracker up the hill. But he was afraid now it might go off again, for Dan would probably recognize the sound.

"Let's go inside," he suggested, and in his relatively attractive apartment he offered Dan some tea.

In the kitchen—Dan was the tallest person to visit Mark's kitchen since he'd moved in, and his wild black hair, less wild now that it was more thin, stood gloriously on end, and his stubble possessed a fine and noble aspect—Dan looked vaguely uneasy, perhaps a little disappointed, perhaps a little bit afraid.

It was true that Mark had not been diligent in cleaning since Elaine left. He had mopped the floor, but the books he left everywhere, in case he wished to start reading them again. Plus there were the dishes. "I'm sorry about the mess," he said. "It was worse this morning."

"No, it looks fine," said Dan, looking around unhappily. "I was just wondering . . . is this the only tea you have?"

All Mark had was Lipton. He and Elaine had cut some corners, in part because they had to, and because they'd been raised that way, and finally because Mark spending money meant less money that Elaine could spend, and vice versa. But Lipton! It was a lousy, tasteless tea. It was a bit like drinking colored water. It was an excuse, essentially, to eat a brownie. A poor excuse.

"You're right," he said.

"Oh, no, I was just wondering," said Dan. "Idly. It's fine."

"No, it's not fine. This is important."

They drove to Wegman's, where they bought many varieties of excellent tea, including some that were not on sale—and white grapes and smoked gouda cheese, which were. "We should really learn how to *live,*" Dan said on the way home, cutting a piece of gouda with Mark's pocket knife. "The tastes of cheeses, the names of foreign towns. We should improve our French, learn Czech. We should reread Shakespeare. Maybe give *Origins of Totalitarianism* another shot." That night, Dan slept on the couch. The walls themselves breathed truth. They were swimming in it.

In this new world, free of disputes about dishes and laundry and sexual timing, the days were not full enough, the nights were not night enough, and soon the couch was not wide enough. Rich, Mark's old college roommate, quit his financial advising job and his fiancée in San Francisco and arrived at the airport three days after Dan pulled into the driveway. Rich was, comparatively, enormous, and blond, and still in love with alcohol. His girlfriend of four postcollege years had initially pressured him to get engaged, to which he acceded, and then to move in with her, and had then demanded that he stop drinking, at which he drew the line. And here he was. If Mark had separated from the lovely Elaine because his life was cluttered, like an office, with lies, and if Dan had left New Haven because he felt that, before the bar of eternity, his union with Debbie was wanting, Rich had a more familiar, an almost archetypal tale. He slept on the couch while Dan shared the bed with Mark.

They continued to come. From all over they came—from the great concrete city, the far-flung steppes, the famous universities. One by one the friends of Mark tossed their meager belongings, their carton of books and case of burned CDs into the backseats of cars. And then to Syracuse they came. A city that during the 1980s had lost a larger portion of its population than Detroit was appearing on Google searches, was being studied on MapQuest.com. There was plenty of parking.

Toby came from Minneapolis, where he'd tried to write a novel about Berlin; Ferdinand came from 116th Street, where he'd accidentally enrolled in the law school; Alex came from Princeton, where he'd studied the dry difficult musings of the political scientists. "Under the influence apparently of Rawls," he said on his first night in Syracuse, as they gathered on what was still Rich's couch, "most liberal theorists now seem to write only about imagined polities. It's very strange."

Milan came from Brooklyn, giving up his editorial assistantship at a magazine that arrived each week in Mark's home. He was perhaps living further from truth than any of them, taking other editors out to drinks and writing semi-informed reviews for weekly book supplements. Milan had resolved to give truth one more chance. He sat down on Rich's couch and began to flip through the magazine he used to work for. "You'll forgive me," he said in his beautiful editorial voice, almost a purr, a voice that sounded like laser printing, "if I immediately cancel your subscription to this venerable publication."

"By all means," said Mark. He had nothing against the *New Yorker,* particularly. The cultural reporting he could take or leave, but the political stuff was top-notch and the cartoons made him laugh and laugh. Still, it had apparently led Milan astray, and Mark would not stand in the way of any man's truth.

"It is eloquently written," Milan explained, "and the font gives me a hard-on. But it is not for men like us. It does not front the essential facts."

The essential facts were these: within a month of Mark's declaration of truth, there were seven of them living together, seven men both large and small, fat and fit, dull and brilliant, handsome every one. It was, any way you looked at it, enough for a hockey team, and they signed up for the men's league. They bought a ramshackle old house set back on a steep slope from Lancaster Avenue (Toby had actually sold his Berlin novel, though he no longer intended to finish it) and moved in most of Mark's furniture—his parents' old gray Brookline couch, and some of the bookshelves, and the big beautiful green-marble-tiled kitchen table, at which Mark's father used to sit for hours, grimly drinking Lipton tea. Each of the men had his own stereo and his own bed, but they all chipped in to purchase a supercomputer for a special room they designed for their most shared solitary need. They outfitted the self-pleasuring pavilion with all the latest technology—a cable modem, a huge LCD display, subscriptions to all the best sites. There were posters in the room and a large leather couch. "It's the sort of room you might see on *MTV Cribs,*" Dan said approvingly when they were done, "if the featured house belonged to eccentric millionaire perverts."

To avoid conflicts there was a sign-up sheet outside the room, and in any case their days were strictly regulated. In the mornings they practiced hockey, in the afternoons they sat in meditation or scattered to the library to prepare their assigned weekly lectures—original reinterpretations of the literary and philosophical tradition. They read Tolstoy to increase their moral appetite and Henry James to sharpen their sensibilities, and in the evenings they held long discussions on the nature of the soul, on beauty, on truth.

"If *beauty* is truth," Dan said during one of their first evening discussions, "I don't think I can handle it. There is too much. It's overwhelming."

He stopped as the others nodded. Dan had decided to go ahead with his dissertation, though one of his surrenders to truth was that he would abandon Hawthorne and the Puritans and write instead on the Holocaust. "It's all I want to think about," he admitted. As a result he was now spending hours in the library surrounded by undergraduate women, and the sight of all that flesh, and the various new underwear technologies, was driving him mad. "The force of it," he said. "The—breasts! I am at a loss, I am disoriented. And yet I'm fairly sure I didn't leave Debbie so I could chase after nineteen-year-olds in sweatpants with STICKLEY written across the ass.

"I just feel like someone should arrest me. I should be arrested!

"But no one," concluded Dan, desolate Dan, "no one will arrest me."

Mark agreed: They were on their own. What they were doing and thinking had been done and thought so many times before that the precedents had essentially canceled one another out. They were free to seek an original relation to the universe, if that's what they were into.

Ferdinand had nonetheless complained, when he first arrived, that it all felt too much like *Fight Club*.

"Did they play hockey in *Fight Club?*"

"You guys play hockey?" Ferdinand was intrigued. "Still, they fought each other, you guys play hockey. It's not exactly a paradigm shift."

"We have an exalted ideology," Dan a little queasily suggested, "forged in the fire of Eastern European dissidence?"

"And we're not planning to garden the way those gayolas do in *Fight Club*," Rich put in.

"Actually," said Alex, "we should probably clear those weeds out front, there." He pointed.

"Maybe it *is* like *Fight Club*," said Mark. "Which was itself a pretty derivative film. But we're not making a movie here, Ferdinand. We're living in truth."

"Which is also derivative!" the newcomer said happily.

"Do you want to play goalie for us or not?"

"I guess I wouldn't mind playing a little hockey," shrugged Ferdinand. "I got a little time."

And so they did—they played hockey. The stadium beckoned to them in the mornings; it called their names in the afternoons. In the evenings, as the sun set over Syracuse, they climbed to the roof and watched the huge white dome retain for just a few moments longer than the day its queer, radioactive glow. They discussed possible line combinations. They dreamed of more speed and vigor, of the elegant pass play, the perfect blue line slap shot. And they were good, they were pretty good. Ferdinand was a preposterous netminder, so vain that he could not assume anything but the most traditional goaltender's stance and movements, even if this meant that, refusing to flop down, he was powerless to arrest a shot that dribbled in to him.

But even Ferdinand occasionally thrust out his glove and felt the puck landing inside. The others had similar moments in which truth in hockey was a quality of their being, and then there was Toby. Toby was a strange sort of guy, a little stiff and awkward despite his Camper shoes, he sometimes left the toilet seat up in the third-floor bathroom. He read much and deeply, yet was barely articulate and sometimes lapsed into morose silences. But Toby was from Minnesota. He was from Minnesota. When his skates touched the ice it was magical. He scored many goals.

And as for Mark, he had played for many years, and though older, stiffer, less in control of his limbs, he could still take the puck behind his own net and emerge rocketlike on the other side. He could still, coming east-west across the neutral zone, pull the little black disc onto his backhand, dip his shoulder up-ice, and accelerate with a few forceful strides around two or three defenders. Aye, and he could still, coming full speed up the right wing, the puck leading him like a rising balloon into the zone, cut across the top of the slot and release a wrist shot past the wrong-footed, screened-in goaltender. He couldn't always do these things, but sometimes he did them, and among the many human feelings he had read about, it was in himself the only feeling he still recognized. It was grace.

He thought about this late at night, about what it meant. And sometimes, too, after everyone was tucked safely in their beds, Mark could hear what sounded like a thousand whispered conversations on a thousand private cell phones. But perhaps it was the wind, for they were on an exposed hillside. The sound of sobbing reached his ears as well, though just as likely those were the heating vents, the water drips. He would have to check on those in the morning.

Mark, too, had a cell phone. He was not a monster, after all, and he was happy to listen to Elaine's complaints about her job, her ugly week-to-week studio on East 3rd Street. Aggressively incompetent, she had at first refused to buy a telephone, so Mark finally sent her one. And yet when they spoke on the much-traveled device, it was as if nothing had happened. Freed from the obligation of spending the rest of his life with her, Mark could think of nothing he would rather do. This was problematic—it was horrible—but he was convinced that eventually it would go away. It would have to.

He still wept, occasionally, but now his tears were holy tears, the tears of a guru. He cried on the phone with Elaine, though mostly they talked of business and their tax returns. Had she bought an answering machine?

"Did you buy an answering machine?"

"I'm in a week-to-week studio, Mark. It's not imperative that everyone leave their voice message."

"But you can take the machine with you when you move. Have you been looking? You should really consider Tribeca. I checked some Web sites and the prices are really low. It's just a matter of time before it recovers."

"I'd be like a vulture, swooping in on a dying housing market."

"No, no, you'll be a great patriot. People will give speeches thanking you." Softly, very softly, he added, "Sweetheart."

She asked, "When will you come see me?"

He said, "I don't know. Soon."

"Do you love me?"

"I love you very much."

"Then why are we doing this?"

"We have to. We were unhappy."

"We're unhappy now," she said.

"We're unhappy now," he agreed.

But he held firm, he pretty much held firm.

2

Having brought them all together under one roof, just as at his wedding, Mark considered his friends. Like a group gathered to perform some fantastic heist in a high-budget film, each of them had a particular exaggerated quality, and Mark was soon conscious of the fact that these qualities were all his. Ferdinand was his vanity, Milan his ambition, Rich his good-humored gluttony, Dan his Jewish-intellect, Toby his conscience, and Alex his worries, his care, his buried secret fastidiousness. If one created a composite of them they would equal . . . Mark, though a few inches taller.

And like him the men experienced guilt for the women they'd left. They recited their names and discussed their fates as if keeping a secret alumni bulletin for a school to which they never contributed. And Mark made a speech on the subject of guilt:

"It is difficult now," he said, "to remember the exact chronology of marriage-leaving and in-truth-living, and in a way it hardly matters. What I know with absolute certainty is that my union was a fragile creature dancing on the back of a thousand little lies. They piled atop one another—the erased Internet history, the secret e-mail accounts, the stolen evenings, I'm talking evenings, not nights, harmless flirtations and maybe once a year, with other women. But even more than that, it was the barely registering lies, the unmentioned half hour in the café, the Strand bag dumped into a trash barrel on the corner . . ."

"The evening with an old friend . . ." someone said.

"The fifteen dollars for a CD . . ." said another.

"I didn't take the bus down to New York, I drove. I could have taken her."

"I told that girl I was single."

"I spent the weekend in Vegas and lost ten thousand bucks."

This was Rich. They all turned to him.

"I won it all back the next weekend," he said. "But I lied about that, too."

"And the guilt!" Mark went on. "For everything. For every moment of unshared joy, and, during shared joy, for every moment of resentment. For every woman I looked at—and there came a point when I found myself looking at *every single woman*."

"Mmm," said the others. "Ahhh."

"But why so guilty? Aren't we, as Americans, entitled to all this? Wasn't that the whole idea of this country?"

"No," said Alex, quickly. "Not at all."

"But isn't that the whole idea of it *now?*" Mark insisted.

"Okay."

"So but here's what I'm saying—there arrived a point in my life with Elaine when guilt became the only feeling of mine that could be classified as decent. I would say things to her, accidentally, occasionally, and then for days I would feel anguish. But guilt is not good enough. It is not a sign of life; it is not a sign of virtue. I am telling you, gentlemen, from the depths of my Jewish heart, that the feeling of guilt alone, for all its fluctuations, variations, its tribulations—is not enough to make a permanent soul."

"All right," the men agreed. "What now?"

Peace now! thought Mark, but beyond that he didn't know. He really didn't know. Secretly, provisionally, momentarily, he had Samara. They'd met at a party in Boston and had been talking ever since. She was like Elaine in her sophisticated girlishness, but younger, less well-read. Courting her on the phone was a pleasure: Mark was allowed to lecture at some length on the intricacies—they were not without interest—of Menshevik history. He had visited her twice and despite an obvious attraction they had yet to consummate the relationship.

"Why not?" Mark wanted to know.

"I have a boyfriend," she said. "It would be dishonest."

"It's dishonest *not* to sleep with me!" Mark declared. "If you want to sleep with me, you must. Otherwise you're not living in truth."

"You know, we ran into someone in Harvard Square the other day who was talking about your little colony."

"Really? He was? Who?"

"Some guy from the *Phoenix*."

"Oh, them. Who's *we?*"

"Paul and I."

"Yeah, I know, but you could have just said me."

"Whatever, Mark."

"And did he spend all night talking about the Patriots?"

Silence.

Mark smiled. He found himself pleasantly capable of this sort of cruelty with Samara, as he was not with Elaine, indicative perhaps of some new possibility in Mark-ness. To Elaine he could only be cruel in the final thing, while moment to moment his heart went out to her, his happiness was predicated on hers. And this was not—well, maybe it was, maybe it was love—but it was not what he'd had in mind. And that, too, that thing he'd once had in mind—it counted for something. It counted for a great deal.

And he searched for it, for his own younger self, that self's intentions. He reread his old diaries, he tried to track down his college e-mails. He sought it in the dull eyes of his students. There were moments in class when time froze and he, having posed a question on NEP, simply stared at them, and they stared, half seeing, back. What are you thinking? Mark wondered, gazing into that semicircle, pretending to wait for an answer. What do you want?

He recalled, in this connection, the Parable of Beard-Face—and off they went to the bars. At Armory Square Mark was pleased to note they formed a well-showered, good-looking group, but, like an unhappy family, they were all good-looking in their own way. Only the gorgeous Ferdinand could thrive in any female environment, because he had devoted so much energy to precisely this, but each time the others tried to interest Ferdinand's admiresses in themselves they learned that the affection of these ladies was, like an airline ticket, nontransferable.

The whole thing, in fact, was a little embarrassing. Ferdinand selected Rich as his wingman. The rest of them sat on high stools around a table, tipping the stools backward and forward and watching girls walk by. And they began to wonder, each to himself, whether they'd left their women in order simply to find—other women? And other women, what was more, that they couldn't even get? Because that—that would be really stupid, considering how wonderful, how soft and funny and affectionate, how *theirs,* their women had been. I mean, that would be really colossally fucking dumb.

The thought hung dangerously in the air. But then: a fragrance, a prelude, and, accompanied by Ferdinand, a swarm of female flesh. "Gentlemen of truth," he said, "meet Sandy, Suzie, Sally, Silly, Sleepy. And," turning to Mark and nudging a plump and pretty blond in his direction, "Prancer."

That night, in the house of truth: drunken, fumbling sex. A triumph of the human spirit. Cell phones shut off; stereos turned on. The masturbation room was empty.

3

So it must have been the next morning, or the morning after that, when Toby wondered over breakfast—they passed around a box of cereal, reaching in for handfuls—how Elaine felt about Mark's living in truth.

"I didn't tell her."

Rich, who'd been washing his cereal down with a swig from the milk bottle, spit it out in surprise.

Toby: "What do you mean you didn't tell her?"

"I didn't want her to think she'd been sacrificed on the altar of some idea."

Mark let his gaze sweep the kitchen. "Look," he said. "I don't think we ought to confuse living in truth with living in cruelty. Decency," he said, grabbing the cereal box from Rich, "decency is pretty high up there, too."

And it was, it was. He must be free, yes, but when he could without a significant constriction of that freedom decrease slightly the sum of the world's pain, perform a sort of high-altitude humanitarian intervention, damn it all he would go down to New York and perform it. Not that he advertised this generosity of Mark.

"Where are you going?" Toby asked him one Friday after Mark announced that he'd be back in time for the game on Monday.

"Just for a drive," said Mark. "You ask a lot of questions, dude."

"A three-day drive?"

The men seemed to encircle him. Mark was already in his leather car coat, the men bunched together near the kitchen. A tension, a jealous orangutan fearsomeness, was palpable in the front hall. Were they sniffing him?

"No," Toby said. "Seriously."

"For god's sake!" Mark cried suddenly, his eyes flashing, "I did not unyoke myself, from the most beloved and beautiful creature on earth, in order to yoke myself to you. To any of you! Is that clear? Because if yoking's your thing, there's plenty out there." He gestured to the door. "Plenty of yoking for the having."

This was a threat, not particularly veiled, of expulsion from the colony of truth, and they fell in line. They did not ask further questions and, what is more, they did not speculate among themselves. Because whom could they trust? Not each other. All the rooms in the house were occupied, while Ferdinand had nominated a friend ("in the event of expansion," as he put it), and so had Toby. There were maneuvers, conspiracies. Mark would receive anonymous tips regarding the late-night phone conversations of one or another of the men. "Milan has had phone sex every night for the past week," one of the notes slipped under his door reported. "In his silky voice, with his ex-fiancée. Unless he's asked a 1-900 girl to use Leanne's name."

That night they tramped into Milan's room. He was in bed already, the tiny silver phone pressed to his ear. Mark tore it from him.

"Who's this?" he demanded.

"It's Leanne," said Leanne. "Is that you, Mark? What are you *doing* up there? It sounds like a cult."

"You wouldn't understand, Leanne." Mark tried to sound poisonous: "How's film school?"

"Put Milan on the phone, please?"

"Milan's busy."

"If Milan's not back here in a week," Mark heard her say as he closed the Motorola handset, *"I swear I'm calling the ATF!"*

"She says she's going to contact the ATF," Mark told the men, who'd surrounded the terrified Milan. "That's where your little phone conversations have landed us, slick."

"We don't have any firearms," Milan pleaded, his voice sounding less and less like a laser printer. "And the liquor and cigarettes we can consume."

"That's not the point," said Mark. "Untruth, gentlemen, is the point. Behold it now!" And so saying he tore the covers off Milan, editor-at-thirty Milan, who was revealed in all his shame—his boxer shorts around his ankles, and his hand still gripping, as if it alone could weather this storm, his sagging, sallow little mast.

"It's horrible, that untruth," Rich commented as the rest followed Mark out of the room, leaving the self-pleasuring Milan to his sobbing.

"Unsightly," someone agreed. "Really gross."

Mark felt a little sorry for Milan, but really they'd all been done a favor. The men had moved too early and had chosen poorly—weak-chinned women, or bad-tempered ones. They had settled on women with unshapely legs. But Mark's case was different. Elaine was the love of his life. They had a private language, and he could not imagine ever developing such another intricate system again. Their little jokes. Her voice on the phone. She still called him whenever anything bad happened. "Mark," unhappily, "I think there's a spider in my room." "Mark," at two in the morning, "I had a dream. It was awful." "Mark, I hurt my finger." "How?" "I singed it. On the stupid pot without a handle." She'd taken the pot without a handle and refused to buy another. Every one of her movements broke his heart.

Mark called Samara to announce his trip to Boston.

"Great!" she said.

"I want to see you."

"Sure. Let's have lunch."

"Lunch?"

"Or the museum. Something afternoon-y."

"Are you joking? I'm coming for the weekend. Cancel everything."

"I can't just do that, Mark."

"Because of Paul? Paul? Do you know what Paul is going to be like in four years?" He knew enough to know that she knew. "Do you know what Paul is like now?"

"Look, Mark," she interrupted. "What do you want from me? Not that I disagree, exactly, about Paul. But what's the point of you saying all this?"

"I want you, is my point."

"But what, exactly? Just sex? You could get that somewhere else. This is quite an investment you're making, phonebill-wise, just for sex."

"No, it's not that. Though that, too. Do you know the address of this place where I can get it?"

"Mark, I'm twenty-five. I'm not in college anymore. I want—I want someone who'll be around. I want someone I can go out with on weekends. Maybe I want someone to spend the rest of his life with me."

Mark greeted this with silence.

"No," she read it well, "probably it won't be Paul. But with Paul I can at least pretend like it's going to be the rest of my life. Can you offer me that? And I can show him to my friends. You're like some sort of maniacal cult leader. I can't take you around."

They hung up—no time for arguing, that sort of conversation only led to impossible promises, and anyway he had a game that night. Though Samara hadn't mentioned it, Mark was also the captain of a failing hockey team.

The Baumberg Blades faced all manner of opponent that fateful, single season. There were frat teams from the university, the beer still rancid on their breath. One team wore all black, as if it were a gang, or in mourning. There was, once, a team without a goalie, whose six skaters swarmed the rink like bumper cars. The Blades found it disconcerting—to skate down the ice and discover, in place of a fearsome, bepadded goaltender, a skinny unimpressive defenseman, his body cringing in anticipation of the puck. Ferdinand was, perhaps, the most disconcerted, to find himself a worse goaltender than no goaltender at all.

And so they lost again—oh, they lost! They didn't mean to. Toby was magnificent, if no longer young, and even the worst of the Blades was filled with a passionate intensity, and Mark, at defense, roamed the blue line like a masked and predatory Lear—but in the end, they were more scored upon than scoring.

Their losses threw them each Monday into an increasingly desperate funk.

"Emerson," Alex began one emergency meeting—they held it right on the bench as the Zamboni circled the rink—after they'd lost 3-2 to a team calling itself the Oswego Otters, which had not only outscored them but had brought their wives to the game. "Emerson says that every man is a ruined god. We, however, are a ruined hockey team."

"Nietzsche says that man is something to be overcome," Dan added. "It appears that it is merely we who are to be overcome."

"We suck."

"On October 25," (this was Mark) "Trotsky consigned the Mensheviks to the dustbin of history. Whoever would have thought we would be consigned to the dustbin of the Syracuse Men's Under-40 Hockey League?"

"Were those guys under forty?" Rich asked.

"Yeah, I think."

"They looked awful old."

"We look that way, too," announced Ferdinand, who had given up the last goal when he refused to flop ungracefully onto the ice and the puck was tucked underneath him. "We're not getting any younger in Syracuse. *We* look awful old. Especially in our defensive zone."

This in turn appeared to be a dig at Mark—he'd had some lapses. "I suppose," he began, as the Zamboni, that wondrous machine, covered the mangled surface with another layer of water, so that all the scratches from their game, the spit and sweat and snot, froze over and receded into the past. "I suppose that we are witnessing the lie being slipped—under the goalie pads, so to speak—to one of our hypotheses. It was an Emersonian hypothesis, maybe. We believed that if we renounced all the superfluities and falsehoods of modern life, if we left our wives, canceled our subscriptions to the *New Yorker,* and lived exclusively in truth, we could do anything. Look inside your-self, said Emerson, and we looked. What did we find? That we could not be everything. We could not be a great hockey team. We could only be what we were. What we are. Maybe, just maybe, what we've become... But not a great hockey team, or even a good one. And, my friends, I'll admit it: That is almost more than I can bear."

Slowly they all skated back across to the locker room, gently, gently, trying to leave no traces of themselves on the fresh new ice.

The lecture series was canceled a short time later when Ferdinand, as-signed a talk on *Dr. Jekyll and Mr. Hyde,* blatantly plagiarized from Nabokov. At first they were embarrassed for Ferdinand, recognizing as they did the original, but by the time he had finished they were embarrassed only for themselves.

That week they tried to depose Mark—he hadn't, they said, an-swered any of their questions, nor had he picked up another defense-man for the stretch run—but he fought off the challenge with demagoguery and promises of reform. Then Ferdinand tried to es-cape, almost leaving them without a goalie. "But earlier you were threatening people with expulsion!" Ferdinand cried as the men choked off the exits to the room. "Poor Milan didn't read the *New Yorker* for a month he was so afraid."

"Things change," said Mark. "History advances. Borders close."

"He's led us into the desert," Ferdinand said to the others. "And now he won't let us leave!"

"That's pretty much the nature of being led into a desert," replied Mark. "And we might still make the play-offs."

But Ferdinand was right, of course, like those Mensheviks who were always right, for all the good it did them. The men soon all got what they wanted, and never had they been so miserable. Reports began to filter in from the abandoned women that they had finally taken up with others, almost uniformly described, by the women in question, as "better" than the truth-tellers. More reliable, perhaps, less dishonest. The evening phone calls abated. No longer was the house filled with a thousand whispered apologies, a hundred stifled sobs.

As for Mark, he slept at last with Samara. It was fine; it was great; it was everything he'd expected. She had a receptivity to all his movements. She made little noises that built into bigger noises, into—he could hardly believe it—an arcing of her back. She shuddered. But in the midst of it, or in the periodic breaks afforded in it, in the spaces given the free range of his mind, he recalled the polemics he'd engaged in, the promises, many of the worst of them implicit, that he'd had to make. And in this way she became what he'd declared he didn't want: a conquest—#12 or #14, depending on your methodology.

Elaine finally found an apartment across town. She took the phone along and gave Mark the number, but she seemed never to be there. Perhaps she had a cell phone? He paced his little room in the house, his books pressing in around him, and hung up repeatedly on the smooth reception of her new voice-messaging. She had always pressed him to order it, but he'd resisted. "You pay the same in a year as you would for a great answering machine," he'd argued. "And what do you have at the end of the year? Nothing. This way you have an answering machine." Then they waited for their old machine to die. "You're just like my father," she'd said. "Like an old Jew." "This is bad?" Now, even when he left a message, it often took her up to a week to return his calls. When she did she seemed to have increasingly less to complain about, and more where to go. Bit by bit, his guilt abated. He looked out the window of the house and saw that the leaves were returning; perhaps, he thought—and that was as far as it went. Perhaps what? Perhaps they'd get back together? Perhaps he'd find someone else? Perhaps he'd done the right thing? The wrong thing? Perhaps they'd make the play-offs? Ah. Perhaps they'd make the play-offs.

That week they played the Cicero Preachers for the final play-off spot. The Baumberg Blades came out scoring—Toby from a scramble in front, Toby from low in the slot. They moved with ferocity, with conviction. But the Preachers, more traditional, more methodical, scored more often. One goal came after a Preacher poked the puck between Mark's skates, stepped nimbly around him, and wristed the black disc, on that black day, into the upper right-hand corner. Late in the game, the Blades still within striking distance, Mark intercepted a pass at center ice and moved up the left wing. Both Preacher defensemen were back—he could try to split them down the center or outflank them on the left. But he was tired—oh, he was so tired. Too many people wanted too many things, and he, for all his promises and pretensions, his speeches and allusions, knew only about a few months of 1917, about some Menshevik lives in exile, and sketchily at that—he hadn't even finished the seven volumes of the Menshevik Sukhanov's magisterial memoirs. Crossing the blue line he lined up a slapshot and fired. His stick smashed against the ice but he had not captured enough puck. It rose a foot into the air and then wobbled, and wobbled, and wobbled, before finally bouncing lamely off the backboard, a demented bird, wide of the net by yards.

After the game, Toby called Mark over to the bench, where all the other players were gathered. Sheets of paper rustled in his hands, and he handed them to Mark.

They were printouts of his e-mails—to Elaine, and to Samara. To some others.

Mark looked around: Their faces had turned to stone. "You were checking e-mail in the MB room and you forgot to sign out," Toby explained. "We accidentally started reading. Then we couldn't stop."

"You write a mean e-mail," Milan told him, smirking. "But I don't think they're publishable. *Tu te répétes.*"

"We called you a lot of names when we first read these," Toby went on.

"Hypocrite," said Rich.

"Recidivist," Alex suggested kindly.

"Pervert," said Ferdinand.

"But finally we settled on just one," Toby spoke for them all. "You're a liar."

It was a subtle distinction to make, thought Mark, when there were so many hockey sticks poised in the air, but he didn't get a chance for this witty rejoinder, after a life of witty rejoinders, because as he raised his head to speak the blows began to rain on him like warm-up shots. With Kohos they hit him, and Sherwoods, and Easton aluminum-graphite hybrids, which never break. He went down on a knee and they continued to hit him: for all the hours they'd spent in Syracuse, for all the boredom and the anguish, for the women they'd lost, for every cartoon in the *New Yorker* they'd missed. And when they stopped, and he lay there on the cool, cruel ice, the sun pressing down on the great white tarp above their heads, he thought only of Elaine, and of how he'd told her she was the sweetest girl in the world, and she'd asked, "Sweet as in pretty?" and he'd said, Yes, yes, she was so pretty. He felt his sadness spread around him like the blood now pooling on the ice. And he recalled the phone call he'd received just a few days earlier, from Havel himself, who'd read about Mark's quest in the international papers. "Mark," said Havel, wise and charming with his strong Czech accent (Mark had never learned Czech!). "Just remember that life is very complicated. Even in the bad old days it was complicated. Just remember what you have," said Havel. "Hold on to it."

RATTAWUT LAPCHAROENSAP

University of Michigan

FARANGS

This is how we count the days. June: the Germans come to the Island—football cleats, big T-shirts, thick tongues—speaking like spitting. July: the Italians, the French, the British, the Americans. The Italians like pad thai, its affinity with spaghetti. They like light fabrics, sunglasses, leather sandals. The French like plump girls, rambutans, disco music. They also like to bare their breasts. The British are here to work on their pasty complexions, their penchant for hashish. Americans are the fattest, the stingiest of the bunch. They may pretend to like pad thai or grilled prawns or the occasional curry, but twice a week they need their culinary comforts, their hamburgers and their pizzas. They're also the worst drunks. Never get too close to a drunk American. August brings the Japanese. Stay close to them. Never underestimate the power of the yen. Everything's cheap with imperial monies in hand and they're too polite to bargain. By the end of August, when the monsoon starts to blow, they're all consorting, slapping each other's backs, slipping each other drugs, sleeping with each other, sipping their liquor under the pink lights of the Island's bars. By September, however, they've all deserted, leaving the Island to the Aussies and the Chinese, who are so omnipresent one need not mention them at all.

Ma says, "Pussy and elephants. That's all these people want." She always says this in August, at the peak of the season, when she's tired of farangs running all over the Island, tired of finding used condoms in the motel's rooms, tired of guests complaining to her in five different languages. She turns to me and says, "You give them history, temples, pagodas, traditional dance, floating markets, seafood curry, tapioca desserts, visits to silk-weaving cooperatives, but all they really want is to ride some hulking gray beast like a bunch of wildmen and to pant over girls and to lie there half dead getting skin cancer on the beach during the time in between."

We're having a late lunch, watching television in the motel office. The Island Network is showing *Rambo: First Blood Part II* again. Sylvester Stallone, dubbed in Thai, mows down an entire regiment of VCs with a bow and arrow. I tell Ma I've just met a girl. "It might be love," I say. "It might be real love, Ma. Like Romeo and Juliet love."

Ma turns off the television just as John Rambo is about to fly a chopper to safety.

She tells me it's just my hormones. She sighs and says, "Oh no, not again. Don't be so naive," she says. "I didn't raise you to be stupid. Are you bonking one of the guests? You better not be bonking one of the guests. Because if you are, if you're bonking one of the guests, we're going to have to bleed the pig. Remember, luk, we have an agreement."

I tell her she's being xenophobic. I tell her things are different this time. But Ma just licks her lips and says once more that if I'm bonking one of the guests, I can look forward to eating Clint Eastwood curry in the near future. Ma's always talking about killing my pig. And though I know she's just teasing, she says it with such zeal and a peculiar glint in her eyes that I run out to the pen to check on the swine.

I knew it was love when Clint Eastwood sniffed the girl's crotch earlier that morning and the girl didn't scream or jump out of the sand or swat the pig like some of the other girls do. She merely lay there, snout in crotch, smiling that angelic smile, like it was the most natural thing in the world, running a hand over the fuzz of Clint Eastwood's head like he was some pink and docile dog, and said, giggling, "Why hello, oh my, what a nice surprise, you're quite a beast, aren't you?"

I'd been combing the motel beachfront for trash when I looked up from my morning chore and noticed Clint Eastwood sniffing his new friend. An American: her Budweiser bikini told me so. I apologized from a distance, called the pig over, but the girl said it was okay, it was fine, the pig could stay as long as he liked. She called me over and said I could do the same.

I told her the pig's name.

"That's adorable," she laughed.

"He's the best," I said. *"Dirty Harry. Fistful of Dollars. The Good, The Bad and The Ugly."*

"He's a very good actor."

"Yes. Mister Eastwood is a first-class thespian."

Clint Eastwood trotted into the ocean for his morning bath then, leaving us alone, side by side in the sand. I looked to make sure Ma wasn't watching me from the office window. I explained how Clint Eastwood loves the ocean at low tide, the wet sand like a three-kilometer trough of mud. The girl sat up on her elbows, watched the pig, a waterlogged copy of *The Portrait of a Lady* at her side. She'd just gone for a swim and the beads of water on her navel seemed so close that for a moment I thought I might faint if I did not look away.

"I'm Elizabeth. Lizzie."

"Nice to meet you Miss Elizabeth," I said. "I like your bikini."

She threw back her head and laughed. I admired the shine of her tiny, perfectly even rows of teeth, the gleam of that soft, rose-colored tongue quivering between them like the meat of some magnificent mussel.

"Oh my," she said, gesturing with her chin. "I think your pig is drowning."

Clint Eastwood was rolling around where the ocean meets the sand, chasing receding waves, running away from oncoming ones. It's a game he plays every morning, scampering back and forth across the water's edge, and he snorted happily every time the waves licked over him, knocked him into the foam.

"He's not drowning," I said. "He's a very good swimmer, actually."

"I didn't know pigs could swim."

"Clint Eastwood can."

She smiled, a close-mouthed grin, admiring my pig at play, and I would've given anything in the world to see her tongue again, to reach out and sink my fingers into the hollows of her collarbone, to stare at that damp, beautiful navel all day long.

"I have an idea, Miss Elizabeth," I said, getting up, brushing the sand from the seat of my shorts. "This may seem rather presumptuous, but would you like to go for an elephant ride with me today?"

Ma doesn't want me bonking a farang because once, long ago, she had bonked a farang herself, against the wishes of her own parents, and all she got for her trouble was a broken heart and me in return.

This was when English was still my first and only language, and the farang was a man known to me only as Sergeant Marshall Henderson. I remember the Sergeant well, if only because he insisted I call him by his military rank.

"Not Daddy," I remember him saying on many occasions. "Sergeant. Sergeant Henderson. Sergeant Marshall. Remember you're a soldier now, boy. A spy for Uncle Sam's army."

And for the first three years of my remembered life—before he went back to America, promising to send for us—the Sergeant and I would go on imaginary missions together, navigating our way through the thicket of tourists lazing on the beach.

"Private," he'd yell after me. "I don't have a good feeling about this, private. This place gives me the creeps. We should radio for reinforcements. It could be an ambush."

"Let 'em come, Sergeant! We can take 'em!" I would squeal, crawling through the sand with a large stick in hand, eyes trained on the enemy. "Those gooks'll be sorry they ever showed their ugly faces."

One day the three of us went to the fresh market by the pier. I saw a litter of pigs—there were six of them—squeezed tightly into a small cardboard box amid the loud thudding of butchers' knives. I remember thinking of *moohan* then, of the little piglets I'd seen skewered and roasting over an open fire outside many of the Island's finer restaurants.

I began to cry.

"What's wrong, private?"

"I don't know."

"A soldier," the Sergeant grunted, "never cries."

"They just piggies," Ma laughed in her stilted English, bending down to pat me on the back. Because of our plans to move to California, Ma was learning English at the time. She hasn't spoken a word of English to me since. "What piggies say, luk? What they say? Piggies say oink-oink. Don't cry, luk. Don't cry. Oink-oink is yummy."

A few days later, the Sergeant walked into my bedroom with something wriggling beneath his T-shirt. He sat down on the bed beside me. I remember the mattress sinking with his weight, the chirping of some desperate bird struggling in his belly.

"Congratulations, private," the Sergeant whispered through the dark, holding out a young and frightened Clint Eastwood in one of his large hands. "You're a CO now. A commanding officer. From now on, you'll be responsible for the welfare of this recruit."

I stared at him dumbfounded, took the pig into my arms.

"Happy birthday, kiddo."

And shortly before the Sergeant left us, before Ma took over the motel from her parents, before she ever forbade me from speaking the Sergeant's language except to assist the motel's guests, before I knew what *bastard* or *mongrel* or *slut* or *whore* meant in any language, there was an evening when I walked into the ocean with Clint Eastwood—I was teaching him how to swim—and when I looked back to shore I saw my mother sitting between the Sergeant's legs in the sand, the sun a bright red orb on the crest of the mountains behind them. They spoke without looking at each other, my mother reaching back to hook an arm around his neck, while my piglet thrashed wildly in the sea foam.

"Ma," I asked a few years later, "you think the Sergeant will ever send for us?"

"It's best, luk," Ma said in Thai, "if you never mention his name again. It gives me a headache."

After I finished combing the beach for trash, put Clint Eastwood back in his pen, Lizzie and I went up the mountain on my motorcycle to Surachai's house, where his Uncle Mongkhon ran an elephant trekking business. MR. MONGKHON'S JUNGLE SAFARI, a painted sign declared in their driveway. COME EXPERIENCE THE NATURAL BEAUTY OF FOREST WITH THE AMAZING VIEW OF OCEAN AND SPLENDID HORIZON FROM ELEPHANT'S BACK! I'd told Uncle Mongkhon once that his sign was grammatically incorrect and that I'd lend him my expertise for a small fee, but he just laughed and said farangs preferred it just the way it was, thank you very much, they thought it was charming, and did I really think I was the only *huakhuai* who knew English on this godforsaken island? During the war in Vietnam, before he started the business, Uncle Mongkhon had worked at an airbase on the mainland dishing out lunch to American soldiers.

From where Lizzie and I stood, we could see the gray backs of two bulls peeking over the roof of their one-story house. Uncle Mongkhon used to have a full *chuak* of elephants, before the people at Monopolated Elephant Tours came to the Island and started underpricing the competition, monopolizing mountain pass tariffs, and staking their claim upon farangs at hotels three stars and up—doing, in short, what they had done on so many other islands like ours. Business began to sag after the arrival of MET and, in the end, Uncle Mongkhon was forced to sell his elephants to logging companies on the mainland. Where there had once been eight elephants roaming the wide corral, now there were only two—Yai and Noi—aging bulls with ulcered bellies and trunks that hung limply between their crusty forelegs.

"Oh, wow," Lizzie said. "Are those actual elephants?"

I nodded.

"They're so huge."

She clapped a few times, laughing.

"Huge!" she said again, jumping up and down. She turned to me and smiled.

Surachai was lifting weights in the yard, a barbell in each hand.

Uncle Mongkhon sat on the porch bare-chested, smoking a cigarette. When Surachai saw Lizzie standing there in her bikini next to me, his arms went limp. For a second I was afraid he might drop the weights on his feet.

"Where'd you find this one?" he said in Thai, smirking, walking toward us.

"Boy," Uncle Mongkhon yelled from the porch, also in Thai. "You irritate me sometimes. Tell that girl to put on some clothes. You know damn well I don't let bikinis ride. This is a respectable establishment. We have rules."

"What are they saying?" Lizzie asked. Farangs always get nervous when you carry on a conversation they can't understand.

"Oh," I laughed. "They just want to know if we need one elephant or two."

"Let's just get one," Lizzie smiled, reaching out to take one of my hands. "Let's ride one together." I held my breath. Her hand shot bright, surprising comets of heat up my arm. I wanted to yank my hand away even as I longed to stand there forever with our sweaty palms folded together like soft roti bread. From inside the house, I heard the voice of Surachai's mother, the light sizzle of a frying pan.

"It's nothing, Maew," Uncle Mongkhon yelled back to his sister inside. "Though I wouldn't come out here unless you like nudie shows. The mongrel's here with another member of his international harem."

"These are my friends," I said to Lizzie. "This is Surachai."

"How do you do," Surachai said in English, briskly shaking her hand, looking at me all the while.

"I'm fine, thank you," Lizzie chuckled. "Nice to meet you."

"Yes yes yes," Surachai said, grinning like a fool. "Honor to meet you, Madame. It will make me very gratified to let you ride my elephants. Very gratified. Because he"—Surachai patted me on the back now—"he my handsome soulmate. My best man."

Surachai beamed proudly at me. I'd taught him that word: *soulmate.*

"How long have you been married?" Lizzie asked. Surachai laughed hysterically, uncomprehendingly, widening his eyes at me for help.

"He's not," I said. "He meant to say 'best friend.'"

"Yes yes," Surachai said, nodding. "Best friend."

"You listening to me, boy?" Uncle Mongkhon got up from the porch and walked toward us. "Bikinis don't ride. It frightens the animals."

"*Sawatdee,* Uncle," I said, greeting him with a *wai,* bending my head extra low for effect; but he slapped me on the head with a forehand when I came up.

"Tell the girl to put on some clothes," Uncle Mongkhon growled. "It's unholy."

"Aw, Uncle," I pleaded. "We didn't bring any with us."

"Need I remind you, boy, that the elephant is our national symbol? Sometimes I think your stubborn farang half keeps you from understanding such things. You should be ashamed of yourself. I'd tell your mother if I knew it wouldn't break her heart.

"What if I went to her country and rode a bald eagle in my underwear, huh?" he continued, pointing at Lizzie. "How would she like it? Ask her, will you?"

"What's he saying?" Lizzie whispered in my ear.

"Ha ha ha," Surachai interjected, gesticulating wildly. "Everything okay, Madame. Don't worry, be happy. My uncle, he just say elephants very terrified of your breasts."

"You should've told me to put on some clothes," Lizzie turned to me, frowning, letting go of my hand.

"It's really not a problem," I laughed.

"No," Uncle Mongkhon said to Lizzie in English. "Not a big problem, Madame. Just a small one."

In the end, to placate Uncle Mongkhon, I took off my T-shirt and gave it to Lizzie. As we made our way toward the corral, I caught her grinning at the sight of my bare torso. Though I had been spending time at the new public gym by the pier, I felt some of that old adolescent embarrassment returning again. I casually flexed my muscles in the postures I'd practiced before my bedroom mirror so Lizzie would see my body not as the soft, skinny thing that it was, but as a pillar of strength and stamina.

When we came upon the gates of the elephant corral, Lizzie took my hand again. I turned to smile at her and she seemed, at that moment, some ethereal angel come from heaven to save me, an angel whose breasts left round, dark damp spots on my T-shirt. And when we mounted the elephant, Yai, the beast rising quickly to his feet, Lizzie squealed and wrapped her arms so tightly around my bare waist that I would've gladly forfeited breathing for the rest of my life.

Under that jungle canopy, climbing up the mountainside that morning on Yai's back, I told her about Sergeant Henderson, the motel, Ma, Clint Eastwood. She told me about her Ohio childhood, the New York City skyline, NASCAR, T.J.Maxx, the drinking habits of American teenagers. I told her about Pamela, my last American girlfriend, and how she promised me her heart but never answered any of my letters. Lizzie nodded sympathetically and told me about her bastard boyfriend Hunter, who she'd left last night at their hotel on the other side of the Island after finding him in the arms of a young prostitute. "That fucker," she said. "That whore." I told Lizzie she should forget about him, she deserved so much better, and besides Hunter was a stupid name anyway, and we both shook our heads and laughed at how poorly our lovers had behaved.

We came upon a scenic overlook. The sea rippled before us like a giant blue bedspread. I decided to give Yai a rest. He sat down gratefully on his haunches. For a minute Lizzie and I just sat there on the elephant's back, looking out at the ocean, the wind blowing through the trees behind us. Yai was winded from the climb and we rose and fell with his heavy breaths. I told Lizzie how the Sergeant and my mother used to stand on the beach, point east, and tell me that if I looked hard enough I might be able to catch a glimpse of the California coast rising out of the Pacific horizon. I pointed to Ma's motel below, the twelve bungalows like tiny insects resting on the golden shoreline. It's amazing, I told Lizzie, how small my life looks from such a height.

Lizzie hummed contentedly. Then she stood up on Yai's back.

"Here's your shirt," she laughed, tossing it at me.

With a quick sweeping motion, Lizzie took off her bikini top. Then she peeled off her bikini bottom. And then there she was—my American angel—naked on the back of Uncle Mongkhon's aging elephant.

"Your country is so hot," she said, smiling, crawling toward me on all fours. Yai made a low moan and shifted beneath us.

"Yes it is," I said, looking away, pretending to study the horizon, rubbing Yai's parched, gray back.

"Hey," she whispered, grabbing my chin, looking me in the eyes.

After *Rambo* and lunch with my mother and a brief afternoon nap, I walk out the door to meet Lizzie at the restaurant when Ma asks me what I'm all dressed up for.

"What do you mean?" I ask innocently, and Ma says, "What do I mean? What do I mean? Am I your mother? Are you my son? Are those black pants? Is that a button-down shirt? Is that the nice silk tie I bought you for your birthday?"

She sniffs my head.

"And is that my nice mousse in your hair? And why," she asks, "do you smell like an elephant?"

I just stand there blinking at her questions.

"Don't think I don't know," she says finally. "I saw you, luk. I saw you on your motorcycle with that farang slut in her bikini."

I laugh and tell her I have hair mousse of my own. But Ma's still yelling at me when I go to the pen to fetch Clint Eastwood, standing in the office doorway with her arms akimbo.

"Remember whose son you are," she says through the day's dying light. "Remember who raised you all these years."

"What are you talking about, Ma?"

"Why do you insist, luk, on chasing after these farangs?"

"You're being silly, Ma. It's just love. You make it sound like I'm a criminal."

"I don't think," Ma says, "that I'm the silly one here, luk. I'm not the one taking my pet pig out to dinner just because some foreign girl thinks it's cute."

I make my way down the beach with Clint Eastwood toward the lights of the restaurant. It's an outdoor establishment with low candlelit tables set in the sand and a large open pit that the bare-chested chefs use to grill the day's catch. The restaurant's quite popular with farangs on the Island. Wind at their backs, sand at their feet, night sky above, and eating by the light of the moon and the stars—it's romantic, I suppose. Although I'm hesitant to spend so much money on what Ma calls second-rate seafood in a third-rate atmosphere, Lizzie suggested we meet there for dinner tonight so who am I to argue with love's demands?

When we get to the restaurant, Lizzie's seated at a table, candle-light flickering on her face. Clint Eastwood races ahead and nuzzles his snout in her lap, but Lizzie's face doesn't light up the way it did earlier this morning. The other customers turn around in their seats to look at Clint Eastwood, and Lizzie seems a bit embarrassed to be the object of his affections.

"Hi," she says when I get to the table. She lights a cigarette.

I kiss one of her hands, sit down beside her. I tell Clint Eastwood to stay. He lies down on his belly in the sand, head resting between his stubby feet. The sun is setting behind us, rays flickering across the plane of the sea, and I think I'm starting to understand why farangs come such a long way to get to the Island, why they travel so far to come to my home.

"Beautiful evening," I say.

Lizzie nods absentmindedly.

"Is there something wrong?" I finally ask, after the waiter takes our order in English. "Have I done anything to offend you?"

Lizzie sighs, stubs out her cigarette in the bamboo ashtray.

"Nothing's wrong," she says. "Nothing at all."

But when our food arrives, Lizzie barely touches it. She keeps passing Clint Eastwood her sautéed prawns. Clint Eastwood gobbles them up gratefully. At least he's enjoying the meal, I think. On week-end nights, I often bring Clint Eastwood to this restaurant, after the tables have been stowed away, and he usually has to fight with the strays that descend on the beach for leftovers farangs leave in their wake: crab shells, fish bones, prawn husks.

"Something's wrong," I say. "You're not happy."

She lights another cigarette, blows a cloud of smoke.

"Hunter's here," she says finally, looking out at the darkening ocean.

"Your ex-boyfriend?"

"No," she says. "My boyfriend. He's here."

"Here?"

"Don't turn around. He's sitting right behind us with his friends."

At that moment, a large farang swoops into the seat across the table from us. He's dressed in a white undershirt and a pair of surfer's shorts. His nose is caked with sunscreen. His chest is pink from too much sun. There's a Buddha dangling from his neck. He looks like a deranged clown.

He reaches over the table and grabs a piece of squid from my plate.

"Who's the joker?" he asks Lizzie, gnawing on the squid. "Friend of yours?"

"Hunter," Lizzie says. "Don't do this."

"Hey," he says, looking at me, taking another piece of squid from my entrée, "what's with the tie? And what's with the pig, man?"

I smile, put a hand on Clint Eastwood's head.

"Hey you," he says. "I'm talking to you. Speak English? Talk American?"

He tears off a piece of squid with his front teeth. I can't stop staring at his powdered nose, the bulge of his hairy, sunburned chest. I'm hoping he chokes.

"You've really outdone yourself this time, baby," he says to Lizzie now. "But that's what I love about you. Your unpredictability. Your wicked sense of humor. Didn't know you went for mute tards with pet pigs."

"Hunter."

"Oh, Lizzie," he says, reaching out to take one of her hands, feigning tenderness. "I've missed you so much. I hate it when you leave me like that. I've been worried sick about you. I'm sorry about last night, okay, baby? Okay? I'm really sorry. But it was just a misunderstanding, you know? Jerry and Billyboy over there can testify to my innocence. You know how those Thai girls get."

"We can talk about this later, Hunter."

"Yes," I interject. "I think you should talk to her later."

He just stares at me with that stupid white nose jutting out between his eyes. For a second, I think Hunter's going to throw the squid at me. But then he just pops the rest of it into his mouth, turns to Lizzie, and with his mouth full says, "You fucked this joker, didn't you?"

"Please, Hunter."

I look over at Lizzie. She's staring at the table, tapping her fingers lightly against the wood. It seems she's about to cry. I stand up, throw a few hundred bahts on the table. Clint Eastwood follows my lead, rises clumsily to his feet.

"It was a pleasure meeting you, Miss Elizabeth," I say, smiling. I want to take her hand and run back to the motel so we can curl up together on the beach, watch the constellations. But Lizzie just keeps on staring at the top of that table.

I walk with Clint Eastwood back to the motel. It seems like we're the only people on that beach. Night is upon us now. In the distance, I can see squidding boats perched on the horizon, fluorescent searchlights luring their catch to the surface. Clint Eastwood races ahead of me, foraging for food in the sand, and I'm thinking with what I suppose is grief about all the American girls I've ever loved. Girls with names like Pamela, Angela, Stephanie, Joy. And now Lizzie.

One of the girls sent me a postcard of Miami once. A row of palm trees and a pink condo. "Hi Sweetie," it said. "I just wanted to say hi and to thank you for showing me a good time when I was over there. I'm in South Beach now, it's Spring Break, and let me tell you it's not half as beautiful as it is over there. If you ever make it out to the US of A, look me up okay?" Which was nice of her, but she never told me where to look her up and there was no return address on the postcard. I'd taken that girl to see phosphorescence in one of the Island's bays and when she told me it was the most miraculous thing she'd ever seen, I told her I loved her—but the girl just giggled and ran into the sea, that phosphorescent blue streaking like a comet's tail behind her. Every time they do that, I swear I'll never love another again, and I'm thinking about Lizzie and Hunter sitting at the restaurant now, and how this is really the last time I'll ever let myself love one of her kind.

Halfway down the beach, I find Surachai sitting in a mango tree. He's hidden behind a thicket of leaves, straddling one of the branches, leaning back against the trunk.

"Hey," I say, walking over to the tree.

When we were kids, Surachai and I used to run around the beach advertising ourselves as the Island's Miraculous Monkeyboys. We made loincloths out of Uncle Mongkhon's straw heap and an old T-shirt Ma used as a rag. For a small fee, we'd climb up trees and fetch coconuts for farangs, who would ooh and aah at how nimble we were. A product of our island environment, they'd say, as if this ability could be attributed to the water and had nothing to do with the hours we'd spent practicing in Surachai's backyard. For added effect, we'd make monkey noises when we climbed, which always made them laugh. They would often be impressed, too, by my facility with the English language. In one version of the speech I gave before every performance, I played the part of an American boy shipwrecked on the Island as an infant. With both parents dead, I was raised in the jungle by a family of gibbons. Though we've long outgrown what Ma calls "that idiot stunt," Surachai still comes down from the mountain occasionally to climb a tree on the beach. He'll just sit there staring out into the ocean for hours. It's meditative, he told me once. And the view is one of a kind.

"You look terrible," he says now. "Something happen with that farang girl?"

I call Clint Eastwood over. I tell the pig to stay. I take off my leather shoes, my knitted socks, and—because I don't want to ruin them—the button-down shirt and the silk tie, leaving them all at the bottom of the trunk before joining Surachai on one of the adjacent branches. As I climb, the night air warm against my skin, I'm reminded of how pleasurable this used to be—hoisting myself up by my bare feet and fingertips—and I'm surprised by how easy it still is.

When I settle myself into the tree, I start to tell Surachai everything, including the episode on the elephant. As I talk, Surachai snakes his way out onto one of the branches and drops a mango for Clint Eastwood down below.

"At least you're having sex," Surachai says after I finish my story. "At least you're doing it. Some of us just get to sit in a mango tree and think about it."

I laugh.

"I don't suppose," Surachai says, "you loved this girl?"

I shrug.

"You're a mystery to me, *phuan*," Surachai says, climbing higher now into the branches. "I've known you all these years, and that's the one thing I'll never be able to understand—why you keep falling for these farang girls. It's like you're crazy for heartache. Plenty of nice Thai girls around. Girls without plane tickets."

"I know. I don't think they like me, though. Something about the way I look. I don't think my nose is flat enough."

"That may be true. But they don't like me either, okay? And I've got the flattest nose on the Island."

We sit silently for a while, perched in the mango tree like a couple of sloths, listening to the leaves rustling around us. I climb up to where Surachai is sitting. Through the thicket, I see Clint Eastwood jogging out to meet a group of farangs making their way down the beach. I call out to him, tell him to stay, but my pig's not listening to me.

It's Hunter and his friends, laughing, slapping each other's backs, tackling each other to the sand. Lizzie walks silently behind them, head down, trying to ignore their antics. When she sees Clint Eastwood racing up to meet her, she looks to see if I'm around. But she can't see us from where she's standing. She can't see us at all.

"It's that fucking pig again!" Hunter yells.

They all laugh, make rude little pig noises, jab him with their feet. Clint Eastwood panics. He squeals. He starts to run. The American boys give chase, try to tackle him to the ground. Lizzie tells them to leave the pig alone, but the boys aren't listening. Clint Eastwood is fast. He's making a fool of them, running in circles one way, then the other, zigzagging back and forth through the sand. The more they give chase, the more Clint Eastwood eludes them, the more frustrated the boys become, and what began as tomfoolery has now turned into a mission for Hunter and his friends. Their chase becomes more orchestrated. The movements of their shadows turn strategic. They try to corner the pig, run him into a trap, but Clint Eastwood keeps on moving between them, slipping through their fingers like he's greased.

I can tell that Clint Eastwood's beginning to tire though. He can't keep it up much longer. He's an old pig. I start to climb down from the mango tree, but Surachai grabs me by the wrist.

"Wait," he says.

Surachai climbs out onto one of the branches. He reaches up for a mango and with a quick sweeping motion throws the fruit out onto the beach. It hits one of the boys squarely on the shoulder.

"What the fuck?" I hear the boy yell, looking in the direction of the tree, though he continues to pursue Clint Eastwood nonetheless.

They have him surrounded now, encircled. There's no way out for my pig.

I follow Surachai's lead, grab as many mangoes as I can. Our mangoes sail through the night air. Some of them miss, but some meet their targets squarely in the face, on the head, in the abdomen. Some of the mangoes hit Lizzie by accident, but I don't really care anymore, I'm not really aiming. I'm climbing through that tree like a gibbon, swinging gracefully between the branches, grabbing any piece of fruit—ripe or unripe—that I can get my hands on. Surachai starts to whoop like a monkey and I join him in the chorus. They all turn in our direction then, the four farangs, trying to dodge the mangoes.

It's then that I see Clint Eastwood slip away unnoticed. I see my pig running into the ocean, his pink snout inching across the sea's dark surface, phosphorescence glittering around his head like a crown of blue stars, and as I'm throwing each mango with all the strength I have, I'm thinking: Swim, Clint, swim.

JOSHUA FERRIS

University of California, Irvine

More Abandon

They're leaving. An exodus. Out of the elevators, onto the street. Into the waning mild Midwestern sunlight. Taking their first real breaths of the day. Thank god to be done with that. Lighting up cigarettes, loosening ties. Clustering at corners to await the light change. Joe Pope's window on sixty-two looks down on only a small tight angle of this manic outrush. The women returned to tennis shoes. The men without wives stopping in Burger Kings and Popeye's Fried Chickens for dubious meals laid out on laps during the express ride home. If they don't leave on the 6:12, they're stuck riding the milk train, making all the stops along the route—can't do that. Their evening hours are time-sensitive material made personal: They shimmy and jaywalk, jook and dart toward their destinations in a pathological state of hurry up and get home. Looking down on an open courtyard, he watches people cut across angles of least resistance, heading toward buses and taxis. Just beyond the courtyard, there's the entrance ramp to the Outer Drive, and the cars are lined up in tight formation to get on. Light descends. It is the settling in of dusk, the draining, abandoning psychology of dusk, and in a few minutes there will be an ebbing, a point of no return. But there is work to do, work to do, and that, he tells himself, is why he stays. It is nothing that can't wait until tomorrow. But he is incapable of breaking free.

Genevieve Latko-Devine has left. Chris Yop has left. Jim Jackers has gone for the night—Joe Pope's coworkers, his friends. Two doors down the hall, Yop keeps a pair of binoculars handy for the closer inspection of unsuspecting women on the rooftop pool of the Holiday Inn. The office without Yop is airless and quiet, stilled as it seldom is when Yop occupies it. But the guy has long cut out, and aside from the neon Yuengling sign and collection of World Series caps on the walls, his office appears anonymous. Joe Pope stands hovering over the desk. He gets down on his haunches and rifles through its drawers. He wonders how creepy he looks. Finally he finds the binoculars under a stack of back issues of *Sports Illustrated,* and he takes to the hall again.

He goes to the office full of pigs. Oh, how fatiguing, he thinks, not for the first time—how vaguely oppressive. Pig calendars, pig posters ("It's been a trough day!"), stress relievers in the shape of pigs on top of her computer. Her name is Megan Korrigan and she loves pigs. Pig pencils, pink pig notepads, pig jokes taped to the door. Pigs hung from key chains pinned into corkboard. Her screen saver is a repeating pattern of dancing pigs, and the credenza is filled with pig figurines, piggy banks, stuffed animal pigs, pigs made of glass and crystal, of eraser and plastic, porcelain Porky Pigs, and a Babe the Pig that talks when you pull its string. She keeps two copies of *Charlotte's Web* on her bookshelves alongside marketing textbooks and binders full of branding guidelines, and hanging from her wall is a metal sign of a bibbed pig licking its lips, promoting the eating of itself by crying, "This way to the BBQ!" Why pigs? He walks past them and approaches the window. There is an orchid and three small rows of unbudded herbs in red clay pots. The need for green at work. This he can understand more clearly than pigs. Traps to catch the sun in. He lifts the gray binoculars to his eyes.

This is the reason he's here: from Megan's northern office on the sixty-second floor, there is a clear view of the building opposite. He can see into fifteen floors of it, about twenty offices from left to right—roughly a total of three hundred windows set in the steely black glazing of skyscraper easily penetrated by Yop's binoculars. The pattern of lit windows is switchboard random. Looking into the first window—what is he hoping to see? What relief will it bring? Must be a woman in one of them.

More abandon. Light's on but no one's home. He eyes these interiors that resemble the interiors of the building he's in, but strike him, because they're in a different building, as exotic, rife with sexual possibility. People in other offices have trysts on desks. It doesn't happen here—doesn't happen to him—but that it happens in that building over there seems possible. Plants along windowsills cascade over air conditioning vents. Chairs are turned awry, screen savers churn. In one office, a small mobile, a red Calder reproduction, hangs from the soft tile ceiling, turning slowly in the central air draft. There are only a handful of windows still lit, and those are empty. Finally, he finds a woman two floors down, a dozen windows over, sitting fortuitously near the window, turned to him and applying herself to paperwork. He trains and refocuses. Not his type. Hair like a fern, tight glossy curls. Bad blouse. He looks for some crack in it, revelation of body beneath. She's all sewn up. He keeps the glasses trained on the space between buttons, where the fabric sometimes poufs out, for the possibility of a glimpse. But no luck. And after a while it becomes no different than joining her at her paperwork. What relief there? What pleasure that?

He missed the window almost directly across from him, one floor down, from which light emanates. He quickly swings the binoculars around front and center, but no sooner does he do so than the light goes out. It bursts like a sunspot in his eye. What, leaving? Why and where to? What plans have *you* made? He pictures a man. The man enters the hallway and heads toward the elevator banks. He is handsome and dressed in a gray suit with a starched white shirt mildly wrinkled after the crush and wrangle of a day, briefcase in hand, holding the suit coat over a shoulder with two fishhook fingers. Where does this image come from? Does it exist in real life, or only in the opening print ads of *GQ?* Well, *some*one just left, Joe saw the light go out, and just because he made it a man (it could as easily have been a woman) in a gray suit with a blue-and-tan striped tie and handsome features, doesn't mean the man doesn't exist. He is just now taking the elevator to the lobby floor. He will climb into the back of a waiting cab. Where to, pal? Home? Meeting a woman in a bar? Now the cab is speeding away. The back of the man's head in the rearview window is disappearing toward the Inner Drive, and Joe's curiosity about the man's destination turns quickly into envy: He has the vague conviction that other people are happier and getting more out of life than he is. He is at work, still at work, no place to be but work, where there is work to do. Difficult to do work, though, when he wants to be out there with them. Where are they all going, those people in the backs of cabs?

He ventures into other offices with views onto other buildings. He goes down the wall-mounted stairs and passes the hardwood-floor reception area with its calla lilies and pitcher of cucumber-and-lime water. All the ice is melted and the sofas are empty. He opens the glass door and enters another hallway. He goes into the first office on the right, which looks west. Ten minutes later, he leaves that office and takes the elevator to the sixty-sixth floor, passes the coffee bar and stops for a few bad pretzels in a bowl. He continues past a cluster of cubicles and into a conference room to a wall-length window. Standees of Tony the Tiger and the Pillsbury Dough Boy lurk anthropomorphically in the corners. Here is where Yop goes to look down on the hotel's rooftop pool. Joe trains the binoculars out the window, but it is too dark now and the pool is empty. No swimming after sundown. He walks to the north side of the building and enters another office—whose is this? Oh, what's his name—the guy collects snow globes. Go somewhere, bring back a snow globe and he'll pay you for it. Appropriately harmless distraction, or a real passion? Joe can't imagine it either way. Turn it over and make it snow. There's some kind of pleasure in that? It sustains you? He walks up to the window. The sun's fully down now. Building tops reflect the black sky, roof spurs blotted out, the construction crew working a half-finished skyscraper gone home long ago. Stilled cranes angle in the air. Farther out is a blinking manic circuit board of light. Signal lights pulse faintly as airplanes circle holding patterns above O'Hare. Objectless longing again: Where do people go when they board planes? Who awaits them in the terminals, in purring SUVs, in warm beds across the hushed and longing land? He is office-locked, deskbound, and how did that happen? He trains the binoculars down on the building across the way and into an angle of windows where no human presence offers itself again.

Joe, Joseph—go home, for god's sake. He can hear someone telling him. His father: get your ass home, son. Call someone. Make plans. Enjoy yourself. You're too damn young. Have yourself a time.

But who could he call that doesn't work here? Who could it be that he wouldn't see tomorrow?

He window shops like this till late in the evening. Part of the night he gives over to the contemplation of why his colleagues put such things on their walls. What it means to be the person who hangs autographed 8 × 10s, African masks. There is one office—Tommi Gorjanc's office—filled with pictures of her abducted child. Everyone knows the story. The child was taken from an unlocked car. Then the body was found several months later and after more months Tommi came back to work and brought pictures of the girl with her. Everyone avoids the office if they can. Most of the frames are two-leaf 8 × 10s meant to be placed on a flat surface. They sit on her desk and bookshelves, the filing cabinet, the credenza along the back wall. The pictures crowd in, elbowing each other for room. Some hang from the wall—Jessica straight on, with her profile floating in white cloud; Jessica in tee-ball outfit; Jessica on her father's knee. The three on the wall facing Tommi's desk are the most mournful things Joe has ever seen, like when a soldier dies, and the wall becomes a shrine. The first time he entered the office and saw the frames in the room—there must have been a hundred—he found himself reluctant to move. It was like someone who, turning a corner in a cavern, finds hundreds of moths on the walls all around him. One moth's wings fan out, then close shut. Another does the same a second later. He felt that the frames were like living things with wings which, if he moved too quick, might flutter up around him with a flapping, metallic sound.

Without his knowing it, the lobby guards change shifts. It is that time of night. So do the security men monitoring the television banks flickering in the small white rooms in that no-man's-land between the lobby and underground parking. Hispanic women in uniforms emerge from the elevator banks, trundling supply carts and industrial vacuums. This is the other side of things, the time of lockdown and cleanup, when the tenders of the building replace its daytime occupiers in order to keep the occupiers from noticing the things to which they tend. One of the vacuumers, with the full lips and sad oval eyes of a dispossessed princess, sees Joe as she pushes her cart down a hallway. He emerges from an office holding binoculars, walks across the hallway and enters another office. He doesn't see her. Then he wanders out of the second office just as quickly and begins to walk toward her. They are both startled—she that he is coming toward her, and he that she is present at all. He's wearing a navy blue button-down and belted pleated slacks, a shiny pair of black oxfords. He reminds her of a person in a catalog. She thinks he commands a presence in this space more important than her own, and she averts her eyes. She is beautiful, he thinks, and must be wondering why he is still here long after he should be gone, and he averts his eyes. They pass down the hall.

An hour later, he is sitting in Jim Jackers's office in a chair of re- markable comfort, an ergonomic triumph, holding Jim's phone in contemplation. Not to his ear but in the cradle of his shoulder. He can hear the faint hum of the dial tone. He likes Jim's office better than his own. Shaped the same. The same ceiling tile count. But somehow Jim has made his more anonymous—absolutely nothing here that couldn't be packed away within minutes. He looks around for even a single personal item. People must wonder about Jim more than they do him. Is that what it means to put stuff on your walls— that people don't have to wonder about you? He reaches out and re- news the dial tone. Well, should he call?

Oh, what the hell. He dials, knowing the phone will ring, ring, ring until it goes into voicemail. Not your average voicemail. That voice. Tone of hope, pitch of happiness. If the small of a woman's back could sing. What's she saying? "Hello, you've reached Genevieve Latko-Devine at the Brand Investment Group. I'm away from my desk at the moment, but if you'll leave—" This is normally as far as he gets. He calls to hear the voice, not to leave a message. He cups the phone in his hand. He shifts in the chair. He should hang up and call back, play the message again. There are nights, make of them what you will, when he repeats the exercise beyond the reasonable. Sometimes calling from his apartment, midnight, two in the morning. Four, five beers roiling in his stomach, television blaring mutely, alarm set for six. He feels moderately less unhealthy now calling from Jim's office. Its cold officeness gives the enterprise a veneer of legitimacy, as if he might be reminding her of a meeting tomorrow morning or changes that need to be made to a document. Is he going to hang up now or what? "...encountering an emergency, please press one now, and you will be directed to—" He hangs on nervously, anguished by the possibility that he might say something into the machine without knowing what that could be, that he might have nothing to say but might say something anyway. He's afraid of himself. Time is never so real—never so forcefully marching on—as when he hears her voice unfurling scripted instructions to leave a message and when, at the end of it, after the beep, he's forced to confront himself. That longing for the inarticulate, recorded, irredeemable confession that he has always managed to refrain from issuing into the pathetic soundlessness of the telephone.

(beep)—

"Hey, Eve—"

Do two little words give him away? Bittersweet that she might know his voice so well. But could he hang up now, and deny it tomorrow? "Did you begin to leave me a message last night?" *Message? Huh? What?*

"—this is, uh—"

Not if he says his name...

"—it's Joe—"

He pauses. *What the Jesus god almighty do I think I'm doing?*

"—it's about, uh—"

Do not be honest about the time.

"—8:30, 9:30, something like that, I'm still at the, I'm still at the office, if you can believe it, just trying to, uh, just finishing—getting a lot of stuff that's been piling up lately, like, well, you know, you know how—. And I was looking over your, uh, your—the ads you did for the hardware convention? The banner ads. And I thought, I should call, because those are really, the images are really beautiful. Hard to believe we're selling hammers. We should be selling, I don't know what. They're that good. What they reminded me of was, they reminded me so much of those screenprints we saw at the Contemporary. Remember? We were there for lunch, I think, like, when was that, six months ago? I forget the woman's name. But when I saw these, I thought of those screenprints. You'll have to remind me of her name. Ha, ha, am I just blabbering into your machine?"

Here begins a long pause. He should cut his losses and hang up. But something strange happens as the pause expands. He comes to realize that it might be possible to separate what he's now saying into the phone from the anxiety he feels at the prospect of her listening to it in the future. Separating the message he's leaving from the message she'll play back in the morning, separating them into two distinct realities—one that he commands and sanctions and is all about him, the other vaguer, involving her (something he doesn't have to think about just yet)—takes the pressure off. He can nearly pretend that he's leaving a message for himself, and he has the freedom to let the entire thing explode with silence if he wants. He can worry about her listening later. Right now, he's just talking. The recording might cut him off soon, but ignoring the consequences for the moment—the pause continues to grow—he leans back, settling into Jim Jackers's chair.

"Yeah," he says, "I am just blabbering into your phone. Can't you tell? Are you still there? You still listening?" Another pause. "What do

I want to say?" A third pause. "I did call for a reason, believe it or not. There were any number of people I could have called, but you were the first one I thought of when I thought to call someone. And I know that it's not really talking when you leave a message, that's not really talking, but I'd feel weird calling you at home right now, obviously. You might be sleeping, or your husband might pick up. It's really more like 10:15 to be honest. 10:30. Maybe I should feel even weirder leaving a message. It's a little, I don't know, a little one-sided—. It's just so one-sided. But I really, I wanted to, uh, to say how lately I've been feeling—. What I want to say is how great you are,"—oh, Jesus. Why *great?*—"how great I think you are, and that we've worked together for, how long, like, three years now, and in that time I've—"

"If you're satisfied with your message, please press one now. To listen to your message, please press two. To rerecord your message, please press three."

Well, he thinks, it all works out in the end. Joe Pope doesn't have to send his personal message after all. Press three and it's all erased. The sped-up heart, the stomach full of jumble—all falsely inspired. Even his minor triumph—his refusal to be cowed by the indelible recordedness of the things he was saying, and by his future accountability to them—can be rendered moot now by the press of a button. He should be grateful. So why is his finger poised above the one button? Why is there part of him that *wants* to send it?

He leaves her a total of five messages. He's cut off from each one after three minutes. When the recorded voice interrupts to give him options, he presses one. Fifteen minutes of message, in which he tells her everything. How he loves her. How she is the reason he gets up in the morning and is eager to return to work. How her presence beside him in meetings, that arbitrary arrangement, means everything to him. How unmoored he feels lately, how rudderless. How lunch with her gives him some sense of north, and how quickly lost he becomes after five o'clock, when she leaves for home. He knows she can't love him back. The irrefutability of it has been made clear by the fact that she is pregnant. And now he fears losing her because the baby is due soon. He attacks himself for this selfishness and says into the phone that he could not be happier for her, honest. And that leads him into darker, more vulnerable territory: Why does her life cast a shadow over his own? Why does her happiness, hers and her husband's, follow him everywhere he goes, quietly qualifying the things that might normally bring him delight? Walking his dog of a Sunday—why does this simple pleasure turn into something irredeemably sad? Why does a cab ride through the city without her make him an empty and unrealized dreamer? And since when, and by what right, has he hitched his happiness to hers, and forsaken the power to be the source of his own contentedness?

His relief, when he finally hangs up the phone, is immense. How long he has wanted to tell her these things. Three long years of days. Consider the discipline it takes. Consider the agony of a single weekend, when she flees the space in which he loves her, for her real and substantial life—the one she shares with someone else—leaving him with the pathetic desire for the weekend to speed by so that *his* real and substantial life can begin again. Fool! What depths of despair are you trawling when your happiness hinges upon work—the meetings you both attend, projects you share, the gossip she lets you in on? Is that why you're still here, when there is all that life to be had out there, beyond the office? Joe Pope had tried to tell himself he was here to do work. But there is nothing that can't wait until tomorrow. He is here because he feels closer to Genevieve at the office than he does at home.

He *had* to tell her, didn't he? Had to unburden. Otherwise the years would continue to pass, and he would end up, what—a slight and regretful old man. Feel good about yourself. It was long overdue. Husband, baby—none of that matters. For Joe Pope, they are beside the point. He's not even sure the torch he carries concerns *her* anymore. Point is this: his days are hell, his nights are worse, something had to give.

So why does he feel a little anxious? Well, it's not easy to confess love, not to anyone, not even to an immense heart like Genevieve's, that boundless heart, that ever-widening and sympathetic heart. What power a confession of love yields, what opportunity for a flattening. But look at what's been gained. There's reclamation. There's taking charge of the world in some vague and hopeless way. And the unburdening—the unburdening can't be underestimated. And that was his purpose, wasn't it, to unburden? Because what could he hope to gain by telling her of his love, when she has a husband, and a baby on the way? Yes, the unburdening was all.

Frank Brizzolara, dying ten years now of emphysema, keeps packs of generic cigarettes in his desk drawers. Joe heads down to sixty-five and teases a bent pipe of a cigarette from one of Frank's packs and walks back to Megan Korrigan's office to smoke among the pigs. He lies down on the carpeted floor of Megan's office and, smoking in defiance of building and city ordinaces, ashes into the orchid he's dragged down with him. Despite a kindling anxiety, he feels good. Laughing the spontaneous, mysteriously prompted, rock-bottom laughter of the recently shrived, he stabs out the cigarette in the orchid's vase and rests for a moment, a blue forearm thrown over his eyes. Light here never goes out completely. Always a little hallway light. Stay the night and no true rest will be had. But at a point when he's dazed enough not to notice the soft trundling of a supply cart down the hallway, the cleaning woman, the dispossessed princess, catches a glimpse of what might be a heel, two heels, a pair of legs— is that a person? Is someone asleep on the floor in there? Having

missed the sound of her, the momentary heat of her stare is enough
to make him remove his forearm. He sees a doorway figure. He sits
up just as she moves on, and both of them shiver uneasily over the
next moment or two, her down the hall, him on the office floor, in
the recognition of being caught in something oddly, embarrassingly,
human.

There's something embarrassingly human, too, about those pigs.
He looks around him: He's not sure he's seen it before just now. The
sheer number of them on display has made it impossible to pay attention to any particular one. It's their combined effect that domi-
nates. But from where he sits on the floor he begins to make out
individual pig expressions: ruddy cheeks, heads half cocked, drowsy
brows at half-mast. They sit like babies in a Michelin commercial.
They stand on tip-hooves in a balletic twirl. He rises and approaches
the credenza. A little dusty, woefully penned in. That's when the anxiety he has been suppressing explodes inside him: He has just left fifteen minutes of unchecked confession on Genevieve's voice mail.
And what was the purpose again? He's lost it. The purpose was to feel
better about himself? To unburden? He's not remembering clearly. It
was something, something prompted him only a half hour ago, when
it all seemed so appropriate . . . Yes, to unburden. But was that it? No,
there was something more. Husband, baby—despite them, he can
see he had allowed himself to be hopeful. Hopeful that she would
play back those messages in the morning and that she would then
confess her own love, too. Fool! He has to find a way to erase them.

But first something needs to be done with the pigs. It's worse
for them here than life on a farm. At least in pens they can oink
around, nose each other's asses, roll over in the warm muck. Here
they look infinitely more imprisoned. They never leave. They never
move. They're ignored, undusted, calling out. They should prefer the
slaughterhouse.

He returns from Marnie Telpner's office with one from her collection of shopping bags, into which he begins to carefully place one pig after the other, thinking, Feel good about yourself. It's liberating. Like these pigs here. It had to be done. For your own sake, if not for hers. Joe is spinning himself the other way again, back to the feel-good story. He tells himself, it had to be done, right? It had nothing to do with hope. It was about how he was beginning to feel a little dusty himself, looked past. How Genevieve responds to the information doesn't even matter. Keep that in mind. It's beside the point. Hope is beside the point. What's important is, what's important.... What exactly is it you think you're doing with these pigs?

He removes the last of them—the wall calendar, the BBQ sign—and carries them down the hall.

Idiot! He spins himself back just as quickly. Two times an idiot! Once in leaving the message and once in sending it! What leave of the senses just occurred here? Confessing into a machine? How do you *think* she's going to respond? Revealed: he's a lonely, anguished, lovesick, delusional fool. Confessing has defeated his very purpose. And what was that purpose again? To let her know that he was available to be loved back. It had *everything* to do with hope. I'm here, if you want me. But could Genevieve love a fool?

He takes the bag full of pigs and enters Tommi Gorjanc's office. When Tommi returned after her child's funeral, she cried during input meetings. Once she cried walking into the men's room without realizing her mistake. She encouraged everyone who came into her office to read the newspaper clippings she kept in an album, and to pick up the frames on her desk and look into the blue eyes of the dead girl. Joe takes one of the frames in his hands—it is now as dusty as Megan's pigs. He collects all the frames from the desk and the credenza and those hanging on the wall and puts them in a corner. Everyone has grown so familiar with your tragedy, he says to the little girl, they don't see your face anymore. Not even your mother, who on some days can be very busy. With nervous energy he replaces the frames with Megan's figurines. Pigs begin to multiply: across wood grains, over disheveled papers, on the dusty top of Tommi's clock radio. He hangs pig key chains from frame hooks, the calendar and BBQ sign from nails that once supported pictures of the girl. The pigs appear refreshed in their new setting, ridiculous smiles renewed. Then he packs the frames into the shopping bag and carries them down the hall. He sets them up across all the pig-free surfaces of Megan's desk, pointing the lost child's smiling face into the hall, so that everyone will have no choice but to notice her again, in the morning, as they walk by.

Around one now. He ends up in Genevieve's office, a floor below his own and a better place to be. It's carefully decorated with merchandise from art museum gift shops—a clock that bobs on a stem, miniature Eames chairs on the windowsill. On the wall behind the desk is a Rothko reproduction in a red plastic frame. And on her desk are photographs of her adoring husband. The message light on her phone beats a red steady pulse. Might it give out by morning? No more likely to than his own sturdy heart. He picks up the receiver and presses the message light. The same conspiring female voice that prompted him to press one now instructs him to input Genevieve's PIN number. He tries her birthday. He tries her address. He tries 1-2-3-4. He spends a good half hour going through various combinations. In a moment of truly lush preposterousness he tries his own name plus zero. Then his own name plus one, plus two, et cetera. Eventually he resigns to not knowing what four digits are closest to her heart.

Maybe it's the phone. Are messages stored in the phone, or in the wires, the connections, some central processing hub? What *is* a message? What if he were to disconnect the cord and replace it with a different phone—say, his own? He could easily switch it with one from a closer office, but her receiver, he's noticed, emits a musky variation on her shampoo, something he'd like for himself. So he carries it up to his office and returns down the stairs with his phone in hand. He gets the feeling of being watched. He turns his head quickly but finds only the diminishing pattern of office doorways and, at the end of the hallway, the blank expression of a blond door that was closed by someone gone home long ago.

When the switcheroo fails to stop her message light from blinking, he considers the wholesale theft of Genevieve's phone. But Kathy Moretti, the office manager, would quickly find her a new one, and when Genevieve got around finally to checking her messages, who would she suspect had stolen the old one?

Teddy Reiser keeps a toolbox full of good stuff under his desk in the event something should go wrong on a photo shoot. Joe takes a Phillips-head from Teddy's office and returns to Genevieve's, where, with the door closed, he opens the silver wall plate supporting the phone cord. With a pair of dull scissors, he works his way through many thin, multicolored wires. The phone goes dead, thank god. But he doesn't stop there. Only cutting the phone lines will look suspicious. People will wonder why they were cut, and if ever the messages surface—who can say whether a message can survive cut phone lines—they will know it was him. But they won't think it was him if he does more than cut her phone lines. The only solution is to gather up all her personal things, including the pictures of her husband and the Rothko reproduction, and to put them in a corner, and then to begin the careful vandalizing of her office. No one would blame Joe Pope for *that*. With the deliberation of an artist, then, he lays the phone on the ground in a way to suggest mindless, tossed-off violence. He does the same with the papers on her desk. He unshelves the books and eases the bookshelves down on the floor and places them at a rakish angle. Standing on her chair, he pulls on the latticework of metal that holds the soft ceiling tiles together. The ceiling buckles. A few of the tiles he removes, setting them where they might likely have fallen. He turns over the chair and the computer monitor. Then he retrieves her undamaged belongings and places them, including the picture of her husband, gently upon the ground, between gaps of destruction. The last thing he does is re-hang her reproductions.

They're coming back. To the footstep, the wheel turn, returning the ways they left. Some seem not to have remembered leaving at all. El cars are crammed, each a tinderbox of body heat and morning breath. The highways beginning at city limits are lined with cars compacted like crushed bellows. Everyone destined to converge upon the center of gravity, the skyline in the distance. If the Loop's tallest buildings shout across the land their strength and height, the brightening sun cuffing their frosted glass is the land's cry back. It begins to slake the buildings' black-metal thirst for heat. The sun's slow predominating brings dread, warning them of another long day ahead. They deboard, hundreds of them, from buses and taxis, gaining the street from platform stairs, the metal gratings dripping with opalescent rainwater. Shouldering backpacks, pulling luggage carts over the curbs and potholes, they're vaguely aware of last night's storm. Otherwise not much thought in the head at this hour. Expressions range from the endorphined glee of the morning person to the shock of those still dazed from being reborn. Their paths include inefficiencies that must be indulged: how far afield they go for lattes, fruit cups, fat-free muffins, packs of cigarettes, aspirins. Their mouths are soured by coatings of toothpaste, their tongues feel furry. Their bowels are jangly. Don't want to go back there. Have to go back there. They march onward, toward the outer reaches of the Loop, that hairy knotted fist, and up the Magnificent Mile's long elegant index finger aiming north. The design of their city is a silent pointing command that says *Go!*

He wakes in Sonya Hutton's office, sharing her upholstered couch with a racquetball racquet and a guitar. Sonya is at her desk early, eating scrambled eggs from a deep black container and listening to NPR on an antique Bakelite radio. He feels he is waking into a dream, a soft-lit and underwater world of cold sunshine, broadcast voices, and cooked eggs. Sonya is uncomfortably near—not much room between the sofa and desk. She is looking right at him, tree-stump calf and combat boot elevated to desk level, egg trough in one hand and plastic fork in the other.

"Comfortable?" she asks.

"Not really," Joe replies, rising to sitting position. One left-side lick of hair stands straight as a wall of tiny black feathers. What's he doing, he wonders, with this guitar and this racquet? And then, Oh. Oh, yeah.

"Sorry about sleeping on your couch," he says.

"It's, you know," she says, eyeing it, "company issued." With egg quivering on her fork, she says, "What's with the guitar?"

He needs to return it to the guitar stand in Gary Need's office, where he took it up as a distraction before bedtime, the tricky, anxious hour between the decision to sleep and sleep itself. Bad choice of distractions, a guitar. Too cumbersome to wield on a sofa, and a cold bedmate. The racquet belongs to Trish Miller. After destroying Genevieve's office, he found himself with a lot of nervous energy he thought to burn off playing racquetball, found Trish's racquet and gym bag, keyed into the gym, and played barefoot against himself until a Rorschachlike stain blossomed down the front of Trish's snug University of Wisconsin T-shirt. He found that in the gym bag, too. He looks down. He's still in it.

"What time is it?" he asks.

Sonya, peering up into a wall-mounted Hamm's beer light box and clock display, where a fountain of white water flows eternally into a crystal stream behind the black hands of time itself, revolving hands, moving inexorably the world into irreversibility—Sonya squints and admits to not having her glasses. Eight-thirty, she guesses. "Were you here all night?"

"Sure was," he says.

"What have you been doing?"

"Well," he says. He leans back on the sofa, and it breathes out through a cigarette burn. "First, I looked out the windows with Yop's binoculars. He has a good pair of binoculars. I did that for about three hours. I was looking for women."

"Interesting," she says.

"But I couldn't find any. So then I smoked one of Frank's cigarettes. And then I took all of Megan's pigs out of her office, and I switched them with all the pictures in Tommi's office."

"What do you mean," says Sonya, "switched them?"

"I took the pigs in Megan's office, and I brought them down to Tommi's office, and then I took all the pictures of Jessica that Tommi has in her office and I brought them down to Megan's office. So now the pigs are in Tommi's, and Jessica is in Megan's."

Sonya lets her combat boot fall to the floor. "You serious?" she asks. Between "you" and "serious," a pellet of egg flies from her mouth and lands somewhere between her and Joe. They acknowledge it unspokenly.

"How does that strike you?" he asks.

"So I could go up there right now and see all the pigs in Tommi's office."

"Uh-huh."

"And all the pictures of the girl in Megan's office."

Joe nods.

She sets the plastic container of eggs on her desk and picks up her coffee. She gets up and looks down at Joe. Her underwear is bunched under her cutoff fatigues and she wiggles to free it. "This," she says, "I got to see."

"If you hurry," he says, "you can be the one to tell them who did it."

She walks out and leaves him on the sofa. His back aches and his head aches and he is not thinking any more clearly than last night if he is telling Sonya Hutton about the switch. The anticipation of shame combined with the smell of eggs makes him want to flee the building. Run, never to return. But it is necessary to stand and stretch for a few minutes. Start the day off right. Stay in defiance, even if it will be short-lived in the face of building security. So he stretches. He walks over to Sonya's desk and leans into it and works his calves. Then he realizes he should get out of Trish's clothes.

He's not sure why he tells Sonya about what he's done. He's the one responsible, he supposes, so he should face the consequences. Maybe he wants to be fired. The only cure to loving Genevieve. He didn't tell Sonya about *that*. Not to prevent them from knowing that he vandalized her office, but to keep them from knowing that he's in love. So what if he blabbered it into fifteen minutes of voicemail? What business is it of Sonya Hutton's? These people around here, they gossip. Word would travel quick. Even if he gets fired, he doesn't like the idea of them talking about something so personal.

Neither Gary nor Trish is in yet. He discovers his blue button-down draped across Trish's chair and quickly changes out of the tee. It's a little stretched-out and musty with sweat, and not as neatly folded as he found it. But it's back in the gym bag now and, frankly, low on the scale of his concerns.

He heads down to the lobby and out the revolving doors. Brooks Brothers on Ohio opens at eight. He buys himself a suit, seersucker, something to be fired in. He'd hate to be fired in yesterday's clothes. There are eight of him in the mirror, and all look awful. He tries to work down sleep's cowlick like a cat. Stubborn little fucker. Giving up, he stands straight again. Pants need a little hemming, but as it turns out the tailor's in early this morning, bulbous nosed and all business. They put his old clothes in a bag and staple it shut. He takes the stapling as an affront. Then he heads back to the building. The hallways are just waking up. Behind his desk, he wipes the screen saver clean, calls up a new browser window, and goes to eBay's home page, where he spends the next hour waiting for them in case they come to take him away, and looking for something he might like to put on his walls in case they don't.

VIVEK NARAYANAN

Boston University

ROSIE

A new wave of burglaries hit the capital. Ravi, who was nine years old, said, "Appa, Appa, I want a big doggy that bites!"

Kalyanaraman looked up nervously from his paper. He said, "What Ravi, why you want to get animals and such things?"

Ravi said, "So that it can bite the Africans and kill them!"

The father swirled the last of the coffee in his tumbler. "You should not talk like that outside, Ravi. Say robbers, not Africans, okay? *Robbers.*"

"Kablalas!" Ravi said.

"Yes, *kablalas,* that's better."

Kalyanaraman thought of the curs he had encountered growing up in a village in Tamilnadu, far from Southern Africa, where he was now. He thought of their red yellow eyes and the mangy patches on their skin, how they liked to hang together in packs of two or three and go to the riverbank to play. He remembered the one dog that all the neighborhood boys liked to throw stones at, how it used to feign a limp. Those village strays were shrewd and even dignified in their own way, he thought. Independent. Every day after lunch, they showed up to eat the leftovers. But owning a dog? That was a different matter. The petting could be left to children, but what would you do if it wanted to come into the house? And what would it eat? Meat?

"I want a puppy dog, too!" said Ravi's sister, Kavita.

Kalyanaraman looked over at his wife, who sat on the sofa, knitting. They frowned at each other. "You can get a dog," his wife said to the children, "but who will take care of it, eh? You know how much trouble it is to take care of a dog? Yes? Now do your homework."

Whites, of course, had always owned guard dogs, just as they had owned guns, but it was a new fad for Indians. Kalyanaraman and his wife were agreed—at first—that they were not the kind of family that owned animals. Not that they had anything in particular against animals. Being vegetarians they didn't, after all, eat them.

The summer wore on. The night burglaries became more brazen. Rather than bothering to break in through a window, robbers now preferred to ring the front doorbell. The newspapers alleged that freedom fighters in the neighboring country had been selling their guns to the capital's criminals. Kalyanaraman had installed barbed wire on his compound's glass-lined high wall, but could the security guard be trusted if the robbers came? Shouldn't he have some canine company by the gate? The Ravanans thought so. So did the Venkatesans, Mishras, Jaitleys, and the Danges. Ravi, clever boy, was keeping count. Or rather, his friends were keeping count for him. All the Indian children seemed to be teaching themselves a great deal about the different breeds of ferocious dogs and what qualities and colors were peculiar to each; they seemed to be picking up extra details from their White and Black friends at school. Rottweilers? Rhodesian ridgebacks? Kalyanaraman had heard of Alsatians and Dobermans but certainly not these.

The children also seemed to know rather a lot about guns, about both air guns and the more serious kind that were illegal to own. Every White family had an air gun. If you spotted the intruders while they were still at the gate and fired a shot, it sometimes discouraged them. It was from his son that the Indian expatriate learned that he should invest in a Webley or a Walther PPK/S.

A businessman was shot point-blank in his car while waiting to pick up his daughter from school. The next day, following some advice from his colleagues about a shipment from South Africa, Kalyanaraman went to the house of a senior official in the national airways and brought back a compact air pistol and cleaning fluid. It felt smart and tough in his hands, and he spent long hours studying the maintenance instructions. Could he fire it under pressure?

Kalyanaraman considered himself to be one of the very first Tamil Brahmin arrivals in Southern Africa. He had come in the mid-1960s, shortly after independence, to a capital city bustling with dozens of newly founded industries. He had been impressed by the charm and unfailing good manners of the Africans he'd met then. His superiors vaunted impressive educations received in England, and the streets had been full of gullible, smiling country bumpkins streaming into the city looking for jobs and a new life, always ready and eager for work. Without quite planning it, he and his wife stayed on for nearly twenty years, renewing five-year contracts without ever contemplating citizenship. They had remained pukka Brahmins in every way. But during this period, the national economy gradually soured. There were debilitating civil wars in neighboring countries. Everyday life became dangerous.

The Ravanans were held at gunpoint in their house for five terrifying hours while the intruders searched for cash. When this happened,
all the other families on Gondwe Road except for the Kalyanaramans
bought dogs. There were German shepherds, pitbulls, bloodhounds,
bull terriers, and Irish wolfhounds. Their owners were Indians,
Whites, Coloureds, and a few middle-class Africans. Many chose to
buy their dogs full-grown, so they could serve their purpose immediately. Some went to the trouble of sending their pets to special training
classes that made them more effective killers. A few Whites—though
this may have been just a rumor—decided to import breeds of attack
monkeys, such as Barbary apes. Kalyanaraman began to feel a little
jealous when he saw how dogs followed their owners around. He
began to think more fondly of the strays in the village where he'd
grown up.

Each time an African laborer walked down the road, a long chain
reaction of barks and howls began. Often, Kalyanaraman would hear
this rough-hewn melody continue for several minutes at a stretch,
reaching two or three crescendos, supplemented even—or so he
thought he heard—by monkeys' screeches, before dwindling down
to a final coda of whimpers and whines. This racial attunement was
notable, though no one on Gondwe Road found it remarkable. Not
once did a dog have to be taught what a poor African smelled like.
Instinctively each adopted the prejudices of its owner.

This phenomenon had troubling effects. A few dogs barked at all
Africans, even if they were owners of property; many dogs barked at
Coloureds, some at Indians, and one or two even barked at Whites.
If a dog escaped from its yard, it picked fights. African-owned dogs
fought it out with White- or Coloured-owned dogs; White and
Coloured dogs fought with each other, too, to the great embarrass-
ment of their owners. Occasionally, dogs from rival compounds
mounted each other in the middle of the road, at which point neigh-

bors of different races gathered together to separate them by beating them with sticks. The Indian dogs were more tentative, and rarely dared to leave their yards.

From time to time dogs made indiscriminate attacks, too. The security guards, who were inevitably Africans, were at risk. A young girl from the road was terrorized by a German shepherd, and once a resident admiring flowers in an adjoining yard was mauled. It became necessary for early morning walkers to carry switches or dog-repellent sonar devices.

After much thought, Kalyanaraman suggested the idea of buying a dog to his wife: "We have been in this country so long, Vaidehi. Shouldn't we get a dog also?"

"But will we let it into the house then?" his wife asked.

"No, no," he said. "It can sleep in the guard's quarters."

"But what if it gets used to *him,* and not to *us,*" she said.

"The children will play with it. And I don't mind giving it a pat or two from time to time."

"And what will we feed it? Meat? Fish?"

"Why? We can feed it curd-rice. If in India dogs are eating that, why not these African dogs?"

"What if it doesn't eat the curd-rice?"

"I think it'll eat the curd-rice, Vaidehi. Look—I was just reading in *Reader's Digest* about a vegetarian dog at the Saint Francis of Assisi mission."

But Kalyanaraman was himself unsure on the dietary issue. So he consulted his knowledgeable friend Dr. Cherian, who had converted to vegetarianism on joining the Mai Baba movement.

"No problem," said Dr. Cherian. "No problem at all. My dear friend, the issue here is nature versus—what? Nurture. Nature versus nurture. Let us take the Doberman pinscher—why don't you buy the Doberman pinscher. After all, he is the best example of nature. Now, some German fellow was experimenting with all this in 1800, okay, and he has discovered, after careful breeding and crossbreeding, that the Doberman pinscher is the best dog for both attack *and* companionship. So deep is the military spirit simply bred into the genes that you should never, even in play, wrestle with him! Now there is an example of a guard dog that will be a guard dog no matter what diet he consumes! In fact, a vegetarian sattvic diet may be just the thing that calms him down. Okay, all right?"

Kalyanaraman began to scour the papers for a cheap, well-raised Doberman pinscher. He went to a farm on the outskirts of the city to call on an Irish dairy farmer who kept dogs. He honked outside the entrance to the farm and, receiving no reply, opened the gate and walked in. The smell of manure was in the air and the buildings were dirty. It was not clear to him which was the farmhouse and which was the shed. He heard a low growl and before he knew it, a short scrap of a dog had lightly clamped its jaws around his ankle. It did not bite into his pants, but Kalyanaraman knew that it would, if he moved. He stood there for six minutes—by his watch—before the farmer, a widowed woman, appeared. He was impressed.

"Is this dog for sale?" he asked.

"No, dearie," she said, "but I'm sure I have just the right thing. You're not wanting pups are you?"

"I am wanting a full-grown Doberman pinscher, cheap. Trained for attack, but quiet."

"I have just the thing for you. A fawn-colored Doberman. They are very rare, of course. But I have a trained one on discount. Under a year old. She doesn't mind Indians, you know, " the woman said, winking.

The dog already had a name that Kalyanaraman liked: Rosie. She seemed small and skinny to him, but was well behaved. And, like the village dogs he liked best, she followed him after a little coaxing. He put her in the backseat and she fell asleep on the drive home.

Ravi said, "If it's a Doberman why isn't it black? I want a black Doberman."

"No, Ravi, this is a fawn-colored Doberman. Very rare."

Kavita said, "But she doesn't look like she would ever bite anyone."

It was true: Though she was trim and pretty, Rosie did not act like a Doberman at all. She sniffled often, shed tears into the rust-colored markings around her eyes, walked with a strange uncoordinated gait that made her seem old beyond her years and—the first sign in the car had been an omen—she slept a great deal. She was sometimes affectionate, sometimes aloof, but never ferocious. The guard liked her, and Kalyanaraman often heard him singing to her in his cabin in the evenings. Strangest of all, she loved curd-rice. She ate such large amounts of it, mixed with half-cups of diced tomato or lentils and bits of banana, that Vaidehi Kalyanaraman began to make a special pot each day just for her.

"Perhaps she may even be the reincarnation of a famous soul," Dr. Cherian said. "Has anyone ever beheld a wonder such as this! Such a noble dog! I will write a letter on your behalf to Baba."

Everyone liked Rosie when she was awake and playing dreamily, but it was a serious, puzzling problem that she was not belligerent at all. She had been bought on discount, but not for an insignificant amount of money. She had come for almost the same price as the air gun. When she encountered other dogs on the street, she immediately fell to her side and let them rest their teeth on her neck. Even the smaller dogs—male and female—tried to climb onto her, and so it was decided by the guard that she should stay inside at all times.

Ravi wanted to put some fighting spirit into Rosie, but Kalyanaraman ruled out wrestling. Instead, the father tried to take her for long walks on a leash. When they went for strolls, the locked-up dogs howled and their owners came out to snigger at his tame-looking Doberman. Mishra suggested that the problem was diet, that Dr. Cherian had been proven empirically wrong. "At least give her some eggs," he said. And so they did, but Rosie did not become energetic. She put on weight.

The newspapers complained that many innocent pedestrians were being harassed and injured by racist guard dogs. A special committee was formed to address the issue in the city council, and there was talk of strictly enforcing the "pauperies" law. Owners insisted on their right to defend themselves. There was a burglary at the Peters's residence, on the far end of Gondwe road. The Peters's dog had had its haunches cut with some kind of machete while the security guard had fled. The Great Dane now wore a plastic bucket around its neck to keep it from licking its wound. This piece of news upset Kalyanaraman. If such a dog has suffered this fate, he thought, how will Rosie protect us? He began to prod Rosie with a switch in an attempt to make her aggressive, but she responded with more sleepy whimpering. He concluded that Rosie was either missing the attack gene or having some very serious psychological problems.

"Depression?" pondered Dr. Cherian. "Existential crisis? Or perhaps, why don't you face it, Kalyanaraman, perhaps it is that Gandhi has been reborn as a dog, ahn? There are more things than what science can explain."

"Wait a minute, hello?" Mishra said, narrowing his eyes. "How can the Mahatma be reincarnated? You're going too far, Cherian."

"No, no, why not?" Dr. Cherian insisted. "That dog is here to teach us something."

He doesn't have children, Kalyanaraman thought, that's why he can have such fancy ideas. The next day, he sent his office boy to buy a side of beef at the butchery. It came wrapped in a brown paper parcel. Kalyanaraman had to spray the car with air freshener to hide the smell. He waited until his wife had gone to sleep. He instructed the security guard, who was sitting doubled over in his cabin, to open the parcel.

"How's a bonus, boss."

"Yes, yes, no problem. You give the meat to Rosie, don't tell anyone, and I promise I will give you a bonus. No problem."

The guard reached into the parcel and took out the dark pink beef. He peeled away the newspaper the meat was wrapped in, and Kalyanaraman felt like gagging. He said, "Throw it, I say! Throw the meat to Rosie."

The guard looked at the meat. "How's some meat for *me,* boss?"

"I'll give you a bonus, and you can buy as much meat as you want, meat for your whole family! But kindly feed Rosie first."

The guard put the meat before Rosie. She ambled over, sniffed the side of beef and turned away. Kalyanaraman prodded her back to it with his stick. This time she went closer, licked the flesh, even took a bit into her mouth, then dropped it and walked off into the garden. The security guard stared at the side of beef on their gravel driveway. Then, on Kalyanaraman's instructions, he picked it up and dropped it back in the parcel. From that night on, it was official: Rosie was a vegetarian by choice.

Kalyanaraman began to practice regularly with his air gun. He wanted to defend his family with a real weapon bought on the illegal market. Meanwhile, the children lost interest in the dog. The guard kicked her out of his cabin. Kalyanaraman continued to take her for walks, beating her with a stick to make her walk faster. She was almost a buffalo in her manners. Sometimes he looked into her eyes, and she mournfully into his, and he was convinced that she had fallen into a deep depression. He took Rosie to a special trainer who operated out of the sports club.

The trainer took one look at Rosie and said, "She's sick, mate. There's someing the wrong wif her."

"Not at all! What is wrong with her? Nothing. I have paid good money for that dog."

"Is she eating all right, then?"

"What is wrong? Please. Her problems are from birth. Some psychological insecurity is there."

"I don't know about that, mate. But I'd take her to a vet if I was you."

It was a wonder that no one had recommended this before. Rosie had so much "personality" that Kalyanaraman and his family had assumed there was nothing medically wrong with her. The vet, however, had different, saddening news. Rosie was suffering from a genetic disease known as "Wobbler's Syndrome," which meant that she had a malformed spinal canal, and that she might someday become partly paralyzed. She would never be the guard dog they wanted her to be.

Violence in the city took a gruesome turn. The Bannerjees, who lived on the next street over, fired their domestic servant for stealing a bottle of whiskey. Later he came back to torture Mrs. Bannerjee, cutting out her tongue before killing her. In the Kalyanaramans's own home, the security guard became obsessed with Mrs. Kalyanaraman. Often, she felt his eyes on her and turned to see him staring through the window. The security company was informed and a jovial old man arrived as a replacement.

Through his contact in the airlines, Kalyanaraman bought an Armscor .38 handgun. He told the security guard to make Rosie sleep outside the guard's shed, at least for show. Often, in the night, he had a recurring dream: waking in the middle of the night to find wind blowing through the windows and the burglar bars pried apart. The dining room light is on. He walks toward the room with his revolver and finds the previous security guard sitting at the table with a number of other African men in suits. On the table is a massive stuffed animal, sometimes a pig, sometimes a turkey, sometimes a goat. Kalyanaraman fires his revolver at the men and hears hyenas howling.

On Sundays, Kalyanaraman took walks through his garden, cocking and uncocking his air gun as Rosie rambled behind. He thought of his first years in the country, when he had directed and supervised educational documentaries for the newly founded national television station, before the information ministry had run out of funds for roving projects. He traveled all over the country, to remote villages and game reserves, and met hundreds of people. Throughout this time, he had never missed a daily prayer, nor cheated on his wife, nor endured the slightest compromise in his diet. Then, as now, they lived in this lovely bungalow in the suburb of Woodlands.

White settlers had built the bungalow. When the Kalyanaramans first moved in, it had come with a rose garden, a gardener, and a maid, in addition to the frangipani and jacaranda trees that still grew in the yard. The property was encircled by high, white walls, which had been raised during the Mau-Mau scare, a false alarm. Now his family could only leave the safety of their yard in a car. The poor were starving in the capital city. They were killing in the daytime. Or was it even the poor who were killing? It was impossible to know. Then, he thought of his ancestral village: his father with his few teeth in old age, sitting on the *thinnai* with his feet splayed. The brothers had sold the ancestral house. Perhaps he could buy land in the area again? Whatever else, with the savings and gratuity from one more year, Kalyanaraman reasoned, he and his family could return to India when his contract expired.

One night, he was awakened by a high, warbling howl that he first mistook for a dream. He locked his wife and children in the bedroom and then stepped outside with his flashlight in one hand and his Armscor in the other. He fired a warning shot from the front door then walked around to the back. The guard's cabin was deserted. Nearby, he saw a hobbling, mangled thing. It was Rosie; he approached her. Someone had cut off one of her hind legs. He thought he saw a figure scale the side wall; he fired twice at the moving shadow. Then he felt a stab in his left calf. Rosie had bitten him.

"Come on, Rosie, sweetie, dearie!" Kalyanaraman yelled. "Stop it. Stop it, all is well." But she didn't loosen her clamp. He looked down at her. She had a red madness in her eyes. With the pain shooting up his leg, Kalyanaraman bent down and fired as gently as he could into the dog's side. The sound of barks, howls, car alarms, and human shouts was near deafening. Up and down Gondwe Road, yard lights came on.

LACHLAN SMITH

Cornell University

SILENT SKY

Jason plucks tiny flowers from the grit and releases them to the wind. Resting on the hard slope, he feels as though he might tumble down the mountain spontaneously or be blown off it. He has left the green hills and black-tailed deer of his father's California hunting ranch to stalk sheep in this godforsaken place with his stepbrother, Brad.

His shoulder presses Brad's. Their guns lean on the rock. Hunting season doesn't open until tomorrow, but Brad claims it's foolish to hike without protection in bear country. Jason knows the truth, that his stepbrother can't stand to be in wilderness without a weapon, or to see Jason unmanned in that way. Despite the annoyance of carrying the rifle, it feels good to have it beside him, if only so that from time to time Jason can hold it to his shoulder, put his finger to the trigger, and imagine dropping a ram at five hundred yards. The outcrop shelters them from the autumn wind blowing down off the heights.

Brad chips at the rock with his knife. A shale fragment sparks against Jason's cheek. Jason never knew his real mother. Brad's father ran away when he was a baby. Jason, Pop, Brad, and Jason's step-mother were destined to make a family together, his stepmother used to say. Then she got cancer. It went away, but ten years later she got it again.

There are fossils in this mountain. Jason remembers hunting as a young boy on their ranch for dusty imprints of seashells and the oc-casional webbing of fish bones in outcroppings like this one. For Pop, the marine fossils were evidence that the world was ancient. There'd been enough time for the hills of California to rise from the bottom of the sea. For Jason's stepmother, the stamped forms of shells and fishtails in the rock were mysteries that humans weren't meant to un-derstand, except as proof that flood waters had recently drowned the earth and that the final apocalypse was coming.

Across the wide, flat valley a line of gentle mountains rises against the deep blue sky. The fireweed on the upper slopes is brilliant red; lower down, the colors of the mountains blend into the valley's yel-low and green. Sunlit, molten channels fray and tie together through the willow brush on the valley floor. To the south, glaciers hang over cliffs. Blackness mars the creases in the ice, like something rotten at the core. The snouts of the glaciers are furrowed, filthy.

Brad closes his now-blunted knife. He takes the map from his pocket and tries to share it with Jason, but Jason doesn't grip the cor-ner as he might to steady the map against the wind. The paper kinks on itself, blowing against Brad's arm. Jason brushes shale fragments from his jacket. The straps of the backpack, which is full of gear, dig into his shoulders as he stands. "It'll be twice as far as you say, and three times as steep. I don't need any map to know that."

Brad folds the map and stuffs it into his pocket. He stands, an inch taller and thirty pounds heavier than Jason. Squinting through the magnifying scope, he points his weapon at the sky. At first Jason thinks that he means to shoot a hawk that holds its position against the wind, rising through empty space over the valley. Then he hears the airplane's tinny whine. His eyes focus on the more distant target. "Collins?"

"I think so. Who the hell do you think he is?" As the Cessna turns, becoming a brilliant pinprick in the flat sky, Brad slings the gun over his shoulder. He flicks his dip into the wind and pulls the tin from his pocket for another. He offers it to Jason, his cupped hand sheltering the tobacco inside.

Jason takes a pinch and folds it beneath his lip. "That's the million dollar question." He feels a tingling warmth as the nicotine starts through him. Pop seemed to know Collins, the pilot they hired in Anchorage. What's more, the two men didn't seem surprised to see each other, though Pop had said nothing about Collins before the three of them ran into him at the airport. Collins gave them a price five hundred dollars below the quote of any of the local bush pilots Brad had talked to on the phone.

"You saw the way he was looking at me," Brad says.

Jason laughs as Brad angrily turns up the mountain. On second thought, it's good to be away from home. For the first time in months, there's nothing that needs to be done. They should waste no more than an hour or two sweating and spend the remainder of the day resting, doing nothing, maybe drinking a little; they work hard enough at home. He has never understood Brad's need for constant motion.

At first the climbing is easy. The strawlike grass soon gives way to crumbled shale. Brad's boots leave messy furrows that Jason can follow without looking up. The music of trickling rock is in his ears, along with the wind and his own wheezing breath. Soon Brad's footprints cross the slope to a brushy defile with a brook running in its bottom, and Jason feels spongy turf under his boots again. The sound of running water replaces the noise of skittering shards. Squinting against the brightness, Jason sees Brad sitting on a big rock beside the stream.

"Seen any sheep?" Brad calls.

Jason takes out his dip and throws it into the stream. He submerges his canteen, the cold penetrating instantly to the bones of his hand. He drinks, then fills the canteen again. "A whole flock of them. With wings. I'm surprised you missed them. They flew by a minute ago."

Brad stares at Jason. "Where's your rifle?"

Pretending to search his pockets, Jason grabs his dick. "Here it is." He lies on the turf and waits for his lungs to open, wishing that he'd returned for the gun as soon as he realized he left it; he isn't about to go all the way back to get it now. It'll be there on the way down. He closes his eyes, and immediately feels himself slipping away.

Something eclipses the sun. Jason awakens to Brad holding the rifle above him, Brad's boot just inches from his face. Brad stares fixedly down at him. He sits up fast, and Brad lets the rifle fall across his lap. He picks up his own gear. "I can't figure out why you even came on this trip."

"It's sure a hell of a lot warmer in California." Jason pictures himself sweating in the late summer sun, drinking a beer on the redwood deck before dinner, leaving muddy fingerprints on the bottle. Then he thinks of the work left undone on the ranch. They can't afford this trip. The old truck won't last more than another year. The roof sprung another leak just before they left. "Did you think the squirrels were going to take it?"

"Leave the gun if you don't want it. Let it rust."

In the final months of his stepmother's illness, the deer only got fed once or twice a week because Jason had to do everything. He hates to think of the ranch failing, he and Brad and Pop being forced to go their separate ways. He stands. "What's the first thing you're going to eat when you get back?" he says when they start climbing again.

Brad stops. He gives Jason a hard look. "Pussy."

Brad doesn't make any effort to wait for him now. He lifts his knees high, no pause in his stride for rest. The rifle bobs on his shoulder. As Jason's lungs begin to close, he drops his eyes to the slope ahead, concentrating on each step, one at a time. When he does look up, he sees Brad facing down the mountain, gazing out into space. Jason turns in time to catch the Cessna's shadow fleeing southward over the willow flats.

The afternoon's getting on, the wind off the heights growing colder. Soon Jason climbs in a gully filled with tumbled, lichen-covered boulders. Squirrels run from him, squealing as they dart away. Blood pounds in his aching temples. His feet punch into treacherous crevices beneath last winter's snow. He tries to walk in his stepbrother's boot marks. The sun blinds him for just an instant as he comes over the dry, rocky pass, and he pauses on the edge of a plateau tens of miles square, meadows falling away to rolling hills. Though the horizon seems to conceal a precipice, Jason knows that these uplands go on and on.

Sitting curled against the nearest grassy ridge, Brad makes an urgent downward gesture with his palm. He cradles the 30-06 in his arms. The wet tundra soaks Jason's knees and quickly numbs his hands. The sling of the rifle keeps slipping from his shoulder, the butt dragging in the mud as he crawls. Finally he crouches at Brad's side.

"It's your lucky day," Brad says. "Peek over."

Raising his head over the little hill, Jason sees that the plateau slopes gently away. There's a silver lake in the next valley, many miles distant and thousands of feet below. Clouds billow over snow-covered mountains to the southwest. In the foreground, sheep nuzzle at the coarse grass, among them a glorious ram. Brad hands him the binoculars. "Now you're glad I went back for your gun. There's another one over the hill. I saw him when I was waiting. I was just about to give up on you and take this one myself."

Jason puts the binoculars to his eyes. The ram's chestnut horns spiral back, down, forward, and back again from the top of its skull, tapering to dull points. Muscles ripple under the ram's yellow white hide, and Jason's heart beats faster. Imagine, an animal like that walking around in the open air, for the taking. The ram sniffs and wanders a few paces from the ewes and lambs, then lowers its trophy head. Letting the binoculars dangle around his neck, Jason sits against the slope at his stepbrother's side. "They probably never heard gunfire before," he says, breathless.

"They'll hear some today. The other one should come over after you shoot. He's mine."

"Season doesn't start until tomorrow." The rams are right there, but they don't have the tools to dress the carcasses or the bags to hold the meat. They'd have to go all the way down the mountain and come up again before sunset, then camp here overnight. That decides it. "Let's go and have dinner, something to drink. They'll still be here tomorrow. No sense ruining the trip."

Brad turns onto his knees. He braces the rifle on his thigh, putting one hand in the grass. His eyes are fixed on the spot where the ram would be if the slope were invisible. "Why don't you quit whining and take your shot. You can't shoot, so I'm giving you the easy one. Maybe the other ram won't even come over the hill. Maybe he'll run the other way. You won't get a better chance all week. Come on, get up here."

Jason lays his gun in the grass. It's not even loaded. Brad would have a fit if he knew. Jason's surprised that he didn't check it when he went back to fetch it. "I'm just along to freeze my butt. You're the mighty hunter."

Brad crawls up and props his elbows near the top of the little ridge. "Move your rifle."

Jason's stepmother could calm Brad from his rages, but only rarely. Since she died, there's no one in the world who can talk Brad down when he wants to throw himself into the pit of an idea. Jason crouches at his stepbrother's knee, aware that anything he says now will only make things worse, that he has said too much already.

Brad's elbow twitches, and the barrel of the gun stills. When Brad pulls the trigger, Jason has to put his hands on the grass to counter the sensation of the earth tilting up, dumping him off.

The ram scrambles up, whirling. Jason raises the binoculars. Blood seeps from its flank, staining the yellow white shag. Jason puts a hand on his stepbrother's shoulder. As Brad works the rifle's bolt, the dense muscles flick beneath his touch. The ram takes three steps, sniffing the air. It kneels, then lowers itself into a sitting position, tucking its hooves under its body as though bedding down. The weight of the rack bends its thick neck sideways. The animal strains to hold its trophy upright, its eyes and nose still searching.

Scattered by the gunshot, the sheep begin to return and to graze again, though in a tighter bunch than before. They keep their distance from the fallen ram, but otherwise seem undisturbed. The ram, on its knees, bends its head to nibble at some last, close forage, and the movement topples its body. The carcass lies on its side with two legs off the ground. The ewes come up to graze around it.

"There's the other one," Brad says as the other ram comes over the rise, its head high, face locked in their direction. The muscles of

Brad's shoulder tense again beneath Jason's hand. He adjusts his aim, then pulls his eye from the scope. "Last chance."

Jason lets his hand drop to his side. Brad bends to the weapon. "That's a pretty long shot," Jason says. He's about to say more, but the crack of the rifle silences him. The ram leaps straight up, its legs higher in the front than in the rear, and lands on its side, dead before the echo of the gunshot has faded.

"You really got that one." Secondary echoes return from a rise about a mile away. Jason walks over the crest of the hill and down. "You sure proved something with that shot," he says. The ewes and lambs stampede for the cliffs. He turns. "We probably won't see another sheep this week. They won't come back for a dozen years. Boy, a black day for sheep. You got them, all right."

White-faced, Brad gets to his feet. A shell casing glints in the grass. He lays the gun against the hill. "Did we get them?"

"Oh, you got them, all right."

They walk across the open ground to the first ram, about three hundred yards from the hill. Jason hefts the trophy by the medium-thick part of one horn, then lets it down and continues on to the second ram. He examines the trophy, then walks back past Brad all the way to the little ridge where he left his pack and gun. His hands are cold. He takes out his eighteenth birthday present from Pop, a silver flask filled with good strong bourbon, and returns to where Brad stands, halfway between the first ram and the second. He offers him the flask, but Brad waves it away. Then, seeming to change his mind, he takes it, drinks, and wipes his mouth. "We'll just pretend we shot them tomorrow."

"Pop's an honest man. You had to go and poach record-book rams, didn't you? When you knew you couldn't get away with it? When you knew you could've just come back tomorrow?"

Brad squats. "What'll we do?"

Jason takes the flask out of his stepbrother's hand and screws on the cap. "You know what we have to do."

"What about the meat?"

"You tell me."

Brad stands. "The hell with the meat."

With Brad trailing behind him and to one side, Jason walks to the first ram and takes it by one horn, then waits for Brad to seize the other. They drag the bleeding, slack-bodied carcass over the grass. Jason wouldn't have thought a sheep could be so heavy.

After sunset, they stand at the western rim of the plateau. Both rams lie on the cliff edge, the animals' heads propped on their dingy horns. Their amber eyes are clouded, their hides ripped and frayed. The sky before them is the same color as the ice-capped mountains that rise against it, a watery violet-blue.

"Back to the earth," Brad says. "They would have died on their own."

"Or Pop could have shot one tomorrow."

"You hungry? Liver's supposed to be good raw."

"Sheep have parasites. I'm going to be sick as it is."

Together, they shove the larger ram over the cliff. A dull thud floats up, followed by a trickle of rockfall, and then more muffled impacts as the carcass rolls into the willows at the base of the cliff. They push the second ram over, and it tumbles into concealment with the first. Brad wipes his hands on a patch of moss. "We'll start fresh tomorrow."

It almost seems possible that they'll climb the mountain in the morning to find the rams still grazing, the trip not ruined. Perhaps when they return to California, Jason's stepmother will be alive, the hunting ranch as it was a year ago, the deer not ravaged by drought and lack of feed. "That pilot even looks at me tonight, I'm going to kick his ass. That's all I know," Brad says.

As darkness falls, even the smallest depression becomes a well of shadow. It's impossible to tell a ledge from a cliff, an easy step down from a deadly tumble. Jason's legs weigh a thousand pounds. His feet are like broken shards inside his boots. The muscles of his arms feel stretched past tearing, tightening so that each step jolts his shoulders with pain. His voice is hoarse. "How are we going to get down? We'll kill ourselves trying."

Brad walks a step ahead. "Just follow me."

HASANTHIKA SIRISENA

Bread Loaf Writers' Conference

PINE

That year Lakshmi yielded and bought a Christmas tree. In sixteen years of living in the States and eight years of marriage, she had never seen the need. If asked why, she explained this was a tradition with no place in her home. But now she could not keep one more thing from Sareth and Aruni—not after everything they had lost. So when Sareth, who was seven, asked for a tree, as he had for the past three Decembers, she said yes. It was, after all, only a pine tree with decorations thrown on it. Still, karma has its effects, and, when she recognized her uncle's voice on the phone, she felt as if he had caught her in an act of betrayal.

"Lakshmi, I need a favor," her uncle said. "The Sinhala Society has a priest from the temple in Atlanta coming for a *dhana*. He's flying into Raleigh-Durham this afternoon. I was supposed to pick him up, but I'm on call tonight. Can't you pick him up, darling? He can stay with you tonight, and I'll come by tomorrow morning."

"It's Christmas Eve, Vijay-*mamma*."

"What's that got to do with you?"

"Is it okay for the priest to stay with me? Isn't it against his vows to stay with a woman alone?"

"He's almost doddering, Lakshmi. I doubt he'll do anything to you, and I equally doubt you'll want to do anything to him. It's hardly fodder for a scandal. You have time for us, no?"

"I'm not trying to put you off. It's just that Nimal is coming tonight. He has some kind of request he has to ask in person."

"Isn't he your ex-husband now? Doesn't he have a new wife?"

"No, she's just his girlfriend."

"Well, the priest is flying in at two. Won't that give you enough time?" He paused, "It will be good for Sareth to meet a priest. Don't you think?"

Lakshmi sighed, "Yes, of course you're right."

After they finished speaking, Lakshmi walked into the living room. Amid the devil-bird masks with hissing cobras wrapped around sharp beaks, the brass plates engraved and pierced with scenes from Sinhala mythology, the batiks depicting dancers with arms flung wide and legs bent in traditional poses, the small pine tree— only a head taller than Lakshmi herself—looked comically out of place. At the abandoned lot turned boreal forest, she had surveyed the felled trees tethered together and displayed like carcasses in a butcher shop and felt dismayed by the waste. When she bought the tree the salesperson informed her, after she had asked how she was supposed to make it stand up, that she would also have to buy a tree stand, a tree skirt, and a humidifier to keep its needles from becoming dry and brittle. And she had to find decorations. At the local Kmart, she scoured rows and rows of Santa Clauses, gaudily painted reindeer with red noses, crèches, and stars, all of which she deemed too holiday specific, before she settled on a box of silver and gold globes, tinsel, and colored lights.

She and Sareth decorated the tree while her two-year-old, Aruni, sat and watched, clapping her hands and reaching for the glistening ornaments. When they finished decorating, Lakshmi stepped back to assess their work. The tree sagged under the weight of its tinseled finery and with lights blinking—red, yellow, green, red, yellow, green—it lost any resemblance to its natural form. It reminded her of a plain-faced prostitute vamped up and strutting under the neon lights of a sunset strip. But Sareth did not see it that way. Her heart tightened when she noticed him standing there, his dark, beautiful face radiant and warm like a piece of coal in a fire. He turned to her and smiled, "*Amma,* isn't it amazing?"

Two days later, he returned from school with a small package wrapped carefully in newspaper. He held it in front of him and walked gingerly, as if he were an unsteady waiter balancing a tray of glasses.

"What are you carrying?" she asked.

He held it out to her, "Open it, *amma.*"

Lakshmi unwrapped the paper. A misshapen papier-mâché star, twice the size of her hand, covered in tinfoil and decorated with glass beads, lay inside. "What is this?"

"It's the star of Bethlehem. When I told Mrs. Pratt we got a Christmas tree she was so happy she helped me make it. She said that we have to wait and put it on top of the tree on Christmas Eve."

"You shouldn't have told Mrs. Pratt we have a tree."

"All the kids have Christmas trees," he beamed, "Now I'm like them." She rewrapped the star and gave it back to him.

"Then why don't you keep it in your room until Christmas Eve."

He wrinkled his nose. "Aruni will eat it. I'm going to keep it here, where everyone can see." He unwrapped the star and placed it on the middle of the kitchen table. After a few minutes of consideration, he placed newspaper wrapping underneath the star. So it would not get hurt he told her.

She felt as if she lost him little by little each day.

That had been over a week ago. Now the tree looked even more pathetic. And, as if it were registering displeasure at its fate, a thin carpet of stale pine needles surrounded its base despite the stream of cool, moist air provided by the humidifier. She tried to keep the floor clean, but a new layer reappeared within minutes. There was nothing she could do about the tree now. She would just have to hope that the priest would not notice it.

She took a back road to the airport to avoid holiday traffic. The rural landscape was barren and lonely; large swaths of black and ochre stretched toward a sunless sky. A rare, early winter snow had fallen two nights earlier. Much of it had melted the day before and refrozen during the evening. A hard sheath covered the ground and trees. The patches of ice were cloudy and dense in the formless light of the gray December afternoon, and the landscape looked trapped under a fragile coating of glass. As she drove, she imagined reaching out and shattering the brittle world with just one warm touch.

Lakshmi arrived early at the airport so she could grab a smoke. She had tried to quit a couple of times since the divorce, without success. She had, however, reduced her habit to the occasional drag while sitting in the car just before entering or just after exiting the offices of the software company where she worked. The stress, however, of the impending visits of the priest and her ex-husband, Nimal, proved too much. The pack of cigarettes and a silver cigarette lighter with her initials engraved on the side—a gift from Nimal—now sat on the car seat beside her like faithful friends. She was not sure why she kept the lighter when she had packed up and stored everything else that reminded her of him. After months of trying to get her to quit, he had given it to her with the admonition that, if she were going to kill herself, she might as well do it in style—a bad joke. Still, the lighter reminded her of a time when they were able to laugh at each other's choices.

They had met during her sophomore year in college. Lakshmi had moved to the States when the Sri Lankan government closed the universities in order to crush student-led opposition. The shutdown, which was only supposed to last a few months, appeared as if it might, like the civil war, go on indefinitely. Her family had decided she shouldn't wait. So at eighteen, she enrolled in a small college outside of Winston-Salem with the expectation that she would go back home when she finished school.

In Sri Lanka, she had grown accustomed to the war; the violence and even the fatalistic acceptance of a life attenuated by violence had become routine. But once in North Carolina, surrounded by the pristine Appalachian landscape, she had recognized the perversity in that existence. Then, she had met Nimal at a Sinhala Society party. A business student in Chapel Hill, Nimal had lived his whole life in the States, the child of immigrant parents who believed their son would succeed only if they pushed him to be as American as possible, without any influence from their Sinhala culture. When she met him, Nimal had just started to explore what he referred to as his roots.

When she reached the terminal gate, the priest was already waiting for her. She placed the palms of her hands together and started to drop to her knees. He stopped her before she could reach the floor. "It will make all these people jealous seeing such a beautiful woman kissing the feet of an old man."

The priest was tall and fleshy. At the tip of his bulbous nose, wire spectacles balanced precariously; they seemed flimsy and ludicrously useless dangling in the middle of the priest's expansive face. He wore a black wool coat over his yellow robes; a black wool cap covered his shaved head. His left arm shielded a small bag that hung from his shoulder, and in his right hand he clutched a metal cane, though he did not seem to need it. In fact, he moved so quickly that Lakshmi, who was much smaller, had trouble keeping up.

At her car, she opened the back door, but he waved his hand in protest and opened the front passenger door instead. He paused when he noticed the pack of cigarettes and the lighter on the seat. Lakshmi reached around the priest and placed both objects on the dashboard. Great first impression, she chided herself.

During their marriage, she created for Nimal an ideal of what it meant to be Sinhalese. Cooked for him—*kirri*-bath, string hoppers, cha-patti—all the food he had never tried. Took him to temple. Lakshmi described to him what it was like growing up in Sri Lanka. What it was like to be an adult and to touch snow for the first time. Or how strange it was to have to listen to weather reports every day in order to know what to wear. When Nimal left, two years earlier, shortly after Aruni's birth, saying that maybe he had married too quickly and that he still was not sure who he was but he knew he was not Sinhala, she felt he had betrayed his family and his culture, but now she felt she had to contend with her own betrayal. She was thirty-four, no country, no marriage, and remnants of a family. Were these losses, she wondered, the price she paid for her unwillingness to return?

After Lakshmi pulled into the garage, she sat wondering if she should help the priest out of the car. He made no move, so she got out and walked around to the passenger side, but as she reached his door, the priest pushed it open quickly, and she nearly fell. He was out of the car and almost to the house before she regained her balance.

Lakshmi steered him to the back door of her house. She knew she probably would not be able to keep him from seeing the Christmas tree, but she did not want it to be the first thing he noticed. The priest, however, was more nimble than she had expected. He slipped past her and made his way into the living room. He walked straight to the tree as if, somehow, he had known it would be there.

"Your husband is Christian?"

"No *swamin-wahanse*. The tree is for my son. He's had a hard time this year, and he really wanted one."

"You're raising him as a Buddhist?"

"Yes, but it's hard here. The temple is eight hours away. I try to teach him the prayers, but he's only seven years old. I saw no harm in letting him have a Christmas tree."

The priest remained silent for a few minutes. He supported one of the silver globes in the palm of his hand and rubbed his finger across the silver veneer. The ghost of his thumbprint appeared on the shiny surface and slowly shrank away. Still holding the ornament in his palm, he said, "But you are the mother, no? You must set him on the right path. Buddhism is like a path on which we journey. We might feel tired and think that there will be no harm in stopping at an inn beside the path. But the inn is warm. The food is good. We may never leave, and then we will not reach our true destiny." A dry shudder shook the tree as the priest released the ornament; the piquant smell of pine needles was exuded like a gentle breath.

Lakshmi nodded, "Then *swamin-wahanse*, you will pray with us tonight? It will be good for my son."

"As you wish. I will pray with you and your family tonight. Your son and husband will be here soon?"

"My children are with a babysitter. She'll drop them off in a little while," she paused, "*Swamin-wahanse*, I'm no longer married, but my ex-husband is coming here tonight."

"No matter, we will still pray with him."

Lakshmi bowed her head further, "My ex-husband is coming with a friend."

"We will all pray then."

"She's not Sinhala."

The priest turned away from the tree. "This is a very American house, no?"

Lakshmi had come, now, to wonder if she had ever really loved Nimal or if he had simply represented a reason—a very good reason—not to return to Sri Lanka. Still, the divorce had been painful, and she wanted very much to ease the pain of it for Sareth and Aruni. She felt she gained nothing by keeping Nimal and his girlfriend from seeing the children. But, when she opened her front door and saw them—Nimal and Wendy—standing so close to each other, her stomach dropped.

Wendy walked immediately to the tree, "Oh, wow, it's beautiful!"

"I helped decorate it," Sareth said.

"Well, you did a good job." Wendy tousled Sareth's hair. He scowled and rubbed his hair flat with his hand.

"I thought you were against having one?" whispered Nimal.

Before she could answer, Sareth asked, "Dad, do you like it?"

"Dad?" asked Lakshmi surprised. "He's your *thathi,* Sareth."

Sareth looked up at her, eyes wide. "That's what the kids at school say."

"Your *amma* is right, " said Nimal. "You should call me *thathi.*"

Wendy smiled and nodded. "That's okay, honey. In America we call our fathers all kinds of things." She winked at Lakshmi.

Lakshmi invited them to sit on the sofa. As she sat down, Wendy scooped Aruni into her arms and held the squirming girl firmly on her lap. Aruni's tiny hands reached for a silver cross dangling from a chain around Wendy's neck.

"No, no, sweetie," Wendy cooed as she gently separated Aruni's entwined fingers.

"That's pretty," said Sareth.

"Thank you. It's an early Christmas gift from your daddy." She smiled and corrected herself, "Your *thathi.*"

Sareth turned to Nimal and asked, "Are you going to give us Christmas presents?"

Lakshmi gave Nimal a warning look. He looked away and said, "No, Sareth. No Christmas gift. But Wendy and I will give you and Aruni a New Year's gift."

Aruni grabbed for Wendy's necklace again.

"Let me take her." Lakshmi made a move toward them but Wendy waved her off.

"No, I'll just take it off." Still grasping Aruni with one hand, Wendy unlatched the necklace with the other and quickly caught it as it slowly slipped down her chest. She placed the necklace on the end table next to the sofa.

When she had first met Wendy, Lakshmi had noticed immediately the physical difference. Lakshmi was so small she bought her shoes in the junior miss section of the department store. Wendy was tall and athletic, with red hair and a round, pretty face. Tiny freckles like pin pricks covered pale, almost translucent skin.

Sareth told Wendy and Nimal about the priest staying in his room. They listened to him nodding as he described saying hello to the priest. Lakshmi was distracted from their conversation by the sound of doors opening and closing in another part of the house. She got up and walked to the kitchen. The priest stood next to the kitchen table. He wore a long, dark cardigan over his golden robes.

"*Swamin-wahanse,* can I get you something?"

"It's time to pray," responded the priest. "I will pray with you and your son in the sitting room."

"My son will sit with you now, and I will join you once my guests leave."

Lakshmi returned to the next room, and explained to Nimal and Wendy that they would have to move to the kitchen.

"That's fine. We're not planning to stay long," replied Nimal. Wendy touched his arm lightly and he continued, "We have a favor to ask you."

Sareth took Wendy's hand in his and looked up at her. "Can I sit with you in the kitchen?"

"Let's ask your *amma,*" Wendy answered, looking at Lakshmi for approval.

Lakshmi grabbed Sareth's shoulder and pulled him to her. "No, *putha,* you have to stay here and pray."

"Do I have to?" whined Sareth.

"Yes. Sit on the ground in front of the sofa and keep your sister on your lap. Listen to what the priest tells you."

With a loud huff, Sareth slumped on the floor. The priest, who had been listening in the doorway, came in and sat with them. He leaned forward and started to speak softly to the children.

In the kitchen, Lakshmi turned to Nimal. "Before I forget. Can you help me put this on top of the tree?" Lakshmi started to show him Sareth's star, but it was no longer on the table.

"That's strange. Sareth made an ornament for the top of the tree. But now it's gone."

"Maybe he took it to his room," Nimal said, "We'll ask him about it in a minute. But first I have a favor to ask you. I'm going to be baptized two weeks from now. That's a Sunday when you have the kids, but I'd like them to be at the baptism."

"You're what?"

"Wendy's family is coming, and I would like it if Sareth and Aruni could be there. It's an important day for me."

"You're converting?"

"*Amma,* Aruni won't sit still." Sareth stood in front of them holding Aruni's hand. Lakshmi pulled Aruni onto her lap.

"Go back and sit with the priest."

"I don't like him. He's weird."

"Don't talk like that about a priest, *putha.*"

"That's right, Sareth. A priest is a holy man. You should show him respect," explained Nimal.

"Do it for me. Won't you?" Lakshmi asked gently.

Sareth pulled on Nimal's sleeve and pleaded, "But he smells funny."

Lakshmi felt her face grow warm. "If I hear you say anything like that again I will punish you." She grabbed Sareth by one shoulder. "Listen to me! You're never to say bad things about a priest. Now go back and sit down!" Aruni hid her head against Lakshmi and began to whine. Sareth stood staring at Lakshmi, blinking. He turned to go.

"Sareth," Nimal stopped him, "Your *amma* said you wanted me to put your star on the tree. Do you have it?"

Sareth bit his bottom lip and pointed at the table. "I put it there."

"*Putha,* please? Just tell the truth."

"Its okay," said Nimal. "Go sit with the priest." Sareth hunched his shoulders and walked slowly away.

As Nimal turned to watch Sareth leave, the light struck the convex surfaces of his glasses and made them white and opaque. He nervously crossed and uncrossed his long, thin legs before turning back to her. "I'm sorry, I didn't think this would upset you so much, but this is important to Wendy and to me."

"Sareth is confused enough as it is."

"Look, it's not like this doesn't happen all the time in Sri Lanka. Think of all the people we know who were raised in mixed families."

"That's different. They live in Sri Lanka. Sareth has to have some grounding, Nimal. You can't just push and pull him at will."

They sat staring away from each other, the only sounds the faint electric hum of the refrigerator and the coarse rustling of fabric as Nimal continued to cross and uncross his legs. Wendy leaned over and placed her hand on Nimal's arm, "Okay, honey, let's go." To Lakshmi she said, "I'm sorry. This was a lot to put on you. We don't want Aruni or Sareth to become Christian."

"We?"

"I have respect for your culture. I think it's beautiful."

Ignoring Wendy, Lakshmi turned to Nimal and said, "You ask too much."

Nimal bowed his head. "Wendy is right. We'll go now, but please think about it."

Lakshmi buried her face in Aruni's hair without answering.

A light rain had begun to fall. Lakshmi dodged chilly droplets as she walked to her car. She slipped into the front seat, closing the door so that she could sit in the cold, crisp darkness. While her eyes were still growing accustomed to the dark, she reached for the cigarettes and lighter on the dashboard, but then drew her hand back in surprise. She switched on the car light. The pack of cigarettes was there but the lighter was gone. She felt carefully along the dashboard and checked under the seat. After a few more minutes of searching, she decided to wait until the morning, when there would be enough light to see. She sat back and closed her eyes.

She thought about Sareth and wondered what he had done with the Christmas ornament. He held so much inside himself; she could see it in the tightness of his mouth and the stiffness of his small shoulders. He had been having trouble at school lately. Some older students had taunted him. Sareth had pushed one of them before the teacher could intervene. The teacher apologized to Lakshmi, assuring her no disciplinary action would be taken against Sareth. She also told Lakshmi she was planning a special class to teach the students about the cultures in India and asked if she would like to make a presentation. We are from Sri Lanka, not India, was all Lakshmi could think to respond. Sareth refused, even when she pressed him, to talk about the incident. And after a while she stopped trying to talk to him about it, afraid to push him too hard and wondering why he would not trust her more.

The next morning Lakshmi was sitting in her kitchen, cradling a cup of coffee, when she heard the crunch of gravel as a car rolled to a stop on her driveway. She looked out the kitchen window, expecting to see her uncle. Instead it was Nimal. She opened the kitchen door for him as he walked up to the house. He came in shivering and blowing into gloveless hands. Lakshmi closed the door behind him.

"Look, first I wanted to apologize for last night. I should have come on my own, but Wendy likes the kids and she wanted to see them." Nimal laughed nervously. "Also Wendy left her necklace here last night. I just wanted to pick it up for her."

"I haven't seen it."

"She said she left it on the end table in the living room."

Lakshmi led Nimal into the next room.

"It's not here."

Nimal dropped to his hands and knees and looked under the sofa. He stood up shaking his head.

"Maybe Sareth saw it." She called to Sareth, who came running from the back of the house. When he saw Nimal, he ran and hugged him. Nimal picked him up and sat him on the sofa.

"Sareth, Wendy left her necklace here. Have you seen it?" asked Nimal.

Sareth bit his lip and shook his head slowly.

"*Putha,* we won't be angry. Just tell the truth."

"We know you just took it to put it someplace safe."

"I didn't take it!"

"Then, *putha,* who else could have?"

"The priest took it!"

Lakshmi crouched in front of Sareth and looked up at him. "I'm not mad. Just tell the truth."

"I am telling the truth. The priest took it. I saw him put it in the pocket of his sweater."

"If you saw the priest take it, why didn't you say something earlier?"

"You said you were going to punish me if I said anything bad about the priest."

Lakshmi sat back from him, resigned. Then, as if realizing the significance of a detail half seen from the corner of her eye, she turned and looked at the tree.

There was a bare space among the branches—a space where a silver ornament had once hung. Sareth followed her gaze. "He took something from the tree, didn't he?"

Lakshmi nodded, "Alright, *putha.* I'm not going to punish you. But go to my room and wait for me. I have to finish talking to your *thathi.*" Sareth pushed himself up from the sofa and ran off.

"What the hell just happened?" Nimal asked.

"My lighter is gone and the priest was the only one in the car. The star is gone and the priest was in the kitchen last night. He was in the living room alone when Sareth came into the kitchen."

"You're kidding me," Nimal groaned. "What am I going to tell Wendy?"

"Wendy? What am I going to tell Sareth?"

"Oh, he's a kid. He'll get over it. But Wendy really liked that necklace."

"Why don't you go and confront the priest? Maybe you can wrestle the necklace from him."

Lakshmi stood up and walked back to the kitchen. Nimal followed behind. "Look, I'll figure out something to say to Wendy. But now won't you at least consider letting them come to the baptism?"

Lakshmi swung around, "What do you mean 'now'? You'll lie to Wendy if I give in to you? Protect our family honor? Protect our cultural honor? Or maybe this is proof they should be Christian."

"That's not what I'm saying!" Nimal exclaimed, palms open. "I just want them to be there. They're my family."

"What about them? What about not confusing them?"

"Look Lakshmi, you don't know what it's like. To get ahead in this country you have to fit in. No one notices everything that's the same about you. Just what's different. My job is closed unless I try to fit in. These guys I work with. They actually make deals at church socials."

"You're converting so that you can advance your career?"

"No, I'm converting because that's the world I live in. My friends, my coworkers, Wendy. Wendy is very important to me. I want to share my life with her, and her religion is important to her. I personally don't care what religion I am. Hell, it's more of a sham to pretend I'm Buddhist just to make a point."

"What are you going to tell Sareth when he asks?"

"I'll tell him the truth. I thought it was the right thing to do."

"For Wendy?"

"Yes, for Wendy."

She leaned against the edge of the kitchen counter to steady her-self, "What does that say to our children?" she asked softly. "What does that tell them about who they are?"

"Lakshmi, you're not the only one who loves them. You're not even the only one who understands them. I do know what they are going through. Has it ever occurred to you I know that better than you?"

"You should go." She opened the kitchen door. As he stepped out-side, he turned to her and asked, "Seriously, what do I tell Wendy?"

"Tell her what you really think. Tell her you can't trust *those* people." She slammed the door and locked it. She kept her burning forehead against the cold wood long after Nimal's footsteps died away.

Her uncle stared at the Christmas tree for a few seconds before sitting down on the sofa.

"Don't say anything, *mamma*."

"One of my good friends—that Wikremesinghe fellow, you know him—never had a Christmas tree in Sri Lanka. He has a Christmas tree now. You know the reason this bugger gives? He's afraid his pa-tients are going to drive by his house, see he doesn't have a Christmas tree, and stop coming to him. We Sinhala are a mixed up people," laughed her uncle. "The priest gave you no trouble I hope?"

"Well—"

"Very sad life that one. His family gave him to the monastery when he was a boy because they were too poor to feed him. Can you imagine? Living seventy odd years in a monastery."

"That seems sad—to have that choice made for you."

"Still, what a hardship his life would have been without the monastery."

"Nimal's converting, *mamma*."

"All that glitters."

"He must love her very much." An emptiness tugged at her chest as she said the words.

"There's nothing you can do about that."

The priest came in, followed by Sareth, who was holding Aruni's hand. Lakshmi's uncle kneeled and bowed his head to the ground in front of the priest's feet. The priest leaned forward and gently touched the top of his head. After her uncle stood up, Lakshmi dropped to her knees before the priest and touched the ground with her forehead. When she bowed, she heard her uncle tell Sareth to do the same.

She watched from the corner of her eye as Sareth knelt in front of the priest; he looked, for a moment, just like a little Sinhala boy. As Sareth sat up, Lakshmi smiled and winked at him. He smiled bashfully in return.

As her uncle was leaving, he put his arm around her shoulder and kissed her on the top of the head. "You are coming for the *dhana*? It will be good for the children to see."

"Of course, Vijay-*mamma*. I will come."

By the time they returned from her uncle's home three days later, the tree had begun to turn brown. Lakshmi sent Sareth and Aruni back to her room to watch television. Then she started to take the ornaments off the tree. She placed one carefully in its original box. After she was done, she took the boxes, the tinsel, and the lights and crammed them deep inside one of the outside garbage cans. Back inside, she pulled the tree off the stand. Pine needles pricked at the skin revealed between her coat and gloves as she dragged the tree outside.

When she reached the garbage cans, she caught her breath and stared at the tree at her feet. Despite the bare patches where needles had fallen away, it was again a simple pine tree, sheared from its roots and resting on its side. She leaned forward, pulled it up, and balanced it carefully against one of the cans. With her foot, she arranged the gravel and dirt around the base to stabilize it further. After she was finished, it looked, at a cursory glance, as if had been planted there. Now, she mused, the tree would exist again, for a short time, as it had once been—even if it were only an illusion, even if it could never thrive.

ARYN KYLE

University of Montana

⁓

BRIDES

The first man I slept with kept his eyes closed the whole time. We did it in the prop room of my high school theater on the leather sofa my parents had donated to help me get a part in *Seven Brides for Seven Brothers.* It would have been better if my mother could have sewn costumes or if my father could have built scenery. But since my mother didn't sew and since my father said that he would rather drive a nail through his tongue than spend his weekend building cardboard shrubbery, they gave the theater department two hundred dollars for programs and the sofa we'd moved out to the garage after our dog chewed the armrest. And voilà. Townsperson Number Three. I had a line, too: *Somebody get the pastor!*

On the first day of rehearsals, I stood to the side while other cast members wrapped their arms around each other's necks and kissed each other on the cheek.

"We're all *so* close," one of the brides told me. "We're like a great big *family.*"

The brides and brothers were all juniors and seniors and the rest of the townspeople were sophomores. Our drama teacher, Mr. McFarland, didn't usually cast freshmen. He believed in working your way up.

"You learn by watching," he said. "Nobody walks in here a star."

Dilly Morris was the exception to this rule. A junior, she'd been cast as Milly—the main Bride. Besides myself, she was the only person who wasn't jumping up and down and shrieking about how happy she was to see everyone. Dilly had been the lead in every musical since she'd started high school, and there were stories about tantrums, about Dilly breaking props when she was angry, screaming at stagehands, making sound managers cry, and storming out in the middle of re-hearsals. Supposedly, she had thrown a shoe at the tuba player during *Hello, Dolly!* when he messed up the big parade song. And halfway through rehearsals of *Oliver!* she'd had Bill Sykes replaced for making farting noises with his armpit during one of her solos.

After we introduced ourselves, Mr. McFarland had us sit on the stage in a circle. We were supposed to go around and explain our characters' motivations to the rest of the cast. Everyone else had done this before. I could tell. They didn't just have lines; they had histories. Jack Owens, who was cast opposite Dilly, adjusted his baseball cap while he talked about the hardships of living off the land. Jenny Crews's character milked cows. Lisa Anderson carried water from a well. And Allison Mosely had survived an Indian attack.

When it was my turn, I stared down at my hands.

"Well, Grace?" Mr. McFarland asked. "What's your character like? What do you want?"

I squeezed my fingers around my thumbs. "I want for someone to get the pastor?"

The brothers rolled their eyes and the brides giggled into each other's hair. Dilly stretched her legs in front of her and leaned back on her hands. "But *why* do you want someone to get the pastor?" she asked.

I tried to remember what happened in the scene. "Because I hear a baby crying?" She smiled.

"Yeah?" she said. "So?"

My fingertips went cold and I could feel my throat tightening. Dilly leaned toward me. "It's because you don't think they're married," she said. "You hear a baby and you don't think they're married yet. Get it?"

I hadn't thought of that, but it made sense. It was a pivotal moment. In my single line, I was speaking on behalf of an entire history. Those frontier people were probably really strict about premarital sex.

"Thanks," I said, and Dilly winked at me. It figured that she would know about babies and religion and not being married. The year before, her older sister had gotten pregnant and dropped out of school. It was a pretty big deal, since they were Catholic and all.

After rehearsal Dilly stood at the side of the stage, whispering to Mr. McFarland, while the rest of us gathered our scripts and backpacks. The brides clustered together on stage, winking at each other and nodding in Dilly's direction. I stepped closer to them, hoping that they would let me into the circle, speak to me with the silent language of their eyes. Suddenly Dilly laughed out loud and covered her mouth with her hand. "That's *terrible!*" she cried, and Mr. McFarland tapped her forehead with his finger.

When she turned and saw us, the brides scattered, and I looked at the floor so that it wouldn't seem like I'd been watching her.

"Hey," she called and trotted across the stage to me. "Hey, you." She snapped her fingers. "What's your name again?"

I looked behind me, but there was no one there. "Grace?"

"That's right. Grace. You're a freshman, right?" I nodded. "Well, you did real good today." Her eyes dropped down the length of my body and I covered my chest with my arms.

"Thanks," I said. "You, too."

"I really like your skirt," she said, and I looked down. "It looks like something Milly might wear, don't you think?"

Something fluttered in the back of my throat and I let my arms fall back to my sides. "You can borrow it," I told her. "If you want."

"Could I?" She ran her hand down the fabric of my skirt, gathering it in her fingers. "The costume department is absolutely grotesque. It's an embarrassment."

"I have others," I told her. "Blouses, too. If you want to come over and look." I thought of my clothes adorning Dilly Morris on opening night, the fabric touching her collarbone, the curve of her throat. It was the kind of thing I would be able to tell my children one day.

Dilly drove me home and when we stepped through the front door, she stood lock-kneed in the hallway. "Ho-ly shit," she said. "Is your dad, like, a movie star?"

"He's a doctor," I told her.

"I feel like I should take my shoes off."

I sat on my bed while Dilly stood in front of the closet. "Jesus, Gracie. Look at all this." I could feel my heartbeat in the roof of my mouth. No one ever called me Gracie.

"My mom really likes to shop," I told her.

"I guess so," she said. "You're lucky. *My* mom likes to watch infomercials in bed." She pulled out garment after garment, holding them up to herself in my full-length mirror and swishing her hips back and forth.

"This is really nice of you," she said and met my eye in the mirror. "You know, most people in the department don't like me much."

I tried to picture her nailing the tuba player with her shoe. "They're probably just jealous."

She nodded. "That's what Mr. McFarland says, too."

Dilly took out every item of clothing that looked old-fashioned and piled them beside me on my bed. I was getting used to the little noises she made in the back of her throat every time she saw something she liked, the clicks she made with her tongue as she pulled clothes off hangers, the way she sucked the air in through her teeth when she held them up to herself. But then her arm went stiff in my closet and her mouth fell open like there was no air left inside her body. "Are these suede?" she asked and pulled out the pants I'd gotten for Christmas.

"Yeah," I told her, and she held them away from herself like she was afraid to touch them. "But I don't think they're something that Milly would really wear. You know, since it's during pioneer times?"

Dilly didn't answer. Slowly, she held up one pant leg and touched it to the side of her face while she closed her eyes and pressed an open hand against her heart.

"But you can borrow them for yourself if you want," I said, and she reached out and took my hand.

"Seriously? I mean, really, seriously?" Her palm was cool in mine and I could smell her hair, sweet like cocoa butter.

"Sure," I said, and she shrieked as she clutched the pants to her chest.

"You know what I think?" she asked as she slipped off her blue jeans and stepped into the pants. "I think you should be my understudy." She pressed one hand to her pelvis and the other to the small of her back as she twirled in front of the mirror.

The air emptied from my lungs and I saw into the future, the way that everything would be: I saw the two of us sitting on the empty stage, eating red licorice and running lines. In the cast picture, Dilly and I standing front and center, arms linked. Dilly having dinner at my house, spending the night, going on vacation with my family. No one would know her the way I would.

"But doesn't Mr. McFarland decide that?" I asked, and Dilly circled with her hands above her head.

"Gracie," she said, "you haven't been around long enough to know this, but things almost always work out the way I want them to."

During rehearsals, if she wasn't on stage, Dilly sat beside Mr. McFarland in the audience with her feet propped up on the seat in front of her. While the rest of us worked through songs or scenes, they would tilt their heads together, whispering through their fingers. Their voices sometimes carried across the auditorium, and their laughter erupted during scenes that weren't funny.

The day after she came to my house, Dilly watched with Mr. McFarland while the townspeople worked through our big scene. I tried to be in the moment, to feel the weight of what I was saying, to really *inhabit* Townsperson Number Three.

"Somebody get the pastor!"

When the scene was over, Dilly dipped her head toward Mr. McFarland and whispered to him through her hair. He cocked his jaw to the side and nodded. "Grace!" he called and I stepped to the edge of the stage. "Nice job with that."

"Thanks," I said.

"How would you feel about working with Dilly as her understudy?" In the audience, the rest of the cast widened their eyes. "What!?" they mouthed. The brides slumped in their seats, and Jack

Owens covered his chest with his hands and fell to the floor like he was having a heart attack.

"Okay," I said. "That would be fun."

At the end of rehearsal, Dilly came up and squeezed my shoulder. "Ignore them," she said. "The boys are morons and the brides are bitches. Oh, and also," she said. "I saw this blouse in a window downtown. Cream-colored lace." She feathered her fingers down her torso. "It would be *amazing* for my ballad in the second act. Think your mom would buy it for you?"

"Maybe," I said. "I'll ask."

"You're the best." She hugged my neck. "The absolute best. You're going to be a great understudy."

I highlighted Dilly's lines in my script and took notes while she was on stage. She started coming home with me after rehearsal. She said it was too hard to memorize lines at her house with her sister's baby crying all the time. We would sit on my bed and talk about the play, about rehearsals, about who couldn't act and who couldn't sing and what Dilly should do with her hair for the different scenes. I was her protegee, her faithful confidant, ready to step in at a moment's notice.

I imagined Dilly on opening night, deathly ill with something really serious, like tuberculosis or brain fever. I would hold her hand and brush her hair off her forehead while she twisted and moaned. "Don't worry," I would say. "*I'll* go on." It wouldn't be long before I was sitting beside Mr. McFarland during rehearsals and telling him the way *I* thought things should be. It didn't seem unreasonable. Dilly wouldn't be around forever. *Someone* had to take her place when she was gone.

In some ways, I was better than she was. I knew the words to all the songs, for one thing. In the scene where she was supposed to be singing a lullaby to her newborn baby, Mr. McFarland had to stop Dilly midsong.

"This is just embarrassing," he told her. "You don't look anything like a new mother singing her baby to sleep. You look like you have a migraine."

"It's because I'm trying to remember the words," Dilly snapped. She walked to the front of the stage, dangling the baby doll by one leg. "This is a retarded song. Can't we just cut it?"

Mr. McFarland stood up in the audience and the brothers made a big show of diving to the floor. "Look out!" one yelled, and they all covered their heads with their hands. "Get out of the line of fire!"

"I'm not cutting a song just because you don't like it," he said. "Learn the words, Dilly."

"It's so sappy," she moaned. "Wah, wah, wah. It makes me gag." She held the doll out by its leg and shook it at him.

"By next time, I want to see a loving mother up there, a mother who knows the words, a mother who doesn't waste my time by coming here unprepared."

Dilly flung the doll toward Mr. McFarland and it landed at his feet. Everything went still, and the rest of us waited while they stood, staring at one another. Slowly, Mr. McFarland bent to pick up the doll, keeping his eyes locked on Dilly's. They watched each other like two angry cats as he moved forward to hand the doll to her. "I mean it," he said when she reached down to take the baby back. "Learn the goddamned words."

Mr. McFarland interrupted the next rehearsal just before we got to the lullaby scene. Only the girls were there. The brothers had gone to a costume fitting, and the brides were trying to work through the wedding scene without them. Mr. McFarland paced in front of the stage.

"What's the matter with you?" he asked. "You're bland. You're boring. You look like a bunch of kids up there!" He looked at the ceiling and shook his head. "How do you expect three hundred people to pay money to watch you if you can't even hold my interest for fifteen minutes?" He hit his hand against the edge of the stage. "You think you can just show up and dazzle them? It's a job. You have to work for it."

We moved into the first few rows of the auditorium while Mr. McFarland pushed my parents' sofa onto the center of the stage and sat on one side of it. "Okay," he told us, "this is an exercise in charisma." Some of the girls groaned, and I turned in my seat.

"What is this?" I asked. Allison Mosely shook her head.

"The worst five minutes of your life."

"Five minutes," Mr. McFarland said, holding up one hand with his fingers extended. "Each of you gets no more than five. Don't speak to me. Don't touch me." His voice dropped and he smiled at us like it was a dare. "Just make me notice you."

He didn't make it easy. He didn't give anybody a break. One by one, the girls crossed the stage to sit beside him. They smiled, batted their eyes, and played with their hair while Mr. McFarland stared into the audience with an empty face. The harder girls tried, the worse it was. Allison Mosely kept clearing her throat. Lisa Anderson tripped and asked if she could start over. Jenny Crews tried to blow in his ear, but her aim was off and all she did was make a piece of his hair stick up.

When it was my turn, my body went stiff and I couldn't find the right way to sit. I was all edges, all knees and elbows and knuckles. I traced the chew marks on the armrest with my finger until I had to press my hands between my knees to keep them from shaking. I tried to smile, but my lips were heavy and numb and I could see the other girls watching with blank, bored faces. I turned to face Mr.

McFarland's profile, to catch his eye with the power of my mind. *Look at me. Look at me. Look at me.* But he didn't. In the audience, Dilly dipped her chin to her chest and covered her face with her hand.

When Dilly walked on stage, Jenny slumped in the chair beside me and looked up at the lights. "Here we go," she said.

Dilly crossed the stage like she was in no hurry at all and sat down beside Mr. McFarland without looking at him. Slowly, she extended her legs in front of her, crossing them at the ankles as she reached her arms up behind her head. She laced her fingers and pushed up with her palms until her whole body had curved and lengthened. She held the stretch, arching her back and closing her eyes as she tipped her chin from side to side.

"Shit," Jenny whispered and the rest of us stared up silently.

Dilly slid one foot to the side and leaned forward to adjust the strap of her shoe. Her fingers moved down to the ball of her ankle and then across the leather top of her shoe. When she sat up, she brought her leg up with her, pulling her knee to her chest and circling her arms around her leg. As Mr. McFarland began to turn, Dilly cocked her head slightly and rested her temple against her knee.

Everything went still. The space between them filled with something large, something that swelled and spread and pushed all the air from the auditorium. I felt everything else shrink under the weight of it. I thought I might be crushed. Dilly and Mr. McFarland just barely smiled before they each turned away.

As Dilly walked off, Jenny held up one hand. "How fair is that?" she asked and I looked at her.

"What?"

She leaned forward and shielded her mouth with her hand. "As long as she's fucking him, I don't think the rest of us can really hope to compete."

"That isn't true," I said. Jenny rolled her eyes.

"Oh, come on, Grace," she whispered. "It's been going on forever."

I shook my head and she sighed. "Sorry," she said, "I forgot you're Dilly Junior."

After we were all back on stage, Dilly linked her arm through mine. "I have a headache, Gracie. Want to fill in for me?" Her eyes looked heavy, like she was half asleep, and she rested her head on my shoulder. It was the perfect chance to make them all forget how I had messed up the exercise. I took Dilly's place for the lullaby scene, and she walked down and sat beside Mr. McFarland in the audience.

I knew the words perfectly. I rocked the plastic baby doll and sang to it like it was the only thing I cared about on earth. Dilly had never once performed the song like she meant it. As I sang, I thought about the two of them watching me. I was sure that out in the audience Mr. McFarland was leaning into Dilly and saying, "Look at Grace. I had no idea."

As the song finished, I leaned down and touched my lips to the doll's forehead. It was a good move. Genuine. Maybe Dilly would even borrow it when she performed. The music ended and I raised my head to look out into the audience. But the seats were empty. I hadn't lifted my eyes the whole time I was singing. I didn't know they'd left.

Dilly came home with me after rehearsal so that I could help her memorize the words to the lullaby. "I can't have you fill in forever," she said.

"How often do we have to do that charisma thing?" I asked and she smiled without looking at me.

"Why? Didn't you like it?"

"I wasn't very good at it," I told her and she looked up from her script.

"You think about it wrong," she said. "Like with Mr. McFarland. If you walk out there *afraid* of him, you're gonna suck. It's the same thing with an audience. You have to think about power. You have it. They don't. You have to make them want you." She touched my shoulder. "Make them love you. Make them go crazy stupid if they don't get enough of you."

"You were really good," I told her.

"It isn't as hard as everyone makes it out to be," she said. "The next time we do that exercise, don't go out there thinking that you need to make *him* notice *you*. Go out there thinking that he's gonna beg *you* to notice *him*." She shrugged. "Be captivating."

"I don't think I'm a very captivating person," I said, and she tilted her head.

"Then pretend you're someone who is."

Dilly stared at the ceiling and tried to recite the words to the song. She stumbled. "Shit," she said. "This is hopeless. And I can't mess up again. He'll kill me."

"You and Mr. McFarland are pretty good friends, aren't you?" I asked and her jaw tightened.

"I know what people say, and it isn't true, just in case you were wondering."

"I wasn't," I said quickly. "I wasn't wondering."

"Not that I couldn't sleep with him if I wanted to," she said. "He's head over heels for me, in case you haven't noticed. It makes him a little nutty sometimes." She smoothed the pages of her script. "But I'm not sleeping with anyone. And do you know why?"

I bit my lip. "Because you're Catholic?" I asked. "Because of God?"

"God?" she said. "I don't give a shit about *God*. Look at what happened to my sister. Did you know that she used to be a straight A student?" I shook my head. "She could have been a doctor, like your dad. But not anymore." She sighed. "I've got a real shot at something, Grace. I'm not going to screw it away like she did."

"Do you love him?" I asked and something in her face hardened.

"Love has nothing to do with it." She looked down at her knees. "He knows what I am, what I could be. He understands."

Dilly never forgot the words to the lullaby again, but it wasn't because she'd memorized them. She tried a few times, but finally she got frustrated and wrote the words on a tiny piece of paper that she taped to the baby doll's face.

"Look at that," Mr. McFarland said while she was singing. "Do you see that? I want to believe the rest of you as much as I believe her."

But the performance dates were getting closer, and Dilly didn't seem to care about Mr. McFarland's compliments anymore. It was everyone else she was worried about. Nobody did anything well enough. We were clumsy, or off-key, or stepped on her lines. "I hate you all!" she would scream during rehearsals. "Just do it fucking right!" I waited for Mr. McFarland to step in, for him to calm her down or shut her up. But unless she was fighting with him, he didn't seem to notice.

Dilly seemed to enjoy pointing out everything Mr. McFarland had done wrong. The sets were phony, or flimsy, or put together wrong. The props weren't in the right places at the right times. The orchestra was too big, the backstage crew was too small, and the leather sofa looked absolutely ridiculous on stage. It was supposed to be the turn of the century, after all. Would they really have an Ethan Allen sofa sitting around in their log cabin?

Mr. McFarland paced and swore and held his hands up in defeat. "I've done everything I can," he told her. "What else can I do for you?"

She narrowed her eyes at him. "Nothing," she said slowly. "There is nothing else you can do for me." She turned her back and Mr. McFarland hit the sofa with his fist as he walked off stage.

They didn't say another word to each other until the last week of rehearsals, when Dilly was working through her fight scene with Jack. In the middle of it, she pushed his shoulders hard with her fists and stomped to the front of the stage. The pushing part wasn't in the script.

"What now?" Mr. McFarland asked. He was sitting in the seat behind me eating potato chips he'd bought from the vending machine.

"He's supposed to be about to hit me," Dilly said, and I could feel Mr. McFarland's foot kicking against the back of my chair. "He looks like he's getting ready to serve a volleyball!"

Jack stood behind her and raised his hands like he was going to strangle her. In the audience, the rest of the cast laughed and Dilly whirled around to face him. "Sorry," he said. "I don't have a lot of experience hitting girls."

"Have you ever watched a movie?" she asked. "A TV show? Jesus, it's not that complicated."

"Enough!" Mr. McFarland called. They both looked at him. "Dilly," he said. "Stage right. Jack, stage left." They looked out with puzzled faces, but they moved to their assigned sides of the stage.

"Dilly," he said. "Try to get to the other side of the stage. Jack, don't let her get there."

On the stage, Dilly and Jack stared at each other.

"How?" Jack asked and Mr. McFarland held up his hands.

"However you can," he said. "I don't care how. Just don't let her get there."

Dilly's body went still, and I could see the veins in her throat, the tremor in her breath. Her lip quivered slightly as she looked at Mr. McFarland. "What is this?" she asked, but he didn't answer.

"Go!" he said instead.

Dilly took a few tentative steps forward. Jack stood with his feet apart, his arms out to the sides. Behind me, I could hear Mr. McFarland's breath, faster, heavier than it had been a moment before. Dilly glanced into the audience and then turned and ran toward Jack.

"Stop her!" Mr. McFarland called and Jack caught Dilly around the waist. They struggled for a second, a tangle of arms and legs, and Dilly broke free.

"Come on!" Mr. McFarland rose to his feet and grasped the back of my chair. Jack looked confused, but he dove and caught Dilly by one leg. She pitched forward, falling facedown on the stage. The crack of her bare arms hitting the floor reverberated through the auditorium.

"That's it!" Mr. McFarland yelled. I could hear Dilly struggling fiercely.

Jack pulled Dilly backward by the cuff of her blue jeans and she flipped onto her back and tried to kick at his hands with her free leg. But Jack climbed on top of her, pinning her shoulders to the stage.

Behind me, Mr. McFarland kneaded the back of my chair with his hands until it began to rock back and forth under the pressure.

As Jack began to get up, Dilly lifted her knee between his legs and Jack's head wrenched back. He fell onto his side. In a flash, Dilly was across the stage. When she reached the opposite wall, she put her hands flat against it and leaned forward, her shoulders heaving. She stood like that for a moment and then turned toward us. Her lips were wet, her forearms pink and raw where she had hit the floor. On the other side of the stage, Jack lay moaning on the ground.

Slowly, the cast turned to look at Mr. McFarland who stood rigid behind me. "Let's get back to work," he said. I kept my eyes on Dilly, but I could feel the heat of his breath on the part in my hair, the ridges of his knuckles against my shoulder blades.

———

The day of our first performance, Mr. McFarland called the whole cast out of first period. We gathered on the stage with our books in our arms, looking back and forth at each other for an explanation. When Mr. McFarland came out of his office, his eyes were red around the rims. He told us to sit down, that he had something to tell us.

"Dilly isn't here yet," I said, and he covered his mouth with his hand.

"I have some bad news." His jaw was clenched and his Adam's apple trembled in his throat.

"Oh, God," Lisa Anderson said. "Dilly's dead."

"No," he said quietly, and he lifted his head to look at us. "Her sister's baby is."

Everything went still and cold and my head felt heavy, like it had filled with water.

"What happened?" Jenny asked.

Mr. McFarland pressed his fingers into the ridge of his forehead. "They don't know. They just woke up this morning and the baby was . . . They just woke up this morning and found her."

"Dilly's not performing then?" I asked.

Mr. McFarland straightened. "She won't be in school. But she'll be here tonight." He nodded to himself. "Dilly's a professional," he said. "She'll be here."

That night Dilly didn't speak to any of us. A couple of the girls tried to hug her, but she shook them away. She sat alone before the mirror, putting on her makeup. And then she dressed in my clothes and took her place on stage without ever meeting anyone's eye. When the curtain rose, she filled with life. She sang and danced and kissed and fought. The audience cried, and during curtain call she blew kisses to the little girls in the front row. When the curtain fell, she buried her face in her hands. Mr. McFarland put his hand on her shoulder, but she slapped it away and left him standing by himself.

Dilly hung my clothes back in the costume room and left without saying good-bye. She did the same thing the next night. And the next.

On the fourth day, she called me. "The viewing is tonight," she said. "Before the show. I can't go alone."

"What about your mom?" I asked.

"She can't handle it," she said. "She hasn't left her room since we found—since it happened." Her breath was slow and heavy. "Will you come or not?"

When I climbed into her car she held up her hand. "Don't ask me how I am," she said. "Because I'm fine. I'm perfectly, one hundred percent fine."

The room at the funeral home was dim and small. I stood behind Dilly in the doorway and looked at two rows of folding chairs. The room was empty except for a girl, a softer, paler version of Dilly, who sat alone in the front row. A ceiling light cast onto a tiny white casket and I turned my head away when I realized what was inside.

"This is my sister," Dilly said to me. "This is Grace."

The sister looked at me with dead, empty eyes and I wasn't sure what I was supposed to say. "You guys look a lot alike," I said.

"Nobody's here," the sister said to Dilly.

"Who would come?" Dilly asked. "We don't know anybody." The sister nodded and Dilly sat down beside her. "Have a seat, Grace," she said. But I was afraid to lift my eyes off the carpet for a single second. I couldn't trust them. I knew where they would look.

"I can't stay long," Dilly said to her sister. "I have to get into makeup."

"No," the sister said. "No, you can't leave me here by myself." My knees and ankles were beginning to tremble, and I touched the wall to steady myself.

"I don't have a choice," Dilly said quietly and put her hand on top of her sister's. "People are *counting* on me."

The sister's voice caught in her throat. "*I'm* counting on you." She started to cry. "Please don't leave me here by myself." The room was too hot, but I felt cold all over. I clenched my jaw to keep my teeth from chattering, but the motion forced the chatter down into my stomach so that my whole body shook.

Dilly pushed her sister's hair behind her ear with one hooked finger and touched her chin to her sister's shoulder. "I told you I wouldn't be able to stay," she said, and the sister leaned forward to cry into her knees. Dilly stood up and twisted her hands in front of her. "I don't know what to do," she said. Then she looked at me. "Grace," she said.

"No," I said.

Dilly took my arm. "Grace, listen."

"No."

"Just for a little while. So she isn't alone."

I walked into the hallway and Dilly followed me. "You knew this," I said to her. "You knew you were going to do this the whole time."

"Grace," she said. "I have to be there. You know I have to be there." I couldn't stop the shaking. It was everywhere now, in my lips and eyelids, in the soles of my feet.

"I can't," I told her. "I won't know what to do."

"Jesus Christ, Grace. You don't have to *do* anything. You don't even have to talk. Just sit there." I shook my head. "You know I have to be there, Grace. You *know* it."

"So do I," I told her. "I have to be there, too. I have a line."

Dilly hit her hand against the wall. "For fuck's sake, Grace, somebody else can call for the pastor!"

We didn't say much, the sister and I. She asked me how old I was and I told her. She asked me if I liked school and I said yes. I stared down at my lap and tried to think of reasons to leave. I couldn't call my parents. They were at the play.

A couple of people came—the sister's friends from school—and each time one did, I thought how I could get up and walk to the bus stop, how I could get back to school in time for the second act. In time to call for the pastor. But none of the friends stayed longer than a few minutes, so each time, before I could get up the nerve to go, the sister and I were alone again. While I was staring at my hands, she stood up and walked over to the casket.

"Do you like her dress?" she asked me.

"Uh-huh," I said, even though I was looking down and couldn't see it.

"It's a christening dress," she said. "I think it's beautiful."

I pulled my knees to my chest and wrapped my arms around them to keep from shivering.

"Would you like to hold her?"

"What?" I asked and when I looked up, the sister was standing in front of me with her arms full of lace and white eyelet.

"Here," she said and held it out to me. My arms moved without my mind and I stared straight ahead without looking down. It felt like nothing. It smelled like nothing. I watched the wall in front of me. If I didn't look, it wasn't real. It was nothing.

By the time I got back to school, the play was over and everyone was gone. I stood in the darkened costume room and shifted through Dilly's wardrobe until I found one of my skirts and blouses. I had to change my clothes. I had to get the feeling of the funeral home off my body. The costume smelled like Dilly's sweat and perfume, and I imagined I could still feel the heat from her body. I looked at myself in the mirror. She would miss the clothes. But that was just too bad. They were mine, after all. I was allowed to take them back if I wanted to. And I did. I wanted to take back all the things that were mine.

I pulled my clothes off the hangers and piled them next to the door. There would be nothing left for her tomorrow night, I thought. She could wear a potato sack for all I cared. She could go naked.

I thought of my parents' sofa in the prop room. I wouldn't be able to get it home, but I could beat it up if I wanted to. I could rip it apart with scissors and pull out all the fluff. I could peel back the leather and hide it in the Dumpster outside. I couldn't take it back, but I could make it worthless.

The prop room was dark, but it wasn't empty. From the doorway, I could make out the silhouette of a person sitting on the sofa. "I knew you'd come back," Mr. McFarland said.

"You did?" I asked.

"Grace?" he said, and I nodded. "I'm sorry." His voice was dull and sleepy. "I thought you were. . . . You're wearing her clothes."

"They're my clothes," I said. "I loaned them to her."

"Why are you here?" he asked.

"Why are you?"

The air was warm and the room smelled safe, like sawdust and tempera paint. "I don't have anyplace else to be," he said. I could still only see his outline in the dark. He wasn't a real person. He was only the shape of one.

"Neither do I," I said and stepped closer to him.

"Has she said anything to you?" he asked.

I took another step forward. "She's fine."

"But she never says anything," he said. "Does she talk to you?"

I could make out a face now. The whiteness of his skin. The dark sockets of his eyes. I could feel him breathing. I could hear his heartbeat. "She never talks about *you*," I said.

I stood in front of him, close enough to smell his hair, to touch the toe of his shoe with mine. I could make him want me. I could make him love me. I could make him go crazy if he didn't get enough of me.

I slid my knee between his. "I held a dead baby tonight," I said and his legs tightened around mine. His breath was harder. His hands moved up my hips and closed around my waist. As I reached out to touch his hair, he closed his eyes and leaned his face into my chest, pulling me closer and inhaling into the fabric of my blouse. He tightened his grip and breathed openmouthed into my clothing like he'd never tasted air. Like he'd spent his whole life hungry. And then I was underneath him, under the heat of him, under the weight of him, under the moment of him that belonged to me. He didn't kiss me. He didn't say my name. He didn't open his eyes until we were finished.

MICHAEL LOWENTHAL

Wesleyan Writers Conference

You Are Here

Given a clear day, Father Tim was hoping to move confession to the Liberty Deck, where penitents could come clean beneath the pure tropical sun. But this Monday, as on the first two days of the *Destiny*'s voyage, the sky is a sallow mess of cloud, and by lunchtime there's unrelenting drizzle. After the meal he heads for the chaplain's office, a revamped supply room by the Pirate's Cove Casino.

A squat, fiftyish woman waits already by the door. Her hair is limp and lusterless—what his mother, who grew up in Wisconsin, would call "sauerkraut hair."

"Pardon me," she says. "Are you the priest?"

For the cruise Father Tim has ditched his collar, identifying himself only by a blue nametag that says FATHER TIM in cheery sans-serif type and that, he now notices, is camouflaged against his azure guayabera. He points to the tag. "Truth in advertising."

Her gaze follows his finger, then darts back to his head, then takes in the whole of him again. He can tell she expects a priest to be older than twenty-seven, with a puffy, underwhelming body and burst-capillary face, not his firmly gym-enhanced physique. The sunglasses probably don't help, either. He removes them and says, "Step into my office."

Ordained just last month, he's yet to hear his first confession, which is what the *Destiny Daily* touts as his role here. But given the holiday atmosphere, and because it's his twenty-something style, there will be no "Bless me Father, for I have sinned." In this floating village where every imaginable service has been arranged, Father Tim is the hired shoulder to cry on.

The lank-haired woman has apparently gotten a jump-start on the crying. The flesh below her eyes looks like dough that's risen and been punched down. She sits in one of two canvas director's chairs—coral-and-white, the *Destiny's* official colors—and Father Tim takes the other. Aside from the chairs, all that's provided in this makeshift confessional is an end table and a box of Kleenex. The space is sharp with the smell of deodorizer.

"My first customer," he says. "What's on your mind today?"

The woman crosses and recrosses her arms. "I'm bad," she says, and he's about to reassure her that despite our mistakes we are all created in God's image, when he realizes what she really said was, "I'm Babs."

"Nice to meet you, Babs. How's the cruise so far? You here on your own or with someone?"

"My husband, Les," she says. "It's our twenty-fifth anniversary. The Renewal of Vows Package."

"Aha! You know I'll be officiating at the ceremony on Friday."

Babs stares at her ragged fingernails.

"The Renewal of Vows," says Father Tim, treading conversational water. "They spoiling you rotten?"

Through the thin wall between them and the casino, he can hear clicking poker chips, the whir of balls in roulette wheels.

"Oh, it's just perfect," she says in a scraped-thin voice. "It's all just so perfect. His-and-hers bathrobes, fresh orchids every morning. Today, breakfast in bed—took one bite and threw up."

"You're having trouble with Les?" he surmises.

A single tear forms at the lip of Babs's eyelid. He plucks a Kleenex and presses it into her hand.

"It's all right," he says. "We all hit rough patches." But he's never faced marital troubles—and now, of course, never will.

Babs blots the tear from her wan, doughy cheek. She tells him about Les, who's in crop insurance back in Kansas, specializing in hail and twister damage. He's a good man, she says, a solid father. And if he's no Harrison Ford, well, she loves him anyway. She's come to count on his Bud belly and his droopy ears the way you get fond of a tumbledown house, how the pantry floor doesn't quite level with the kitchen.

"But I've never felt," she says, "you know"—her voice downshifts to a whisper—"the way you're supposed to. That way."

That way, thinks Father Tim. How do any of us know how "supposed to" feels? It's why for so long he failed to recognize his own faith.

Now a steady flow of tears begins. He lays the box of tissues in her lap.

"I've always known something was missing," she says, "but I wouldn't let myself see just what. The kids kept me busy. Now they're gone, Jenna to K State and last year Kyle to Notre Dame, and the empty feeling's back, even worse—like, no matter where I go, what's really happening is happening somewhere else. My mother always said that perfect is the enemy of good, and I'm sure I don't need perfect. I just never reckoned good would feel so bad."

He wants to pat her shoulder, but these days boundaries call for overcaution; he's been trained, when it's one-on-one, not to touch.

"With the kids away," she continues, "I got e-mail so we could keep tabs. As long as it was there, why not have some fun? I joined an online bridge tournament. That's how I met Denise."

The rest pours out in hot, hushed, rapturous shame. Denise is from Salina. Tall and blond. They've gotten together a dozen times, when Les was inspecting crops. They've talked and hugged. They've kissed, but nothing more.

"When I'm with her," Babs says, "I feel like I've finally gotten *there*. We're the center. Everyone else is just the fringe."

Father Tim wasn't expecting this from Babs. But can he condemn her thrill in a change he too has felt? She's just described—better than he's ever managed to—the centripetal force of opening himself to God, when suddenly he started living at life's hub. The crush of it: turmoil and romance.

But his love was God; hers is a woman. He looks hard at her and asks, "Does Les know?"

"He suspects something, but he'd never guess what." Babs's hair has now fallen across her eyes—drooping, damaged hair, like shocks of wheat battered by a squall. "It's wrong," she blurts. "I know it's wrong."

He can't tell if she wants him to absolve her or to say, *Yes, it's a sin and you must stop.*

"Marriage is a sacred commitment," he begins. "A commitment to Les and to God." It comes out hesitant and tinny, first notes from a borrowed instrument. "But you also have a commitment to yourself. How can you honor God's truth if your own life is false?" That's closer, almost his normal voice. "The key," he says, "is telling what feels true from what is."

A cheer is audible from the casino, then a faint metallic jackpot clang—someone else's luck, distant and muted. Father Tim looks into Babs's runny eyes and sees in them, blurry and reduced, himself. He asks, "Do you feel like renewing your vows would be false?"

She bows her head. "I feel like jumping overboard."

After she's gone, Father Tim waits out the rest of the hour. He wants to keep the door open so other visitors will know he's available, but like all the *Destiny*'s doors, this one shuts itself with coffin-lid finality. He pulls his chair to the threshold and makes himself a human doorstop.

He's stiff with frustration. What more could he have done for Babs in the wake of her dire disclosure—told her to pray, to recite the rosary? All he gave her was another minute of clunky advice and an offer to meet again, as much as needed.

He listens to ukuleles tinkling from a lower deck, the kind of music that might accompany a limbo contest. (On this ship, it probably does.) A month ago at the Catholic Games, the tongue-in-cheek seminary Olympiad, he placed second in the Don't-Get-Stuck-in-Limbo event. Already, he sorely misses Saint Thomas: the expectancy, the joyful striving. That was all just preparation for this, now. But what if it turns out that he enjoyed the long rehearsal better than he enjoys the show itself?

The hour passes without another caller. People take cruises, he figures, to indulge in fresh sins, not generally to reconcile those past. He replaces his chair, debating whether to head directly to his cabin, or to hit the spa for some ionotherapy.

The door slams behind him, and his still-full stomach lurches as though a wave has broadsided the ship. He's steadying himself when someone calls his name.

"Tim?" she says again. "It *is* you!"

He turns to face a woman in a *Destiny* uniform, eyes hidden behind mirrored shades but a mile of leg exposed. Her skin is tanned to the hue of his crème brûlée from lunch.

"Don't you recognize me?" She whips off the glasses, shakes her hair free from a coral baseball cap.

When he sees all of her, his gut lurches again. "Alison," he says. "I can't believe it." She has the same beauty he remembers: catlike, all arches and grace. But gone is the college girl's look-away expression, replaced by a disarming, full-bore stare.

"It's so good," he says, forgetting to add "to see you." "Are you here for—" He gestures to the supply room/chaplain's office. "Something you want to confess?"

She looks at him perplexedly, then at the door, then back at him. "You aren't? Oh, my gosh, you really are." She taps his nametag and hoots. "Father Tim! No, Father, I have nothing to confess. I mean, other than what you already know."

"Then what are you—"

She points at her uniform. "Shore Excursion Manager. But right now I'm on my way to the goombay drumming show. It's fun. Come on, we'll have a blast."

And so he's tugged to the Paradise Lounge.

What'll I wear? was the first thing Tim wondered when he opened his last semester's grades. The seminary had a deal with Sun Line Cruises, filling one slot each year in the chaplaincy rotation. The cushy Caribbean stint went to the Saint Thomas MDiv with the highest marks in his class; Tim's final set of As clinched the spot.

He knew the week at sea wouldn't be a totally free ride. But he thought of old *Love Boat* episodes in which kindly Doc, the shipboard physician, dispensed Band-Aids and an occasional aspirin, but mostly socialized and lived the good life. Tim imagined himself on the *Destiny* as a similarly carefree doctor of the soul, applying spiritual Mercurochrome: Say two Hail Marys and meet me at shuffleboard.

Comparing himself to a television personality wasn't especially far-fetched; strangers did it to him all the time. "You're that guy from CNN," they would guess, stopping him on the street; or, leaning across his booth in a restaurant, "Wait, don't tell me: the guy who kissed Ally McBeal in the Christmas episode?" He had a best-supporting-actor sort of handsomeness, softened by just enough im-perfection that people felt they could approach him, but that doing so was a privilege. The dimple between his eyebrows gave him an affect of compassionate concern. A chronic crick made him tilt his neck un-consciously to the left so he always seemed to be listening for trouble.

Already in his role as a deacon, Tim had seen how good looks worked to his advantage. Other seminarians, with their frail figures and acne-scarred chins, gave off a eunuchy air of hopelessness; people pitied them, discounted their advice. But Tim's bullish eyes and veiny forearms won the attention of even the most agnostic parishioners. For him, they assumed, the priesthood was not a fallback but a choice. And if the church's message was compelling enough to win this hunky man, maybe they, too, should listen up.

Tim's turn to the church was unexpected. He'd always called him-self a Catholic because his father had been one, and that trumped his mother's lapsed Lutheranism, despite—or perhaps because of—his father's absconding when Tim was six. But without his father to im-part its rituals, Tim's Catholicism lived in him as a palpable absence, like the whiff of incense that haunts a room long after the stick is snuffed.

At eighteen he chose Boston College, not for its Jesuit tradition but because they offered the best scholarship. He enrolled in the

School of Management, intending to manage his way into the upper class. He was not ashamed of his family's poverty, but it wearied him. Almost every night of his childhood he'd been woken at 1:00 A.M. by his mother's return from moonlighting at the diner; her car door's slam was the very sound of her prospects being shut off. She'd been caught unprepared when her husband walked away, too reliant on her faith in love alone.

He breezed through first semester, acing Statistics and Intro to Accounting, although the courses, like most everything, bored him. He liked his classmates, or at least wanted to be liked by them, investing in their attention as if purchasing futures in social standing. He was asked to pose for the "Men of Boston College" calendar, and he agreed because the photographer let him keep a varsity wardrobe Tim could never have afforded. He strode across campus with ground-gulping strides, dressed in the clothes of a man he thought he longed to be.

In his second year he met Alison, the star shortstop of BC's softball team. She was pixyish and lean and looked finely bruiseable, but there was infield dirt beneath her fingernails. He got a kick from her alertness, the way she charged into conversations as if each comment were a double-play ball to be nabbed. Their sex was all hustle, headfirst.

For spring break, Alison was joining an immersion service project: ten days at an El Salvador orphanage. Tim signed up, too, wanting to prove himself worthy of her affections. Maybe her faith in him would boost his faith in himself. On the plane they sat together and squeezed hands during gut-drop turbulence.

The orphanage director was Padre José, a priest who, with his unflinching stare and hydrant-thick neck, would have made a convincing fireman, someone whose net you would happily plunge into. In fervent English he explained his mission's method: The orphanage was an active construction site. The boys worked hard—framing walls, tiling roofs—and as they built their home, he built them into men. These were boys who had never felt secure, the priest said, so they lacked the right emotional infrastructure. He was teaching them love from the ground up. "After all, Jesus was a carpenter! 'God the Father' is not merely a metaphor to these boys. The Church becomes their home, their family."

Afterward, Alison wanted to explore the town's cafés, but Tim said he'd look for her later. He stayed up past midnight with the fire-eyed priest, sharing philosophy and rum.

In the morning they excavated a new foundation hole for a bedroom to house the youngest boys. Tim's palms blistered, but he didn't mind the pain. When the shovel hit a rock it hummed like a tuning fork, and Tim's body, too, reverberated. With every shovelful he dug out for the orphanage foundation, he felt his own hollowness filling up.

That Sunday, in Padre José's whitewashed church, Tim received his first communion in years. When the priest asked the congregation to join hands in a prayer of peace, Tim gripped the clay-caked fingers of two orphans. The comfort was comparable to holding hands with Alison, but deeper, an anchoring.

Back at school, he began attending Mass every week, then every day. BC's gothic towers and its golden eagle bust—once emblems of all he wanted to achieve—now seemed flimsy backdrops to a much more urgent drama. He'd always been skeptical of see-the-light accounts. This wasn't like that, he assured himself—but it almost was. No glittering revelation, no bolts from on high, but an unforeseen inevitability. Before, he had felt like a river's fickle current; now, he felt like the riverbed. He woke each day with a trembling heart, as if in love.

It was softball season. Alison had on her game face when he tried to explain himself. They stopped assuming they would spend weekends together. The spare toothbrush in his bathroom went unused. On Easter Monday, through his soft tears and Alison's sharp silence, Tim officially broke things off.

In May, during finals, he got an e-mail. "I've been thinking of you," wrote Padre José. "That look in your eyes when you hugged the boys good-bye. You have so much to give. Will you let yourself?"

Tim withdrew from the School of Management and transferred to Saint Thomas. His classmates couldn't fathom the switch. Did he realize the income he'd give up? But money—like romance, like a father—could disappear. The need to serve would always remain.

The day he moved he saw Alison at the campus bookstore, trading in her used texts for petty cash. She was dating the ace reliever on the baseball team, she boasted, but her smile was so tight it must have hurt.

Father Tim scans the Jolly Roger Room. He's four minutes early for their nightcap. This afternoon, as they were sitting down for the goombay drumming show, Alison was summoned by her office—some problem scheduling a parasailing trip. She proposed this late-night drink as a rain date.

The Jolly Roger Room is where, in the morning, Father Tim celebrates Mass. At that hour, with its velveteen hush and suggestive dimness, the space is not altogether unchurchly; crowded now with brandy-breathed revelers its decor strikes him as "bordello lite." The looseness is too forced to ring true, like a businessman's blue jeans with ironed creases.

On a table just inside the entry sits a twice-life-sized bust of a woman. Oddly jaundiced, the sculpture looks familiar. He's puzzling over the resemblance when a thin, goateed man presents himself. Visitors to the Jolly Roger Room, he explains, have their photos taken and dumped into a bowl. Each day he selects one snapshot randomly and carves a corresponding "Butter Bust."

Catchy, Father Tim acknowledges—he saw something similar at the Wisconsin State Fair—but he tells the man no thanks, not for him. "Oh, you must," the artist insists, aiming a Polaroid before he can duck away.

At the front of the lounge, bathed in black light that makes their teeth fluoresce, Kip's Kalypso Kings libidinously perform. Kip, a jowly, ash-skinned man who, according to his bio on the drinks menu, once sang backup for Jimmy Buffett, croons "Day-O" as if it were a love song. Father Tim taps his foot but resists humming along. He decides to leave and walk the deck for a minute, hoping Alison will be here when he returns. As he pivots, a hand on his waist halts him.

"Hey, Father," says Alison in the same cozy tone she used back in college for "Hey, Twinkle." ("Hey, Star," he'd respond, and kiss her nose.)

"Hi there," he says, winking. "Come here often?"

She leads him to a booth at the side. Where she touched him he feels a phantom grip.

Alison orders a strawberry margarita. When Father Tim asks for Glenlivet on the rocks, she arches a roguish eyebrow.

"What'd you expect?" he says. "A Virgin Mary?"

"I'm just surprised you'd spring for the good stuff, is all. You were always a well-drink kind of guy."

He likes how they've slipped back to their old repartee. It's all the more enjoyable now for being safer, their boundaries defined, so that neither one is trying to gain advantage. "You look wonderful," he says. "Really great."

"You're the one who's buffed and polished." She squeezes his biceps. "'Father What-a-Waste.' That's what my mom always called guys like you. Who'd have guessed that Mr. Men of BC Calendar would wind up a priest?"

He says, "That was a long time ago."

Alison plays with the parasol that came with her margarita, the same magenta as her fingernails.

She never used to paint her nails, he thinks. "Tell me," he says, "how'd you end up here?"

She fills him in on the missing years: a softball coaching stint at a prep school in Rhode Island, then back to Boston, a Back Bay PR firm. "A real job, you know? Put the communications degree to work. Communication? Ha. Ended up being me, alone at a desk, writing press releases and faxing them to who knows." She swigs an antidote of margarita. "I'd always dreamed of taking a cruise, so when I quit, it's the first thing I did. I liked it so much, I made them hire me! Oh, don't look so shocked. Not like you never had a quick conversion."

"If you know what you want," he says, "great."

"I'm not going to do this forever. But for now? I couldn't be happier."

The Jolly Roger Room has filled to capacity. At the next table a portly black man and his Japanese lady-friend sip from a scorpion bowl with two Crazy Straws. Behind them sit an older, lei-wearing white pair, feeding each other calamari. The Kalypso Kings warble "I Want to Hold Your Hand." The couples moon at one another and sway along.

Father Tim feels the space between him and Alison shrink and swell, like a balloon in fluctuating air pressure. It's been months since his last private, nonchurch conversation with a woman.

"What about you?" she asks. "When you transferred, I was sure it was just a phase."

He shrugs. "If it's a phase, it's a pretty long one."

"I just wondered." She twirls her miniparasol, then sucks its wet stem. "Was I that bad in bed? To make you swear it off for good?"

"It's always the celibacy! Give me a huge break." Seeing her chastened face, he softens. "But no, not any fault of yours. Trust me." In fact, he remembers her expertise vividly. And more than that, just her presence, her jazz. In these cloistered years he's held tight to certain images: Alison head-sliding into home to beat a throw, a crescent moon of belly visible; in El Salvador, Alison gobbling an empanada, salsa in dribbles on her chin.

She takes his fingertips, a slight but ardent touch. "Can you try to explain? Why did you do it?"

How do you explain why even the blind know how to smile? Why whistling and laughter are contagious? "I know it looked sudden. But I'd always felt sort of off-course. After that service project, it was like somebody turned the map around, like I'd always been reading it upside down. Boom, there was that arrow: YOU ARE HERE. The church is where I am. God is where."

As though buffing a gem to determine if it's real, she rubs at the knuckle of his thumb. "I believe in God, too," she says.

"But I want to *serve* him. To make a difference. To help others feel that same groundedness." He envisions Babs's blotchy, frightened face.

"Can't you do that without," Alison says, "you know?"

He yanks his hand away. "Still stuck on sex."

"No, it's just…okay, maybe I am. How can you live without being sexual?"

"I am. Everybody is. That doesn't mean I have to express it genitally." He hears how clinical that sounds and cringes, tries again: "Ally, to be human is to be finite. By choosing one thing, we always give up something else."

"Aren't you scared of being lonely? What about marriage?"

He braces himself with a sip of scotch. "Most people get married for the wrong reasons," he tells her, repeating something his rector once told him. "Or incomplete reasons. Naive ones. But eventually they grow into it, and it's right. Maybe choosing celibacy is the same."

They sit at a silent impasse. When the waitress comes they decline a second round. The neighboring couple—the hefty black man and his fine-boned companion—punch and slap at each other's shoulders. It's a mock argument, a tipsy mating display, but Father Tim senses underlying tension.

"The funny thing," Alison says. She has twisted her swizzle stick into a crooked helix, and stares at it as if it might reveal her future. "I kind of thought you and I would get married."

"Ally, we dated less than a year."

"I know, but I just had a feeling. Nobody else ever seemed so right."

A hot burst of something erupts in his chest, on the edge between soothing and unpleasant. He's swallowed too much scotch, or not enough.

He asks, "What happened to what's-his-name, with the curveball?"

"Topher? Uch, was that a bad rebound. The guy kissed like he was spitting tobacco. He shipped off to the minors, and I didn't return his calls."

They laugh at Topher's expense, and at the distance of their past. Father Tim fills with startling relief.

In the morning he returns to the Jolly Roger Room for Mass. Some dozen cruisegoers are in attendance. There's a couple in matching canary jogging suits who bicker about the husband's need for a shave. Next to them rests a raisin-faced, copper-haired grandmother with her grandson, a drowsy teen in shorts.

Father Tim officiates from a table with a napkin wedged under one of its legs for balance. Wearing full vestments before this holiday congregation he feels uncomfortably overdressed, a tuxedoed judge at a swimsuit competition. (Earlier, he found the previous chaplain's note: "If you get too hot, the a/c control's behind the bar—chasubles weren't designed for the tropics!")

Halfway through his homily something shifts, a change more of subtraction than addition, as when a blaring car alarm finally stops. He sees the effect on the worshippers' faces—they slacken with a kind of beatific relief. He'd like to think they're transformed by his words, or the comfort of the Holy Spirit, but what they're feeling is that the *Destiny* has docked.

Thankful himself to be at this solid mooring, he ministers Communion to the bickering couple, to the woman with the penny-colored hair. He's placing the Host on the palm of her yawning grandson when he sees Babs at the back of the room. She slinks in, accompanied by a man with a corn-stubble crew cut and a plow blade of a jaw. Father Tim beckons them, but they hang back, looking away, as if respecting the privacy of someone scantily clad.

Only when Mass is done do they approach. "Sorry we missed it," says Babs. "This is my husband, Les."

She looks better than she did the day before, her face less puffy, her hair not quite so moribund on her shoulders, but in her voice he hears the chronic misery.

Les's handshake is surprisingly mealy for a man his size. "My fault," he says. "Hate to be late. But I couldn't for the life of me find my sunglasses. Babs says I've got Sometimer's disease—like Alzheimer's but less predictable. Ha ha!" He laughs as if reading aloud from a cartoon bubble.

"Funny," says Babs, "the Sometimer's almost always hits just as we're on our way to church."

"Oh, now," says Les. He takes her hand and pets it with habitual tenderness. "You heading ashore today, Father?"

The priest removes his stole. "Hadn't planned on it."

"Come with us. I predict it'll clear up this afternoon."

"I don't know," says Father Tim. Last night, Alison mentioned Ocho Rios as her favorite port of call, but he decided just to stay onboard, maybe work out in the Buried Treasure Gym. He's found it difficult to partake of the ship's relentless luxury, and spends most of the time alone in his cabin, reading. He can see himself turning into his mother, who always orders the cheapest dish in a restaurant, even when she's being treated, because if she doesn't get used to pampering then she can never miss it.

"You can't skip Ocho Rios," Babs says. Her eyes look fragile, pleading.

"They've got it all planned out," Les adds. "A tour of some old plantation. A fish-fry lunch."

It's not the world's most convincing pitch. Father Tim wonders how much insurance Les hawks. But he thinks of Alison's enthusiasm, the giddy way she said "Shore Excursion Manager."

Alison stands at the gangway, clipboard in hand, looking necessary and ornamental all at once. Her tan is such a contrast to her uniform whites that she appears enhanced, a colorized image. Last night, across from her in the lounge, Father Tim could smell her lush papaya hair conditioner; now his nostrils fill with the same cut-open scent.

"Too late to sign up?" he asks.

"For you? I think we can find a slot."

"Good. I've got my camera and my tacky shirt and my overflowing wallet. Do I look like *Touristicus Americanus?*"

"Yeah. What happened to the vow of poverty?"

"Doesn't apply to parish priests," he says and leans closer. "Ready to manage my excursion?"

"You betcha. I'm going to manage you right on over to Andrew"—she points to a redheaded, Canadian Mountie-looking fellow—"who'll be leading your group to shore."

"You're not coming?"

"I'm too high and mighty now. Got to hold down the fort."

Father Tim adjusts the camera's weight around his neck. The sunscreen on his brow is unpleasantly gummy. Maybe he should bag it, he's thinking, when a hand lands coercively on his shoulder. "Fun and sun, here we come!" says Les. Beside him stands Babs, quietly wincing. Her eyes are red and watery again.

Andrew, the rangy tour guide, blows a whistle.

"Guess we're out of here," says Father Tim to Alison. "But maybe we can find time later. Dinner?"

She frowns. "Sorry, no can do. Booked."

"Maybe tomorrow?"

"I've got a staff meeting, but how about another nightcap? Same time and channel as last night?"

"Sure," he says. "Sure. It's a date."

At the pier a gold-toothed man, his face tiny within a tangle of dreadlocks, pushes Rasta caps and balsa carvings. Andrew warned of these often shady "higglers," so Babs marches stonily on, ignoring his continued list of wares. "Mahogany? Black coral? Batik?" But Les, seemingly enamored of the man's high-rent smile, stops to answer his soul-brother handshake.

"Come on," calls Babs. "We'll be late for the tour."

Les is inspecting a tortoiseshell comb. "Nice? Maybe to bring back for Jenna?"

"Les, that stuff's illegal. Protected species, Andrew said. Right, Father?"

The priest, trying not to get caught in the middle, says flatly, "It might be a risk at customs."

The Rastafarian hides the comb back in his bag, then fingers Babs's sauerkraut locks. "How 'bout da woman's hair—she wan' mi braid it?"

Les claps his hands. "Fun! Like a real Jamaican."

"No," Babs says, ducking away.

"Come on, hon. Live a little. It would look pretty."

"No," she repeats, and strides off, leaving the men to chase behind.

"Don't know what's gotten into her," says Les. He sticks a pinkie into his ear and wiggles it as if trying to pick the lock of his own thoughts. "Do you suppose it could be the change of life?"

Seeing Les's lunkish, unwitting expression, Father Tim is awash with the awful helplessness of watching a sparrow fly into glass. How could two people live together for a quarter-century and still know so little about each other? "Have you tried to talk to her?" he suggests.

"She's not much of one for talking. She'd rather sit alone, fooling on her Internet."

Father Tim looks ahead to Babs's trudging form, her fallen-soufflé bottom within lime Bermuda shorts, and tries to imagine her with Denise. "I'd be happy to do what I can," he offers.

Les waves him off. "We'll work it out. Always have. That's why we're married."

They catch Babs and reconnoiter with the cruise ship group. Andrew—who, despite his aggressive chipperness, turns out to lead tours only to fund grad school in social work—brings them to Good Hope Plantation. They learn about the life cycle of the banana plant, the proper way to carry a load of coconuts in a head basket.

Then it's on to a nearby waterfall—popular, Andrew informs them, as a marriage proposal spot. This prompts a round of story-telling, as each couple recounts where they popped the question. Two newlyweds, by the sound of them Brooklynites, describe the thrill of saying yes on the Coney Island Cyclone, just as the roller coaster plunged. The pair from this morning's Mass, in the canary jogging suits, quibble over the site of their engagement: "Depends," says the man. "First or second time?" Babs and Les don't volunteer their story, but Father Tim watches a shadow of private memory pass between them.

The waterfall is an intricate liquid rope, braided from a dozen streaming strands. Over its exuberant noise—an endless *yes*—he hears the Brooklyn wife bidding for his attention. "...favor...just married...you wouldn't mind?" She plants a sleek black Leica in his hand.

"My pleasure," he says. "There, against the falls?"

The couple pose in the self-evident spot, by a mist-brightened, heart-shaped outcropping, and Father Tim captures the shot. It's an image, he realizes, that must reside in a thousand honeymoon al-bums. But isn't that exactly the point, linking yourselves to a vast married chain? At last you've joined the club. You're in.

The jogging suit duo finally agree on something: They want a snapshot, too. "Us next?" says the man, more a statement than a question, as he foists his Nikon on Father Tim. The priest focuses, frames the shot; the shutter clicks.

All turn to the last pair, Babs and Les. As Father Tim meets her gaze, Babs crouches to wash her hands in purling water. She dunks her fingers as if they're something to be drowned.

Respectfully, the others avert their eyes. But Les, belly jiggling, hams it up. "My wife," he announces, so loud that everyone is forced to hear, "is part Cherokee, her father's mother's side. She's scared a picture is going to steal her soul." As if his Instamatic is a savage jungle beast he thrusts it at her, growling extravagantly.

Babs glares. "I am no such thing," she says.

"Oh, yeah? If you're not Indian, what are you then?"

She shakes her hands dry. "Nothing. And you know it."

"Not to me," he says. "You're everything. You're mine."

Babs startles, then shyly blinks her eyes. Her firm frown warps into a smile. "Oh, quit fussing," she says. "Hurry up and get the shot."

Father Tim accepts the camera from Les and snaps a photo; then, just in case, he snaps another.

The man from Brooklyn jokes that if church life gets too slow, the priest could always go into business. "A sideline," he says. " 'Heavenly Photos.' "

Father Tim's own camera remains around his neck. Nobody offers to take his picture.

Lunch is at a grubbily authentic corrugated tin shack back in town. They're fed goat stew, fried dolphin, and salt cod pancakes that the cook calls "stamp-and-go." Everyone guzzles Ting, a local grapefruit soda that Father Tim decides, as it trills down his throat, achieves a kind of gustatory onomatopoeia.

He remembers something he's meant to tell Alison: a hole-in-the-wall Salvadoran lunch shop he discovered in East Boston, where the *pupusas* are the true *criolla* thing. He'd love to take her there, for old time's sake. He's forgotten to ask where she's based when the *Destiny* isn't sailing. Could she come to Boston? Where would she stay?

Just as dessert is served, the clouds that have dogged the entire voyage peel away, like bandages stripped to bare renewed skin. Andrew announces that the group will split up for the afternoon. There are glass-bottom boat trips, catamarans, horseback tours. Just be back on ship by five o'clock, he warns.

Father Tim approaches Babs and Les. This past while, husband and wife haven't said much to each other, but they no longer appear to be consciously not speaking. Les has a boat-shaped piece of papaya, Babs a plate of sliced sweetsop. In the unconscious balletic movements of a long-established couple, they trade bites of the juice-dripping fruit.

"Remember Marty?" she says.

"Sure," says Les, "that time in Hutchinson."

"When he swallowed—"

"And his face—"

"Porcupine!"

Father Tim stops short and clears his throat. Les turns. "Hey, Father. How about that sun? Did I tell you?"

"You sure did. I thought some snorkeling might be in order to celebrate."

"Sounds fun," says Les. "But we already settled on one of those paddle boats. Take a couple of Red Stripes and drift around the bay."

"Absolutely. That could definitely work, too."

Les and Babs exchange a low-lidded glance. Babs chews on a last piece of papaya. "The paddle boats only have two seats," she says.

"Oh," says Father Tim. "Of course. I wasn't thinking."

By now the others have all gone, so he makes his way alone to the beach. Lovers splash in the surf and families play along the shore, using coconut shells to shape sandcastle domes. The sun stings like the aftermath of a slap.

He strips off his shirt. On his last trip to the beach, a weekend getaway to Plum Island with seminary classmates, they took turns rubbing one another's backs with sunblock. Now, with no one to help him, his skin will surely burn. He replaces the shirt and retreats to the ship.

The next day they dock at Grand Cayman. Father Tim worries that Les might propose another excursion, but thankfully he and Babs don't show at Mass. He wonders what this bodes for their marriage; they could be sleeping late together, or not speaking again.

Returning to his cabin, he takes a longcut past the gangway. Alison is snared in an argument with an underchinned, stumpy man who insists his travel agent touted Grand Cayman's Mayan ruins.

"Could she have said Tulum?" Alison suggests. "Near Cozumel?"

"No! It's Cayman. She definitely said Grand Cayman."

Father Tim flashes a sympathetic smile, but she misses it.

He spends the morning secluded in his cabin. Sprawled on the vast bed with the collected works of Flannery O'Connor, he tries to pick up where he left off in *Wise Blood*. After reading the same page seven times he gives up, his concentration shot by the awareness of all the reputed fun he's missing. He could be tracing figure eights at the ice-skating rink, or sinking putts on the nine-hole green. There's the rock-climbing wall, the Virtual Reality Center with its "motion-based undersea theme rides." If he were home it would be the height of decadence to read in bed in the middle of the day, but in this temple of pleasure, where even the deck swabbers seem ecstatic in their swabbing, anything less than the time of his life feels like failure.

At last he rouses himself for a stroll. For the first time in days he's feeling queasy, so he sticks a motion sickness patch behind his ear. The nausea confounds him: The ship is moored, the weather has calmed. Maybe it was the stamp-and-go.

He ascends to the Liberty Deck, where the sun, as if piqued by days of passenger complaints, reigns with vengeful, be-careful-what-you-ask-for strength. There are no clouds, and the browbeating high-noon clarity makes it hard to believe there ever might be again. With the heat, and so many passengers ashore, the *Destiny* is eerily deserted. Dozens of empty deck chairs face the sea in bleak rows, a graveyard for a boatload of drowned tourists.

His stomach flares, but it's not a seasick sloshing. It's the arid, barren clench of solitude—much worse than yesterday at the beach. *Aren't you scared?* asked Alison. *How can you live?* The "discipline of celibacy," when they parsed it at Saint Thomas, was not a white-knuckled act of self-denial but a choice, a more inclusive way of loving. Now he unsheathes the phrase and it pricks with a different edge: Celibacy is a punishment.

At Saint Thomas, he could manage his longings. He fought pangs of desire and isolation, but didn't everyone? Even married folks? The potholes in his chosen walk were pretty well patched by camaraderie. Three times a day he broke bread, and three times a day he prayed, with the best friends he'd ever known; having one soulmate didn't seem so necessary. How could he not have guessed the loneliness that would vise him once he was ordained and on his own?

Clutching the railing, he stares past the port of Grand Cayman, into the nevermore distance, where sea and sky disorientingly merge. His grief is anchorless, uncloseable, as for a loved one lost at sea, no corpse to bury.

He spies the sculptor a half second too late to pretend he hasn't.

"Oh, good!" calls the artist, who grabs him by the elbow and detains him at the Jolly Roger Room's entrance. "I hoped you would come tonight. Look!" With a flourish he whisks away an invisible curtain to reveal tonight's buttery creation. It's Father Tim—the unconsciously canted neck, the dimpled brow—caught in a look of grudging submission.

The artist, smiling, asks, "Are you happy?"

For a moment Father Tim is too stunned to understand that the question is aesthetic, not existential. The rendition is so accurately cheerless. "Yes," he says. "You're very talented." He pushes into the bar and picks the table where two nights prior he and Alison chatted.

Same time, same channel, she said. The Kalypso Kings break into "Day-O" right on cue, the ten o'clock bell. Even Kip's gestures are identical. Maybe he's not real, but animatronic.

The waitress asks if she can bring the priest a drink, but he says no, he'll hold out for his guest. He rearranges a stack of cocktail napkins in a pointless solitaire. He remembers waiting for Alison after they'd had sex for the first time. He lay in her undone bed, ceding her the five minutes of bathroom privacy she requested—their only separation since meeting that afternoon. He slipped his hips into the hollow in the mattress made by hers. He inhaled the sweet mossy smell of her sheets. Five minutes was unthinkable! He burst in, and they went at it again in the shower.

How easy this is, he remembers thinking, how astonishingly effortless and alive. But was that, over time, the difficulty? Growing up with his left-behind mother, Tim had come to think of love as untrustable, a mirage. Now he wonders if his and Alison's was real. In their molten almost-year together they fused a shape that was neither of them, yet both—a being that kept no secrets from itself. He told her about the sucker punch of his father's disappearance; his drive to feel needed so as never to feel needy. He cried in her cradling arms.

He wants that again, that heat and hope. He wants to confide in her, to confess his qualms about being the one to whom others now confess, his panic at the thought of life alone. He burns to lie with her—not for the physical release, but for the stitched-togetherness, the gut cramp that says five minutes is too long to be apart.

When the waitress returns at quarter past and asks if he's okay, Father Tim orders a Diet Coke. Her staff meeting must have run late, he thinks. Maybe a foul-up with the Cozumel logistics.

At ten-thirty he requests a double scotch. He asks the waitress to ask the barman if anyone's left a message. She returns with the drink and with a shrug.

Jowls wattling, Kip sings, "I feel so break up, I wanna go home." He finishes the tune, then belches some mock-piratical innuendo about the prowess of his restless "Jolly Roger." How many nights has he slung the same old jokes? What life did the young Kip once dream of?

The crowd has thinned, leaving only a half-dozen elderly couples holding arthritic, familiar hands, and at the front a younger pair who, despite the music's lull, still rock to a steady private beat.

At five past eleven, another two scotches downed, but not so much drunk as saturated, Father Tim signs his tab and stands. He shuffles toward the exit, by the now abandoned display table, and as he passes he can't help but see his likeness melted to a sallow, vacant blur.

Thursday's weather is touch-and-go, no rain yet but a sky the bleary milk blue shade of a bum eye. Father Tim hunkers in the chaplain's office.

He hasn't eaten. His hangover hammers him with its claw end, sharp and mean. He went looking for Alison at lunchtime, but according to Sandy, the Cruise Director, she's gone for the day, scouting sites in Cozumel.

To kill time, and because his mind is too mushy for much else, Father Tim has brought along postcards. The first he addresses collectively to Saint Thomas, to the teachers and jealous pals he left behind. "Pilgrim's progress," he scribbles shakily. "Paradise regained? Wish you were here."

Then his mother. The card he's picked for her shows the *Destiny* in scale against the White House, dwarfing it. Before embarking, he thought that if the trip was fun he might sign her up for their New Year's singles' cruise. Now he tells her how much she would hate it: the wastefulness, the enforced merriment.

There's a faint knock that might be the disgruntled table-slap of a gambler next door. When it sounds again, louder, he realizes he has a visitor. He cracks the door and is met by Les, his face and neck sunburned to the shade of cooked shrimp, but his buzzed scalp a halo of lighter flesh. In his hands he holds a Pioneer seed cap, worrying its brim into a frown.

"Hi, Father," he says. "Disturbing you?"

"Not at all. That's why I'm here." He motions for Les to take a seat.

"Case you're wondering," Les says, "Babs went ashore."

"You didn't want to see Cozumel, too?"

Les crimps his cap more firmly. "We had a fight." He recounts how, after breakfast, Babs sicked up her food for the third time already on the cruise. He helped her back to their cabin and fizzed some Alka-Seltzer, but she said the trouble wasn't her stomach, it was her conscience. She sat down on the big bed, not touching him, not looking. There was someone else. A woman. Denise.

"Just like that," Les says. "Like it was already history, a done deal. A day before our anniversary." He rubs at his dry, reddened neck. As if confirming the punch line of a joke he doesn't get, he turns to the priest and says again, "A woman?"

"I'm so sorry," says Father Tim. "You must feel totally blindsided." Not letting on that he already knows feels like a lie; his palms get clammy and cold.

"Actually," says Les, "it's almost a relief. At least now I have an explanation." But his face, like a cliff suddenly eroding, goes loose. "Oh, Father," he whispers. "Oh, Father."

To be called upon like this by a man his father's age is what he's worked for. It should be a confirmation. But a sense of inadequacy knocks the wind out of him.

"She said I could ask for an annulment," Les goes on. "That what feels true is sometimes really false."

Father Tim is humbled to hear his own words quoted. "And what did you say to that?" he asks.

Les straightens his back as though taking an oath. "That I would do absolutely no such thing. That she's my wife and she always will be."

Father Tim stares at this damaged, stalwart man, revising his evaluation. What struck him initially as stony doltishness he sees now as Les's bedrock strength. Here's a guy who has witnessed the devastation of countless storms, the terrible routineness of disaster. It's obviously more than a professional belief for Les that if properly insured, you can always rebuild.

"Listen," Les says. "I'm nothing to write home about. I've never had the looks of some guys." He gestures to Father Tim's musculature. "And maybe I can't be everything to Babs. But I can be a lot. I already have. We've put too much into this to scrap it now."

This is when Father Tim should bolster Les. Annulment, he should say, is a drastic, last-ditch measure. They've got to try everything else first, just as a priest doubting his vocation should explore every path before quitting his vows.

Yet he hesitates. He pictures Babs the first day she came to him: boggled, woebegone. He recalls how she brightened when she spoke of Denise, the film of sorrow skimmed from her expression.

"Father?" asks Les. "Will you talk to her?"

He swallows an acrid emptiness. He nods.

When Les is gone, Father Tim withdraws to his cabin and pumps one hundred-twenty-something pushups, until his own weight is unsupportable. He collapses on the floor, his heart skittery and uncertain, a compass needle in a magnetic disturbance.

He waits for a call from Alison. And waits.

Finally, after dinner, which he fails to attend, he glumly heads out in search of Babs. He checks the spa, the casino, the Jolly Roger Room, eyes peeled for Alison as well. On the Indulgence Deck there's a drum show and a bridge tournament, but neither woman is anywhere to be found.

He climbs to the Liberty Deck, ready at last to quit, and wends his way aft toward the railing. In daytime it's where skeetshooters kill their birds of clay, but now it hosts fantasizers of another sort: sunsetlovers swooning at the sky.

This evening the display is washed out and unimpressive, the sun veiled by tight-knotted clouds. The crowd is sparse and mumbly with disappointment. Which is why he's not surprised to find Babs there. He spots her with her chest pressed against the steel railing, breasts spilling down like batter overrunning a pan.

"I did it," she says softly. "I told him."

"I know. I spoke with Les," he says, after deciding it's all right to reveal that much. "So, how are you now? How do you feel?"

"I feel," she begins, then reconsiders. "Honestly, not much of anything. Like how food tastes when you've got a bad cold."

"That's natural," he says. "You're in shock."

"I thought once I told him, he'd leave me," she says. "He's made it tougher. He's put the choice on me."

Father Tim winces against the stiff sea wind. "Choosing is what makes us human—that we have to, that we know our lives are finite." It's what he tried to convince Alison—and himself—the other day, but now he feels the hairline ache of it in his bones. "If you leave Les, you'll mourn your old life. If you stay, you'll mourn the life you might have had."

"That's just it," Babs says. "How're you supposed to weigh two things when one's on the scale already and the other's just imagined? I was thinking, standing here before you showed: I don't know Denise's middle name. I don't even know if she's got one." She lets out something between a laugh and a grunt. "Then I think: If I always only stuck with what I know, I never would have married Les to start with. I wouldn't've had my wonderful kids. Sometimes to get somewhere the only way's to jump."

Father Tim wrestles with what to say. Part of him wants to tell her, Keep going. Go *there.* Don't turn back from the edge of happiness. But of course he can't openly counsel her to leave and violate the sacrament of marriage. And who's to say that happiness is what she would find if she leaped blindly to the other side? "You're right," he says, "the more risk, the more reward. But couldn't staying put be more of a risk than running off? Sometimes it takes guts to stick it out where you are."

Babs coils a hank of dull hair around her fingers; she twists and twists, but the hair won't hold a shape. High above the deck wheels a lone gray gull. She watches it with a look of stupefaction.

"If you left Les," he asks, "what would you miss most?"

"I'm sick of thinking about who I should be for Les. Or for my kids. Really, even for Denise. I want to be somebody all by myself."

"But nobody's anybody by themselves. Life is with people, and with God."

He turns and stares at the indistinct horizon, where the low sun still muddies the clouds. The sky's the color of apple flesh that's been bruised.

Because he's gazing off, he doesn't notice the woman until she's tapped his shoulder.

"Would you mind?" she says, holding up a camera.

Father Tim shoots a bemused glance at Babs and they both laugh. "Do I look like an easy mark?" he says.

"If it's a problem," the woman says. She steps back.

"No, no, I'd be happy. I've just been asked to take a lot of photos lately."

Father Tim accepts her big-lensed camera. She's his age, he guesses, give or take a year, and has Alison's kind of calisthenic poise. She wears her hot pink halter top with the unabashed aplomb of someone who has nothing to hide. Beside her stands another woman, also halter topped and blessed with similarly bold and striking features. The older sister, Father Tim decides.

"Not much of a sunset," he says, "but do you want me to get it in the background?"

"Perfect," the sisters call in unison.

When they've arranged and rearranged themselves properly at the railing Father Tim begins his count to three. By "two" the women are locked in an all-or-nothing kiss. He swallows "three" but manages to snap the shot.

The women keep kissing, then finally disengage, both of them sparkly and flushed. "Thanks," says the one in pink, reclaiming her camera. "Our one-year anniversary." They flash matching gold bands on their fingers.

Babs stands beside the priest, wordlessly gaping with awe or with horror, he can't tell. Seeing what's possible is sometimes worse than being blinkered.

He smiles at the women and says, "Congratulations."

At midnight, sleepless, he returns to the deck, to the same spot where he and Babs stood. He's been pacing the cage of his cabin for hours. He needs the touch of unconditioned air.

The *Destiny* is at sail once more, chugging on its long haul home. It will cruise around Cuba's untouchable western shore and head at last for Fort Lauderdale. He wondered, when awarded this vacation, why a chaplain would be needed on a cruise. Wasn't the pampering, the escape, ministry enough? But he sees it now—how freeing yourself from the trap of your routine can set the springs of other keen-edged traps.

A sharp moon undermines the privacy of night. The air is fickle with swells of warm and cool. Father Tim turns his face to the sky. He prays.

He prays for Babs, that she'll make the best decision. And for Les, that he won't be left behind. That these two prayers might be mutually exclusive is a puzzle he leaves for God to solve. Let there be more love and less loneliness, he beseeches. Let the lines of love not cross or disconnect.

But he's unsure what an answered prayer would be. Does his sturdy priest's faith—still within him, just as strong—mean he's always got to live a priest's life? Is there room for love of God and someone else?

Then comes the voice. "Hey, Twinkle," she says.

He sees her first not as a woman but a flower, an outsized orchid sprouted from the deck. Sheer and shapely, her evening gown is leaf-green at the legs, and at the bust blooms with violet.

"Alison. I didn't hear you coming."

She shrugs and whispers, "I fly stealth."

They stand there a long fifteen seconds, just breathing, watching the ship's wake diverge. Father Tim hears the blood beat in his ears. Around Alison's neck hangs a strand of fat pearls; her dress is cut so the gems flirt with her cleavage. The last time he saw her all dolled up like this was their sophomore-year Valentine's Ball. Jittery with nerves and with arousal, he pricked his finger pinning on her corsage.

"What's the occasion?" he asks.

"Formal dinner. I was at the captain's table."

A devil of brine-scented air whirls around them, threatening their eyes with salt and grit. There's the thin sound of laughter from somewhere up-deck and, far below, the engines' grumbling.

"Last night," she says. She strokes a pearl in the scoop of her neck. "That was gutless. I'm really sorry. It's just you show up, after all these years, a *priest,* but there's still that . . . I don't know, between us. I didn't know how to tell you—"

"It's all right," he says. "I'm just glad you found me now."

He says the words simply to soothe her, but as they come out he realizes they're true. His budding anger, last night's humiliation—it all rolls away like the *Destiny*'s wake.

Just standing here, feeling graced, at the hem of her moonshadow, he's not unconvinced of divinity at work. He needs her right now, and she's appeared; what clearer sign should he expect? He steps into the lee of her tall, exquisite form, her body heat a faint radiance.

"There you are," booms a man's baritone.

They turn back to the deck to find its source. Andrew, the redheaded trip leader, strides toward them, his dinner jacket catching wind like a sail.

"I know," he says, "tour guides should be on time." He grins for a calculated instant, then ducks to land a kiss below her ear.

"Andrew," she says, pulling away, "I think you know Father Tim?"

"Sure, of course. You came along at Ocho Rios." Andrew traps him in a double-handed shake. "Did you have fun there in the afternoon, on your own?"

"I turned in early," says Father Tim. He reclaims his hand and hides it in his pocket.

Draping his arm around Alison's waist, Andrew tips his head skyward. "Wow. Talk about beautiful." It's not clear if he means Alison or the moon. "What's the plan? More dancing? Champagne?" He whirls on the toes of his wingtips.

Alison tries to smile, but it comes off as a cringe. She looks uneasily at Father Tim.

"Oh, no problem," Andrew says. "Do you want to tag along, Father?"

"No," says Alison. "This was just an accident. I mean, coincidence. Tim was taking a midnight stroll."

"Actually," he says, "I was kind of looking for you." He feels his biceps, still sore from this afternoon's workout, contract beneath his cooling skin.

A web of silence falls upon them, but Andrew cuts it with an overreaching laugh. "Hey, three's a good number. The Holy Trinity!" He laughs again—short, spanking bursts of sound.

With a muddled gaze, Alison turns to Father Tim. "What I wanted to say. Andrew and I . . . we're engaged."

"Proposed at the falls in Ocho Rios," he says. "A couple of cruises ago."

Father Tim glances down to her ring finger, sees the diamond. She must have taken it off for their Jolly Roger date. "You couldn't have told me?" he says.

"I was going to. I should have. I just didn't want it to be the first thing—like you didn't want to be seen as celibate, right off. And after that . . . well, it seemed harder."

It's a chickenshit excuse, he thinks—as lame as his own defensiveness the other night.

Andrew reinvites him to come with them downstairs to the Paradise Lounge for ballroom dancing. Father Tim declines. He can't look at Alison. Instead he turns, as the sound of their double footfalls fades, to the railing and its view of the wake. The water recedes in ever-widening furls, two lines that will never intersect.

The Wedding Chapel is on the Fantasy Deck, catty-corner from the duty-free shop. It's a smallish room, painted in sunny stained-glass shades as if to compensate for the absence of windows. Unaccountably, there's an overboiled, industrial-food smell that reminds Father Tim of waiting in a line.

The ship's photographer, a schnauzer-faced, fidgety man, caps and uncaps his camera's lens. By the altar, at parade rest, stands Captain Dickerman in a blue uniform with golden epaulets. The priest has warned them this will likely be a bust; only one couple prepaid for the Renewal of Vows, and that couple is Babs and Les.

They've agreed to wait until ten past the hour. It's already 4:08. The souvenir champagne flutes with the Sun Line Cruises logo stand empty on a silver tray. The commemorative certificate, awaiting the captain's signature, remains stowed in its coral cardboard tube.

"Call it quits?" the photographer suggests. "I'm due to shoot some 'after' pics at the spa."

Captain Dickerman consults his watch. Pouting slightly, as if pained to be deprived of the pomp, he nods. The photographer collapses his tripod.

"Better luck next cruise," says Father Tim. He thumps his book of rites against his palm.

"Father," says the captain, lingering. "You're fresh from seminary, aren't you? Might you weigh in on a theological debate?"

"Don't expect any miracles," says the priest.

"I hear you got the highest grades in your class."

"That's right," he says, wishing that he were slightly worse at tests. Isn't that what this trip with Alison has been?

"Here's what I've wondered," the captain says. "The wedding vows are for life, are they not? 'Till death do us part,' et cetera? So how can a renewal of those vows be justified? Is that conceding that they *aren't* permanent?" The captain bares a cunning, trump-card grin.

Dredging his mind for an answer, Father Tim finds only worthless jetsam. Right and wrong seem like dim, distant shores. He's about to admit he's stumped when Babs and Les walk in.

The captain hails back the photographer. "We're in business," he calls exultantly.

Babs wears a sleek satin dress that accentuates her figure's hills and dales. Her face is tanned now to the mousy shade of her hair, which has been frosted and teased aloft with spray.

Father Tim reaches haltingly for her shoulder. They both stiffen with a brief static shock. "We'd almost given up on you," he says.

She rubs the spot where he touched her. "Me, too."

Les, in his tuxedo, shifts and twists his neck, self-conscious as a Great Dane in a sweater. "Sorry," he says. "Sometimer's again. Couldn't remember where I'd stashed the ring." He produces a small, velvet-covered jewelry box and hands it to Captain Dickerman.

"Marvelous," the captain says. "It's just not a cruise without a little 'I do.'"

Wife and husband stand at a measured distance, seeming to regard each other with a mix of fear and hopefulness. In her dress Babs appears breathless, girdled. Father Tim sees where tears have streaked her rouge. But when Les takes her hand she offers a small smile and at long last quietly exhales.

What happened? Father Tim wants to ask. A more responsible priest might halt the proceedings and insist that the couple talk straight. But in the end he can never glimpse the hidden circuitry that keeps alight the filament of marriage. Who is he to say a commitment isn't true?

"My other shoot," the photographer reminds them. He taps twice on the back of his wrist.

"By all means," says the captain. "On we go."

The anniversary pair shuffle half a step closer with the awkwardness of blind dates. Les winks. Babs double-checks her hair.

Father Tim opens his ritual and begins. "Repeat after me," he says to Les. "'I renew my commitment to you, my wife.'"

Les matches his cadence word for word.

With text in hand, his mind is free to drift. He conjures the future and envisions it all too well: the dozens and dozens of weddings he'll oversee, and the others he won't witness or attend—Alison's wedding to Andrew, his own. He'll have God's touch and that will have to be enough.

" 'I promise again to be true to you in good times and in bad, in sickness and in health, to love and honor you all the days of my life.' "

Father Tim states the pledge that from his lips isn't binding; Les repeats it and the words gather weight.

The priest turns to Babs and says, "Ready?"

BHIRA BACKHAUS

Arizona State University

SANGEET

When she married, my sister Neelam surrendered herself to a fate dictated, not by desire or foolish dreams, but by the positions of the stars and planets. She became engaged to a man she had never met, someone she had known merely as the fuzzy image in a photograph, but whose destiny was nonetheless aligned with hers.

We lived on Fremont Road, in a three-bedroom house on the outskirts of the small, northern California town of Oak Grove. Orchards enveloped the town's edges, supplanting a fertile landscape once lush with grasses and dotted with sprawling oaks. The broad domes of Sikh temples competed with the lean spires of Christian churches. Since the immigration laws had changed, the town pulsed to the exotic beat of dohls and the soundtracks of the Indian films that hit American shores. The all-white city council members learned to publish their campaign literature in Punjabi, as though each tumultuous decision made at City Hall had some great bearing on our tight little universe. After World War II my Uncle Avtar, my father's older brother, had taken advantage of cheap land prices and a few weak-willed men to begin securing his holdings. He'd offered my father, Mohinder Singh Rai, a small share of it when he emigrated from India in 1957. By then my mother was already expecting her first child.

A young woman scarcely had time to weave the fragile fabric of her dreams in our town. All too soon the hazy faces and soft mouths of imagined lovers were replaced by hard, real ones. Neelam married Davinder Mahal when she was eighteen; I was fifteen then. It was a hasty affair that left all involved a bit breathless and stunned as she exited the front door carrying the last of her bags. In the days following the wedding, my mother roamed the house with a light, buoyant step.

One fall afternoon, months after Neelam's wedding, I hurried off the school bus into a full, slanted wind, the sycamore leaves tossed around me like brown hands. I was attending Oak Grove High School and afternoons would return home to a living room where my mother, sister, and aunts sat like fleshy fixtures drinking tea. Inside the house, the air felt stiff and dry, as if all their talking had sucked away any moisture. Aunt Teji greeted me when I entered the living room and tapped the sofa seat next to her lightly with an open hand before pushing her smudged glasses back on her nose. I settled beside her, taking in the sandalwood scent of her wool shawl. My mother's attention was focused on her sister, my Aunt Manjit, who perched at the edge of her chair in her erect and ever-alert way.

"If it worked once, why shouldn't it again?" my mother said, casually flicking crumbs from her kameej. Her voice had a slightly ragged edge to it, and I recognized that, with my presence, the conversation had shifted into what I called code talk. I looked from face to face for clues. Neelam turned toward the wall in one long sweep of her lashes, and a streak of crimson rose along the side of her neck.

"There's an ointment that can be rubbed into the feet each night. Santi was telling me," Aunt Manjit said. She had a closet shelf stuffed with ointments and ingredients for salves—tattered paper bags filled with old walnut husks, dried pomegranate skins, and ajuwan—their woody scents mixing with the smell of leather rising from the scuffed collection of boots and sneakers piled on the floor. She was my mother's younger sister, and they were as different from one another as Neelam and I. Only twenty-eight, Aunt Manjit's body hadn't softened and spread after three children, but had sharpened into pointed, bony angles at her chin, shoulders, and hips.

"I think the young bride and groom can handle these matters on their own." Aunt Teji shifted her soft, pliant weight on the sofa and playfully slapped Neelam's thigh. Neelam, who had thus far displayed no emotion, stirred and languidly peeled herself from the sofa back, sitting upright.

Prem burst into the room with a basketball hooked under one arm and, without any greeting, plunged a dusty hand into the platter of pakoras.

"As many as you like, son," my mother said. "Here take some for Deepa, too." She handed him the entire platter, watching the mound of pakoras shift in Prem's precarious grip. Deepa was Aunt Teji's son. The two boys attended junior high together and fancied themselves twin Indian Kareem Abdul Jabars, despite their delayed growth spurts.

Neelam rose, collected tea cups, and disappeared into the kitchen. The door creaked as it swung shut behind her. I wanted to follow her, but remained helplessly sunk into the soft cushions next to Aunt Teji. The sofa rose and fell with a momentous sigh from Aunt Teji, and the others joined in a round of sighing and silent assessing. A fly buzzed and skittered against the window.

"It's all in the Lord's hands anyway," Aunt Manjit said. How could something that a moment earlier was to be assuaged with an ointment now be in the Lord's hands?

"Jeeto, put on another pot of tea." With a snap of her head, my mother motioned me toward the kitchen, where Neelam was running the water and clinking cups. There was something my mother wished to say to the others, something dark and secretive, that required my absence. I would miss it, I thought, as I plunged through the kitchen doorway. I'd been unable to decipher the discussion completely, but I knew it had to do with Neelam and the fact that, after eight months of marriage, she had yet to announce news of an imminent child.

The previous year, over cups of scalding tea, my mother had watched as Charan Kaur pored over the creased pages of astrological charts, settling on the twenty-third of February as an auspicious day for her daughter's wedding. Thus were Neelam's shame and misfortune to be swept away, forgotten altogether if memory were charitable.

The same Charan Kaur had arranged the match. My mother had unfaltering faith in the woman to whom she had turned to ensure her third child would be a boy. Had Charan Kaur merely consulted charts, or was she present in some magical way the night my mother and father had, no doubt, joyously made love believing a son would soon bless our family? The cherished birth of my younger brother Prem nine months later only hardened my mother's faith. In the interim, Charan Kaur had become a much sought-after matchmaker. Those who took interest in such matters could tell you of her successes: She managed to unite the feuding Gill and Thiara families, joining Oak Grove's most eligible Indian bachelor with the starchy, morose eldest daughter of the Thiaras, thereby doubling the land holdings of each. My mother eagerly enlisted her talents to find a suitable boy for her own troubled daughter.

Nothing in life is a coincidence, my mother always told us as a preface to exemplary tales. A favorite of hers: There was my Uncle Dev who once took the wrong train from Jullundar to New Delhi and wound up in a small village in the highlands. At a lunch stand, he encountered a former colleague from the postal service who had retired there with his two daughters. At dinner at this man's home that very evening, Uncle Dev was particularly taken with the eldest daughter, Seema, a ravishing beauty reluctant to marry, though she was nearing twenty years of age. That night, Uncle Dev, unable to sleep with his thoughts of desire, was roaming the dark village streets when a holy man dressed in mere rags approached him. This holy man looked deep into Uncle's fevered eyes and instructed him to drink at dawn from the spring at the hill beyond to purify himself against such injurious thoughts. Uncle Dev did so the following morning, but then collapsed, exhausted, against a rock nearby. Along came Seema, the lovely daughter, her slender arms embracing a ceramic pot to collect drinking water. She revived him, and soon they were married and produced seven excellent children. "Coincidence that he took the wrong train?" my mother would ask, her hands clasped triumphantly. "Impossible!"

On the day the wedding date was decided, the letter still lay on my mother's dresser among the unopened amber bottles of cologne she collected like jewels. Tucked inside the envelope was the black-and-white photograph of Davinder Mahal, a corner of it already beginning to crease from the many hands that had handled it and the few that would handle it many times. Sitting against the mahogany wood and the glittering glass, it became a small planetary object. The three of us—Neelam, my mother, and I—revolved about it like moons held fast by its gravity. I had passed the half-opened bedroom door late one night to see my mother leaning against the headboard, the letter in her hands as she mouthed the words silently. I used pre-

tenses myself—the retrieval of her shawl before an outing, the stow-
ing of folded laundry—to enter her bedroom and glimpse again the
features of my future brother-in-law's face. A thick flush of wavy,
black hair dominated his head as if impatiently waiting for the remainder of his features to catch up and balance the whole. His expression bore the somber quality so common in Indian photographs,
the avoidance of any display of overt joy or satisfaction that might
look undignified, so that the viewer had to search the subject's eyes
for any useful clues. Yet in the corners of his mouth I saw the rudi-
ments of a smile about to bloom, even if the eyes remained serious,
wet-looking, as though he was waiting to blink. He wore a black suit
and tie, the white collar of his shirt slightly loose about his neck.

The letter had arrived on a chilly December afternoon in the
hands of Charan Kaur. It was hardly a day to be out, with a dull,
creeping fog coating everything like pewter. I'd been brooding that
afternoon at having been overlooked for a planning committee at
school, so my mother had finally given up on my sour mood and
gone to the market alone. Charan Kaur stood shivering in the doorway, with only her sea green eyes and delicate nose peeking out from
under a russet-colored shawl. Once inside the house, she reached into
her bag, not a common purse, but a large, woven bag embroidered in
plush thread with fruits—mangoes, lemons, and pears. She would
not hand the letter to me, but kept it pinched between her fingers.
"Your mother will be pleased with the news I have for her," she told
me. I led her across the patchy winter lawn and down the gravel
driveway toward my father's shop.

The old wooden structure had once housed the assorted equipment required for the running of the farm—tractors, trailers,
sprayers, rows of wooden ladders used in the harvest. As a child, during marathon games of hide and seek I would slip inside there and
crouch among what I imagined were the metal flanks of giant insects

or horses, listening for small footsteps as dusty air and diesel burned my nose. The first change my father made when he converted it into an auto shop was to clear it out and pour a concrete floor. Then the entire family had assisted one warm and breezy afternoon in coating the parrot green exterior a neutral gray blue, with fine mists of paint bandying through the air and pelting our faces and arms. We hacked back the tangled branches of the mulberry trees that clung to its walls and roof, then stood back to survey the appalling outcome of our efforts.

I unlatched the cold metal lock and heaved the sliding door open far enough to let Charan Kaur enter the shop. A bright apron of light leaked onto the floor from a bulb slung on an axle beneath a truck. The '65 flatbed Chevy belonged to the Sidhus, and my father had been working on it for the better part of the week. His booted feet jutted out from beneath its front end. A small space heater buzzed and rattled a few yards away.

"Jeeto, bring me the long needlenose pliers in the second drawer," he said, his voice escaping into the hollow metal channels under the truck. He'd learned to recognize his children by the sounds of our footsteps on that concrete slab.

"Masi Charan Kaur is here," I said. My father slid out on his dolly and stood up.

Charan Kaur brought her palms together in greeting. "Sat siri akal." She covered her head once, then again with her shawl, fussing mightily with each fold before clasping her hands at her waist. "Bhaji, we've finally received word on the question of Neelam."

My father scrubbed his hands at the sink a long minute. The back of his coveralls was grayed and faded where it pressed for hours against the dolly. The sound of Neelam's name coming from this woman's mouth appeared unsettling to him as well. He'd argued with my mother over her unreasonable rush to marry Neelam. I could see the tendons working in his neck and pulling at his jaw as he silently dried his hands. "What question of Neelam?"

"The boy's family has written from India. They sound amenable to the marriage. Here, they've sent a photo for your approval." As she unfolded the letter, the photo slipped off its crisp pages and fluttered to the floor. The remote and solemn face stared back from the grimy surface and across thousands of miles. What would Neelam say? She was away visiting a friend for the afternoon. She'd relinquished everything, I thought, for a few words exchanged between my mother and this lady, and now this face looking up from the ground. I handed the photo to my father. Charan Kaur watched closely for his reaction. His thick black brows threw a shadow over his eyes, but his face remained placid and steady. My father was handsome in a lean and angular way, and I had a vague notion that his looks came from having denied himself something essential.

"He's quite fair," Charan Kaur said. "And tall, I hear. Of course, you can't tell that from the photo." She stifled a mild giggle with a corner of her shawl, her eyes fixed somewhere past my father's shoulder. I had never seen her so nervous, so at odds with the movement of her own body, the placement of her feet and hands; the faithful protection of distant stars and planets had abandoned her temporarily. "The family works in mining. A *top* family in Ludhiana." *Top,* spoken in English, made a small uncorking sound.

"We'll go into the house. Jasbir will want to see. And Neelam, of course."

My mother's approval was clear and swift. "A fine-looking young man," she announced. Alongside her on the sofa, Charan Kaur basked in the sublime essence of her good deeds. It had grown dark, and the low windows reflected our silhouettes. We waited for the sound of the pickup truck Neelam had borrowed for the afternoon, and when she came in, her eyes met Charan Kaur's, and she understood.

The engagement was brief and not uneventful, with Uncle Avtar insisting on his particular mischievous brand of involvement in such affairs. The Mahals arrived from India in early February and stayed most of the three weeks prior to the wedding with relatives in the Bay Area. News of their stay came to us in intermittent and unexpected waves. They'd enjoyed a snowy interlude at Lake Tahoe, taken a tour of Alcatraz. Sethi Mahal, an aunt of the groom's who resided in San Jose, had already visited once, plying us with hearsay that swelled his stature among the Rai women. He grew taller, more clever with each anecdote. She herself had not seen him since he was a boy in India, but the way he could swing a cricket bat even then! The close of each story brought a choreographed turning of heads in Neelam's direction (the lucky young lady!), and she bravely summoned the expected blush each time and displayed the proper level of coyness.

Davinder's image rose from the photograph and began to take a clearer shape in our minds. My mother began to speak of him as though he had always been a part of the family, constructing the scaffold of a grand narrative, a life she hoped to ease her daughter into. Hari's name was never to be spoken again within the walls of our home, as if silence could deconstruct that bit of history. Neelam withstood the scrutiny, the whispering, until it was generally agreed that hers had been the briefest of falls from grace.

Hari had left town at the urging of his own family, dismissed the way one would release a child from some odious task. It had seemed a drastic course of action at the time, but one that my family certainly welcomed, since plans for Neelam's engagement were underway.

Hari was someone Indian girls talked about. He was the grandson of Mohta Singh, one of the elders who'd emigrated to California early in the century, someone even Uncle Avtar held in some form of begrudged esteem. Hari was already a second-generation American, but that wasn't what made him interesting. He simply looked comfortable in his skin, and carried none of the awkwardness that tormented other Indian boys as they watched white girls at school swaying through the hallways clad in miniskirts. When our school bus pulled into the parking lot in the morning, his souped-up Impala would cruise by, filled with Indian boys. He would pass me in the hallway, his skittish glance gliding over me with that curiosity, I realized later, felt for a sibling, one so closely tied to the object of one's fixation. One girl in our group said he dated, or ran around with girls, white and Indian.

So it surprised everyone that Neelam, who wore salwaar kameej to school many days, caught his eye, but no one was more surprised than my mother. She came marching through the corridor at lunch period one October afternoon of my sophomore year, the ends of her veil snapping indignantly in the air behind her. I thought someone had died when she plucked me wordlessly from the table where I sat with friends and guided me to the parking lot. Neelam was slouched in the back seat of the car, her skin damp and translucent like the peel of a grape. It had all been found out, and if my mother felt the once-solid walls of her world crumbling around her, my reaction was to view my sister with renewed curiosity. Neelam would not discuss the matter in any detail with me, but she had acknowledged that it was Hari whom my mother could only refer to as "the boy, that boy." But how, and when? Like so many things in my young life, this was left to the furtive workings of my imagination. Neelam would only say that it was for my own good that she left me out of it. When my mother confronted me, and I told her truthfully that I had known nothing, she didn't believe me.

The weeks of gloomy weather that had stretched endlessly since early winter broke suddenly in mid-February. Now the sunlight slanted through the trees out my window and lay in ripples over the tufts of grass that had sprouted everywhere. A steady trickle of visitors began to besiege our home, and we welcomed them, for all the bustle and activity was a respite from the pointed accusations and long silences. Neelam's wedding sari and jewelry arrived and, after a day or so of careful handling and admiration, were stowed in a closet. My father worked long hours in order to clear his schedule before and after the twenty-third, a date that had become a fulcrum for all of us.

The official introduction of bride and groom was to be held at Aunt Teji's. Uncle Avtar, the patriarchal head of the family, took an exceptional interest in the whole business. His wife, Aunt Teji, bustled around as though she were the mother of the bride; her eldest son, Paul, who worked in the restaurant business in the Bay Area, remained unmarried, so it was the first big wedding among the Rai children.

We were to meet the Mahals on a Saturday, one week before the wedding. Aunt Teji suggested a lavish afternoon feast, but my mother insisted that tea and sweets would be more appropriate. The day before the proposed meeting, my mother, Neelam, and I went into town. Neelam wanted shoes to match the satin, shell-white salwaar kameej she'd selected to wear to the meeting, and we visited three shoe shops before she found the right pair. By this point Neelam seemed resigned to the whole affair, even relieved that the big event was now only a week away, and that if she had to do it, she would have the right shoes and bags and matching everything.

When we arrived home, Uncle Avtar's blue Ford pickup was parked in the driveway beside a Caterpillar tractor. He had one foot propped on the tread of the tractor and was gesturing with one hand to a young man whose back was to us while pushing his gray fedora back on his head with the other. He made this gesture often, usually when he was formulating a question in his curious mind. We stepped out of the car, and Neelam called to Uncle Avtar. Hearing her greeting, the young man talking to Uncle Avtar turned. The silence that followed caused my mother—already heading into the house—to stop suddenly and look back. Before us was the figure we had been stealing looks at in that photograph—the wavy black hair, the boyish face. He pulled his hands from his pockets and brought his palms together in greeting, the still, solemn image coming to life. Neelam's hand went instinctively to the strands of hair that, after hours of frantic shopping, had loosened in unruly wisps from her braid.

"It's him!" I blurted out in something considerably louder than the whisper I had intended.

"Hello, ladies," Uncle Avtar said, stepping forward and pushing his hat even further back on his head so that it looked in danger of falling. "The shop is locked. I don't know where Mohinder is. I was giving the young man a quick tour of the place. Showing him what all the Rai family has managed in the U.S." He slapped Davinder playfully on the back, but he didn't appear to feel it, or to hear any of the brief conversation. He had not taken his eyes off Neelam.

Well, the damage was done. Neelam turned sharply and disappeared into the house. My mother attempted the sort of skillful diplomacy required in those delicate moments when murder is on one's mind. The only thing that would have been worse was the premature death of the groom. "You'll come in for tea?" The exaggerated arch of her brows lent a vaguely threatening tone to her words.

"I've got to get the boy back." Uncle Avtar slung an arm through the open window of the truck as if preparing to flee.

"We'll meet all of your family tomorrow then," she said to Davinder. She stormed up the front steps. I found something unbearably humorous about the situation—the "chance" meeting of the two my uncle had so deviously managed to arrange—and doubled over each time I recalled the utterly silly and helpless look on the young man's face. Yet, when I closed my eyes to sleep that night, I could not forget the look he'd given Neelam, and a great desire to be regarded in that same desperate, if foolish, way swept over me.

The following day, a large black Lincoln followed by a second, smaller gold sedan pulled up at Aunt Teji's around two. We had arrived at noon to find my cousin Juni tidying up lawn clippings in the front yard. Their home, like ours, rested back from the main road several hundred yards, so that you drove over a small dirt lane through an orchard to reach it. The white house looked bright and exposed under the bare-limbed cottonwood trees that bordered the lawn. A splatter of daffodils nodded in a corner bed. Inside, sheer white curtains on the open windows flared with the breeze, and a lingering trace of Pine-Sol mingled with the smell of cut grass. Aunt Teji had wiped and polished the furniture and the glassware and the photographs so that everything gleamed. We set out the sweets—layers of golden ladoo, barfi, and besan—on Aunt Teji's best china trays and arranged them on the coffee table. Neelam fussed a while with a vase of daffodils, then moved it from one surface to another, finally settling on a side table next to the sofa.

It was Prem who alerted us to the Mahals' arrival with a piercing "They're here!" We tugged him back from the window, then huddled behind him for a quick peek at the entourage filing toward the house. My father, a bit relaxed after no doubt sharing a shot of whiskey in a back room with his brother, opened the door, and a crowd of Mahals entered. Davinder startled me when he swept down and touched my parents' feet with his hands, a custom rarely seen anymore in California, at least among the Sikhs. Prem and Deepa carried in extra chairs from the dining room and everyone took seats. At the far end of the room, Neelam sat in pearly white satin, like a fresh calla lily poised in a slender vase. She rose long enough to quietly greet her new family.

Tea was brought in. There was talk of London, where the Mahals had stopped for two weeks on their way to the States. "Kensington, actually," Mrs. Mahal clarified in her Indo-British accent. She looked dignified in her royal blue and gold sari. Her hair was not streaked, but splotched with silver. Next to her sat a young, fair-skinned woman, the wife of Davinder's older brother, in whose lap a restless baby boy squirmed.

"I have cousins in Southampton," my mother announced proudly. "And Rugby. They visit every few years, always in the summer when they can complain of the heat."

"Jasbir has family everywhere," my father said. "But the Rais—"

"Only in California and Punjab," Uncle Avtar butted in. He sat forward, resting his elbows on his thighs and clasping his palms together between his knees. Over his light blue shirt he wore a burgundy wool vest Aunt Teji had knitted for him years ago. "It was like a pipeline between Punjab and California for a while. In 1947, when I came over, my first boss—his name was Joe Duncan—spoke fluent Spanish, and he would come over to me and start rattling off directions in Spanish. This was in the onion fields down in Imperial Valley. He wouldn't believe I was from India, until he finally checked the name on the payroll. So you see, I had two new languages to learn."

"I hear there are four gurdwaras here in town," Mr. Mahal said.

"It's not that we are exceptionally religious people," Uncle Avtar said, to laughter.

"There are factions," my father broke in. "It's inevitable when the population gets large enough."

"And, of course, the newest one must be more lavish than the last," Aunt Teji said.

"Many, many changes," Uncle Avtar said. "The first gurdwara was built in Stockton in 1912. Bring out the photo from '50," Uncle Avtar said to Aunt Teji.

She waved him off. "They're not interested in those old times." But just the same she rose and left the room.

"We have wonderful festivals—Baisakhi, Independence Day," my mother piped in. She had only recently complained to my father that all these events were going downhill, even the weddings, where young couples were beginning to request disco music at the receptions.

"It's encouraging to see the traditions maintained. It's a little different in England," said Mrs. Mahal. The baby arched his back, eager to be let down off his mother's lap. She set him down, and he crawled to the center of the room, slapping his palms against the glassy veneer of the polished wood floor, then crawled to Neelam's feet. She scooped him up, and he sat contentedly with her, wiggling his plump toes in the air.

"Are you in school right now or working, bhout?" Mrs. Mahal asked Neelam.

"I've finished high school. I worked in a fabric store this summer, but right now, nothing. I help keep my father's books."

"If you start a business, you'll have an excellent accountant," my father said to Davinder.

"Young brides have plenty to occupy themselves with," Aunt Teji said, returning with a large, framed photograph. "When I married your uncle, I had no idea how busy he would keep me knitting gloves. It would get cold in the winter and his hands would tighten up working outdoors, so I made him a pair of fingerless gloves. Well, when the other men saw his, they wanted them, too. Even his boss. I must've knit fifty pairs that winter." She held the photograph before Mrs. Mahal. In it a large group huddled on the steps before the arched doorways of the Stockton temple. The solid and upright men clad in suits and turbans or hats were gathered at the back, the women and children in front. If you squinted a bit, you could make out Aunt Teji in the second row, with baby Paul slung on her hip.

The conversation took its natural course, the men talking loudly in one half of the room, while the women gravitated to other topics. Neelam and Davinder barely acknowledged one another, but that was in keeping with expectations. And they were spoken of by the others as if they were not even present. I was relieved during that visit of any but the most menial tasks, though my mother asked me once to retrieve more napkins—a ploy to show the others that I was perfectly capable of rising from my half stupor and walking and moving about like a normal human being. I sat nearly motionless next to Neelam the entire time, playing with the hem of the cotton, sapphire blue kameej she had loaned me for the day. The whole scene seemed distant and unreal to me. These two families, brought together by what? The stars? A photograph? At any rate, here they sat, enchanted with each other's company, or at least making every effort to have it appear so. When the Mahals rose to leave, it was like reunited long-lost relatives once again being forced to part.

Sangeets—celebrations of food, song, and dance in anticipation of the wedding—were held over the week. The sofas in our living room were pushed against the walls so the women could perform their dances ostensibly out of view of the men, though Uncle Avtar always found reason to be nearby on these occasions. I blushed as I watched the nimble bodies, young and old, circling the floor, the provocative hip thrusts that tell the story of a virgin bride's sexual initiation. Among them was my mother, swirling, clapping, lithe and light on her heels, laughing like a girl. Neelam declined when a married friend clutched her veil and pulled her toward the circle of dancers. Afterward, as I swept up paper plates and rumpled napkins, the room still pulsed with a sweaty odor and the echo of songs.

The gurdwara we attended had been the first to be built in Oak Grove. It was rather simple in design, though recognizably something other than a Christian church with the single, gold-painted minaret that towered over it and the fine latticework and scalloped edging at the entryway. Those built afterward had tried to outdo one another in ostentation and poorly attempted authenticity; one had a court-yard with shallow, reflective pools running the length of it that had already had to be drained due to faulty plumbing. Another had three grand minarets, one at each corner, with the fourth forgone when funding suddenly dried up. Ours was not the grandest, but it had a dignity earned with the struggles to build the first gurdwara. The oak trees that framed the building were beginning to spread and mature, and our temple looked as if it belonged on that site.

On the day of her wedding, we whisked Neelam through the back entrance of the gurdwara into a small dressing room. She had dressed at home, a process requiring hours before the last gold bangle was fit over her wrist. She swayed and shimmered with the weight of the gold and the gold thread woven through the fabric of her red silk sari. A throng of women and girls—those young enough to regard her with envy—gathered around her. Her friend Mani stood by her side like a sentry with a pinched, flat mouth, viewing others as intruders. My mother soon chased out all but two of my aunts, who would escort Neelam into the cavernous main hall.

The room swelled with a swarming tide of people. Their voices rose in a collective din toward the high carved ceiling. On the women's side, Mrs. Mahal and her daughter-in-law sat on the floor next to Aunt Teji and Aunt Manjit. Across the aisle my father, Prem, and Uncle Avtar crouched uncomfortably, with the Mahals on their far side. We'd once enjoyed the luxury of folding chairs in the temple, but a few years earlier a reformist group had led a protest to return to the more traditional custom of sitting on the floor. After a careful review, one of the clergy discovered that floor-sitting increased the density of worshippers, and therefore revenues, by fifteen percent over chair-sitting, and so the reformists prevailed.

Surinder and I squeezed behind Aunt Teji. Surinder was a cousin of sorts, meaning that we were not related by blood but through a convoluted system of kinship. Surinder made the most of her looks, despite a longish nose and small, narrow eyes. Some of her jet black hair was gathered in a twist at the back, and the rest fell well past her shoulders. Her mother allowed that. She'd called Neelam the night before to offer assistance with makeup, jewelry, and other details ("beauty treatment *karenge*," she said gaily over the phone). We shuffled on the floor to make room for my mother. As the groom was seated, the crowd inched forward in a final push so that my knees scrunched against my face. Someone else's knees repeatedly grazed my back, and I turned to see Charan Kaur wedged close behind me. We waited some moments, Davinder at the front with his head bowed in that saffron-colored turban, before Neelam was led out. Only then did the crowd quiet down.

"She looks beautiful," Surinder whispered.

"You can't even see her," I said, for Neelam was covered head to toe in red and gold. The granthi appeared, dressed in a white kurta-pajama and a charcoal-colored vest. His long beard swung like a silver curtain over his chest as he lowered himself before the low lectern where the holy book, the Granth Sahib, lay under layers of brocade. Two musicians, also dressed in white kurta-pajamas, took up their instruments—a harmonia and dhol—and began to play. The harmonia player, a serious, sunken-faced man whom I recognized from earlier performances, stretched his long hands over the bellowslike portion of the instrument and summoned the most aching and plaintive notes. Soon Aunt Teji was pressing the backs of her hands against her cheeks. The married women bowed their heads in communal reverence. All of us, together, seemed to be yielding to something, submitting quietly and seriously. I had attended countless weddings already in my fifteen years, but I felt the shape of something indistinct, but hard and quiet, lodge within me just as the music faded and the granthi began to pray.

Soon Neelam and her new husband were circling the Granth Sahib, their wrists tied together with a band of white cloth. There was a moment of laughter when the two rose and turned in our direction, suddenly paralyzed, and Mrs. Mahal made a clockwise gesture with her arm as if to propel them into motion around the holy book. As the couple circled the Granth Sahib, Aunt Teji silently mouthed the words the granthi spoke: "Ek Jot Doe Murthi," one spirit in two bodies. After they sat, we circled bills and coins over their heads and laid them in their laps, a wish for prosperity, then showered them with rose petals.

Only relatives and close friends—a small portion of the humanity streaming out the temple doors—were invited to Aunt Teji's for the reception. The decision to hold it there had required little discussion. The house was larger than ours—with two bathrooms, Aunt Manjit mentioned several times—and the large expanse of lawn would hold numerous picnic tables where the men could convene. Uncle Avtar had stopped by one evening a few nights earlier to discuss preparations for the reception, but the way he stood in the doorway spinning his hat in his hands, we all recognized it was really a kind of apology to my mother for the unexpected meeting of bride and groom. He spoke mournfully of the goat he would slaughter and curry for the feast following the wedding. It was one of Melinda's sons, Melinda being his favorite, now aged, goat. I occupied him with idle questions at the doorway, while my mother hovered just within earshot with a broom in her hand, though she couldn't quite bring herself to sweep anything (it was evening and that was bad luck).

Aunt Teji's place appeared quiet, almost sleepy, in the strong, hazy light of midafternoon. A few children ran among the wooden tables and benches lining the front lawn. Small plumes of smoke threaded toward the sky on the north side of the house, and there a group of men gathered around a fire with a large iron pot pitched over it. My mother offered some parting words on moderation to my father as he headed off, and he laughed mildly and told her not to worry. Prem, basketball clutched under one arm, ran off in search of Deepa and his other male cousins.

I'd always liked riding in our car and staring into the houses that rushed by, rows of them, one after the other, and imagining their rooms and the walls that separated them, the people in them. Lying in my own room, I would hear my parents' muted voices seeping through the walls like a slow, thick syrup, speaking words that couldn't be spoken elsewhere. I wondered at how physical spaces dictated our words and actions, mandated our lives. I passed from the cool sunlight into the dusky shadows of Aunt Teji's living room, aware of the sea of faces. They looked at Neelam first, but I knew their scrutiny would turn to me next. If the circumstances of Neelam's life had changed that day, mine had also.

Mrs. Mahal rose and engulfed my mother and Neelam in lengthy embraces. Neelam had changed into a light, peach-colored salwaar kameej and looked remarkably refreshed and rested, though earlier she had snarled at me for coming into the bedroom while she was attempting to nap.

"Your husband is resting," Mrs. Mahal said to her, tapping her lightly on the thigh. "Teji hid him away somewhere. He'll be up soon. If not, I'll go tell him myself that his bride has arrived." Her earlier disappointment, elicited when Neelam declined to go with Davinder straightaway to Aunt Teji's, seemed to have disappeared. I was standing against the wall with my hands pressed at the small of my back. Mrs. Mahal motioned me over, and as I sat next to her she took my chin in her hand and smiled approvingly.

I felt other eyes on me, dozens of pairs of brown eyes (and one pair of green ones) blinking and flashing in my direction. I was being appraised in a new light—as a woman, as marriage material—now that Neelam's future had been settled; I wasn't sure their assessment was entirely agreeable. My toes turned fat under their close gaze, bulging over the tips of my sandals, my ankles knobby, my neck long and spindly, barely able to support my head. I longed for something clever to say, to put them all at ease, to show them I was Neelam's equal and more, but all I could manage was that Aunt Teji's samosas were the best.

"Serjit, you've grown taller than Neelam and your mother," Charan Kaur said to me. The other women nodded at this milestone, presented as a compliment. "But quite thin," she added severely.

I was relieved to hear a male voice behind me. Davinder appeared under a ruffled crown of hair that he attempted to smooth with one hand as he greeted Neelam. His face still wore the dreamy languor of sleep. "You've had some rest yourself, I hope?" Davinder asked, leaning down toward her.

Neelam threw her elbow over the back of the chair and faced him. "A little. There was still some packing to do." She couldn't quite bring her eyes to meet his.

Taking her nephew by the sleeve, Sethi Mahal guided him toward the door. "It's time for you to join the men outside. You'll see plenty of her later," she said to laughter. Davinder threw up his hands as if in surrender and left.

The thrill caused by that brief exchange receded like floodwaters from a low plain. Hunger brought on by the wafts of curry and masala coming from the kitchen began to dull our moods and an acute torpor settled over us. Someone brought up the subject of the upcoming Mann wedding. Not even Charan Kaur's information about the groom, a boy from Fresno, could pique much interest. "The older son or the younger?" someone asked. "The one with his eyes too close together," another answered, putting to rest that little mystery. Neelam traced with one finger the delicate henna pattern scrolled on the back of her hands. These parties could be miserable affairs. Inside, where the women remained sequestered, the walls could barely contain the mix of cooking smells and the hot, slightly acid, breathed-in air.

When Surinder's family arrived, Surinder and I were mercifully called into the kitchen. Neelam shot me a desperate glance as I left the room, but I had sat and listened to the satin folds of my salwaar rustling long enough. In the kitchen, my mother was still rolling out rounds of wheat-flour dough for roti and slapping them on the griddle. Surinder and I ladled bowls of orange chana dahl and saffron rice with almonds and raisins and yogurt kutta dotted with small pakoris and speckled with grains of masala and cayenne pepper. Surinder had fixed her hair differently, into a high ponytail at the back with curled and teased bangs that framed her face. She was an only child, a rarity among Indian families, and her parents doted on her as though she were a boy. We were inseparable at these parties; we hunkered down together and got each other through.

Uncle Avtar poked his head through the back entrance. "Ladies, my goat is waiting," he said, waggling his head. "I've refined my recipe. You'll all be clamoring for more." He was renowned for his fiery cooking.

"Acha, we'll see. Last time you gave your Uncle Sodhi a gall bladder attack," Aunt Teji said. She whisked a stick of butter over a roti, leaving creamy pools that splattered as she tossed it onto a mounting pile.

Outside, under a cluster of orange and lemon trees, Uncle Avtar lifted the heavy, charred pot from the platform onto a wooden table. The fire still smoldered. A phalanx of ribs jutted out as Uncle Avtar stirred the thick, golden sauce. I thought of him standing at our door, spinning his hat in his hands and talking somberly of Melinda's boys as though they were his own. He ladled the curry into bowls with great care.

The house, facing west, cast a wide shadow over the lawn as the sun lowered in the sky. Surinder and I distributed the bowls among the long rows of tables, and the sight of food enticed the men to take seats. The place had the feel of countless other parties my aunt and uncle had thrown here. A maze of light bulbs strung over the tables bobbed in the breeze. Small glasses filled with Aunt Teji's purple violets decorated the tables. A few rusted metal drums, the kind Uncle Avtar burned trash in, were scattered around. Later, when it grew colder, he would light fires in them so the men could huddle there and keep warm; it was his way of extending a night's festivities.

As Surinder and I served the food, we never lingered too long in one spot lest someone's errant gaze fall on us. From the head table, I felt my father's eyes following me. Davinder appeared a little droopy and sullen, propped as he was between my father and his, who were engaged in an impassioned conversation. The lights in the house went on just then, and his face swept toward the window that framed Neelam as she sat inside, a soft bank of light spreading across her back. Her veil fell from her head, caressing her shoulders, exposing the smooth, alabaster nape of her neck. She pulled the veil back over her head, and Davinder turned away.

———

Eight months later, that autumn afternoon in my mother's kitchen, I filled a pot with cold water from the tap to brew fresh tea for the women. Neelam's hands were immersed in a basin of soapy water, and her arms appeared as though they had been lopped off at the wrists. Her thick, blue black braid hung forward over one shoulder, snaking down her chest.

"More tea? Aren't they ready to leave yet?" She spoke as though this were her home, as if after the others left, she would remain with us, where she belonged. Though Neelam still visited the house nearly daily, I missed her constant presence, the slow sway of her shoulders and hips ahead of me in the hallway as I tried to bolt past. Prem missed her, too. She had been motherly to him, fussing over him, plying him with treats and favors, shielding him with her body when things got rough and heated between him and me.

I cracked the kitchen door open a few inches and peered out at the ladies. Aunt Teji sprawled against the back of the sofa, her eyes shut and her chest heaving with each deep, rhythmic breath. "Aunt Teji's snoring," I said, dashing Neelam's hopes that the afternoon's gathering might soon break up. No one dared to wake our aunt.

Neelam rolled her eyes and shook the cups under the steaming stream of water. She vigorously dried them with a white cotton towel and set them on the counter. The sleeve of her kameej slipped off one shoulder, exposing the shell-shaped birthmark that kissed her collarbone. "How's driver's ed going?"

I added milk to the tea and turned down the flame. "I don't know. Mr. Ronin keeps his eyes shut most of the time when I'm driving."

"He did that with me, too. He must know we're Mrs. Rai's daughters," Neelam said, laughing. "I was so relieved when I got my license and Mom didn't have to drive us around anymore."

I nodded, though I was still regular prey to her herky-jerky, foot-on-the-pedal method of getting across town.

"Jeet." Neelam pronounced it in two slow, urgent syllables, jee-*eet*. She was looking down, nervously stroking her braid as if it were an appendage, an arm of plump, dark flesh. When she lifted her eyes to me, my breath stopped. I knew what she was about to say, and dreaded hearing the words. "You're still checking the mail every day yourself?"

I nodded, feeling my blood slow within me.

"But nothing comes for me? You'd tell me first, wouldn't you?"

"Of course."

Her chin trembled faintly. I'd yet to experience that kind of love. All last semester Joey Kaminsky and I had exchanged long, burning glances in the back of the classroom in U.S. Government, but then I had seen him the final week of school behind the crab apples planted against the wall of the gym, his mouth hovering around Cynthia Wold's neck. The memory felt dim and paltry as I stared into Neelam's warm, glistening eyes.

She gripped the edge of the sink with both hands and gazed out the window. A row of red, blue, and purple smoked glass dishes, earned for our mother in fervent coin tosses at the county fair, lined the deep windowsill. Outside, the gnarled fruit trees stood like old men tired of stretching their limbs. In winter, when their leaves had fallen and were matted copper and rust against the muddy ground, you could just make out Aunt Teji's house through the dense criss-cross of branches.

"I don't think he'd try to get in touch with you here. Do you know where he is now?" I asked. The thrill of these secrets fluttered through my body.

Neelam shook her head. "Don't mention it to anyone. I wanted to ask you before, but it seemed ridiculous. I guess it still does."

My mother burst through the door with all the finesse of an invading army tank. "How long does it take to brew a pot of tea? You're standing around while the ladies are waiting." Her face turned from mine to Neelam's.

"Just sisters talking," Neelam said.

"Look, you've cooked it too long." My mother pulled the pot off the burner; the tea had boiled away to half its original volume.

"Aunt Teji was sleeping anyway," I protested.

"Well, she's wide awake now, and quite thirsty. Neelam, bring out more sweets."

In the living room, Aunt Manjit was back on the topic of old Mrs. Sidhu, a favorite of hers. "Did you see what she wore to the Soba wedding? That orchid pink? You'd think she was trying to steal the groom."

"So the poor old thing wants to turn a few heads. There's plenty of lonely widowers to take notice," Aunt Teji said, waving a hand.

The air hung like sticky, thick molasses. I tapped the tip of my sandal against the worn wooden leg of the coffee table, earning a stern look from my mother. Toe tapping was considered brazen and wanton, and all my life my mother had sought to keep my restless legs still. As the women finally rose to depart, Aunt Manjit sneezed. Twice. Everyone retreated to the sofas again for the customary half hour it would take for bad luck to exit our household.

I walked Aunt Teji home later. Neelam had left quietly, after whispering that we would talk more tomorrow. Aunt Teji and I set off down the dirt road that cut through to the other side of the property. The door on my father's shop was padlocked, as he was away making deliveries for the afternoon. Deepa followed behind us or scurried ahead. The late afternoon light had a way of flattering everything that time of day. Aunt Teji looked blushed and radiant, and I could imagine her clearly as the vigorous and willful young woman who had come from India many years ago as Uncle Avtar's bride. Even now, her carriage was strong and erect, and I had trouble keeping up with her. I rolled up my pant legs and slipped the sandals off my feet, letting my toes curl into the dust. It sifted like fine flour around my ankles.

My mother must've waited that night, watching for the crack of light under my bedroom door to disappear before she came in. She rarely interrupted as I did schoolwork, yet made certain that I wouldn't get to it until well after dinner, after the dishes were washed, dried, and put away. *Hoshaar,* smart, she would say to the others, referring to me, but my education frightened her, for she knew one day it would take me away from her.

"Jeeto," she called to me, pushing the door open. Her long wavy hair, loosened from its dignified bun, cascaded well past her shoulders. In the shadowy light she appeared young, as though it were Neelam coming to bed when we shared a room.

I sat up on the bed and flipped on a light. She came in and inspected a page in my geometry book, which lay open on my desk.

"We're learning the Pythagorean theorem, how to find the lengths on the sides of a triangle." With my forefinger, I etched the simple shape in the air.

"Acha," she answered, okay, as if she had gotten the essence of it. She would nonchalantly leaf through a book and I saw wonder seep through her, a guarded amazement that there was a system, a body of logic beyond her gods and goddesses. She smoothed my cotton blankets and rested one hip at the edge of the bed. The lamp on the nightstand cast a bright arc of light over her green kameej and the pink covers on my bed. Her full, unlined face remained in a shadow. "So, what were you and Neelam talking about today?" she asked casually.

"Nothing, really. She might go shopping in Berkeley on Saturday. Can I go with her?"

"With all the clothes she has? She hasn't even worn every outfit once yet."

I shrugged. "She has those empty closets to fill in that new house." Neelam and Davinder had bought a house in a new subdivision on the north end of town. It was called Stonebrook Heights, though as far as I could tell, its elevation was no different than the dull flatness of the rest of Oak Grove.

"Now that I think of it, you could use something for the festival. But I won't pay the prices in Berkeley. I'll have Balwant Kaur make you another one."

I sat forward, resting my chin in my palm and picking at the loose weave of the blanket with my other hand. "She'll make something ugly like she always does. I think she wants me to look ugly on purpose. Last time I had to wear that beige thing with huge, light blue roses. I felt like I was walking around in someone's awful curtains."

She took my arm and patted it. "When you marry, you can have nice things to wear like Neelam." I didn't want to look at her then. "If Neelam's going anyway, you can go along. Davinder's going, too, isn't he?"

"I don't know."

"Well, they had some beautiful chunis at Sardar's. You can pick up one or two for me," she said, rising.

In the dark and quiet, I could hear a faint humming in the walls of the house. A branch on the walnut tree outside my window creaked against the eaves. I could imagine Neelam lying in the bed against the other wall in the grip of a fevered slumber. As I settled back into my pillow, I felt my pulse roaring into its cushiony fibers, and I knew that I would lie again.

MATTHEW PURDY

Binghamton University

CREATURES OF A DAY

DAY ONE

I've decided to live with the chickens. I've been here almost a week,
and even though I made it clear my staying would be temporary,
they've nonetheless invited me to stay. I like it here. I feel accepted
and necessary. They've given me my own coop in the corner of the
pen. This, again, was to be only a temporary accommodation, though
in the time I've been here no one has asked to use it. It's small, as
coops go, though it's enough for me. At first, I hit my head on the
ceiling every morning, and the closeness of the space made it hard for
me to fall asleep. I've since gotten used to it, though; my time here
has been nothing if not a series of adjustments. In fact, I've even
come to like my coop. I like to think it brings me closer to the original egg-state that is a common point of reference for my fellows.

That, I think, is the one thing that most separates me from them, and it's an unbridgeable divide. But if it's brought me closer to understanding them, I'm glad for a little inconvenience.

DAY TWO

I am surprised how quickly I picked up their language. I've never had much of a knack for languages. When I visited Paris several years ago, it was all I could do to order a cup of coffee at a café. I wasn't used to a language that lived so far back in the head, reclining on one's tongue with a distinctly European mixture of indifference and scorn. I stomped where tiptoes were required. Everything is smaller there, not unlike my coop. Here, there is an economy—of food, space, even movement. Take Roselle, for instance, one of my first friends on the farm and still one of my dearest. She's just passing by now, saying hello. "Hello, Roselle!" She never has a feather out of place, nor a movement. None of the flamboyant scratchings in the dirt to which so many of them feel compelled. I realize it's a sign of greeting, but it still makes me feel uneasy. It just seems pointlessly hostile. I secretly think one of them will attack me, when I see it kicking up clouds of dust with those claws. I know it's wrong of me, but still. Anyway, none of that for Roselle. It seems she doesn't even blink her eyes unless it's absolutely necessary. Her steps are careful, and she carries herself with remarkable grace and silence. Ironically, it is primarily her from whom I learned their language. Ordinary things—names, greetings, small talk, forms of address— but important things. As far as I know they don't have a literature, as such; it would have to be an oral literature, if anything. I shall have to ask about that.

DAY SIX

My apologies for not having written sooner. I've spent the past few days exploring some of the finer points of the culture. There's so much to tell! In no particular order, then:

1. Their language is much subtler than I had originally thought. So much depends on inflection; it's not so much spoken as sung. Sitting in the main coop yesterday, awash in the chorus of voices, the beauty of the language—the sheer miracle of it—overwhelmed me. I drew up my knees close to my chest as a small, slow tingle threaded its way through my body.
2. Corn-day is heaven on earth.
3. I'm beginning to feel more at home here, less foreign. More importantly, they've come to regard me as a member of the community. Or, at any rate, they've accepted that I'm not going to leave. I'm a recognizable part of the landscape. There is a certain unease, though, that still persists. Last evening, for instance, I came upon some unfamiliar fellows conversing outside the main coop. As I approached, they immediately broke and ran. I called to them in my pidgin chicken, but to no avail. I must remember to ask Roselle how to say my name in their language.
4. There is no rigid social hierarchy. (I almost said "pecking order"!) Rather, the proximity in which they all live fosters an astoundingly complex web of relationships; they have at least seven words for "friend." Strangely, ties of kinship don't appear to be very important to them. Social standing is intensely relative and constantly fluctuating. If one is an outcast, it is more than likely one's own doing; status is very rarely chalked up to simple fate. (My standing is still unclear, though I suppose I'm an exceptional case.)

DAY SEVEN

I have yet to mention the farmer. His name is Roger; he's old and walks with a limp. Before I decided to take up permanent residence here, he tried to rout me out, brandishing a rake and shouting that my coop was meant for the chickens, that he'd lose money if people found out there was some vagrant living in there. I tried to show him my point of view, but there's no reasoning with people like that. All our shouting, moreover, proved quite unsettling to my fellows, who began chattering and flapping and running and scratching in the dirt like I've never seen. Eventually Roger gave up. As he trudged back toward the door of the pen, my fellows swarmed about him. He called back that, if he found out I hurt his chickens, he would call the police. What kind of a monster did he take me for? And what right did he have to call them "his"? I didn't care, though. My fellows lingered by the door, their clamor unabated, until Roger was safely out of sight.

It was then that I decided I belonged here. My fellows knew it before I did. They recognized me, though still very much a stranger, as one of their own, and they united against our common oppressor on my behalf. I didn't know their language very well at all then, so I don't know what, exactly, they said. But I understood them as clearly as I do today. Strangely, though, I've never heard them talk about the farmer. I don't think they even have the words for it.

DAY EIGHT

Roger told me if I was to stay I'd have to do my share. He gave me a bag of grain and a pail to feed my fellows (not to mention myself) every morning. This, of course, is quite an honor. As they crowded around me, some returning for three or four servings, I was giddy with my own importance. They pushed one another out of the way, and there were even some fights. All because of me! I began to laugh. My laugh is beginning to sound more like crowing, and it inspired some of my fellows to crow themselves. That made me laugh even more.

DAY NINE

"Warm is with day."

Roselle said this to me this morning. It was the first time I didn't have to translate something from their language to mine. Of course, I have to translate it to write it down here, and now that it's in front of me it seems kind of silly, but I knew instinctively what she meant.[1]

"Yes," I said. "Quite with." I glanced up at her from my cot. She blinked once and thrust her head forward several times. This is a sign of approval, a compensation for their inability to smile. I nodded my head in response. She took a hesitant step forward, but then quickly said, "You and the day with happiness," before hastening out the door.

Oh, Roselle. My dear, dear Roselle...

DAY ELEVEN

Blinton was young. He took up with Thelma around the time I first arrived. He was small, but he came into his comb, as they say, fairly

---

[1] The possessive case is almost entirely unknown to them; interrelatedness is the currency of the country. For instance, I wouldn't say, "The coop is yellow," but "The coop is with yellow," or more colloquially, "Yellow and the coop." "Yellow" is seen as an entirely separate entity from "coop." Since it wouldn't occur to them that the coop would "have" yellow, the coop and yellow are thus in a relationship, together on an equal plane of being.

early. Early yesterday morning, Thelma laid for the first time in their courtship. Blinton climbed atop the grain trough and began to wail. It was a strange, brutal music. I put off my feeding chores for nearly an hour so as not to disturb him in his holy fury.

In the afternoon, Roger came to collect Thelma's eggs. Blinton blocked the entrance to the coop. Roger tried to brush him aside, but Blinton shrieked and lunged at Roger's hand. Roger swatted at him; Blinton pecked and scratched in the dirt. Roger clasped his hands around Blinton's head and Blinton scratched Roger's arm with his claws and (as Roger jerked him upward, roaring from the pain and the barbed-wire scar budding and blotting on his flannel shirt, though not for a second slackening his grip) jabbed at his chest, his cheeks, his neck before Roger threw him at the dirt and stomped and ground his shoe against his neck, frothing up the dust into a cloud so thick it lingered in my clothes and stung my eyes for many days afterward. Panting, he finally picked up the limp and strangely tiny body and flung it under his arm. He emerged from the coop a minute later with the eggs in one hand and Blinton's body in the other. On his way out of the pen, he glanced inside my coop. "Fucking vermin, eh?" he said. To my horror, he expected sympathy. He passed by before I could respond.

DAY THIRTEEN

Roselle and I shared a deeply melancholy night. We sat on top of my coop, where we could hear the distant hum of the highway and see the copper-colored smog smeared along the horizon. We witnessed the passing of something. A sediment of pollen and fly parts had collected in the gutter; I scooped out a handful and dumped it over the side. Roselle lowed a soft whine. I lay back and she settled herself on my chest. The cicadas' irregular, mournful rhythm was like something seeping out of the night.

"Roselle," I said, "what do you think happens when we die?"

"What do you mean?" she asked.

I propped myself up on my elbows. "When we die. At some point, we won't be here anymore."

"Yes," she said. "The great dark will leave and the small dark will come, and then the blue with warm."

"But one day the blue and the warm and the brown soft and the great and small darks won't come. You won't see it anymore."

She looked at me suspiciously. I had piled so many idioms on top of one another that by the end I hardly remembered where I had begun. They have no words for death, I now realize, nor even words for sight; what one sees is what one is. Roselle blinked rapidly as she shook her head. "I don't understand," she said.

"It's okay," I said. I began stroking her back, and after a while she began to quiver. She moaned and I cupped my hands around her. She kneaded my shirt with her claws, plucking and tearing. She moaned again, loudly and long, and in a moment a small, pale egg sat like a miniature moon on my stomach. With the egg in one hand and Roselle in the other I sat up. I pressed her close to me and she rubbed her head against my breast several times. We both shivered, she with exhaustion, I with wonder and humility. I lifted the egg into the still, cool night. "Thank you," I said. I said it in my own language, but I think she understood.

DAY FIFTEEN

Roselle spent the last two nights in my coop. No, no, there was nothing untoward. But she did lay again for me late yesterday afternoon. I put them under my cot, where the sun shines in all day and where my body heat will keep them warm all night. I cut off a lock of my hair and tied it around her left leg, as a gesture of friendship. She said it makes walking uncomfortable, but she doesn't walk all that much anymore. She just sits on the eggs, mostly. We had a slight disagreement about where to put the nest—she wanted it in the opposite corner, for some reason—but she finally conceded to keeping it under my cot. It would have been too much effort for her to move the nest, anyway.

Our recent domestic adjustment has been like corn for the gossips, and there are many. I've never had much time for them, though. My male fellows have been civil—or, at least none of them have shown their jealousy outright. Roselle was quite the prize, and in her day she's inspired more than a few brawls. Some of them, I've heard, think she's only interested in me because I'm "exotic." They accuse me of wooing her with tales of strange customs and far-off places. That, of course, is nonsense. She loves me for who I am. And if I don't cock my comb, so to speak, like everybody else, well, that only endears me to her more. Why can't they just leave us alone?

DAY SIXTEEN

Roger came by this morning, looking for Roselle. When he didn't find her in her usual coop, he came screaming into mine. I was able to drive him out and barricade the doorway with my cot. I threw stones at him until he left. He said he's going to call the police. I've tried my best to comfort Roselle, but I'm frightened, too.

DAY EIGHTEEN

I'm writing this from intensive care. The police came after all. Roselle got up and started running. They put handcuffs on me. She fell and her leg bent backward. I could hear her screeching from the car.

Roger carried the eggs off in a carton. My clothes reek of sweat, but I remember the day as being very cold. They said I was severely malnourished. Everything was very fast, then everything was still. Roger held Roselle by the feet. They keep asking me what my name is. Everyone was watching as we drove away. I could have died of starvation, they said. They shone a light in my face and even though it was barely afternoon it stung. My wrists still hurt from the handcuffs. She fell because of the hair I tied around her leg. She laid that egg for me. They put an IV into my arm. Is this what hatching is like? I'm so tired.

DAY TWENTY

They cut my hair and gave me new clothes before releasing me. They made me promise I wouldn't go back to the farm, that I would go right home. The doctor slipped me ten dollars for food. A block away from the hospital I hailed a cab. I thrust my bill at the driver and asked if it would get me where I wanted to go. When we arrived at the farm he asked if he should stick around. I told him no.

I went by the pen. No one recognized me. I tried the gate, but it was locked. I was surprised how quickly I'd forgotten their language. A few came near, thinking I was Roger, but they had never been friends of mine. I sat down in the dirt, wondering if I could die simply by willing it. I clenched my eyes shut, but when I opened them I was still there. Somewhere eggs were lain and squabble-dust rose thick, but I would never know. There was no place for me there anymore. Would I become an exile, condemned to wander the earth without a homeland or a people? I wanted to call Roselle's name but didn't, for fear I had forgotten how to say that, too.

I walked over to the farmhouse and knocked on the door. Roger's wife, Anne, answered it. She was terse and suspicious. She called Roger's name without looking away from me. "It's him," she added. "I'll call the fucking cops!" he yelled, stomping down the stairs. "Tell him to get the hell off my property!" I told them I'd come to make amends; could I please just come inside?

The living room was strangely dark. The sheer density of things—the two couches, the four chairs, the little circular tables with photographs and dishes full of gumdrops, the books, the flowers, the faceless dolls in old-fashioned clothes—made me nervous. I sat down delicately on one of the chairs while they delicately sat down on the couch. I told them I had nowhere to go and no job; I had made up a name in the hospital, but I didn't know if it was right. They were silent a moment, exchanging soft glances. I was humble and soft-spoken, not to say clean and shorn, which I believe helped my case. They left the room to speak, and a few minutes later they invited me to spend the night. Afternoon was waning and Anne was just about to start supper. Roger said he'd take me into town in the morning. I thanked them and they showed me a spare room upstairs. After they left I laid down on the bed and fell asleep.

I awoke to Anne calling my name from the bottom of the stairs. "I've prepared a plate for you," she said. The house was a harmony of smells, modulating and counterpointing as I walked down the stairs and through the living room. Though something primal and word-less pulled at me, I stopped in the doorway to the kitchen. On the table sat a steaming and glistening chicken. Anne pulled out a chair for me and I sat down. I took a bite of the meat; it made my very bones tingle with satisfaction. I finished off the plate before Roger even sat down. Anne tore off one of the legs, which was bent at a strange angle, pointing away from the rest of the carcass, pointing at me. She carved the bone clean and I ate all of it.

TAMARA GUIRADO

Wisconsin Institute for Creative Writing

DOG CHILDREN

In an effort to save their relationship, Maggie and Avashai were watching pornos in Maggie's barn apartment. Both front and back doors were open, and they could hear the soft nickering of the neighbor's horses while on the television screen, a small blond woman in a red neckerchief straddled the supine body of Long Dong Silver. The woman slowly skewered herself, shrieking gamely, as Long Dong lay perfectly still, looking vaguely embarrassed. Maggie was reminded of a feminist philosophy course she had taken in which the professor had suggested that *enclosure* might be a better word than *penetration*. In class they sat in a circle and passed an orange around the room like a talking stick—whoever had the orange had the floor and sometimes you had to wait a very long time to make your point.

She looked up from the TV and out the hay doors at the gathering dusk. It was Indian summer. Star thistle grew rampant all the way to the neighbor's pasture—purple blooms like handfuls of needles. It would die when the rains came, leaving a thin sheet of green.

"It's getting late," Maggie said. "I wonder where the woodman is?"

"No pun intended," Avashai said.

"I wish it were already winter."

"What for?"

"I don't know." A host of images panned across her mind, but they were far too complex to explain. "Snow."

Except for the small bathroom, the barn was one big room with a counter separating the kitchen area from the living room. Above the kitchen was a loft where Maggie slept. The walls were knotty pine with spider webs and little bits of straw still clinging to the upper corners where a broom couldn't reach. The ceiling had silver insulation stapled to it with tufts of pink fiberglass fluff, like cotton candy, sticking out in spots.

Long Dong had closed his eyes and looked almost as though he might be sleeping. The poor man was deformed; when standing his penis hung down to midshin. Maggie wondered what his daily life was like, if he had to strap the thing to his leg somehow—with an Ace bandage or a specially designed piece of cloth and Velcro. Did he wear loose, voluminous pants? She wanted to talk to Avashai about this, but she had promised to watch in silence, as her running commentary tended to disrupt his rather fragile erotic illusions.

She reached out to pet his hair but he dodged her, jaw twitching impatiently. His shaved head had grown a half inch of dark, soft stubble that made his skull look like some kind of appealing baby animal—a blind puppy, or a seal cub. They sat on an old patchwork quilt on the sofa. The quilt was handmade by her mother and contained scraps of cloth from her mother's and father's and stepfather's and Maggie's own clothing—in the center was an edenic embroidered scene of tiny pink naked people lounging in a field of strawberries.

"Is there any more beer, Gretchen?"

"I'm not Gretchen." She felt a stabbing in her gut, followed by the sick, warm trickle of pleasure at being wounded to her advantage. She worked up some water in her eyes.

"Did I say that?" He reached out and gave her a tight, crushing hug, the kind he gave only when he had done something very, very bad. "Shhhh, shhhh, I'm sorry, baby. It was just a slip of the tongue."

Sometimes she hated Avashai, but she saw his fuzzy skull as a separate entity for which she had an enormous fondness. While cradling or petting it, she felt some deeper kind of connection was taking place than they were capable of on a verbal level. She liked to hug him when he would let her, but, aside from sex, he was skittish about being touched. She cut him slack about this because he had confessed to her that when he was four he had been molested in a foster home by a gang of older boys. The more she wanted to touch him, the less he wanted to be touched, and this made her want to do it even more.

She could feel the rusted dog tag chain he wore around his wrist pressing into her shoulder; it gave off a faint metallic odor, like dried blood. The last time he'd hugged her like this was in the alley by his apartment between Biggum's Silver Lion and Ye Old Sweet Shoppe, pressing her into the bricks, minutes after she had discovered her friend's eighteen-year-old baby sister in his bed, "Just sleeping because she needed a place to stay."

Avashai fancied himself an anarchist and a revolutionary, which in practice meant that he compiled a little zine with articles on the plight of the working man and had once defaced a mail truck. Like Maggie, he was twenty-six, a bit old, she thought, to still be punk rock, but he was beautiful—half Irish, half Cherokee, with pale, pale skin and dark red Mick Jagger lips. It was fashionable in Ashland to be Native American but Avashai wasn't particularly interested in that part of his heritage. He identified with his Irish side, romanticized the IRA, and had a Celtic cross tattooed across his snow white abdomen.

They had a lot of semipublic sex. Once recently at the Angus Bowmer Theater very early in the morning, on stage, on a brocade prop sofa facing the rows of empty seats. Avashai was a janitor at all three theaters on the Shakespeare lot and had keys to all the bathrooms and the sets as well as free tickets to the plays. They watched *Pool of Bethesda* and several hours later had sex on the abstract set on a leper's pallet. The play wasn't very sexy—an actress had worn a prosthetic breast with purple and red cancerous lesions, and various cripples and lepers with running sores had hobbled around the set. A fat, naked Asian man with long tangled hair, his groin draped in soiled cheesecloth, had reclined in the straw where they now lay. The stage sloped forward toward the "fourth wall" giving Maggie the feeling of certain falling nightmares she'd had.

Maggie tracked Avashai's eyes to the television screen and saw the blond take in the last five inches. The woman's forehead wrinkled up and she let out a sharp cry of pain, professionally disguised as passion. She wondered if perhaps Long Dong were in pain as well, because surely his penis must be folded up inside this woman, it wasn't humanly possible for it to have all gone in straight—the thing would be up in her heart.

"Ouch," Maggie said.

"I can't watch this with you," Avashai said, releasing her.

"Why not?"

"There's a suspension of disbelief, and you're ruining it."

"Sorry."

"Let's just forget it." He sighed and pushed the Stop/Eject button on the VCR.

On the local news there was a fire watch and burn piles were forbidden. A teenage mortuary worker in Cave Junction had kidnapped a corpse in the mortuary's hearse and was still at large. She'd left a letter confessing to amorous episodes with between twenty to forty dead men. A photo of a young woman hovered in the upper-right-hand corner of the screen. She looked like you'd expect, Maggie thought, a plump, sullen-faced white girl with dyed black hair and a cultivated pallor. Ordinary.

"She's pretty," Avashai said.

"If you like eighties goth." She looked like a heavier, younger version of Gretchen.

The girl's white-trash mother seemed to be enjoying the attention, allowing news cameras into her home, giving a tour of her Satanist daughter's bedroom—a pitiful mix of shabby stuffed animals and pencil drawings of roses and razor blades.

"You need help, honey," the girl's mother hammed tearfully at the camera, sitting on her daughter's floral comforter. "Come home."

"Now watch," Maggie said. "Every teenager in the Rogue Valley who burns incense or candles will be booked for cattle mutilation."

The phone rang. It was the woodman, postponing until tomorrow.

"Let's go eat," Avashai said.

Through the hay doors they saw the lights of the taxi coming down Frank Hill Road. Maggie nearly tripped over a package on the porch—the Bertoluccis, her father's renters who lived in the main house, brought her mail to her. The territorial Mrs. Bertolucci didn't like her much, which Maggie understood; when Maggie moved back to Ashland for college, the Bertoluccis had been forced to evict a tenant so Maggie could have the barn. When she was a kid, her family had lived in the front house until her father began screaming a lot. His face turned very red and he knelt on the living room floor, beating the shag with his hands and yelling, "I want everything. I want everything," while her mother held him from behind. When Maggie asked her mother what her father was doing, she said, "He's having a tantrum, just like you do." Then she and her mother had moved to the barn. It didn't have a bathroom then, and where the balcony was now, the hay doors used to open up onto nothing, just a drop of twenty feet to the ground below.

She had expected everything to be smaller when she came home—the houses smaller, the distances shorter—because that's what everyone said when they returned to their birthplace. But it hadn't been that way at all. Not for her. She was shocked to see the distances she traveled as a child—miles and miles through sagebrush and star thistle along the sluggish green irrigation ditch and into the cedar and poison oak clotted hills, a lonely child nomad accompanied by imaginary animal companions.

The waitress at Kopper Kitchen was in her midforties. Her hair was frosted in brown and blond and lighter blond stripes and her eyes gunked with black liner and mascara, but her lips were naked. She had bumps of adult acne smeared with flesh-toned Oxy-10 concealer. It wasn't blended in, just swiped on, but something about this made her look more appealing rather than less so—kind of rough and sexy like a Dusty Springfield song.

"Enjoy your meal," she said.

Avashai opened up the bread of his roast beef sandwich and peered suspiciously inside. "This meat is raw."

"Here we go," Maggie said.

"What?"

"I just don't understand why you keep ordering it when you're just going to send it back." She cut the tape on her package with a butter knife, sending a flurry of Styrofoam packing snow onto the table.

Her aunt in Seattle had sent her some tins of English tea, wool socks, and a pair of woolen gloves. It was already cold in Washington. One of the cans wasn't tea. The label read, I CAN: 101 CARDS OF PERSONAL AFFIRMATION.

Avashai flagged down the waitress with an officious wave of his hand, the coppery scent of his wrist chains mingling in the air with the smell of eggs and grease and bleach.

Maggie shuffled through the I Can cards while he hassled the waitress.

"Honey, I realize it looks pinkish, but that's just the color of the meat," the waitress said in a hoarse, erotic whisper.

Maggie gave the woman a covert smile and the woman winked back while Avashai poked daintily at his sandwich with a fork.

"No," he said. "I know what roast beef looks like. This meat is not cooked properly."

"Would you like it well done?"

"I'd like you to take it back and cook it some more."

Avashai's tone made Maggie want to grab a fork and stab him.

"Sure thing, honey." The waitress picked up the plate and swayed back toward the kitchen.

Maggie pulled out a card. It read: "Three bricklayers were asked what they were doing. The first replied, 'Laying bricks.' The second said, 'Earning a living.' But the third said, 'I'm building a cathedral.' I can build a cathedral with my life."

That was kind of beautiful, she thought. Maggie averted her eyes from Avashai's hostile pose and took a bite of her eggs. She knew better than to wait for his sandwich; he never sent food back just once. She tried to just accept it, like you would a peg leg or something. He'd been dirt poor and ostracized as a child, so he had respect issues with people in the service industry. It was embarrassing at restaurants but came in handy if she needed to return something at a shop. He had once made an enormous and valiant scene for her at Gucci in Seattle when they wouldn't take back a pair of black patent leather mules.

"If you were stranded on a desert island and you could only eat one thing, what would you eat?" she said, attempting to distract him.

"A roast beef sandwich."

"My mom read me this book once about these two people who crashed in a little plane in the Yukon and almost froze to death. They didn't even know each other—they had hooked up through an ad."

"A personal ad?"

"No, just a platonic traveling companion thing." It would have been a better story if they were in love.

"A lot of rock stars died on those little planes," he said.

"They didn't have any food except for a pack of Wrigley's gum."

"You can survive a long time on just water."

"That's what they did. Every night they would take turns cooking. Whoever was the cook would boil the gum in a pot of snow water and they would pretend it was really food. The cook would make up an imaginary meal—'tonight we're having braised roast and baby potatoes with spring vegetables,' or whatever." The book used to make Maggie hungry.

"My mother used to tell stories," Avashai said.

"Like what?"

"Like stuff about kids being dismembered by ax murderers or drowned in the river in a bag filled with rocks."

"Oh, my god."

"That was the only time she'd hold us, during story time. She'd have us sit in her lap and tell us these really violent stories. My sisters would put up with it for the affection but I eventually refused."

"Jesus Christ." No wonder he was so fucked up.

"I wish you wouldn't use his name that way."

"What?"

"Jesus was a man, not a swear word. Say 'fuck me' or 'cunt' if you want to swear."

"Pick a card, any card," she said, thrusting the I Can cards toward him.

"What are they?"

"New Age fortune cookies."

He plucked one out and read aloud, "People deserve love. I am a person—what is this crap?"

Maggie laughed. "Read the 'I can' part."

"I'm not an 'I can' kind of guy."

The waitress came back and set his plate down gently on the table. He opened up the bread.

"Goddammit, it's still raw."

Maggie shook some ketchup on her hash browns and kept a carefully neutral expression on her face while he signaled the waitress back over; she knew that any perceived lack of solidarity would provoke an explosion. There was so little they could do without fighting. Everything was so fraught; even the most basic activities—eating and sleeping—were dangerous. She didn't like to sleep at his apartment downtown because she always found things, even when she wasn't looking—blouses, bras, notes—"Thanks for the scrambled eggs, ooxx Gretchen," et cetera, supposed mementos from the past. Some nights when they slept at her place, she broke out in hives and wherever she scratched, big white welts swelled up in the shape of her fingernails—she couldn't tell if there were bird mites in the walls or if she had become allergic to him. She had to be on the outside of the spoon or she would suffocate and she had almost unbearable urges to kick him out of bed and off the side of the loft. She sealed layers of duct tape over the knothole by the swallows' nest and scratched her arms until dawn.

"This meat is bloody," he told the waitress, who stood patiently, her hip cocked. Maggie turned toward the window. There were already Halloween decorations on the glass—a crudely painted ghost hovering above a cluster of gravestones, each stone with the initials RIP smeared in black. Outside, the stars were bright against the black sky.

"I can't eat this."

"Avashai, why don't you order something else?" Maggie said.

"Because I don't want something else."

"I'll have him put it back on the grill, hon." The woman sighed and picked up the plate with great restraint, taking it back to the kitchen where she would undoubtedly throw it on the floor and spit on it before slapping it back on the grill.

Avashai narrowed his eyes at Maggie. "Don't ever do that to me again."

"But it gets old, you know? It's the same thing every time. It's like you enjoy it or something."

Avashai scraped his chair back, stood up, and leaned across the table toward her, his face twisted up with two bright spots on each white cheek. "You never have my back," he hissed, spraying spittle on her chin. "You never have my back."

"Oh, for Christ's sake. You act like we're in a gang war instead of harassing the poor waitress at Kopper Kitchen."

He grabbed his green army coat. "It's because of people like you that revolutions fail."

"Are you leaving? You're leaving. And look who gets the check, as usual."

The glass door jingled behind him. She watched him walk across the parking lot out to the edge of the highway, hunch-shouldered, his thumb held out halfheartedly at the passing traffic.

———

Maggie woke to a freak frost. Looking out the window past the ditch to the orchard, she saw that the star thistle and the rows of stunted apricot trees were coated in white sparkles, as were the ruins of what used to be the outcast henhouse—a tiny shed her father had built years earlier for the chickens that got their eyes pecked out by the others due to some mysterious hierarchy in the chicken social order. The barn was not well insulated and she would have to duct tape plastic over the windows pretty soon. She turned on the space heater and wrapped herself in the quilt. Last winter her stovepipe had broken and she had to sleep in the tiny bathroom, curled on the floor with the space heater. She left the water running a little, like the Bertoluccis had instructed her to do, to keep the pipes from freezing, but they froze anyway.

Maggie rummaged through Avashai's grocery bag full of movies, looking for something to watch. There was a Malcolm X documentary, *Ren and Stimpy* cartoons, and *Full Metal Jacket*. She pulled out a video with twin blond sisters in Santa hats on the cover, each woman holding an ice sculpture in the shape of a penis very near her open mouth, stylized drips of water running down their chins and arms. She wondered if the dildos were actually made of ice or were clear plastic. They looked like real ice that had been very intricately carved or frozen in a mold. It was the ice she liked; it stirred up some kind of inchoate longing, something at the edge of her mind. A sharktooth necklace, Spock in an ice-cave, a translucent plastic Barbie shoe. She pulled out another well-worn tape, with the title *Bumping Uglies II* printed on it in Magic Marker. She popped it into the VCR.

At first she thought it needed to be rewound, so she pushed the Rewind button on the remote. Again, after the blackness, a blazingly lit and larger-than-life close-up of anonymous shaved genitalia, midpenetration.

"That's how it goes," she said to herself.

There was no tinkle of seventies Muzak, no kooky little skits of pool boy and rich lady, student and teacher, Girl Scout and cookie buyer. Every scene started out the same way—a bright, clinical study, like a liver transplant on *NOVA*.

This vigorous slapping up of parts did nothing for her. It actually made her a little nauseous; she was a vegetarian and something about the denuded flesh made her think of glistening hunks of raw chicken. As a teenager she'd had a kitchen-prep job in Juneau, Alaska, where she had to touch cold bloody hamburger meat with her hands and slice up slimy chicken strips while concealing her dry heaves from the boss. The night cook, a plump Scot with checkered pants, was a nice guy and would do it for her. He carried his fancy expensive knives and sharpening stone with him in a black bag like a doctor. He often brought his little daughter to work with him, and she would sit on a tall stool and cut up peppers and tomatoes with a big glittering cleaver. "Children only cut themselves on a dull knife," he said. "They're careful with a sharp one."

She remembered that the pudgy night cook had been married to a woman from Thailand with a butch way of walking, but he was in love with a boy only a couple years older than Maggie who worked in the kitchen. The kitchen boy was a crack addict the cook had taken under his wing and taught how to brush his teeth and carve radish roses. He stared at this kid with intense tenderness and longing as the boy deveined shrimp or peeled potatoes.

She lost her virginity in Alaska that summer. She had a crush on a Tlingit guy who wore a shark tooth necklace and faded Levi's and worked at the fish market down by the wharf. She walked by there every day on the boardwalk, past the gift shops full of kachina dolls and woodblock whale prints, to catch a glimpse of him in his blood-stained apron, stacking salmon on the ice. He looked at her one time and held her eyes, smiled knowingly, and she almost died. But she was too shy to ever go in the store, so she ended up doing it with another guy whom she didn't know well or like much, in a room full of basketball trophies and a textured black light poster of a castle. She had reached up to feel the poster, its velvety black fuzz like some kind of phantom Braille.

Maggie heard the rumble of a pickup truck coming up the Bertoluccis' driveway but thought it was too early for the woodman; he was supposed to come around two. When it was almost time for the come-shot, the camera panned out to reveal the whole bodies of the actors, their gymnast arms and shoulders, their bored gymnast faces—the man's oddly immobile, like a draft horse pulling a plow—the woman's a stylized manic rictus, eyes rolled toward a spot or clock on the wall to stage right. After a showy come-shot across the woman's chest, the couple faded to black, and immediately the next pair of giant genitals filled the screen.

There was a knock at the door. She turned off the video. "Who is it?"

"Firewood."

She opened the door. The woodman wore an "Incident at Oglala" T-shirt and crudely patched corduroys with a pair of webbed, orange gloves hanging out of his back pocket. He looked kind of familiar.

"Oh, hey," he said, smiling broadly. "You're Lily's friend."

"Yeah." She couldn't quite place him. He had a long, Titian ponytail, wholesome freckles, and a scraggly thin goatee in a slightly darker shade than his hair. She was going to tell him to watch his step, but the ice had melted, leaving the porch damp and swollen. The rotting stairs wouldn't last another winter.

"Remember? I'm the guy who picks morels, you know, the hermit."

"Oh, yeah. You have a beard now." He was a Buddhist recluse who lived very far out in the Applegate and subsisted on a trust fund and the peddling of fancy mushrooms to the local restaurants. She'd eaten lunch at his cabin once with her friends Lily and Tom. He'd taken them for a tour of his garden—a paradise covered in flowering sweet peas and an elaborate irrigation system of pierced rubber hoses. Lily said he used to be something of a frat boy before he became a hermit. She remembered that he hadn't wanted them to leave, that he had kept making up reasons for them to stay and spend the night. When they left he waved and waved and followed their car down the pitted logging access road.

The woodman raised his arms hesitantly, and at first Maggie didn't know what he was going to do, but then he was hugging her. She tilted her torso back to avoid contact and slanted to the side so that only one breast pressed into his chest. He held her for what seemed an excessive length of time, and she gave him a fluttering pat on the back to signal the end of the hug, but he didn't seem to get it and gave her another squeeze. Her armpits began to prickle and itch. She patted him again and quickly disengaged.

He hovered about awkwardly until Maggie felt compelled to ask if he wanted coffee.

"Do you have any tea? I don't take any substances," he said.

"I don't think I do," she lied.

"I have ginger in my truck." He sprang down the stairs like an eager dog. "I'll get it."

Don't be mean, Maggie thought, it's no wonder he's starving for human contact, living that far out with no neighbors or electricity. She showed him where to park, beckoning to the battered truck, guiding him to back up the hill, past the guitar stem planted in the ground like a headstone, and around to her front door.

He brought in several plastic bags full of dirty vegetables and mushrooms, spontaneous gifts for Maggie, and, without asking, began washing a twisted lump of ginger in her sink. He held it up, dripping water on the floor. "Look." The root was vaguely humanoid, with arms and legs. "It's alive."

"Now I feel bad chopping it up." She put the kettle on and got out the cutting board.

The woodman, whose name Maggie was desperately trying to recall, picked up the ice-twins video, then quickly set it back down as though it had burned him. He took the *Bumping Uglies II* case off the counter and examined it. "*Bumping Uglies I* was better, I thought. That's the problem with sequels."

They laughed.

"That's not mine." Maggie hacked the ginger creature in two. "It's my boyfriend's."

"Who's your boyfriend?"

"Donny Ludwig, but he changed his name to Avashai."

The woodman wrinkled his nose slightly, as though he were smelling something bad but was too polite to say so. "I know him. He cleans the crappers at Shakespeare."

"Yeah."

"I know his girlfriend or, I'm sorry, his ex-girlfriend or whatever—you're his girlfriend." The woodman blushed. "I mean, I know Gretchen."

Maggie grunted noncommittally.

"It's really none of my business," he said, "but I just don't understand how that skinny runt gets so many pretty, intelligent women when he treats them so bad. I'm sorry, that's very rude of me. I live out in the woods and I forget how to interact with people."

"Don't worry about it. I've been wondering the same thing myself."

Maggie took down the I CAN cards and popped off the lid.

"Pick a card," she said.

He felt around enthusiastically, pulled one out, and handed it to Maggie.

She read aloud, "Every ship needs a port during the storm. I can be a person who offers safety to others."

"That's good. I got a good fortune."

Maggie closed her eyes, and felt around in the cards. They were cool and slick, and she shuffled through them, giving the universe a chance to cull the right one. One card seemed to have a special tingle.

"The Eskimo leave sharp knives smeared with meat at the perimeter of their camp. Wolves will repeatedly lick the sharp knives until they cut their tongues and bleed to death," she read. "I am not a wolf. I can eliminate destructive behaviors before they eliminate me."

Maggie laughed out loud—something she hadn't done for a long time. She laughed so hard she had to put her head down on her knees.

"I don't think there's any such thing as an Eskimo," she said. Her stomach was weak from laughing. "I think that's just another made-up word for the indigenous."

At a private school called Tamanous, her fifth-grade class had studied the Eskimo. The teacher had been a good-natured, spindly woman who favored leotards and wraparound Indian skirts and sometimes forgot to wear underwear on yoga day. The class learned that the Eskimo sewed their parkas with whalebone needles, that their shamans went into trance states and took "soul flights" under the ice, and that everyone slept in the same bed on the floor and the parents made love right next to their children.

The teacher said that the Eskimo were a jolly people and that they played many games to while away the boring hours cooped up in the igloo. In one game all the seal oil lanterns were put out and everyone got naked in the dark and had a big orgy, not knowing whom they were lying with. Afterward everyone had to guess, judging by the huffing noises that the person made or the size of their belly, and there was much merriment. Maggie had imagined the glistening walls of the igloo, the fur-lined floor, a few red coals in the fire—not enough to see by—and everyone peeled out of their parkas and all you could hear was their breath in the dark.

"I think Eskimo means 'people,'" the woodman said.

There was another knock at the door. She slid open the bolt to see Avashai standing on the porch. He had bleached his hair platinum since the previous night and his nose was pink. He looked like an albino possum.

"Hi," he said. He put his hands in his pockets and sniffled like he had a cold.

"Hi."

Then he noticed the woodman and stiffened.

"Hey, Donny," the wood guy said. "How's it going?"

Avashai nodded at the woodman. "Can't complain."

They nodded at each other again and the woodman put his teacup down and stood up. "Well, I better get to that cord."

"Trust fund hippie-poser," Avashai muttered when the woodman began tossing logs out of the back of his truck.

"You know him?"

"He was always sniffing around Gretchen." The presence of a potential audience seemed to have perked him up; he sat down and patted the sofa. "Let's watch a movie."

"I'm not going to fuck you while the wood guy is here." She watched as pieces of madrone flew past the open front door against the violet sky.

"Who asked you to?"

"I'm just saying."

"Let's not fight anymore, baby." Avashai picked the I CAN card tin off the shelf and shook it vigorously. "Here, let's see what the magic eightball has to say." He closed his eyes and passed his hand over the can like a magician. "Oh, magic hippie cards, please give me direction."

"Read it."

"Weird." He hunched over the card, his brow furrowed with concentration. "It's the same as last time."

"Maybe someone is trying to tell you something."

He shrugged. "False idols."

Maggie held up the ice-twin video. "How about this one?"

"I don't think you'll like that one."

"I'll like it."

"I don't know, I don't want to hear some diatribe about incest."

"Fair enough," Maggie said. "This is my personal favorite." She pushed *Bumping Uglies II* into the VCR, then pressed the sound down a couple of notches in deference to the woodman.

On screen the genital parade continued, like the endless cycle of samsara, one crotch after another. She started to reach for Avashai's hair, but he flinched, so she turned around and began slowly pulling up her skirt the way he liked. She peeked over her shoulder.

He pursed his lips. "I thought you didn't want to have sex while the wood guy was here."

"No sex, just some frottage. I have a really good idea. I don't like the visuals, I admit it. But I like the sound. So I'll look this way." She climbed onto his lap. "And you look that way."

He was still frowning but picked up the remote and turned up the sound a notch. They arranged their bodies so that he could watch and she could listen, Maggie straddling his thigh, the fabric rubbing against her as she ground into his thigh. He faced forward. She pressed her cheek into the velvet fuzz of his scalp and looked over his shoulder out the hayloft door to the darkening sky. There was the smell of damp weeds and dirt from the road that ran along the irrigation ditch. She had walked that trail many times as a child, often at night. Once, a strange light had hovered in the sky above the hill. She thought it was an alien spacecraft, and she stood there, waiting. Not scared. Just waiting for it to come and beam her aboard. She was surprised when it flew off.

Over the disembodied moans she could hear the barn cats slinking around underneath the loft—the tinny rattle of aluminum pie tins full of dry food, and the thunk, thunk of logs hitting the woodpile. She glanced at Avashai. His glazed eyes never left the screen except once to look at her ass and give it a quick shake with his fingers; he liked to see it ripple. Once she had found a notebook of his where he had written, "Sometimes when i have sex with a woman doggy style it's like i'm seeing a row of women from in the past and into the future, one anonymous chain of flesh, and i grow weary."

"I'm going to beat off, okay?" He unzipped his trousers. They were Dickies brand with the little horseshoe symbol. Union made in the U.S.A.

"Sure. Me, too." She closed her eyes and thought of the whiskey-voiced waitress from Kopper Kitchen and the blond Santa twins and of icicles hanging from a porch railing and of snow. Some people were triggered by the smell of suntan lotion, but sex and snow were closely linked in Maggie's mind and she could trace the origins of this: two films she'd seen as a child—one, *Nanook of the North,* which she'd watched with her mother in the Methodist church. They weren't religious, but it cost only fifty cents to go to the movies there on Tuesday nights. The small screen had flickered black and white, there were fur-rimmed faces, a hole cut in the ice, a spear, a slippery seal carcass being dragged along the ice, a black spot in the snow (seal blood), and the main thing—people kissing by rubbing noses together because it was too cold to stick your tongue in someone's mouth. And the other movie, which she saw around the same time at the Varsity Theater, again with her mother, was about a whaling boat that shipwrecked in the Arctic, stranding European sailors on the ice. The expedition was rescued by a band of Inuit hunters who had never seen outsiders and thought that they were dog children—the offspring of an Inuit and a dog. There was a scene where an Inuit woman and a sailor were fucking in a snowdrift, having pulled down only their bottoms because it was so cold. Maggie remembered the embryonic glimmer of sexual feeling she experienced, at age seven, in the dark theater, watching the parkas and the flash of bare thighs entwined in the snow.

Avashai slammed down the remote.

"What?" she said.

"Do you have to act so martyred and sad?"

"I didn't say a word."

"You were making a face."

"I was not."

There was a throat clearing. "Excuse me." The woodman stood in the open door, a dark silhouette knocking on the frame. Maggie knew that the counter blocked most of his view, but she wondered how long he'd been on the porch.

"I'll be right out," Maggie said. She pulled her skirt down and went to get her checkbook. It was dark outside. The woodman had turned on his high beams; a looming pile of neatly stacked wood and a swath of star thistle were spotlit against the starry black sky. There was the sound of crickets and a snuffling exhale from one of the neighbor's horses.

"Do you have a tarp?"

"No."

"I'll loan you mine," he said.

Maggie wrote out a check while he brushed the sawdust out of his scanty red beard. "Thanks." She remembered his name. "Matthew. Thanks for all the mushrooms and ginger and stuff."

"You're welcome."

He started his truck and leaned out the window to say, "Just let me know if you ever need any produce or anything. I always have extra."

She pulled the door closed and slid the wooden latch into place. Avashai had the news on.

"Would you mind getting me a beer while you're in there, Gre—baby?"

"What's my name?"

"Maggie, Maggie, mi amor."

She opened the refrigerator, which was directly next to the front door. It was very old and had an open freezer at the top completely encrusted in ice and frost. There wasn't anything edible inside—just some Rogue Ale, moldy tempeh, and an empty container that had once held Mongolian barbecue. She looked at Matthew's grubby vegetables sitting on the counter in an orange Fiesta bowl. It would take too much effort to clean and cook them.

"The larder is bare," she said.

"No beer?"

"There's beer." She didn't like it when Avashai drank. After only two beers his lips turned very red and wet and he started acting like an asshole. More of an asshole. But she was trying to be as saintly and un-Gretchen-like as possible so she wasn't criticizing. Maggie didn't drink. Not socially. Not unless she felt really bad and then she drank a lot.

Maggie went up to Seattle to visit her aunt for the weekend and when she came home the first snow had arrived. Her taxi had to let her out on Ashland Mine Road; it didn't have the traction for Frank Hill. She happily dragged her suitcase the mile down Frank Hill to the Bertoluccis' driveway. Everything was white and the air was clean and cold in her nostrils.

Inside, the barn smelled dank and yeasty. She saw remnants of a beer party Avashai and his buddies must have thrown. She climbed up in the loft to see if Avashai had remembered to prop open the little window for the cats. Kneeling on the bed, she saw a tiny spot of dried blood on her pillow. She sniffed the pillow. It smelled strongly of menstrual blood and someone else's vagina.

"I am not a wolf," she said while she broke things. The beer bottles, presents from Avashai, a tacky mirror with stained glass sunburst rays squiggling out of it that she had never liked. The window, with a rock, not her fist, although she hoped Avashai would think it had been her fist.

Avashai walked in to find her sitting silent on the floor among the broken glass.

"What's going on now?"

"Could you at least have the decency to wash my sheets after you fuck other girls on them?"

"What is your problem?"

"There's blood on my pillow."

"There is?"

Avashai climbed up in the loft. She could hear the boards creaking under his weight.

"Huh, there is a little dot of something. Must have been one of the cats—had blood on its paw."

"Do you know how disturbing it is to not only have your boyfriend cheat on you but to have to know that he raised some other girl's haunches on your pillow?"

"It's from the cat, you're paranoid."

Maggie said it was over and he left without a struggle. Then she changed her mind. She called him but he wasn't answering the phone. It was too late for the buses to be running and she didn't have the money for a taxi. She threw a jacket on over her T-shirt and pajama bottoms, slipped on a big pair of rubber boots to slog through the slush and mud of Frank Hill.

Her breath came in clouds and the road was covered in a crunchy layer of sparkling snow. In the moonlight she could see the roof of the outcast chicken house barely visible in the tall thistle and beyond to the valley below to the glowing blue square of the Jackson Hot Springs pool off Highway 99 that was surrounded by a cluster of bungalows. You could walk all the way there from the barn if you wanted to; there was a secret trail off the irrigation ditch. Her father used to take her. The water smelled of boiled eggs from the sulfurous springs. They sold snow cones and you safety pinned your locker key to your suit and there were signs that said, WE DON'T SWIM IN YOUR JOHN, PLEASE DON'T PIDDLE IN OUR POOL. In that world, it did not matter that she was tiny and weak; her father would float on his back with his eyes closed, his great whale belly curved against the blue sky and she would drag him easily through the water by his arm. Fat floats. That's why women make better swimmers, her mother said; that, and they can hold their breath longer. Like the Japanese women pearl divers who dive down to the pearl beds without wet suits or masks, only knives clenched between their teeth.

Downtown, midnight revelers were pouring out of the Rouge Brewery toward the Black Sheep and Alex's. Maggie crossed Lithia Square past the two sets of drinking fountains. The fresh water drinking fountains were done in scrolled copperwork with delicate porcelain basins but the Lithia water fountains were a set of squat, hallway-style fountains mounted around a bare cement block. An older hippie woman in a long wooly tunic was filling a plastic jug full of Lithia water—a revolting sulfurous mineral water sipped only by tourists and the mad.

In front of Chateaulin a round-faced Asian man with bristly short hair was spare-changing the passersby. "Spare change for a foot rub," he said to two blond girls in ski jackets who were leaving the techno thumping of the gay bar frequented by college kids next door.

"It's too cold to take my shoes off," one of the girls said, dropping coins into his palm.

"Spare change for a foot rub," he said to Maggie. She pretended not to hear him. The door to Cook's opened and a snatch of lyrics blasted out: "Touch me baby, tainted love."

Avashai lived above Biggum's Silver Lion, the alcoholics' bar, which was convenient for him. His apartment was the first one at the top of the stairs. It was an old office building, and all the apartment doors had glass windows. As she climbed the stairs she could detect Avashai's favorite incense, Spiritual Sky Number 8, Spring Flowers, and she could see a faint light glowing through the white curtain.

She knocked on his door but there was no answer and she felt the quicksilver trickle of ice spread through her chest.

"Avashai." There was the faint sound of jazz from the stereo. "Avashai."

He was home. He could hear her. She could feel him hear her. Her gut tensed as she peered through the inch-wide crack at the edge of the curtain into his darkened living room. There was an open door at the far side; through it, she could see the edge of the stereo in the bedroom. On the bedroom wall there was the flickering light from a candle, a candle she could not see but knew sat on the bedside table—a large blue and rainbow-colored candle purchased at Rare Earth.

"How very fucking romantic," she screamed, and hit the door hard with her hand, rattling the glass. Then she ran, terrified they might open the door before she was gone. She lunged down the stairs two at a time, the rubber boots making it awkward. Don't fall. Don't fall. She passed the mail slots, where it still said "Donny Ludwig," burst through the outer door, and loped the three yards to Biggum's Silver Lion.

Inside it was too hot. She was soaked with sweat. Peeling off her coat, she realized she was still dressed in a T-shirt and flannel bottoms printed with blue cows leaping over crescent moons and smiling, shooting stars. So what? She'd seen the dirty hippie teenagers in Lithia Park playing Frisbee in tattered slips and button-front long johns with their rosy asses hanging out. Her face hurt. It was a strange thing that happened to her sometimes—her cheeks and forehead would get sore and swollen like someone had been slapping them over and over.

She didn't have any money but the bartender let her use Avashai's tab. She ordered six tequila shots with beer backs in rapid succession.

All of a sudden she couldn't hear very well; everything was muted. Muted laughter. Pool balls clicking gently together.

"Like snow," she said aloud. The way it muffles sound.

"What's that, darling?"

She couldn't tell who had spoken. To her right sat an old man with liver spots on his hands and a jaunty red beret. To her left, a couple seats down, was a freckled man in a flannel shirt; he had a ponytail and scraggly beard. Looked a little like the woodman but it wasn't him. A lot of people looked like that.

"Nothing," Maggie said, looking forward at the row of shiny bottles. "I wasn't talking to you."

"Talking to yourself." The ponytail guy was missing a front tooth. Definitely not the woodman. "Well, don't let me interrupt, darling."

She looked up at the chalkboard where people's names were scrawled and she couldn't remember what that was for, though she knew it was something mundane she'd forgotten. The television above the bar was tuned to a football game.

She recognized a guy playing pool that she had made out with twice before when Avashai cheated on her. He had a shaved head also and was really cute in an Aryan Nazi kind of way but for some reason she had no chemistry with him. Maybe because he was a Virgo, or maybe because every time he'd stuck his tongue in her mouth she had been so drunk she was on the edge of vomiting. She ran into this guy only a couple times a year, when she happened to be dead drunk, and she knew he must think she was like this all the time. Last time she gave him head on the floor of her friend Lily's living room and Lily's roommate walked in on her, but it was no big deal. Everyone was like that over at that house—boys and girls, and girls and girls, and pseudopagan orgies, while the kids slept upstairs curled up in a riotous mess of clothes and school papers on Lily's bed.

Maggie noted a stir in the other bar patrons; everyone was looking at the television. It wasn't the game anymore; the news was on. The photo of the necrophiliac girl floated in the corner over the manic blond newscaster's head. "The police found Annalisa Gabelien in Klamath County this morning, overdosed on codeine Tylenol. She is listed in critical condition at Providence Medford Medical Center and has been charged with illegally driving a hearse and interfering with a burial." The newscaster looked up with seriousness. "There is no law in Oregon against necrophilia."

"That's just sick," said a woman in a fringed leather vest sitting at the poker machine.

The bearded man on Maggie's left spoke across her to the old man in the beret to her right.

"What I want to know," he said, his beer mug tilting dangerously, "is how did she do it? How the hell did she get their equipment to stand up?"

"People lack imagination." The old man winked at Maggie. "Penetration is not the only way to make love."

The guy she sometimes made out with had spotted her and was heading toward the bar. The effort of remembering his name and trying to talk without slurring was more than she could take, so she braced herself on the counter and eased off the stool. The walk across the bar to the door was perilous and she knew she fooled no one with her landlubber sway.

The Asian panhandler had moved to a wrought-iron bench in front of the fountains in the square. "Spare change for a foot rub?" he said. Steam rose out of his mouth.

He had a clean shave and wore a new-looking REI jacket. He was overweight but not bad looking. He looked familiar. Maggie was drunk enough to feel like it was okay to stand and stare at him and figure out who he was. She knew she was listing to one side and she didn't care. It came to her that he was the fat leper from the play *Pool of Bethesda,* but with short hair. He'd probably been wearing a wig. She recalled that Avashai had said that the actor had been in a movie they had both seen about a serial killer who stalked an agoraphobic. The guy had a bit part as a cop who gets killed.

"I don't think so," Maggie said, narrowing her eyes at him. "I think you'll pay to touch my feet."

The leper tilted his head at her. "Okay. How much?"

"Thirty dollars."

"Okay." He withdrew a leather wallet from his pants pocket and pulled out a ten and a twenty. "Here."

Maggie sat down on the bench and awkwardly pulled off one of her rubber boots and threw it on the sidewalk. She flopped her stocking foot into the actor's lap.

"Can I take off your sock?" he asked.

"Go for it."

He daintily peeled off her dirty tube sock and placed it on the bench like he was handling a delicate gardenia. The actor began kneading her foot with his chubby fingers. The air was cold but his hands were warm. It probably would have felt good if she had allowed herself to relax, but even as drunk as she was, she was rigid, a cold little part of her brain curled up stone sober inside, watching her toes being handled by a fat foot fetishist.

"So, you go to college here?" The actor stroked her sole.

"Don't talk."

He nodded and kept massaging. His breath came through his nostrils in soft snuffles. He sounded like he had a cold. She remembered that during *Pool of Bethesda* one of his artificial sores had fallen off his leg and onto the stage.

He put her sock back on in a ritual manner. "Other foot," he said.

Maggie kicked off her other boot and stared at the rusted water fountains, the brown mineral deposits oozing down their lips reminded her of a row of urinals.

"You ever taste the Lithia water?" she asked, guessing he was from out of town.

"No, is it special?"

"Tastes like Perrier. Some people think it has magical properties."

"A fountain of youth?"

"I don't know, I guess they think it has lithium in it, which maybe it does, but in such trace amounts that it wouldn't do anything." She pulled her foot from his hands and pointed it ballerina-style at one of the fountains. "Try it."

The actor bent over the fountain and sniffed it. "Smells kind of weird."

"That's the minerals. It's good for you."

He took a sip and immediately sprayed it back onto the fountain. "Shit." He spat on the ground twice. "Okay, funny. You got me."

She tilted her head back and looked past the dark pines of Lithia Park to the black hills dotted with the lights of wealthy homes, then Venus and the moon. She got the spins, like she was on the scrambler at the fair, peeking out through the cage at the cold, starry sky.

"I got a joint at my house," the man said. "You smoke weed?"

"No."

"I'll pay you a hundred dollars to step on my dick."

"What?"

"With some high heels on. I have some at my place. I won't touch you."

"That's what they all say." Maggie lurched for her rubber boot.

"No, really, all you have to do is step on my dick and I'll pay you a hundred dollars. You can choose which shoes. I have brand names. Manolo Blahnik. I'll let you keep a pair."

"No, thanks." She yanked her boot back on, noticing one pajama leg was out and one was in.

"How much do you want?"

"We're done here," she said. She started back up First Street, and the actor tried to follow her.

"Sit," she said. And he did.

Maggie walked to the pay phone in front of Biggum's Silver Lion. Inside, she fumbled with her change, the sober thing in her brain observing her spastic fingers. She slowly dialed Avashai's number and listened to his tape-recorded voice superimposed on Elvis Costello's.

"Be a man and answer the phone you weak sociopathic whore. You think Jesus was a punk rocker? You think Jesus would have wanted you backing him up? Jesus would have hated you. I have no idea why I ever—I don't even like you. Not as a human." She babbled into his answering machine until the beep cut her off. Then she did it again.

She did it five more times, alternating between threats and pathetic pleas for closure, and the fifth time, Gretchen picked up the phone.

"Have a little self-respect and dignity," Gretchen said, and hung up.

Maggie sank down onto the floor of the phone booth. She could feel the cold, textured metal through her pajamas. For a moment she indulged in a maudlin fantasy of death by exposure, conjuring up an image of herself—fetal and blue—on the floor of the phone booth as morning broke. She looked through the smeared glass at the sidewalk glittering with frost. She closed her eyes to the spins and imagined herself way, way out on the frozen tundra.

Far away there is a twinkling light from the ice-cave. Ice window warped and shimmering. Inside the hot damp igloo there is the sputter and pop of embers, steam rises from the bodies coupling on the fur-lined floor, knees scraping hide, hands clutching seal fur, smell of a leather poncho. She watches from the perimeter of camp, wet tongue hanging in ribbons.

IAN DAVID FROEB

University of Iowa

THE COSMONAUT

April 12, 2001

Edward,

I came across the enclosed recently and of course thought of you. Fi-nally, to learn whatever happened to Mikhail Ilyich Korff! I must admit: I was surprised to see he had returned to Russia. Once the USSR fell, I suppose there was no reason not *to return. Still, it's sad in a way. If he wanted to die alone, he could have done it here just as well.*

It gives me a chill to realize Mikhail died less than a year after we lost contact with the Brahe module. Does this mean I'm turn-ing into a superstitious old fool? Seeing signs and portents in the patterns of stars? But I suppose I shouldn't be that shocked by such a coincidence. We're old men now. You and I. Mikhail. The Brahe module.

Forgive the maudlin tone. I think of you often, my friend. Give my love to Jeanne.
   Ping

Stapled to Ping's letter was a photocopy of a page from a Russian newspaper. Edward hadn't read Russian since his retirement from NASA, but it was like Ping to presume he hadn't forgotten a word. He took the Russian dictionary from his bookshelf, brushed the dust from it, then carried it and the letter to his desk.

Ping had marked the relevant item on the newspaper page. It was a short notice. The photocopy was poor: the ink too light, the print fuzzy. Each word floated above the page and wavered on the periphery of his vision, as in a test an ophthalmologist might give. He removed his spectacles and pinched the bridge of his nose. Surely such a simple task wasn't beyond him. He perched his spectacles where his nose broadened and, following the text with his index finger, his left hand poised above the dictionary, began to read.

Mikhail Ilyich Korff. Died on January 10, 2001. Seventy-six years old. Lived in Saint Petersburg. In his apartment gave piano lessons to children. Decorated for valor in the Great Patriotic War. No known living kin.

He read the obituary again, but with the same result: In the end, Mikhail had returned to Russia. It was surprising, surprising and sad, although for reasons far more complicated than Ping believed. Ping considered Mikhail a figure from the cold war, a historical curiosity. But Edward's surprise and sadness had nothing to do with politics—the Soviet Union's collapse was beside the point. The Mikhail Edward had known would not have returned to Russia. Then again, if this obituary was accurate, the Mikhail Edward had known had died years ago.

Jeanne called him to dinner. He put Ping's letter aside and went to the kitchen.

"What does Ping write?" Jeanne asked.

"He says hello." He kissed her cheek. "And someone we worked with died. Mikhail."

"My god. I haven't thought of him in years." She ladled beef stew into two bowls. "He was ancient when we knew him."

"He's my age."

She pursed her lips, a patient smile. "I meant ancient in spirit. Do you think they buried him in that funny hat he always wore?"

Edward carried the bowls of stew to the table. "I don't know what hat you're talking about," he said.

Of course, the Mikhail Ilyich Korff in the newspaper might not be the Mikhail he had known. Mikhail was a common first name in Russia, and Ilyich a common patronymic. The obituary didn't mention Mikhail's role in the Soviet space program—that if not for an irregular heartbeat he, not Yury Gagarin, would have been the first man to orbit Earth. It didn't mention his wife, Sofya.

"A deerstalker," Jeanne said as they cleared the table.

"What?"

"That funny hat he wore. It's called a deerstalker."

"He never wore a funny hat."

"No need to snap." She waved a dish towel at him. "Go. You're in one of your moods. I'll clean up faster by myself."

He returned to his desk and read the obituary again. Mikhail was dead. It was ridiculous to think otherwise. The age was right, and the detail that he'd taught piano in his apartment was persuasive. From his bookshelf Edward took a photo album and opened it to the final page: a shot of Mikhail, Ping, and himself in the backyard of his house in Greenbelt, celebrating the launch that day of the rocket carrying the Brahe module. Mikhail, in blue jeans and a white T-shirt, the outline of a pack of cigarettes visible in his chest pocket, looked no less comfortable an American than Ping or he himself did. Mikhail had seemed happy then, satisfied that he'd had an impact on the Brahe project, looking forward to his next assignment with the government. He'd had no reason to return to Russia. None whatsoever. But he had.

The shot was tilted five degrees on its z-axis. Linda had taken it. She couldn't hold a camera steady at that point but had insisted on joining the celebration. Even now her strength during those final months impressed—no, staggered—him.

Jeanne was already asleep when he came to the bedroom. He padded across the carpet and turned back the covers on his side of the bed.

"I'm awake," she murmured.

He lay down and pulled the covers to his chin. "You're angry I snapped at you."

"No. You lost someone." She nuzzled her head against his shoulder. "Do you want to talk?"

"You're too understanding. I don't deserve it."

She kissed him on the mouth: her lips were soft, the tip of her tongue ticklish against the tip of his. His hands moved through the dark toward the gentle slopes of her hips. He fumbled with the hem of her nightgown. He couldn't lift it from her without pinning her head in between her upraised arms. She told him to lie down. With one hand she grabbed the bottom half of her nightgown in a bunch and held it above her waist; with the other she yanked his pajama pants to his ankles. She straddled him, her hands against his sternum for leverage, and he swayed slightly with the rocking of her hips. The tilted picture: Linda's trembling fingers struggling to focus the lens. His muscles quaked with exhaustion; he clutched Jeanne's hips to halt her movement.

"I'm sorry," he said.

"Don't." She laid her head against his chest. "The thought was lovely."

The warm pulse of her breath on his neck slowed. She'd fallen asleep. The pressure of her body against his made his joints ache, but he didn't want to move her to her side of the bed. He stroked her face, marveling at the soft, smooth skin, at the dusting of freckles on her cheeks. He was more attracted to her now than when they'd met, twenty-six years earlier.

Jeanne had stopped by his office to introduce herself: Ping's new secretary. A short, plump woman in her early thirties, curves that might have been pleasing flattened by a poorly tailored pantsuit. Face pale and unpainted, hair pulled back into a bun. Certainly not as beautiful as Linda had been at her age.

He was tall and quite thin then—not handsome, exactly, but with what he thought a good face: his nose a bit too thick, his forehead a bit too high, but his eyes bright green, his jaw strong. Now his hair had gone silver and he'd lost a few inches from his height—several operations for a slipped disc and the natural curving of age—and after he quit smoking and stopped walking to his office every day he'd developed a soft, sagging paunch. He now had to study his reflection for minutes to find the green within his rheumy eyes.

Only when his son visited from college could he recall how he'd once looked—and even then this recollection was faint. William was tall and lanky and had his green eyes, but William's features were softer—they had the rounded quality of Jeanne's—and his hair, like Jeanne's, was curly and a rich, chocolate brown. William, a drama student also taking premed courses, had the world ahead of him. Edward wouldn't live to see all that William might make of his possibilities. This he'd known since William's birth. Yet these bittersweet feelings always turned to frank amazement. He was seventy-six years old, past the age when the world expected anything from him, yet he could claim to be the father of this young man. This young man, soon to become a doctor, an actor, or both, still phoned him for advice on car repair, to ask his opinion on politics or baseball. He thought this one of the miracles of life.

He'd wanted a child with Linda. It would be easy now to say he hadn't, that they hadn't been meant to be parents. But, oh, he'd wanted a child—he'd wanted everything—with her. Linda was a tall, slender girl with sharp features—almond-shaped eyes and a thin, sleek nose. Her face seemed to split the air as she moved forward. He thought her a movie star, the tough-talking dame in detective pictures, the one with a wounded heart. She would have looked good wearing a hat with a black veil, smoking a Turkish cigarette in an ivory holder.

They made love for the first time in the backseat of his father's Packard the night before he enlisted in the Navy. Her expression then—her head turned aside, her eyes half shut, biting a corner of her bottom lip—suggested however close he might be to her at that moment, he'd never learn her secrets. Three years they were apart. On the deck of the *Enterprise* in the Pacific, when the evening sky was cloudless and bright with what seemed millions of stars, he would get dizzy at the thought of those secrets and the mystery of their future together looming above him, infinite, unknowable.

They married a month after he came back from the war and a week before he enrolled at Johns Hopkins. Linda didn't become pregnant right away, but he didn't worry. His time in the Navy had taught him patience. It was easy to forget they were young—twenty-one, and already a veteran!—but they still had their entire lives ahead of them. Besides, he believed it wise not to have children so soon. There was the workload of his studies, at Hopkins and then at MIT. There was the move from Baltimore to Boston, then from Boston to Las

Cruces for his first assignment with NASA, then from Las Cruces back to Maryland, to Greenbelt, for his permanent assignment at the Goddard Space Flight Center. This was 1959. They were settled now, but no longer so young. He was thirty-four, Linda thirty-two. Still, no child came. They sought medical advice. The doctor was compassionate but clear: Linda could not bear children.

Linda accepted the news much better than he would have imagined. She was firm in her conviction they would raise a child—they would adopt. But as they undertook the process, as they filled out forms and sat through interviews, she grew quite angry with him. Why had they waited so long to consult a doctor? Why had they wasted so much time?

They'd been too busy, he told her. Besides, no adoption agency would have considered them when they'd moved so many times. He understood her anger but didn't share it. He didn't think it rational. They'd already wasted too much time being frustrated. Their lovemaking had become as rote as the tests he performed at work. Worse, even. It held no mystery, no chance of discovery at its conclusion. Now, they had an explanation for, and a solution to, their problems. For this, he was grateful.

The adoption agent called them an ideal couple. Edward painted the spare bedroom light blue. Linda knitted booties, caps, and a sweater. Then her first bout with illness: a lump in her right breast. The doctors eliminated this cancer, but Linda said she wasn't yet strong enough to endure the adoption process again. He was on the Apollo program then and could and did work twelve or more hours each day. Then he was named codirector of the Brahe project. The slow, steady progress of the project absorbed him: visiting Las Cruces or Houston for weeks at a time; debating with Ping where to place the radio transmitter on the Brahe module to provide the most accurate telemetry; having to wait over five years before the module would begin to send back results. It gave him the sense he was part of something far greater than himself, something that would outlive generations.

Linda took a job at the public library and in her spare time got involved in Greenbelt's civic pride association. She put her knitting in a box in a closet in the basement. The light blue bedroom remained unfurnished. It was 1975. He was fifty years old, his hair had turned silver, and he considered his and Linda's efforts to be parents an idea that a better scientist would have scribbled down, then discarded without lifting his pencil from the page. He spent too much time at work. Linda never fully recovered her strength after her illness. The great bawling energy of a child would have overwhelmed them both.

His work could so absorb him that someone wanting to speak with him had to knock on his office door or call his name several times. Jeanne, the day they met, knocked once. Later, he would ask her how long she had stood in his doorway, watching him, before he happened to look up. "Long enough," she would say.

She introduced herself. She'd started the week before. He'd been in Houston then. He noted as discreetly as he could her plain clothing, her simple hairstyle, her lack of makeup. She would be an excellent worker, he concluded, quiet and efficient.

"Don't let Ping work you too hard," he said. He meant it as a joke, but he spoke sternly, biting off the end of each word.

"Oh, he's not. He has me doing calculations for some project," she said. "The Tiki Bar project? That can't be right. Anyway, it was a piece of cake once I rounded the decimals up."

He stared at her.

"I'm kidding," she said and laughed softly. Her teeth were small and white, her laugh a low, husky bubbling. "He wanted me to give you this." She approached his desk and handed him a manila folder.

He didn't meet her eyes.

That night, as he did most nights, he heated dinner for Linda and himself in the oven. They sat on the living room sofa and watched television while they ate. During a commercial break, Linda put her plate, mashed potatoes and gravy still heaped upon it, on the coffee table and told him she was going to bed.

"It's only eight-thirty," he said.

"I'm exhausted."

"Because you don't eat properly."

"I eat fine." She stood from the sofa. "But right now I'm not hungry."

"You said that last night."

"Edward, please, I just want to go to bed."

Her skin was gray in the room's dim light, the bags underneath her eyes blue tinged with black. The face he'd loved for its secrets was now too sallow and pinched to hide anything. She seemed less a person than a sketch of a person. She was sick again, he thought, and this thought immediately became a certainty. Suddenly, he wanted to embrace her as he had after that first time they'd made love: lying spooned across the backseat of his father's Packard, her back to him, her breasts resting in the crook of his arm, his nose pressed to her neck, burning the scent of soap and sweat into his memory. The ferocity of this desire shocked him, but as he stood to embrace her, he found it wasn't desire he felt but rage—rage that thirty years had brought them no farther than this: she standing over a plate of cold mashed potatoes, exhausted, barren, miserable; he able only to put his arms around her and tell her what she already knew.

"You should see a doctor," he said. "It's probably nothing. But if it's not—if it's not, you know we have to find out as soon as we can."

She rested her forehead against his shoulder but said nothing and didn't return his embrace.

"I'll call tomorrow to make an appointment," he said. "I'll schedule it for when I'm back from Las Cruces. We'll go together."

Even as he said this, he wondered what they would do if it wasn't nothing. They'd lived so long in the shadow of her first illness that darkness and solitude seemed the normal course of their life together. He feared another illness would reveal their marriage to be a sham, a way to pass time between crises. No, he didn't believe this. Not really. What was a marriage if not two people constructing something to withstand the relentless passage of time? But Linda's first illness had ended the hope of their becoming parents, and he didn't know what remained for a second illness to end, except for the marriage itself. As estranged as that marriage might be, he couldn't imagine himself separated from it—from her.

In Las Cruces, at White Sands, he observed a test-firing of the Brahe module's thrusters. The thrusters ignited, twin ribbons of white heat against the desert's hazy gold. Then the entire apparatus—thrusters, engine, the test platform—exploded. Debris fell hundreds of yards away. Black smoke towered above the test site. A catastrophe, said the head engineer of the thrusters, covering his face with his hands.

Edward called Linda that night and said he would be coming home several days later than he'd planned. She should reschedule the appointment he'd made for her.

"I already went," she said.

"What?" He switched the receiver from one ear to the other. "Why?"

"I wanted to get it over with. I went yesterday. I'm fine. Nothing's wrong. I'm taking a week off from the library. It's what the doctor suggested. Rest."

"We were going to go together."

"Edward—" it sounded as if she were stifling a yawn. "When have

we done anything together? If you'd come home when you were supposed to, you'd have found another reason not to come."

"I wanted—" he began, but she'd hung up. He slammed the receiver into its cradle. Of course he was relieved Linda wasn't ill, but in
one sense it was as bad as he'd feared: The threat of illness had revealed
the fissure between them. A small fissure perhaps, but some engineers
at White Sands speculated that an even smaller fissure, a microscopic
rupture in a fuel line, had caused the destruction of the thrusters.

He accompanied a few colleagues to a bar in Las Cruces to com-
miserate over the accident. They bar was dim and smoky, not much
bigger than the living room of his house. The hostess led them to a
table in the back, and a waitress brought them pitchers of beer. He
drank several glasses of the watery beer, then ordered a scotch. One
of the engineers laughed at his drink order, but then thumped his
back with the palm of a hand, no hard feelings. He'd wanted to nurse
the scotch but downed it in two burning gulps. Johnny Cash was
playing on the jukebox. It was too loud to follow conversation. A
woman now sat beside him. She had red hair teased into a cascade
and wore a black dress that showed a constellation of freckles above
her large breasts. He ordered a second scotch and asked the woman
what she wanted to drink. She shook her head no. He asked what she
did. She was a singer, she offered. She was working to earn money to
go to New York City to audition for record companies. He finished
his scotch in one swallow. She rested her hand above his knee and
asked what he liked to do. He spoke of the Brahe project, its general
idea: to establish a sensor platform beyond Earth's gravitational pull;
to learn how this distance would impact long-term data accumulation; to build the foundation for future devices—a space telescope,
say—that wouldn't be restricted to Earth's orbit.

"No," she said. Her lips brushed his earlobe. "I mean, what do
you like?"

She led him to a small bedroom on the floor above the bar. There was a thin mattress on the hardwood floor, beside it a jar of Vaseline and a strip of condoms like the coiled skin of a snake. The room smelled of incense and bleach. She sat on the edge of the mattress and removed her dress in one motion. Stretch marks striped the mound of her stomach. Yellow bruises splotched the lengths of her pocked thighs.

He leaned against the wall to keep his balance. "I left my wallet downstairs," he said. "I think I'd better go."

He sat by himself in the bar, sipping from a glass of water, waiting for the other engineers to return from upstairs. It was four in the morning back east, too early to call Linda. He pinched the bridge of his nose. His stomach was bubbling with guilt and scotch. He didn't think he could wait several days to talk with her. But hadn't he waited thirty years already?

In fact, he returned to Greenbelt the next day. The director of Goddard called him back for an emergency meeting. The failure of the thrusters had panicked NASA. They feared the project was losing momentum. It needed a stronger sense of direction. Edward took this to be a criticism of his leadership and offered to resign. The director laughed and said it wasn't *that* serious. NASA was sending a senior consultant to work directly with him and Ping. Mikhail Korff. Once the shining star of the Soviet space program. A test pilot and an engineer. He'd had a crisis of conscience in the early 1960s after his wife's death in a plane crash and defected to the United States.

Linda was asleep when Edward got home that night. He wanted to wake her but thought of her doctor's advice that she rest. He went into the bathroom. When he came back, she was sitting up in bed.

"You scared me," she said. "I was going to call the police."

"I'm sorry. They flew me out first thing this morning. I didn't have a chance to call." He changed into his pajamas, telling her about failure of the thrusters as he did. "If I don't get my act together soon, I think they might replace me entirely."

She yawned. "Can we talk tomorrow?"

"I think we should talk now." He sat down beside her. "I want to know why you went to the doctor without me."

"I told you it's no big deal. I'm fine." She fluffed her pillow between her hands. "I need rest, Edward. That's all."

He considered telling her he'd slept with the whore in Las Cruces, but it occurred to him she might not even care. This realization wounded him more deeply than the guilt he carried for following the whore upstairs. He removed his pajamas and put on the clothes he'd worn all day. Linda sat up and asked where he was going.

"I feel restless," he said. "I'm going to my office."

"It's almost midnight." Then, more softly, she added, "You need rest, too."

"I have too much work to catch up on."

Goddard was quiet but by no means empty. In scattered windows of every building the fluorescent lights flickered. As he approached his building, he saw a light in a window of Ping's office. He unlocked the door to his office, then went down the hall to say hello. Jeanne stood at her desk in the office's anteroom, loudly declaiming a poem. When she seemed to have finished, he cleared his throat. She looked up, her mouth round with surprise, then smiled.

"Don't worry," she said. "Ping's not making me do this."

"I saw the light."

"The acoustics are better here than at home." She pointed to a plate on her desk. "I made brownies."

He told her to be sure to lock Ping's office when she left. In his office, he began sorting through the paperwork that had accumulated while he'd been in Las Cruces. He'd made almost no progress when Jeanne knocked on his door and said she was leaving.

"Are you sure you don't want a brownie?" she asked.

He eyed the plate, held now beneath her chest. "Maybe one."

She crossed the office to his desk. He took one and nibbled its corner.

"Ping told me what happened with the thrusters," she said. "I'm sure it's a temporary setback. Maybe you can just adjust the fuel-to-oxygen ratio rather than redesigning them from scratch."

A brownie crumb fell from his lip to his lap. He brushed it aside.

"I majored in physics," she said. "Acting's just a hobby. Which reminds me." From her purse she took a sheet of paper. "We're performing *Julius Caesar* this weekend. The Greenbelt Dinner Theater Collective. I'm playing Calpurnia."

He took the sheet from her and placed it atop his pile of paperwork. "Thanks," he said. "For the brownie."

Edward had no intention of seeing Jeanne's play. But as he walked home from work on Friday evening, he found the idea of spending the evening with Linda—or, rather, spending it alone in the silence between them—unbearable.

The Greenbelt Dinner Theater Collective had set up camp in a Chinese restaurant in the town center. He took a table, ordered dinner, and awaited the performance.

The other diners did not seem aware that a play would accompany their meals. There was no stage, nor were the tables arranged in such a way that everyone would face the same direction. The performance began with two men in suits emerging from the kitchen and addressing the diners as if they were the populace of Rome. Then a man stood up from a nearby table and spoke the role of a carpenter; at another table a man stood and delivered a cobbler's lines. By the first scene's end, it became apparent to Edward he was the only person in the restaurant who wasn't part of the performance. With the beginning of the second scene—Caesar, played by a man made-up to look like Richard Nixon—the conceit of the performance also became clear. Edward did want to consider this conceit seriously, but when Caesar called for Calpurnia in a horrendous impression of Nixon's voice—speaking as if gargling—Edward began to chuckle and might have continued to chuckle throughout the performance had Jeanne not appeared at that moment. She was, Edward supposed, Calpurnia as Pat Nixon, but given her age and the way her pantsuit, clearly a size too small for her, highlighted her curves, it was difficult to imagine. She was not a particularly good actress. She enunciated each word too distinctly, her lines were too obviously memorized, and her body language and actions were so pronounced as to be melodramatic, but he thought her effort to raise herself above the other performers' simplistic satire endearing—noble, even—if doomed.

He waited for her outside the restaurant. Half an hour passed before she emerged. She'd changed into a sweater and jeans. Her hair hung around her face in damp ringlets. Her eyes were red and puffy from crying. She hugged him. Surprised, he briefly touched his hands to her back, then stepped back an arm's length.

"Thank you for being here," she said. "I can't believe you're the only one. I left fliers at work, all over town. We put a notice in the *Post*. Tell me what you thought. Be honest."

"It was—the Watergate angle was interesting."

"It was awful. You can say so."

"You were very good."

"I need a drink. Will you buy me a drink?"

They walked to a nearby bar. She ordered a gin and tonic. He wanted a scotch and soda but ordered a club soda with lime.

"I'm sorry no one came," he said. "I wanted to bring my wife, but she isn't feeling well."

"It's probably best. It's an awful production."

"It wasn't that bad."

She laughed. "If you thought that wasn't awful, you don't know a thing about theater."

He looked away from her.

"I'm sorry," she said. "I need to make a confession." She took several sips from her drink. "I lied about leaving fliers at work. You're the only person I told."

He took a sip from his drink. It sloshed onto his hand.

"Oh, god." She lit a cigarette and took a long drag. "I can't believe I just admitted that."

With the end of his straw, he poked the lime wedge to the bottom of his drink.

"As long as I'm being honest," she said. "When I said I majored in physics, that was a lie, too. But I'm fascinated by your work. I've been reading up on it."

"Fascinated by what I do."

"You have a passion for it."

"I work hard. I like what I do. I don't know that I'd call it a passion."

"A lot of people work hard." She reached across the table and covered his hand with hers. It was damp and trembling. "You have a passion. Intensity. It's why I'm attracted to you."

"No one's found my work that fascinating. No one who wasn't already involved in it." He finished his drink and studied the melting ice cubes. "I should go."

Her apartment was an efficiency. The sofa unfolded into a bed. They didn't bother to put sheets down. Her body was soft and rounded and comfortably bore his weight. He imagined he wasn't very good;

he'd forgotten how much energy desire demanded when the act was more than simple mechanics. But she cradled his head against her chest afterward and murmured how wonderful it had been, and he thought perhaps it had been wonderful. If not the act itself, then the desire that had driven him to it.

This feeling faded as he walked home. In its place came neither guilt nor shame, but dread and a sense of futility. What he'd done had felt right, but he thought only negative consequences could follow. When he got home and saw Linda asleep on the living room couch, he feared the worst. She'd waited for him. He couldn't tell her he'd gone back to his office after the play. His clothes reeked of Jeanne's perfume. He went upstairs, changed into his pajamas and washed his face, then returned to the living room. He touched a hand to Linda's cheek. She opened her eyes slowly and for a moment seemed not to recognize him.

"What time is it?" she muttered.

"I came home hours ago," he said. "I didn't want to wake you."

He didn't want to think of himself as someone having an affair. Could he call it an affair when it was possible Linda, should she discover it, wouldn't mind? Besides, his feelings for Jeanne weren't rooted in the kind of desperation and aimless lust he imagined underlay others' affairs. He hadn't been looking to cheat on Linda. He'd slept with Jeanne because he wanted her. That it was an affair was a technicality.

A few days after their first night together, Jeanne asked him if he saw this as a fling or the foundation of something serious. They were in an empty storage room down the hall from his office, lying naked on the blanket he had in his office for nights he worked too late to bother walking home. It was the lunch hour. Ping and the others who had offices on the hall had gone to the cafeteria. That these circumstances were much like those he'd always associated with affairs—a room dimly lit, uncomfortable, unclean—made it difficult to say clearly what he meant.

"My wife's a good person. I loved her very much. I don't know what happened." He looked away from Jeanne. "I don't know what's happening."

"Do you think we're bad people?" Jeanne asked. "Because I don't."

Someone knocked on the door. Jeanne's eyes widened, but he pointed to the dead-bolt lock. She nodded but pulled the blanket around her shoulders. The doorknob rattled, then they heard the click of a key fitting the lock. Jeanne yelped. He got to his feet to hold the door shut, but he was too slow. He stood now between this intruder and Jeanne, a trembling hand cupped over his groin.

"I am looking for the office of the Tycho Brahe project," the intruder said. He had a thick Russian accent. "Perhaps I have the wrong building?"

"Down the hall," Edward said. His voice was soft and reedy. "I'll be right there."

The intruder smiled and nodded, then walked away. Edward closed the door and rested his forehead against it. "I don't think he saw you," he told Jeanne.

Jeanne giggled. He turned and frowned at her.

"Sorry. I couldn't help but think. If Brezhnev saw Ford naked, the cold war might end right then and there."

"I'm glad you can laugh about this—" his voice wavered on the last word. He cleared his throat. "What the hell are we supposed to do?"

She stood, the blanket falling from her, and embraced him. Her skin was warm and damp with sweat. Still, he shivered. "He doesn't know us yet," she said. "Pretend nothing happened, and he'll understand it's not an issue. For all he knows, I'm your wife."

His stomach roiled. His pulse hammered his temples. He dressed and trudged down the hall to his office. He couldn't match Jeanne's calm. In truth, her calm disturbed him as much as the intrusion itself. How much experience did she have in these situations? Such thoughts were irrational. He laughed once, a bitter bark. The nonsense he'd spouted about theirs not being an affair. He was an amateur, through and through.

Mikhail sat waiting in the anteroom to Edward's office, rifling the pages of a black binder he held in his lap. He was a stout man with a large, square face. He had a broad, flat nose and heavy jowls, and as he looked up from the binder a slight curl suggesting bemusement or disgust came to the corners of his mouth. His eyes were small and gray and almost completely hidden beneath bushy black eyebrows. He wore a black trench coat and a deerstalker, its flaps tied above cauliflower ears.

Without speaking, Edward walked past Mikhail into his office, sat at his desk, and cleared the papers from the ink blotter. Mikhail followed him, sat in the chair opposite the desk, as if he'd been in Edward's office countless times before, crossed one leg over the other, and whistled a complicated series of notes.

"About what just happened," Edward said.

Mikhail gestured with one hand as if to swat a fly. "It is none of my business. Believe me, I am used to keeping quiet. Like those monkeys. See no evil. Hear no evil. Speak no evil. Definitely speak no evil." He smiled. "I am here to help make your satellite work. Something else is going on? I could not care less."

"You shouldn't have the key to that room."

"They gave me the master key to this building but did not tell me which room. I heard voices, so I entered." He shrugged. "Now, why your thrusters exploded. I know exactly what you did wrong."

"The team at White Sands has been working around the clock to correct the flaws in the design. They assure me they've got a handle on it."

Mikhail repeated the swatting gesture. "It is like I said to Yuri Alexseevich. He was so excited to travel into space, he did not see the point of all the test flights. I told him, you can be sure or you can be absolutely sure. Sure is blasting off into space. Absolutely sure is sending a chimp up there first."

Edward narrowed his eyes. "We tested the thrusters. That's how we discovered the problem in the first place."

Mikhail smiled again, very broadly. His teeth were yellow and crooked. "I will give you the calculations I made. If you had studied them before you tested the thrusters, you would have seen an explosion was inevitable."

Mikhail's calculations did prove this, but Edward took offense at any implication he and the others on the Brahe project hadn't done their jobs properly. The failure of the thrusters was a setback, but it was the kind of thing that happened often in the early stages of NASA projects. As the former shining star of the Soviet space program, Mikhail should know that. This was rocket science. Things went wrong.

"He's insufferable," he told Jeanne the next day. Despite Jeanne's insisting otherwise, they'd returned to the storage room. He didn't want to risk being seen walking to her apartment together. "I feel like he's already judged me for what he saw here and for what's gone wrong with the project."

"Silly," Jeanne said. She traced figure-eights on his bare chest. "You've known him for one day."

"He talks to me like I'm a child."

"Well, you *are* acting a bit like a baby."

He sat up and turned his back to her. "You don't understand. I'm fifty. My marriage is a shambles. I don't have children. I have this. Now he comes along and says I'm screwing even that up?"

She wrapped her arms around his waist and pressed her face to his back. "The project might not be all you have," she whispered.

"Don't be dramatic. We've known each other a few weeks."

She let go of him, lay back down on the blanket, and wrapped its ends around her. "Tell me which has been longer. Since you slept with your wife, or since the two of you had a real conversation?"

"What does that have to do with anything?"

"I'm curious. Because you obviously aren't used to talking about your problems with another person. I'm trying to understand what you're going through. Don't try to cut me off with a petty comment like 'Don't be dramatic.'"

He turned back to face her. "You like provoking me, don't you?"

"Right now, I'm not sure how else to get a response out of you."

"I'm not used to someone trying to understand me."

She sat up and touched the tip of her nose to the tip of his. "Then I'll make you get used to it."

"I still don't know what to do about Mikhail."

"Invite him to dinner."

"With Linda? After he saw us together?"

"You said yourself he didn't seem to care. Look, you need him to be on your side. It'll show you're welcoming him to the project. Invite Ping if you want. It will reduce any tension."

"I think maybe you enjoy provoking me like this."

She smiled but said nothing.

He doubted Linda would want him to invite coworkers to dinner. She'd taken a second week off from the library, and while she said she'd done so because she'd enjoyed her first week of vacation so much, he now believed that she was sick again. It would be easy to confront her with his suspicions, but he knew doing so would force him to admit to her that he was having an affair, and he wasn't ready to do that.

Nevertheless, he asked her about the dinner so he wouldn't be lying when he told Jeanne he'd tried to follow her advice. To his surprise, Linda wanted to know only if he expected her to cook. When he told her he would make all the preparations himself, she said it was fine as long as it ended at a reasonable hour.

"It might be nice to have people over," she said. "The house could use a little life."

Of course, he could have told Jeanne that Linda had refused to host a dinner—but, in truth, he was beginning to warm to the idea. Not because he thought it would establish a good relationship with Mikhail—in fact, when he invited Mikhail, Mikhail said only, "As long as you do not serve chicken. Americans eat chicken and nothing else it seems," and Edward could tell then the dinner would be an awkward, tense occasion—but because he wanted to show Jeanne he appreciated her advice, that her concern had touched him.

He set the dinner for Saturday. He bought fresh salmon and two bottles of an expensive white wine. Mikhail and Ping arrived together, Mikhail in a gray suit that matched the color of his hair, Ping in his usual work clothes: white shirt, black tie, blue slacks. Staring at his feet, his black hair rumpled as if he'd just gotten out of bed, Ping seemed a child next to Mikhail.

Edward burned the salmon, the wine tasted vinegary, and no one said very much as they ate. Or as he and Ping ate. Mikhail scowled at his scorched fillet. Linda took a bite of hers, a forkful of rice, then pushed her plate away.

"So," Edward said. He took a long drink from his wine and winced. "So."

Mikhail looked at Ping. "I met your new secretary the other day," he said. "She is quite nice."

Edward glared at Mikhail. Mikhail met his stare, but his expression was inscrutable, a slight indentation of his eyebrows, which looked like two caterpillars greeting each other.

Ping, chewing slowly on a piece of salmon, said, "Jeanne. A nice girl. She wants to be an actress. She just had a part in a play. *Julius Caesar.*"

Mikhail waggled his eyebrows. "I am as constant as the northern star," he said.

"There's a meteor shower next Saturday night," Edward said. "At four in the morning. Goddard usually hosts a party to watch showers. You should go Mikhail. We should all go."

"Why stay up so late to see some lights in the sky?" Linda asked.

"It's like fireworks," Edward said. "Nature's fireworks."

"Lightning," Ping said, still chewing. "Lightning is nature's fireworks."

"I agree with your wife, Edward," Mikhail said. "Meteor showers are not so spectacular. If you see one, it is enough."

The conversation lagged. The only sound was Ping scraping his food onto his fork with his knife. Edward served dessert. Linda didn't eat any of hers.

Mikhail cleared his throat. "I notice you have a piano in your main room."

"Linda used to play," Edward said.

"I still play," Linda said. "When you're at work."

"Could I perhaps play for you?" Mikhail asked. "I have not played in a long time."

Edward and Linda sat on opposite sides of the living room sofa. Ping ignored Edward's gestures toward the love seat and stood awkwardly beside them. Mikhail sat at the piano, lifted the cover from the keyboard, and struck notes at random. Edward couldn't recall when he'd last had it tuned, but Mikhail seemed satisfied. He held his fingers above the keys, shut his eyes and began to play. Edward knew little about music, but to his untrained ear the slow, elegiac melody sounded lovely. It put him in mind of the melancholy that descended on him like a fever whenever he parted from Jeanne, knowing he could never leave Linda for her. It simply wasn't in him.

Linda sobbed, a deep, cracked sound, and fell forward from the sofa onto her knees. She used the coffee table to push herself to her feet and stumbled toward the staircase. Mikhail took his fingers from the keyboard and stared at Edward. Edward's mouth went dry. Calmly, as if Linda did this every night, he stood from the sofa and followed her footfalls to their bedroom.

She was standing at the window, her face pressed to the glass.

"It was beautiful," she said. She was no longer sobbing but crying softly with a low, pulsing sniffle. "His playing was so beautiful."

"Linda. Please tell me. You're sick again, aren't you? You've been hiding it from me, I know."

"You stupid, stupid man," she said.

"Linda." He frowned. Had she guessed he was having an affair? Suddenly, he wanted her to accuse him. "Please tell me what's wrong."

She turned from the window. "I'm dying, you stupid bastard. I'm dying, and you don't even care."

At first he didn't believe her. She'd uncovered the affair but had waited to confront him, wanting to embarrass him in front of his coworkers. He wanted to laugh—wanted to say she'd timed her dying perfectly, since he was falling in love with someone else. But she stepped toward him and widened her eyes slightly, and he realized that she wasn't angry at him but waiting for him to say something—anything. His scorn dissipated. In its place came a great wave of sorrow. He'd promised to learn all of her secrets. Three years she'd waited for him to return from the war, and then she'd waited another thirty years. She was waiting still.

"Oh, god," he said. "Oh, god, Linda, I'm sorry."

She said nothing. He slumped against the bedroom door. His hands shook.

"I'm so, so sorry," he said.

She gasped. Her eyes were no longer focused on him but at a point beyond him. He turned. Mikhail stood at the top of the stairs.

"Come," Mikhail said. "Come downstairs and let me finish playing for you."

"Mikhail—" his voice croaked. He coughed violently. "You'd better go. Linda isn't feeling well."

"No," Linda said. Her voice was soft but clear. "No, I want to hear the rest."

Mikhail nodded once, then turned and went downstairs. Edward looked at Linda, but she walked past him without a word, drying her eyes with the back of her hand as she went. After a moment, he followed. Mikhail had resumed his place at the piano. Ping sat on the love seat now, but with his back turned to the rest of the room, staring out of the window. Linda lay across the sofa and covered her eyes with the back of one hand. Edward perched on the arm of the sofa and tried to concentrate on Mikhail's playing. He was on to a different piece now, something stark and somber.

Linda had fallen asleep by the time Mikhail finished. Edward put a finger to his lips and led him and Ping to the door. Ping thanked him for dinner and walked to his car. Mikhail turned to follow Ping, but Edward touched his arm. Mikhail stopped, turned back, and studied Edward with his eyebrows furrowed and his lips pursed. Edward saw pity in this expression—pity and, Edward believed, a measure of distaste.

"Thank you," Edward said.

"It was nothing," Mikhail said. "My technique is quite rusty. I will do this. I will come back tomorrow to play. I promise it will be much better than tonight."

Edward nodded. "I'd like that."

"It is not for you," Mikhail said, then turned and walked to Ping's car.

Edward knelt beside the sofa and stroked Linda's hair. Her eyes fluttered. "What can I do?" he asked. "Whatever you want, tell me."

"There's nothing you can do," she said, her voice slurred.

"Tomorrow, we'll talk. I'll make sure you get the best doctor. We won't give up unless God himself delivers the test results."

"Edward, we both know you don't believe in God." She closed her eyes and turned her body to face the back of the sofa. "Please, just let me sleep."

He went upstairs to their bedroom and took the telephone from the nightstand. He held the receiver to his ear and dialed the first six digits of Jeanne's number, then replaced the receiver in its cradle. He put the phone back on the nightstand and returned to the living room. He took the quilt from the back of the love seat and draped it over Linda. Then he lay down on the love seat and watched her sleep.

She was still asleep when he woke the next morning. His first thought was to phone her doctor and confirm her prognosis, but it was a Sunday, and he was sure her doctor would not be in his office. He made a cursory search of their bedroom and the cupboard in the dining room in which they kept their papers but found no record of her most recent visit to her doctor except a canceled check for seventy-five dollars "for services rendered." He brewed coffee, then took his cup into the living room and again sat on the love seat to watch her sleep. She had kicked off the quilt he'd laid over her and her naked foot dangled over the edge of the sofa. He took this foot in his hands. It was light and dry and had the texture of a crumpled paper bag; the skin was almost translucent, lacy blue veins like rivers on a map. He kissed the tip of her big toe, then guided her foot back to the sofa and laid it to rest beside its mate.

He showered and dressed and left a note saying he was going for a walk and would be home shortly.

Jeanne greeted him at the door to her apartment, her eyes closed and her lips pursed for a kiss. He pecked the corner of her mouth then strode past her to her sofa bed, still unfolded from the night before. He sat on the edge of its mattress and buried his head in his hands.

She sat beside him, wrapped an arm around his waist, and rested her chin on his shoulder. "It went badly," she said.

He took a deep breath then, his voice low and raspy, told her what had happened.

"Oh, my god," she said. Tears glimmered in the corners of her eyes. "Oh, god."

"I really don't know how I'm supposed to handle this."

He stood from the sofa bed and paced the length of the apartment.

"Please let me help you," she said.

He shook his head. "This is a mistake."

"Sit down. We have to talk."

"I can't do this. Not anymore."

She was sobbing now. "Please, just sit down."

"I haven't done a single thing in thirty years to make my wife happy. The least I can do is take care of her now."

"And who's going to take care of you?"

"Maybe I'll just move into my office." He ran his fingers through his hair. "Once she's gone, I can live in my office and never bother anyone again."

"This isn't a sign from above. You couldn't have known this was going to happen. It doesn't mean what we're doing is wrong. It's more complicated than that. Please tell me you think it's more complicated than that."

"If you think it's better we're in separate buildings, I'll have Ping transfer you. He'll be discreet about it, I promise." He kissed her forehead. "Good-bye."

"Edward—"

He sat on a bench at a bus stop and tried to light a cigarette. He dropped three matches before he managed to strike one. A bus lumbered to a halt in front of him. With a hiss like an exasperated sigh its doors opened. He met the driver's eyes. The marvels of this technological age he'd helped to make. You could board a bus near Washington at lunch, be on a plane to Argentina before dinner, then be on a boat to Antarctica by breakfast the next day. He was one of the builders, not one of the travelers. The driver yanked a lever: the bus's doors creaked shut. Edward flicked the end of his cigarette under one of its wheels then stood and resumed his walk home.

He could hear piano music from the far end of the path from the sidewalk to his house. He approached the front door but didn't open it. Instead, he peered into the living room window. Linda sat on the sofa, still in the dress she'd worn for the dinner party. She'd shut her eyes and was swaying slightly to the music. Mikhail was hunched over the piano, his eyes shut as well, his fingers striking the keys in a jerky, up-and-down motion like a marionette's.

Edward let himself in when he thought Mikhail had finished, but he took only a few steps beyond the entryway. Linda didn't open her eyes at his approach. Mikhail leaned back on the piano bench to regard Edward and cocked his head toward the sofa.

"I don't want to intrude," Edward said.

"No, take a seat," Mikhail said. "I am about to begin the second movement."

Linda opened her eyes then. "No, that's enough, Mikhail," she said. "It was lovely."

"I will return tomorrow?" Mikhail asked.

"Yes," Linda said. "Please."

Edward looked from Linda to Mikhail then back to Linda. "I was going to make lunch," he said. "If you'd like to stay, Mikhail. No chicken, I promise."

"I'm not hungry," Linda said. She stood from the sofa, bracing one hand against the arm of the sofa as she did. "I'm going to go lie down."

"I'll be up in a minute," Edward said. "I'll see Mikhail out."

"No," she said. "Go make lunch for you and Mikhail. I'd rather be alone right now."

Slowly, feeling her way from sofa to piano as if she were blind, and then from piano to banister, she made her way across the living room and up the stairs.

"I am going to step outside to have a cigarette," Mikhail said. "Please join me."

Mikhail lit two cigarettes and handed one to Edward. Edward inhaled deeply and gagged at the sharp taste.

"They are generic," Mikhail said. "They are more like Russian cigarettes."

"Thanks for the warning," Edward said in between coughs.

"I am sorry," Mikhail said. "I do not mean to intrude in your personal life. It seemed a good idea last night to come back today. But now I think I should have phoned first."

"What the hell," Edward said. "You caught me with another woman. You know what happened here last night. I don't know what constitutes intruding at this point. At least you have some idea what she wants."

Mikhail shrugged. "I am here to play the piano. It gives her something to listen to for a few minutes. Even if it is my inadequate playing."

They were silent for a moment, then Mikhail said, "I knew a boy in Russia. Burned over his entire body. Everywhere but his left hand." He held out his left hand, palm up, as if Edward might never have seen a hand before. "The doctors could not explain why the left hand was not burned. It did not really matter to them. This was the Nedelin disaster. Have you heard of it?"

Edward shook his head. He knew the name Nedelin from briefings at NASA. An upper-level officer in the Soviet military, some knowledge of rocketry, killed in a plane crash years ago.

"They've kept it quiet. At Baikonur Cosmodrome. Fifteen years ago. A terrible thing. An explosion on the launchpad. Many people dead." He took a drag from his cigarette. "The lucky ones were incinerated. The others, like that boy." He shrugged. "I could not describe the horror. Five days he lived. I was at the hospital every day. Not to see him. But an old woman was always there when I was there. You could not get permission to visit patients in the trauma unit, of course, but every day she argued with the nurse on duty until she was allowed to see this certain patient. One day, I followed her. She is sitting at the bedside of this boy. You could not even tell he was a boy. Covered totally in bandages, except his left hand. She sits beside his bed and squeezes this hand between hers for hours. Says nothing. Does not move except to squeeze his hand. The fifth day, the nurse on duty tells the woman the boy died during the night. She is quiet. She makes the sign of the cross. She walks away. I stop her. I tell her I am sorry for the loss of her son. She says, 'He was not my son. I do not know who he was.' After she left, the nurse told me her story. This woman came the day of the accident to find her son. She thought the burned boy was him. She sat with him all that day, thinking he was her son. That night, she learned the hospital had already identified her son's body. Still, she came back the next day, and the next day, to sit with this other boy. Can you imagine?"

Edward thought he understood. It was an apology, of a kind, from Mikhail to him—an apology and an explanation. Mikhail had never meant to interfere in his problems. If anything, Mikhail was the only person who might truly understand what he was going through right now. Mikhail had lost his wife. That loss had precipitated his decision to leave the Soviet Union, the director of Goddard had explained. Edward couldn't imagine what it would be like to lose your wife and betray your country in such short order—knowing you could never visit her grave site, never again see the house you shared with her, the bed in which you first made love—knowing you yourself had chosen this exile from your past. And yet he didn't think this much different from his situation. He had lost his wife—in spirit, if not in fact—many years ago. He'd exiled himself and now, when his wife would have needed him most, he couldn't return to her. It was not a perfect analogy, but he and Mikhail weren't that different. Both of them were learning, under extraordinarily unusual circumstances, how to grieve.

"I know what you're trying to say," he told Mikhail. "I know what you must be going through."

Mikhail punched him then, a clumsy uppercut that struck the edge of his right jaw. He staggered backward, more stunned than hurt.

Mikhail stepped toward him, both hands balled into fists. "You cannot know what I am going through. You will be able to say goodbye to your wife when the time comes." He lowered his hands and took a few steps back. "The woman in the hospital, what did she think when she found out that boy was not her son? What did she tell herself about the first day she spent with that boy? Did she think it was as if she was holding her son's hand? Is that why she came back? But did she think maybe her son had been alive in the hospital at the same time—maybe her son was desperate for someone to hold his hand as well? Did the possibility, even if it was small, even if her son lived only a few minutes while she was with the other boy—did it drive her mad?

"You know where they buried the boy? The one burned except for his hand? A mass grave. Like in wartime. Almost a hundred dead, and most of them went into one grave. They made everyone say there had been a plane crash. They would not admit the disaster happened. They still do not. If you go to the Soviet Union and look up the records of Marshall Nedelin, it will say killed in plane crash, the twenty-fourth of October, 1960. My wife's records, the same thing."

"Oh, my god," Edward murmured. "I'm so sorry."

"It is my fault. She was so bored living at the cosmodrome. Baikonur, it is in the middle of nowhere. Wastelands. She had no friends, no life. I told her we would leave, but first I must finish training the cosmonauts. I didn't have a choice. We had to beat you Americans into space.

"I had influence. I got her a job. She was a chauffeur. For important visitors to the base. It was boring, yes, but it passed time. So when Marshall Nedelin visited the base, she drove him. He was there to oversee a missile test. A ballistic missile. There were many problems. Leaks in the fuel line. Computer systems failing. They should have scrapped the test. Nedelin said they must go ahead. So, they went ahead. Some say he was being pressured by Khrushchev. I do not know. I prefer what Sofya said the first day she drove him. 'The man is a pompous ass,' she said.

"The day of the test, he had Sofya drive him right up to the launch site. As close as he could get. Wanted everyone to see how confident he was. So they were right there at the time the missile exploded. What an explosion. A fireball like the sun. I was on the other side of the cosmodrome, but I could feel the heat. So powerful. I thought it must be a nuclear attack.

"I spent the next week at the hospital. I refused to leave. I wanted some proof Sofya was really dead. A piece of clothing. A bone. They found nothing. Or they said they found nothing. There probably was nothing to find, if she was at the front of the launch area. Still, I wonder sometimes. All those bodies in a single grave. There is not a single part I could say is Sofya? Not a hand in the hospital I could have squeezed? It is awful to think, I know. I am a sick man, I think. But not half so sick as a people who would bury those bodies all together. I swear to you, Edward, even if I could go back there, I would not. They want Sofya's entire life to vanish like her body did. I will not accept it." He rubbed his eyes. "It is later than I thought. I should go now. I hope I did not hurt you too badly."

"No," Edward said. "Will you come tomorrow to play for Linda?"

"Perhaps not tomorrow. I am very tired."

Edward nodded. He, too, was tired. He couldn't remember when he'd last felt this bone weary.

In their bedroom he found Linda curled beneath a single sheet. Gooseflesh rippled the skin of her arms. She stirred slightly at his approach but didn't wake. He noticed her lips were dry, the color and texture of chalk. He filled a paper cup with water from the bathroom spigot. He brought the cup to the bed and held it to her mouth, tilting it as slightly as he could so only a few drops spilled over her lips. What Mikhail had wanted: to give a moment's comfort. She raised her head from her pillow and bent forward to drink from the cup, sipping at first, then slurping, water running down her chin in rivulets. He dabbed the water from her skin with his shirtsleeve. She reached up with one hand and touched his cheek.

Jeanne lay beside him, snoring softly. When she woke, if his body was willing, he would make love to her with the ardor of a man a third his age—although he would, in truth, settle for a deep, long kiss. Later, he would call their son solely to provoke an argument over the designated hitter rule. Now, though, he would bury his head underneath his pillow so his weeping wouldn't disturb Jeanne and grieve for Mikhail and Linda—that their lives hadn't been as miraculous as his own.

REBECCA BARRY

Ohio State University

⤜⤛

SNOW FEVER

Madeleine Harris appeared out of nowhere in the late fall, when the sky was damp and gray and depression came drifting in for the winter. She just showed up at Lucy's Tavern one night, a medium-sized woman with big feet and a perfect throw. The first night Bill Wilcox saw her, she beat Hank Stevens three times in a row at darts. Bill watched this with interest, partly because Madeleine was good-looking, and partly because Hank owned the diner where Bill made soup and baked pies and he liked to see him lose.

"She has a good arm," said Hank, sitting down next to Bill after the third game. "I haven't seen that on a woman since that lesbo mail carrier, Fat Betty."

"I haven't seen that on a man since the last time your mother was in town," said Bill, since Fat Betty was his friend and she was a meter maid, not a mail carrier. Then he changed the subject as if he weren't

354

interested. He had sworn off women since his last girlfriend, Trish, left him for a piano tuner, but because Madeleine was new, and because she didn't seem to care if he lived or died, Bill found himself keeping an eye on her.

Over the next few weeks, he learned that she was dating an organic vegetable farmer from Lodi, a fantastic drunk who had once been arrested for driving his truck home naked. But Madeleine came into the bar alone and left alone. Unlike the other women at Lucy's, she drank her liquor straight and almost never let anyone buy her a drink. After three bourbons she usually left, unless she had to finish a game, in which case she'd start drinking water.

"She drives a school bus over in Newfield in the morning," said Tommy, the weeknight bartender who had gone to high school with Madeleine.

Bill laughed. "Nothing but a bunch of retards and rednecks out in Newfield," he said, since he was from there and could say it without being rude. But he liked the idea of Madeleine Harris, her big hands resting on the oversized steering wheel of a school bus, up early in the morning before husbands and wives started bickering. He imagined the kids on her route: the red hat girl, the crying kid, the family of four melon-headed boys whose father left a deer carcass on the clothesline to save money on dog food, the boy who smelled like cows, the two girls who brought their violins on Thursdays. He saw her managing the clutch of the bus with her smooth-toed work boots, taking those kids to school and away from their homes.

"I don't think she's very good at her job," Tommy said. "She was driving the bus when that eighth grader was giving a blow job to another eighth grader."

"I heard about that," Bill said. "On a school bus. What's wrong with these kids?"

"That's what Maddy said," said Tommy. "She stopped the bus, got up, pulled the girl off the boy and took her outside. Then she said, 'Now you listen to me. Never, ever, do that for free.'"

"It's not bad advice," Bill said.

"No," Tommy said. "But I think it got her into trouble."

Bill watched Madeleine a lot after that.

One Monday in the beginning of December, Hank closed the diner early and he and Bill went to Lucy's because they were tired and wanted to be drunk. It was 3:30 in the afternoon and the place was almost empty. They sat at the bar, talking about people they hated (cops, the mayor, Rita, the weekend bartender who had cut them off the night before), and women they thought would be hot in bed (Rita, Rita's girlfriend, Sheila, and the weather girl on Channel 7). They had just started telling dirty jokes when Madeleine came in and sat down a few stools away from them, her back straight as a Mormon's. She didn't say a word to either one of them and didn't ask Tommy for darts. Instead, she asked for bourbon, neat, which she drank quickly. Then she ordered another.

Bill noticed she was drinking more than usual and hoped it would make her more friendly. He and Hank swapped a few more jokes, and Hank loudly overused the word *pussy*. Normally this wouldn't have bothered Bill, but tonight, with Madeleine sitting right there, Hank's crassness was embarrassing, and Bill stopped laughing when Hank got to the one about Little Red Riding Hood.

Madeleine didn't seem to care. She was talking to Tommy about her vegetable farmer, who, if Bill heard right, had left her for someone else two weeks before.

"He's in love with a stripper," she said. "You know how I know that? He came over today to pick up his things and I asked him. I followed him around like a seventh-grade girl saying, What is her name? What does she do? Do you love her? Do you love her? Do you love her?"

Madeleine shook her head in disgust and Tommy poured her another bourbon, her fourth by Bill's count.

"I didn't want to ask him that of course," Madeleine said. "I wanted to shoot him with rock salt. But I couldn't stop. 'Yes,' he finally said, 'Yes, I love her, not you.'"

In the minute that no one spoke, Bill remembered that when Trish left he hadn't said the right thing either. Before she'd gone he'd said the words a hundred times: "Don't leave me, don't ever leave me." It was stupid, since things were good then, but he was always drunk when he said it, and he was always embarrassed the next day.

When Trish finally did go, he hadn't said a word until she got into the car. Right before she drove off, he came out and banged on the window on the driver's side. "Hey!" he yelled. "Hey!" When she rolled the window down, her face was so tired, almost old. I did that, he thought, and this made him so deeply sad that he just said, "Well, see you later."

"He was afraid of cows," Madeleine said. "How can you be a farmer and be afraid of cows?" She looked at Bill, and as she turned he caught a smell from her jacket. It was a clean, spicy smell. Like sage.

"You farm corn," he said.

Madeleine laughed. It was a low, warm laugh, and when he heard it Bill thought, That's how a woman should sound. His ex-girlfriend had a voice like a screech owl.

"That's like being a bus driver and being afraid of the kids," said Hank.

"Right," said Madeleine. She took one of his cigarettes without asking, and Hank tried to look down her shirt. "Except I'm not afraid of the kids."

"Nope," said Hank. "Telling them not to give out free blow jobs is definitely not being afraid of the kids."

"That's not exactly what I said," Madeleine said irritably. "I told her not to give a boy a blow job unless he took care of her first."

"It wasn't bad advice," said Bill.

"It was very good advice," Madeleine said. She tried to rest her foot on one of the rungs of the stool, but missed and almost lost her balance. Bill caught her arm, which he noticed was muscled like a man's.

"Those girls think blow jobs are just part of making out," she muttered. "They do it like kissing."

Bill nodded and placed the hand that had just touched her on his thigh. He wanted to kiss her himself, blow job or no blow job, and curled his fingers into a fist to keep from touching her again.

"Fucking farmer," Madeleine said. "That man was a fucking drunk anyway."

"Come on, Maddy," said Tommy. "Let me call someone to take you home."

Madeleine smiled almost sweetly at her drink. "That's nice, Tommy," she said. "But exactly who do you think is going to come pick me up?"

Tommy didn't say anything, and Bill was just about to say, "Me, please," when Madeleine said, "Oh, Christ, I'm just kidding. I can get home fine."

She drank half her drink and put her feet on the floor. Then she steadied herself, and walked slowly out the door.

Bill saw Madeleine a few times after that at the bar and tried to meet her eye, but each time she looked right past him. Then she disappeared altogether. She probably went back to her boyfriend, he thought, as he looked for her by the dartboard. Who cares? he thought, even though he knew he did, since the only people over there now were Jake Hradisky, Little Eric, and Fluffy Mahoney, who had earned his nickname from the collection of pubic hairs he kept in his wallet.

Then in late February a snowstorm hit. No one expected it; in fact, the weather girl on Channel 7 had predicted clear skies and good driving for the next few days. But sometime around four o'clock, the sky turned lavender gray and the snow began to fall.

An hour later Bill was on Route 13, pushing slowly toward the diner in his truck, although he had a nagging suspicion that it was a wasted effort. He figured there would be at least a foot of snow on the roads by midnight. There would be plows and roadblocks and cops, cops, cops. For the fourth time that week, he uttered some unkind words about the officer who had nailed him with his latest DUI.

The truck crossed some ice and skidded, almost hitting a guardrail. Bill straightened it out and checked the rearview mirror for spectators. Seeing none, he readjusted the THINK GLOBALLY DRINK LOCALLY hat he wore for sanitary reasons in the kitchen and drove on, thinking about the soup he was going to make that night: a mushroom broth with scallions and potatoes.

Bill loved potatoes. Unlike carrots, peas, or peppers—glossy vegetables, with no stamina at all—potatoes were survivors. They could go anywhere, be put into anything, and if you didn't need them, they could sit quietly in a kitchen for weeks. When their bodies shriveled, they would send out long shoots: fierce, red eye-arms looking for light. You had to admire a vegetable for that. Potatoes could last for months that way, even in the bottom of a suburban kitchen pantry.

The snow was falling hard when Bill reached the restaurant and saw Hank's sign in the window: CLOSED DUE TO INCREMENT WEATHER.

Increment weather, Bill thought. What the hell was that? Little bits of snow, little spurts of hail? He fished in his coat lining for a loose cigarette and cupped a bare hand against the wind to light it. Ten miles through the snow on a suspended license, and the restaurant was closed. That lazy son of a bitch. He walked next door and into Lucy's.

The place was almost full, which was unusual for a Tuesday night. Scarves, hats, and mittens lay in piles along the brick walls. Behind the dark wood bar, Tommy poured drinks. In front of him, Fat Betty the meter maid sat with Stewart Levine, a former marine who lived with his mother.

Bill saw Hank and Frankie, the dishwasher, sitting at a table with a bottle of tequila and six lemon rinds nestled limply in the ashtray. Frankie's girlfriend had just had a baby, and since Frankie wasn't usually out, or a hard liquor drinker, Bill wondered if he and his girlfriend had broken up again.

"Good to see you, brother!" yelled Hank, and Bill guessed the diner had been closed for at least two hours.

"You closed the restaurant," he said, sitting down heavily.

"The roads are terrible," Hank said. "No one is going to come out in this weather. Not for roast chicken. Shit, not even for hot cherry pie."

"It's a snow night," Frankie giggled. "Like a snow day at school, only at night."

"You could have called," Bill said. "Your hands aren't broken."

Hank offered him a shot to make peace, although they all knew Bill would have ended up at the bar, call or no call. Bill decided instead to get a Guinness. He went back up to the bar and waited for Tommy's attention.

Stewart Levine was talking to Fat Betty. "What's nice about it is that she only charges me three hundred a month, and I get to use the TV and the toaster oven. Not that many landladies let you use their toaster oven for free."

"I know, Stewart, you told me already," Betty said.

"That's right," said Stewart. Stewart used three hopeless, unappealing lines to pick up women. One was that he would have been a concert pianist if his fingers hadn't been so fat and clumsy. Another was that he was a very rich man and had always tipped the hookers well in Vietnam. The third was that his mother rented him a great room.

Bill finally got Tommy's attention and ordered a pint. "Bad night out there," Tommy said.

"Wouldn't want to be homeless," Bill said, and then, because he hated the way he made small talk, he turned his back to the bar and let the beer settle into his blood like it was coming home. Out of habit he looked at the dartboard, where he saw Madeleine taking careful aim, her dark hair in a long braid down her back.

Bill's belly flipped and his throat began to burn. All that time getting used to not seeing her, and now here she was, thick-haired and good-boned and beating Little Eric at darts. And it's a snow night, Bill thought.

He made himself stop staring before she saw him, and turned back toward the bar again. Stewart had gone to the bathroom and Fat Betty waved a cigarette in his direction. Bill reached for his lighter.

"Well," she said, "what's cookin'?"

"Not a thing," Bill said. "The restaurant is closed due to increment weather."

"Isn't that a shame," said Betty. "Those increments will get you every time."

Fat Betty bought Bill a woo-woo and they toasted the storm. From where he was sitting, Bill had a good view of Madeleine, who was now playing Fluffy Mahoney. The woo-woo made him kind toward everyone, and for a moment Bill even forgave Fluffy for his disgusting collection. He looked at Madeleine's face and noticed a scar, a little half moon, on her cheekbone. He wondered if she was a woman who picked at things. Trish had picked at everything. Try washing a dish once in a while, she'd said. Do you have to buy the expensive juice? You should stop drinking. Please stop drinking. If you don't stop drinking, I will slit my own throat, and then I'll slit yours.

Hank came over to the bar. "Frankie's starting that drinking game where you list places you've had sex in alphabetical order." He ordered a shot of Jack Daniel's. "I hate drinking games."

Bill looked at Madeleine again. Hank noticed.

"Madeleine Harris," he said.

"What do you think of her?" Bill said.

"Nice ass," Hank said. "A sweet, sturdy, truck-bumper ass. She has the kind of ass women are always trying to get rid of. Why do they do that?" For a minute, Hank looked very sad. "Just when they have something you can grab onto, they start eating some crap like rice cakes."

Bill shrugged. Madeleine shot three straight bulls.

"She could knock a man's teeth through his balls with those arms, though." Hank finished his shot and ordered one for Bill.

"Amen to that." Bill finished his pint and began to feel handsome. He looked at Madeleine and imagined grabbing that sturdy ass, kissing that thick braid, and it was a good feeling. He drank his shot and remembered that Madeleine had called her last boyfriend a fucking drunk, and had a good feeling about that, too. In his experience, women who said they hated drunks went home with them over and over again.

"I'm going to go home with her," he said.

Hank kept a straight face. "I'm sure you are, Bill."

"What do you mean by that?"

Hank laughed. "What, you talk to her once and you think you'll go home with her? That woman won't even let anyone buy her a shot."

Bill didn't say anything, but he firmly put down his pint glass on the bar so that it made a small, definite warning sound. Over at his table, Frankie was yelling something about a bathtub.

"Bill, you barely even talk," Hank said. "What are you going to say? What are you going to talk about?"

"Potatoes." Bill said this by accident, and it made him mad at Hank.

"Potatoes," Hank said. "You're going to sweet-talk her with sweet potatoes. You'd have better luck getting Fat Betty to switch sides."

Bill stood up and considered punching Hank in the face. Hank, he knew, wouldn't have minded hitting him back.

Then Hank started to laugh. "Potatoes," he said, swatting Bill lightly on the arm. "You're a jerk."

"You're an asshole," Bill said, and walked off to the bathroom.

Outside the snow fell and fell. It silenced the streets, covered driveways, cornfields, and pastures. Inside the bar, people continued to drink and toast the storm.

A little before midnight the power went out. For a few moments everyone was hushed by the warm darkness and the quiet outside. A few people moved toward the door to leave, but then Stewart sat down at the piano and began banging out some kind of a rumba. He cocked his head and growled at his clumsy fingers, which sometimes landed on the wrong keys. Hank started heckling him. Stewart played louder until his fingers obeyed and Fat Betty began to dance. She danced slowly at first, her plump hands kneading the smoky air like sea anemones. She closed her eyes, and as the music picked up she rocked her hips. Hank clapped, and Frankie stood up in front of her, swiveling his own hips. Madeleine stopped her game to watch, her shoulders swaying slightly. Fat Betty and Frankie circled around each other, and then out shot Frankie's hand and Fat Betty was stuck to his side, dwarfing him with her giant bosom. Bill watched them and felt good about Frankie. When Frankie drank too much, he'd sing and dance with anyone. When Bill drank too much, he'd call his own mother a son of a bitch or hit people he wanted to like.

Hank ordered his third pitcher and put his arms around two young women standing beside him. Snow fever, Bill thought, watching Frankie's small hands caress Fat Betty's bottom. This whole place has snow fever. He tried to tell Tommy about it, but it came out sounding like *cleaver,* and Tommy asked him if he was going to throw up.

Bill sat back and let the room grow thick and liquid. When the music stopped, Frankie brought out a deck of cards and tried to convince Hank to play. Fat Betty drank some vodka and began to long for past loves. Stewart came back to the bar and put his industrial-sized cranium down for just a little rest.

At midnight Hank stumbled home and Frankie wobbled over to the pay phone to call his ex-girlfriend. Madeleine finished her last game of darts and came over to the bar to settle up with Tommy. She stood about two feet from Bill, but if she noticed him, she didn't let on. Bill tried to think of something to talk to her about—darts, maybe, or her ex-boyfriend, or this unexpected storm.

Madeleine leaned forward to get Tommy's attention and Bill got a whiff of her clean scent. He thought of all the times just one or two words, *please* or *you're pretty,* would have changed everything, and how he could never say them when he needed to. He thought about how this was going to happen again, right now, and how stupid that was. And then, because he couldn't stand to watch the moment pass, he did something that surprised even him. He reached out and put his palm on her head and touched her hair.

Madeleine didn't move, but watched him in the mirror across from the bar. He moved his fingers along her temple and then tucked a loose tendril of hair behind her ear, and for a moment they stayed there, his hand in her hair, her money on the bar.

Then she leaned into his hand. He moved his hand down the nape of her neck and felt the dampness caused by sweat where the braid began.

Tommy came over and picked up her money. Madeleine straightened, and Bill's hand dropped to his side.

"Maddy," said Tommy, "I thought you might have left town."

"Not yet," she said. She paid Tommy and turned to look at Bill. Bill looked at his beer.

"Well," she finally said. "See you later."

Bill wanted to tell her how funny it was that he had said those same words to his ex, but he was afraid of slurring, so he said nothing. Madeleine put on her scarf, stepped around him, and walked out into the snow.

Bill watched the door shut behind her. In the background he could hear Frankie yelling into the pay phone: "You listen to me! I'm the one talking! Don't hang up! Please." Bill wanted to punch himself in the eye.

Frankie got off the phone and sat down next to Bill where Madeleine had been. "Shit," he said. "My ex-girlfriend wants to be my wife. Can you believe that?"

Bill looked at him. Frankie's face bobbed slowly, a little white moon lost at sea.

"I'm only twenty-three," Frankie said. "I'm just getting used to being a father. I don't know if I'm ready to be a husband."

Bill picked up his drink, and as he caught their reflections in the mirror behind the bar, him with his beer, Frankie staring sadly into the remains of his milky White Russian, he thought about that door shutting behind Madeleine. He imagined a hundred doors shutting on an endless line of women, all beautiful, all walking away from him into the snow, all chances he had missed and would continue to miss, because women were smart and he was dumb and at thirty-two years old, he still didn't know how to get them to stay with him.

"Aw, the hell with her," he said out loud, only his heavy tongue mangled the words and Frankie misunderstood.

"No, the hell with you, man," Frankie said. "Fuck you."

Bill watched him put on his coat and stumble out into the storm. He ordered another pint, and his anger turned to shame.

At about one o'clock the snow finally stopped and the moon came out. It lightened the sky and turned the pastures and cornfields a soft, pale blue. At the bar, Stewart began to snore and Bill decided it was time to go home. He closed one eye and let the jukebox, the bar, and Stewart's big sleeping baby face come into focus. He put on his hat and wove his way to the door.

Outside, the air was cold and still. Bill started to turn left, toward his car, but the thought of going home to his empty house, to his bed with no sheets, just seemed too exhausting. So instead he turned right and slogged back to Hank's restaurant, which would at least be warm. When he got there, he jimmied the lock on the back door and broke in. He stood for a moment in the kitchen, letting the smells of disinfectant, rubber, and steel sink into his skin. He looked at the knives, pots, and pans waiting for him, still and eager as church folk. He imagined that this was how Madeleine felt, looking at her empty bus every morning, before the children got on and started doing unspeakable things.

Perhaps it was the thought of Madeleine on her bus, or maybe it was expectancy he felt in the silent kitchen, but the next thing Bill did was open the walk-in cooler. He took out onions, tomatoes, potatoes, greens, and all of Hank's precious seafood. He took off his coat and put on an apron. Then he went to work.

Bill Wilcox chopped, boiled, diced, and minced. He laid out the carrots, onions, scallions, and seafood in four careful stacks, nodding with satisfaction at their colors. Tenderly he deveined the shrimp, peeling away their translucent skin. He breathed in fresh parsley and thought of Maddy's hair. He chopped vegetables, squeezed tomato juice, and peeled potatoes.

He was opening a clam when he slipped and cut his finger with a kitchen knife. He was drunk enough that it didn't hurt, but it did bleed, so he bashed around the kitchen until he found some duct tape and stopped the blood. Then he went on boiling, chopping, licking, and tasting, thinking and dreaming of Maddy.

The hours went by and the kitchen grew full and steamy. The smell of Bill's soup grew and grew, until it was too big for the kitchen. Bill imagined it trickling out, slowly at first, then gaining force and tumbling into the night sky. He saw it pass the bar, where Tommy, tired and sore, was putting chairs on tables. It wrapped around Stewart, who was standing on the street corner, bellowing to anyone who would listen that he was a star in Vietnam, a god-damned star, ask anyone. Ask the ladies. It roared and it laughed, and it wafted on over to Frankie, sitting at home, smoking a cigarette, wondering if he could be the right husband for his son's mother. Finally it found Madeleine Harris, in her house flanked by wheat fields and dairy farms, and let her know that Bill knew as well as she did what it was like to come and go places alone.

A week later Bill saw her again. He was on his way to the grocery store to pick up some vegetables and Madeleine was walking toward him on the street. Their eyes met, and he wondered if she'd heard (the way everyone else had, from Hank's big mouth) about how he'd broken into the restaurant, cut open his finger, made a pot of soup, and then passed out on the rubber matting by the sink, leaving the walk-in cooler open and twenty pounds of fresh seafood out on the counter, where it turned and became of no use to anyone.

Maybe if he'd been at Lucy's, on his first or second drink, he would have joked about it being the best soup he ever made. That it was too bad he couldn't remember how he did it. He might have shown her his stitches. And he imagined that in the right mood he might have asked her if she wanted to go home with him, or at least go out for a beer.

But it was daytime. The sun was out and the rules were different. He dropped his eyes and they passed each other without speaking, the way people who drink at the same place often do once they step out of the bar and into the world.

CONTRIBUTORS

BHIRA BACKHAUS holds a degree from the University of California, Davis and received her MFA at Arizona State University. She received the Robert C. Martindale Educational Foundation Fiction Award for her story "Sangeet," which is excerpted from her first novel, *Among the Faithful.*

REBECCA BARRY is a graduate of the Ohio State University MFA program. Her fiction has appeared in *Ploughshares, One Story,* and *Tin House.* Her nonfiction has appeared in many places such as the *Washington Post,* the *New York Times Magazine, Real Simple,* and the *Best American Travel Writing.* She lives in Ithaca, New York, and is working on a collection of short stories.

JOSHUA FERRIS received a BA from the University of Iowa in 1997 and an MFA from the University of California, Irvine, in 2003. His work has previously appeared in the *Iowa Review.* He is currently at work on a novel and lives in Brooklyn.

IAN DAVID FROEB was born and raised in Baltimore, Maryland, and now lives in St. Louis, Missouri. He was an Iowa Arts Fellow at the Iowa Writers Workshop, and upon graduation received a James A. Michener–Copernicus Society of America Fellowship. He has written a collection of fiction—from which "The Cosmonaut" is taken—and is currently writing a novel.

KEITH GESSEN was educated at Harvard and Syracuse—as well as Newton South High School, where (no offense meant to the Hruby brothers or the Nick brothers) he was the finest hockey player of his day. His criticism has appeared in *Dissent, The Nation,* and *Feed.* He lives in New York City and is completing a collection of stories.

TAMARA GUIRADO received a Sacatar Foundation Fellowship on Itaparica, Bahia, Brazil, in summer 2003. She was the 2002–2003 Carl Djerassi Fiction Fellow at the Wisconsin Institute for Creative Writing at the University of Wisconsin and a 2000–2002 Wallace Stegner Fellow at Stanford University. She recieved her MFA from Mills College in Oakland, California. She is currently working on a novel.

CHARLEY HENLEY spent much of his youth in Mississippi, but he now lives with his wife and children in Tallahassee, Florida, where he is working on his Ph.D. in Creative Writing at Florida State University. He holds a BA in Philosophy from the University of Montana and an MFA in Creative Writing from the University of Alabama. He has been previously published in *Another Chicago Magazine.*

FRANCES HWANG is a graduate of the University of Montana and a former fellow at the Fine Arts Work Center in Provincetown. She is currently the James McCreight Fiction Fellow at the Wisconsin Institute for Creative Writing and is working on a collection of short stories. This is her second story to appear in Best New American Voices.

ARYN KYLE recently received her MFA from the University of Montana. Her fiction has appeared in *The Atlantic Monthly.* She is currently working on a novel.

RATTAWUT LAPCHAROENSAP was born in Chicago in 1979 and raised in Bangkok, Thailand. He received his BA from Cornell University and his MFA from the University of Michigan, where he was a recipient of the Avery Jules Hopwood Award and the Fred R. Meijer Fellowship in Creative Writing. His work has appeared in *Granta* and *Glimmer Train.* He is at work on his first collection of short stories.

MICHAEL LOWENTHAL is the author of the novels *Avoidance* and *The Same Embrace,* as well as short stories that have appeared in the *Southern Review, Kenyon Review, New England Review,* and in many anthologies, most recently *Lost Tribe: Jewish Fiction from the Edge* and *Bestial Noise: The Tin House Fiction Reader.* The recipient of fellowships from the Bread Loaf and Wesleyan writers' conferences, the Massachusetts Cultural Council, and the Hawthornden International Retreat for Writers, he has also written for the *New York Times Magazine, New York Times Book Review,* and *Washington Post Book World,* among many other publications. He can be contacted through his Web site, www.MichaelLowenthal.com.

VIVEK NARAYANAN was born in India, and grew up in Zambia and Tanzania. He was trained as a historical anthropologist at Stanford University. His stories have appeared in *Agni,* the *Post-Post Review* (Bombay), and *Mamba* (Durban, South Africa), and his poems, in the *Harvard Review, Fulcrum,* and in the anthology, *Reasons for Belonging: Fourteen Contemporary Indian Poets* (New Delhi: Viking Penguin, 2002.)

ERIC PUCHNER is a Wallace Stegner Fellow at Stanford University. His short stories have appeared in *Zoetrope: All Story, Missouri Review, Glimmer Train,* and other magazines, as well as the 2004 Pushcart Prize anthology. He was the recipient of the 2002 Joseph Henry Jackson Award for young California writers. He lives in San Francisco, where he is completing a collection of stories entitled *Music Through the Floor.*

MATTHEW PURDY is currently working toward a Ph.D. in English at the University of Iowa. His work has previously appeared in the *Iron Horse Literary Review, One Story,* and the *Mid American Review.* He has recently completed a collection of stories, *Something Outside Is Clacking.*

HASANTHIKA SIRISENA was born in Sri Lanka and grew up in North Carolina. She is currently living in New York City and completing her MA in English at City College. Her work has been included in the *Denver Quarterly* and *Placemats,* a collection of fiction, essays, and artwork. She is also working on her first novel.

E. V. SLATE attended Boston University, where she won the Florence Engel Randall Graduate Award. In 2003 she received a Saint Botolph Club Foundation Grant and a Rona Jaffe Foundation Writer's Award, which enabled her to travel to Mumbai to complete her collection of stories set in China, Singapore, and India.

LACHLAN SMITH received his MFA from Cornell University and is currently a Stegner Fellow at Stanford. Excerpted here is the opening chapter of his first novel, *Silent Sky.*

PARTICIPANTS

American University
MFA Program in Creative Writing
Department of Literature
Washington, DC 20016-8047
202/885-2973

Arizona State University
College of Liberal Arts and Sciences
Department of Literature – Creative
Writing Program
Tempe, AZ 85287
480/965-3528

The Banff Centre for the Arts
Writing Studio
Box 1020, Station 34
107 Tunnel Mountain Drive
Banff, AB TIL 1H5
403/762-6269

Bennington College
Program in Writing and Literature
1 College Drive
Bennington, VT 05201
802/442-5401, Ext. 4452

Binghamton University
Creative Writing Program
Department of English, General
Literature, and Rhetoric
P.O. Box 6000
Binghamton, NY 13902-6000
607/777-2168

Boise State University
MFA Program in Writing
English Annex 102A
1910 University Drive
Boise, ID 83725
208/426-1246

Boston University
Creative Writing Program
236 Bay State Road
Boston, MA 02215
617/353-2510

Bowling Green State University
Department of English
Creative Writing Program
Bowling Green, OH 43403-0215
419/372-8370

The Bread Loaf Writers' Conference
Middlebury College
Middlebury, VT 05753
802/443-5286

Brown University
Box 1852
Creative Writing
Providence, RI 02912
401/863-3260

California State University,
Long Beach
Department of English
1250 Bellflower Boulevard
Long Beach, CA 90840
562/985-4225

California State University,
Northridge
Department of English
18111 Nordhoff Street
Northridge, CA 91330-8248
818/677-3431

California State University,
Sacramento
6000 J Street
Department of English
Sacramento, CA 95819
916/278-6586

The City College of New York
Graduate Program in English
138th Street and Convent Avenue
New York, NY 10031
212/650-6694

Colorado State University
MFA Creative Writing Program
English Department, 359 Eddy Hall
Fort Collins, CO 80523-1773
970/491-6428

Columbia College
Department of Fiction Writing
600 South Michigan Avenue
Chicago, IL 60605-1997
312/344-7611

Columbia University
Division of Writing,
School of the Arts
2960 Broadway, Room 15 Dodge
New York, NY 10027
212/854-4392

Cornell University
English Department
Ithaca, NY 14853
607/255-6800

Eastern Washington University
Creative Writing Program
705 W. First Avenue MS#1
Spokane, WA 99201-3900
509/623-4221

Emerson College
Writing, Literature and Publishing
120 Boylston Street
Boston, MA 02116
617/824-8750

Fairleigh Dickinson
MFA in Creative Writing Program
285 Madison Avenue, M-MS3-01
Madison, NJ 07940
973/443-8632

Fine Arts Work Center
in Provincetown
24 Pearl Street
Provincetown, MA 02657
508/487-8678

Florida State University
Creative Writing Program
Department of English
Tallahassee, FL 32306-1580
850/644-4230

George Mason University
Creative Writing Program
MS 3E4 – English Department
Fairfax, VA 22030
703/993-1185

Hollins University
Department of English
P.O. Box 9677
Roanoke, VA 24020
540/362-6317

The Humber School for Writers
3199 Lakeshore Blvd. West
Humber College
Toronto, ON M8V 1K8
416/675-6622

Hunter College
MFA Program in Writing
Department of English
695 Park Avenue
New York, NY 10021
212/772-4000

Indiana University
Department of English
Ballantine Hall 442
1020 East Kirkwood Avenue
Bloomington, IN 47405-6601
812/855-8224

The Indiana University
Writers' Conference
Ballantine Hall 464
1020 East Kirkwood Avenue
Bloomington, IN 47405-7103
812/855-1877

Johns Hopkins University
The Writing Seminars
3400 North Charles Street
Baltimore, MD 21218
410/516-7563

Johns Hopkins Writing Program –
Washington
1717 Massachusetts Avenue, NW
Suite 104
Washington, DC 20036
202/452-1280

The Loft Literary Center
Mentor Series Program
Suite 200, Open Book
1011 Washington Avenue South
Minneapolis, MN 55415
612/215-2575

Manhattanville College
2900 Purchase Street
Purchase, NY 10577
914/694-3425

The Manhattanville Summer
Writers' Week
2900 Purchase Street
Graduate and Professional Studies
Manhattanville College
Purchase, NY 10577
914/694-3425

McNeese State University
Department of Languages
P.O. Box 92655
Lake Charles, LA 70609-2655
337/475-5326

Miami University
Creative Writing Program
Oxford, OH 45056
513/529-5221

Michener Center for Writers
University of Texas
J. Frank Dobie House
702 East Dean Keeton Street
Austin, TX 78705
512/471-1601

Mills College
Creative Writing Program
Mills Hall 311
5000 MacArthur Boulevard
Oakland, CA 94613
510/430-3309

Minnesota State University, Mankato
230 Armstrong Hall
English Department
Mankato, MN 56001
507/389-2117

Mississippi State University
Department of English
Drawer E
Mississippi State, MS 39762
662/325-3644

The Napa Valley Writers' Conference
Napa Valley College
1088 College Avenue
St. Helena, CA 94574
707/967-2900

Naropa University
Program in Writing and Poetics
2130 Arapahoe Avenue
Boulder, CO 80302
303/546-3540

New Mexico State University
Department of English
Box 30001 – Department 3E
Las Cruces, NM 88003-8001
505/646-3931

New York University
Graduate Program in
Creative Writing
19 University Place, Room 219
New York, NY 10003
212/998-8816

Northeastern University
Department of English
406 Homes Hall
Boston, MA 02115-5000
617/373-2512

Ohio State University
English Department
421 Denney Hall
164 West 17th Avenue
Columbus, OH 43210-1370
614/292-6065

Oklahoma State University
Creative Writing Program
English Department – 205 Morrill
Hall
Stillwater, OK 74078
405/744-9474

PEN Prison Writing Committee
PEN American Center
568 Broadway
Suite 401
New York, NY 10012
212/334-1660, Ext. 117

Pennsylvania State University
Department of English
112 Burrowes Building
University Park, PA 16802-6200
814/863-3069

Rivier College
Department of English
South Main Street
Nashua, NH 03060-5086
603/888-1311

Sage Hill Writing Experience
Box 1731
Saskatoon, SK S7K 3S1
306/652-7395

Saint Mary's College of California
MFA Program in Creative Writing
P.O. Box 4686
Moraga, CA 94575-4686
925/631-4762

San Francisco State University
Creative Writing Department,
College of Humanities
1600 Holloway Avenue
San Francisco, CA 94132-4162
415/338-1891

Sarah Lawrence College
Graduate Writing Program
1 Mead Way
Slonim House
Bronxville, NY 10708-5999
914/395-2371

The School of the Art Institute
of Chicago
MFA in Writing Program
37 S. Wabash Avenue
Chicago, IL 60603
312/899-7412

Sewanee Writers' Conference
310 St. Luke's Hall
735 University Avenue
Sewanee, TN 37383-1000
931/598-1141

Southwest Texas State University
MFA Program in Creative Writing
Department of English
601 University Drive
San Marcos, TX 78666
512/245-2163

Stanford University
Creative Writing Program
Department of English
Stanford, CA 94305-2087
650/725-1208

Syracuse University
Program in Creative Writing
Department of English
College of Arts & Sciences
Syracuse, NY 13244-1170
315/443-2174

Taos Summer Writers' Conference
Department of English
MSC 03 2170
University of New Mexico
Albuquerque, NM 87131-1106
505/277-6347

Temple University
Creative Writing Program
Anderson Hall, 10th Floor
Philadelphia, PA 19122
215/204-1796

Texas A&M University
Creative Writing Program
English Department
College Station, TX 77843-4227
409/845-9936

University of Alabama
Program in Creative Writing
Department of English
P.O. Box 870244
Tuscaloosa, AL 35487-0244
205/348-5065

University of Alaska, Anchorage
Department of Creative Writing and
Literary Arts
3211 Providence Drive
Anchorage, AK 99508-8348
907/786-4330

University of Alaska, Fairbanks
Program in Creative Writing
Department of English
P.O. Box 755720
Fairbanks, AK 99775-5720
907/474-7193

University of Arkansas
Program in Creative Writing
Department of English
333 Kimpel Hall
Fayetteville, AR 72701
479/575-4301

University of California, Davis
Graduate Creative Writing Program
Department of English
Davis, CA 95616
530/752-1658

University of California, Irvine
MFA Program in Writing
Department of English and
Comparative Literature
435 Humanities Instructional Bldg.
Irvine, CA 92697-2650
714/824-6718

University of Central Florida
Graduate Program in Creative
Writing
Department of English
P.O. Box 161346
Orlando, FL 32816-1346
407/823-2212

University of Cincinnati
Creative Writing Program
Department of English and
Comparative Literature
Cincinnati, OH 45221-0069
513/556-5924

University of Florida
Creative Writing Program
Department of English
P.O. Box 117310
Gainesville, FL 32611-7310
352/392-6650

University of Illinois at Chicago
Program for Writers
Department of English MC/162
601 South Morgan Street
Chicago, IL 60607-7120
312/413-2229

University of Iowa
Program in Creative Writing
102 Dey House
507 N. Clinton Street
Iowa City, IA 52242
319/335-0416

University of Louisiana at Lafayette
Creative Writing Concentration
Department of English
P.O. Box 44691
Lafayette, LA 70504-4691
337/482-5478

University of Maine
Master's in English Program
5752 Neville Hall
Orono, ME 04469-5752
207/581-3822

University of Maryland
Creative Writing Program
Department of English
3119F Susquehanna Hall
College Park, MD 20742
301/405-3820

University of Massachusetts, Amherst
MFA Program in English
Bartlett Hall
130 Hicks Way
Amherst, MA 01003-9269
413/545-0643

University of Memphis
MFA Creative Writing Program
Department of English
College of Arts and Sciences
Memphis, TN 38152
901/678-2651

University of Michigan
MFA Program in Creative Writing
Department of English
3187 Angell Hall
Ann Arbor, MI 48109-1003
734/763-4139

University of Minnesota
MFA Program in Creative Writing
Department of English
207 Church Street, SE
Minneapolis, MN 55455
612/625-6366

University of Mississippi
MFA Program in Creative Writing
English Department
Bondurant Hall C128
Oxford, MS 38677-1848
662/915-7439

University of Missouri – Columbia
Creative Writing Program
Department of English
107 Tate Hall
Columbia, MO 65211
573/882-6421

University of Missouri – St. Louis
MFA in Creative Writing Program
Department of English
8001 Natural Bridge Road
St. Louis, MO 63121
314/516-6845

University of Montana
Creative Writing Program
Department of English
Missoula, MT 59812-1013
406/243-5231

University of Nebraska, Lincoln
Creative Writing Program
Department of English
343 Andrews Hall
Lincoln, NE 68588-0333
402/472-3191

University of Nevada, Las Vegas
MFA in Creative Writing
Department of English
4505 Maryland Parkway
Las Vegas, NV 89154-5011
702/895-3533

University of New Mexico
Graduate Program in
Creative Writing
Department of English Language
and Literature
Humanities Bldg., 2nd Floor
Albuquerque, NM 87131
505/277-6347

University of New Orleans
Creative Writing Workshop
College of Liberal Arts
Lakefront
New Orleans, LA 70148
504/280-7454

University of North Carolina,
Greensboro
MFA Writing Program
P.O. Box 26170
Greensboro, NC 27402-6170
336/334-5459

University of North Carolina, Wilmington
MFA in Writing Program
Department of Creative Writing
601 S. College Road
Wilmington, NC 28403
910/962-7063

University of North Texas
Creative Writing Division
Department of English
P.O. Box 311307
Denton, TX 76203-1307
940/565-2050

University of Notre Dame
Creative Writing Program
356 O'Shaughnessy Hall
Notre Dame, IN 46556-0368
574/631-7526

University of Oregon
Program in Creative Writing
Box 5243
Eugene, OR 97403-5243
541/346-3944

University of Pittsburgh
Creative Writing Program
526 CL
4200 Fifth Avenue
Pittsburgh, PA 15260
412/624-6506

University of San Francisco
MFA in Writing Program
Program Office, Lone Mountain 340
2130 Fulton Street
San Francisco, CA 94117-1080
415/422-2382

University of South Carolina
MFA Program in Creative Writing
Department of English
Columbia, SC 29208
803/777-4204

University of South Dakota
Creative Writing Program
Department of English
Vermillion, SD 57069
605/677-5229

University of Southern Mississippi
Center for Writers
Box 5144 USM
Hattiesburg, MS 39406-5144
601/266-4321

University of Texas at Austin
Creative Writing Program in English
Department of English
1 University Station B5000
Austin, TX 78712-0195
512/471-4991

University of Utah
Creative Writing Program
255 South Central Campus Drive
Room 3500
Salt Lake City, UT 84112
801/581-7131

University of Virginia
Creative Writing Program
Department of English
P.O. Box 400121
Charlottesville, VA 22904-4121
804/924-6675

University of Washington
Creative Writing Program
Box 354330
Seattle, WA 98195
206/543-9865

University of Wisconsin – Madison
Program in Creative Writing
English Department
Helen C. White Hall
600 N. Park Street
Madison, WI 53706
608/263-3750

University of Wisconsin – Milwaukee
Creative Writing Program
Department of English
Box 413
Milwaukee, WI 53201
414/229-4511

Unterberg Poetry Center
Writing Program
92nd Street Y
1395 Lexington Avenue
New York, NY 10128
212/415-5760

Vermont College of Union
Institute and University
MFA in Writing
36 College Street
Montpelier, VT 05602
800/336-6794

Washington University
The Writing Program
Campus Box 1122
One Brookings Drive
St. Louis, MO 63130-4899
314/935-5190

Wayne State University
Creative Writing Program
English Department
Detroit, MI 48202
313/577-2450

The Wesleyan Writers Conference
Wesleyan University
Middletown, CT 06459
860/685-3604

West Virginia University
Creative Writing Program
Department of English
P.O. Box 6269
Morgantown, WV 26506-6269
304/293-3107

Wisconsin Institute for
Creative Writing
University of Wisconsin – Madison
English Department
Helen C. White Hall
600 N. Park Street
Madison, WI 53706
608/263-3800